SHATTER

Michael Robotham

sphere

SPHERE

First published in Great Britain in 2008 by Sphere

A CIP catalogue record for this book
is available from the British Library.

Hardback ISBN: 978-1-84744-177-5
C Format ISBN: 978-1-84744-178-2

Typeset in Baskerville MT by Palimpsest Book Production Limited,
Grangemouth, Stirlingshire
Printed and bound in Great Britain by Clays Ltd, St Ives plc

Sphere
An imprint of
Little, Brown Book Group
100 Victoria Embankment
London EC4Y 0DY

An Hachette Livre UK Company

www.littlebrown.co.uk

This is for Mark Lucas, a friend first.

Acknowledgements

This story was inspired by true events in two countries but not based upon either of them. It could not have been told without David Hunt and John Little who were invaluable in helping my research. Among the others who answered my questions and shared my excitement were Georgie and Nick Lucas, Nicki Kennedy and Sam Edenborough.

As always I am indebted to my editors and their teams, Stacy Creamer at Doubleday US and Ursula Mackenzie at Little, Brown UK, as well as to my agent Mark Lucas and all those at LAW.

For their continued hospitality I thank Richard, Emma, Mark and Sara and their respective broods. My own brood must also be acknowledged – Alex, Charlotte and Bella, who are growing up before my eyes despite my pleas for them to never change.

Last, but not least, I thank Vivien, my researcher, reviewer, reader, therapist, lover and wife. I have promised her that one day I'll find the right words.

The sleep of reason produces monsters.

Goya (*The Caprichos*)

The words of his mouth were smoother than butter, but war was in his heart: his words were softer than oil, yet were they drawn swords.

Psalm 55:21

There is a moment when all hope disappears, all pride is gone, all expectation, all faith, all desire. I own that moment. It belongs to me. That's when I hear the sound, the sound of a mind breaking.

It's not a loud crack like when bones shatter or a spine fractures or a skull collapses. And it's not something soft and wet like a heart breaking. It's a sound that makes you wonder how much pain a person can endure; a sound that shatters memories and lets the past leak into the present; a sound so high that only the hounds of hell can hear it.

Can you hear it? Someone is curled up in a tiny ball crying softly into an endless night.

1

University of Bath

It's eleven o'clock in the morning, late September, and outside it's raining so hard that cows are floating down rivers and birds are resting on their bloated bodies.

The lecture theatre is full. Tiered seats rise at a gentle angle between the stairs on either side of the auditorium, climbing into darkness. Mine is an audience of pale faces, young and earnest, hung over. Fresher's Week is in full swing and many of them have waged a mental battle to be here, weighing up whether to attend any lectures or go back to bed. A year ago they were watching teen movies and spilling popcorn. Now they're living away from home, getting drunk on subsidised alcohol and waiting to learn something.

I walk to the centre of the stage and clamp my hands on the lectern as if frightened of falling over.

'My name is Professor Joseph O'Loughlin. I am a clinical psychologist and I'll be taking you through this introductory course in behavioural psychology.'

Pausing a moment, I blink into the lights. I didn't think I would be nervous lecturing again but now I suddenly doubt if I have any knowledge worth imparting. I can still hear Bruno Kaufman's advice. (Bruno is the head of the psychology department at the university and is blessed with a perfect Teutonic name for the role.) He told me, 'Nothing we teach them will be of the slightest possible use to them in the real world, old boy. Our task is to offer them a bullshit meter.'

'A what?'

'If they work hard and take a little on board, they will learn to detect when someone is telling them complete bullshit.'

Bruno had laughed and I found myself joining him.

'Go easy on them,' he added. 'They're still clean and perky and well-fed. A year from now they'll be calling you by your first name and thinking they know it all.'

How do I go easy on them, I want to ask him now. I'm new at this too. Breathing deeply, I begin again.

'Why does a well-spoken university graduate studying urban preservation fly a passenger plane into a skyscraper, killing thousands of people? Why does a boy, barely into his teens, spray a schoolyard with bullets, or a teenage mother give birth in a toilet and leave the baby in the wastepaper bin?'

Silence.

'How did a hairless primate evolve into a species that manufactures nuclear weapons, watches *Celebrity Big Brother* and asks questions about what it means to be human and how we got here? Why do we cry? Why are some jokes funny? Why are we inclined to believe or disbelieve in God? Why do we get turned on when someone sucks our toes? Why do we have trouble remembering some things, yet can't get that annoying Britney Spears song out of our heads? What causes us to love or hate? Why are we each so different?'

I look at the faces in the front rows. I have captured their attention, for a moment at least.

'We humans have been studying ourselves for thousands of years, producing countless theories and philosophies and astonishing works of art and engineering and original thought, yet in all that time this is how much we've learned.' I hold up my thumb and forefinger a fraction of an inch apart.

'You're here to learn about psychology – the science of the mind; the science that deals with knowing, believing, feeling and desiring; the least understood science of them all.'

My left arm trembles at my side.

'Did you see that?' I ask, raising the offending arm. 'It does that occasionally. Sometimes I think it has a mind of its own but of course that's impossible. One's mind doesn't reside in an arm or a leg.

'Let me ask you all a question. A woman walks into a clinic. She is middle aged, well-educated, articulate and well-groomed. Suddenly, her left arm leaps to her throat and her fingers close around her windpipe. Her face reddens. Her eyes bulge. She is being strangled. Her right hand comes to her rescue. It peels back the fingers and wrestles her left hand to her side. What should I do?'

Silence.

A girl in the front row nervously raises her arm. She has short reddish hair separated in feathery wisps down the fluted back of her neck. 'Take a detailed history?'

'It's been done. She has no history of mental illness.'

Another hand rises. 'It is an issue of self harm.'

'Obviously, but she doesn't *choose* to strangle herself. It is unwanted. Disturbing. She wants help.'

A girl with heavy mascara brushes hair behind her ear with one hand. 'Perhaps she's suicidal.'

'Her left hand is. Her right hand obviously doesn't agree. It's like a Monty Python sketch. Sometimes she has to sit on her left hand to keep it under control.'

'Is she depressed?' asks a youth with a gypsy earring and gel in his hair.

'No. She's frightened but she can see the funny side of her predicament. It seems ridiculous to her. Yet at her worst moments she contemplates amputation. What if her left hand strangles her in the night, when her right hand is asleep?'

'Brain damage?'

'There are no obvious neurological deficits – no paralysis or exaggerated reflexes.'

The silence stretches out, filling the air above their heads, drifting like strands of web in the warm air.

A voice from the darkness fills the vacuum. 'She had a stroke.'

I recognise the voice. Bruno has come to check up on me on

my first day. I can't see his face in the shadows but I know he's smiling.

'Give that man a cigar,' I announce.

The keen girl in the front row pouts. 'But you said there was no brain damage.'

'I said there were no *obvious* neurological deficits. This woman had suffered a small stroke on the right side of her brain in an area that deals with emotions. Normally, the two halves of our brain communicate and come to an agreement but in this case it didn't happen and her brain fought a physical battle using each side of her body.

'This case is fifty years old and is one of the most famous in the study of the brain. It helped a neurologist called Dr Kurt Goldstein develop one of the first theories of the divided brain.'

My left arm trembles again, but this time it is oddly reassuring.

'Forget everything you've been told about psychology. It will not make you a better poker player, nor will it help you pick up girls or understand them any better. I have three at home and they are a complete mystery to me.

'It is *not* about dream interpretation, ESP, multiple personalities, mind reading, Rorschach Tests, phobias, recovered memories or repression. And most importantly – it is *not* about getting in touch with yourself. If that's your ambition I suggest you buy a copy of *Big Jugs* magazine and find a quiet corner.'

There are snorts of laughter.

'I don't know any of you yet, but I know things about you. Some of you want to stand out from the crowd and others want to blend in. You're possibly looking at the clothes your mother packed you and planning an expedition to H&M tomorrow to purchase something distressed by a machine that will express your individuality by making you look like everyone else on campus.

'Others among you might be wondering if it's possible to get liver damage from one night of drinking, and speculating on who set off the fire alarm in Halls at three o'clock this morning. You want to know if I'm a hard marker or if I'll give you extensions on assignments or whether you should have taken politics instead of psychology. Stick around and you'll get some answers – but not today.'

I walk back to the centre of the stage and stumble slightly.

'I will leave you with one thought. A piece of human brain the size of a grain of sand contains one hundred thousand neurons, two million axons and one billion synapses all talking to each other. The number of permutations and combinations of activity that are theoretically possible in each of our heads exceeds the number of elementary particles in the universe.'

I pause and let the numbers wash over them. 'Welcome to the great unknown.'

'Dazzling, old boy, you put the fear of God into them,' says Bruno, as I gather my papers. 'Ironic. Passionate. Amusing. You inspired them.'

'It was hardly Mr Chips.'

'Don't be so modest. None of these young philistines have ever heard of Mr Chips. They've grown up reading *Harry Potter and the Stoned Philosopher*.'

'I think it's "the Philosopher's Stone".'

'Whatever. With that little affectation of yours, Joseph, you have everything it takes to be much loved.'

'Affectation?'

'Your Parkinson's.'

He doesn't bat an eyelid when I stare at him in disbelief. I tuck my battered briefcase under my arm and make my way towards the side door of the lecture hall.

'Well, I'm pleased you think they were listening,' I say.

'Oh, they never listen,' says Bruno. 'It's a matter of osmosis; occasionally something sinks through the alcoholic haze. But you did guarantee they'll come back.'

'How so?'

'They won't know how to lie to you.'

His eyes fold into wrinkles. Bruno is wearing trousers that have no pockets. For some reason I've never trusted a man who has no use for pockets. What does he do with his hands?

The corridors and walkways are full of students. A girl

5

approaches. I recognise her from the lecture. Clear-skinned, wearing desert boots and black jeans, her heavy mascara makes her look raccoon-eyed with a secret sadness.

'Do you believe in evil, Professor?'

'Excuse me?'

She asks the question again, clutching a notebook to her chest.

'I think the word "evil" is used too often and has lost value.'

'Are people born that way or does society create them?'

'They are created.'

'So there are no natural psychopaths?'

'They're too rare to quantify.'

'What sort of answer is that?'

'It's the right one.'

She wants to ask me something else but struggles to find courage. 'Would you agree to an interview?' she blurts suddenly.

'What for?'

'The student newspaper. Professor Kaufman says you're something of a celebrity.'

'I hardly think . . .'

'He says you were charged with murdering a former patient and beat the rap.'

'I was innocent.'

The distinction seems lost on her. She's still waiting for an answer.

'I don't give interviews. I'm sorry.'

She shrugs and turns, about to leave. Something else occurs to her. 'I enjoyed the lecture.'

'Thank you.'

She disappears down the corridor. Bruno looks at me sheepishly. 'Don't know what she's talking about, old boy. Wrong end of the stick.'

'What are you telling people?'

'Only good things. Her name is Nancy Ewers. She's a bright young thing. Studying Russian and politics.'

'Why is she writing for the newspaper?'

'"Knowledge is precious whether or not it serves the slightest human use."'

'Who said that?'

'A.E. Housman.'

'Wasn't he a communist?'

'A pillow biter.'

It is still raining. Teeming. For weeks it has been like this. Forty days and forty nights must be getting close. An oily wave of mud, debris and sludge is being swept across the West Country, making roads impassable and turning basements into swimming pools. There are radio reports of flooding in the Malago Valley, Hartcliffe Way and Bedminster. Warnings have been issued for the Avon, which burst its banks at Evesham. Locks and levees are under threat. People are being evacuated. Animals are drowning.

The quadrangle is washed by rain, driven sideways in sheets. Students huddle under coats and umbrellas, making a dash for their next lecture or the library. Others are staying put, mingling in the foyer. Bruno observes the prettier girls without ever making it obvious.

It was he who suggested I lecture – two hours a week and four tutorials of half an hour each. Social psychology. How hard could it be?

'Do you have an umbrella?' he asks.

'Yes.'

'We'll share.'

My shoes are full of water within seconds. Bruno holds the umbrella and shoulders me as we run. As we near the psychology department, I notice a police car parked in the emergency bay. A young black constable steps from inside wearing a raincoat. Tall, with short-cropped hair, he hunches his shoulders slightly as if beaten down by the rain.

'Dr Kaufman?'

Bruno acknowledges him with a half-nod.

'We have a situation on the Clifton Bridge.'

Bruno groans. 'No, no, not now.'

The constable doesn't expect a refusal. Bruno pushes past him, heading towards the glass doors to the psychology building, still holding my umbrella.

'We tried to phone,' yells the officer. 'I was told to come and get you.'

Bruno stops and turns back, muttering expletives.

'There must be someone else. I don't have the time.'

Rain leaks down my neck. I ask Bruno what's wrong.

Suddenly he changes tack. Jumping over a puddle, he returns my umbrella as though passing on the Olympic torch.

'This is the man you *really* want,' he says to the officer. 'Professor Joseph O'Loughlin, my esteemed colleague, a clinical psychologist of great repute. An old hand. Very experienced at this sort of thing.'

'What sort of thing?'

'A jumper.'

'Pardon?'

'On the Clifton Suspension Bridge,' adds Bruno. 'Some halfwit doesn't have enough sense to get out of the rain.'

The constable opens the car door for me. 'Female. Early forties,' he says.

I still don't understand.

Bruno adds, 'Come on, old boy. It's a public service.'

'Why don't *you* do it?'

'Important business. A meeting with the chancellor. Heads of Department.' He's lying. 'False modesty isn't necessary, old boy. What about that young chap you saved in London? Well-deserved plaudits. You're far more qualified than me. Don't worry. She'll most likely jump before you get there.'

I wonder if he hears himself sometimes.

'Must dash. Good luck.' He pushes through the glass doors and disappears inside the building.

The officer is still holding the car door. 'They've blocked off the bridge,' he explains. 'We really must hurry, sir.'

Wipers thrash and a siren wails. From inside the car it sounds strangely muted and I keep looking over my shoulder expecting to see an approaching police car. It takes me a moment to realise that the siren is coming from somewhere closer, beneath the bonnet.

Masonry towers appear on the skyline. It is Brunel's masterpiece, the Clifton Suspension Bridge, an engineering marvel from the age of steam. Taillights blaze. Traffic is stretched back for more than a mile on the approach. Sticking to the apron of the road, we sweep past the stationary cars and pull up at a roadblock where police in fluorescent vests control onlookers and unhappy motorists.

The constable opens the door for me and hands me my umbrella. A sheet of rain drives sideways and almost rips it from my hands. Ahead of me the bridge appears deserted. The masonry towers support massive sweeping interlinking cables that curve gracefully to the vehicle deck and rise again to the opposite side of the river.

One of the attributes of bridges is that they offer the possibility that someone may start to cross but never reach the other side. For that person the bridge is virtual; an open window that they can keep passing or climb through.

The Clifton Suspension Bridge is a landmark, a tourist attraction and a one-drop shop for suicides. Well-used, oft-chosen, perhaps 'popular' isn't the best choice of word. Some people say the bridge is haunted by past suicides; eerie shadows have been seen drifting across the vehicle deck.

There are no shadows today. And the only ghost on the bridge is flesh and blood. A woman, naked, standing outside the safety fence, with her back pressed to the metal lattice and wire strands. The heels of her red shoes are balancing on the edge.

Like a figure from a surrealist painting, her nakedness isn't particularly shocking or even out of place. Standing upright, with a rigid grace, she stares at the water with the demeanour of someone who has detached herself from the world.

The officer in charge introduces himself. He's in uniform: Sergeant Abernathy. I don't catch his first name. A junior officer holds an umbrella over his head. Water streams off the dark nylon dome, falling on my shoes.

'What do you need?' asks Abernathy.

'A name.'

'We don't have one. She won't talk to us.'

'Has she said anything at all?'

'No.'

9

'She could be in shock. Where are her clothes?'

'We haven't found them.'

I glance along the pedestrian walkway, which is enclosed by a fence topped with five strands of wire, making it difficult for anyone to climb over. The rain is so heavy I can barely see the far side of the bridge.

'How long has she been out there?'

'Best part of an hour.'

'Have you found a car?'

'We're still looking.'

She most likely approached from the eastern side which is heavily wooded. Even if she stripped on the walkway dozens of drivers must have seen her. Why didn't anyone stop her?

A large woman with short cropped hair, dyed black, interrupts the meeting. Her shoulders are rounded and her hands bunch in the pockets of a rain jacket hanging down to her knees. She's huge. Square. And she's wearing men's shoes.

Abernathy stiffens. 'What are you doing here, ma'am?'

'Just trying to get home, Sergeant. And don't call me ma'am. I'm not the bloody Queen.'

She glances at the TV crews and press photographers who have gathered on a grassy ridge, setting up tripods and lights. Finally she turns to me.

'What are you shaking for, precious? I'm not that scary.'

'I'm sorry. I have Parkinson's Disease.'

'Tough break. Does that mean you get a sticker?'

'A sticker?'

'Disabled parking. Lets you park almost anywhere. It's almost as good as being a detective only we get to shoot people and drive fast.'

She's obviously a more senior police officer than Abernathy.

She looks towards the bridge. 'You'll be fine, Doc, don't be nervous.'

'I'm a professor, not a doctor.'

'Shame. You could be like Doctor Who and I could be your female sidekick. Tell me something, how do you think the Daleks managed to conquer so much of the universe when they couldn't even climb stairs?'

'I guess it's one of life's great mysteries.'

'I got loads of them.'

A two-way radio is being threaded beneath my jacket and a reflective harness loops over my shoulders and clips at the front. The woman detective lights a cigarette and pinches a strand of tobacco from the tip of her tongue. Although not in charge of the operation, she's so naturally dominant that the uniformed officers seem more ready to react to her every word.

'You want me to go with you?' she asks.

'I'll be OK.'

'All right, tell Skinny Minnie I'll buy her a low fat muffin if she steps onto our side of the fence.'

'I'll do that.'

Temporary barricades have blocked off both approaches to the bridge, which is deserted except for two ambulances and waiting paramedics. Motorists and spectators have gathered beneath umbrellas and coats. Some have scrambled up a grassy bank to get a better vantage point.

Rain bounces off the tarmac, exploding in miniature mushroom clouds before coursing through gutters and pouring off the edges of the bridge in a curtain of water.

Ducking under the barricades, I begin walking across the bridge. My hands are out of my pockets. My left arm refuses to swing. It does that sometimes – fails to get with the plan.

I can see the woman ahead of me. From a distance her skin had looked flawless, but now I notice that her thighs are criss-crossed with scratches and streaked with mud. Her pubic hair is a dark triangle: darker than her hair, which is woven into a loose plait that falls down the nape of her neck. There is something else – letters written on her stomach. A word. I can see it when she turns towards me.

SLUT.

Why the self-abuse? Why naked? This is public humiliation. Perhaps she had an affair and lost someone she loves. Now she wants to punish herself to prove she's sorry. Or it could be a threat – the ultimate game of brinkmanship – 'leave me and I'll kill myself.'

No, this is too extreme. Too dangerous. Teenagers sometimes threaten self-harm in failing relationships. It's a sign of emotional immaturity. This woman is in her late thirties or early forties with fleshy thighs and cellulite forming faint depressions on her buttocks and hips. I notice a scar. A caesarean. She's a mother.

I am close to her now. A matter of feet and inches.

Her buttocks and back are pressed hard against the fence. Her left arm is wrapped around an upper strand of wire. The other fist is holding a mobile phone against her ear.

'Hello. My name is Joe. What's yours?'

She doesn't answer. Buffeted by a gust of wind, she seems to lose her balance and rock forward. The wire is cutting into the crook of her arm. She pulls herself back.

Her lips are moving. She's talking to someone on the phone. I need her attention.

'Just tell me your name. That's not so hard. You can call me Joe and I'll call you . . .'

Wind pushes hair over her right eye. Only her left is visible,

A gnawing uncertainty expands in my stomach. Why the high heels? Has she been to a nightclub? It's too late in the day. Is she drunk? Drugged? Ecstasy can cause psychosis. LSD. Ice perhaps.

I catch snippets of her conversation.

'No. No. Please. No.'

'Who's on the phone?' I ask.

'I will. I promise. I've done everything. Please don't ask me . . .'

'Listen to me. You won't want to do this.'

I glance down. More than two hundred feet below a fat-bellied boat nudges against the current, held by its engines. The swollen river claws at the gorse and hawthorn on the lower banks. A confetti of rubbish swirls on the surface: books, branches and plastic bottles.

'You must be cold. I have a blanket.'

Again she doesn't answer. I need her to acknowledge me. A nod of the head or a single word of affirmation is enough. I need to know that she's listening.

'Perhaps I could try to put it around your shoulders – just to keep you warm.'

Her head snaps towards me and she sways forward as if ready to let go. I pause in mid-stride.

'OK, I won't come any closer. I'll stay right here. Just tell me your name.'

She raises her face to the sky, blinking into the rain like a prisoner standing in a exercise yard, enjoying a brief moment of freedom.

'Whatever's wrong. Whatever has happened to you or has upset you, we can talk about it. I'm not taking the choice away from you. I just want to understand why.'

Her toes are dropping and she has to force herself up onto her heels to keep her balance. The lactic acid is building in her muscles. Her calves must be in agony.

'I have seen people jump,' I tell her. 'You shouldn't think it is a painless way of dying. I'll tell you what happens. It will take less than three seconds to reach the water. By then you will be travelling at about seventy-five miles per hour. Your ribs will break and the jagged edges will puncture your internal organs. Sometimes the heart is compressed by the impact and tears away from the aorta so that your chest will fill with blood.'

Her gaze is now fixed on the water. I know she's listening.

'Your arms and legs will survive intact but the cervical discs in your neck or the lumbar discs in your spine will most likely rupture. It will not be pretty. It will not be painless. Someone will have to pick you up. Someone will have to identify your body. Someone will be left behind.'

High in the air comes a booming sound. Rolling thunder. The air vibrates and the earth seems to tremble. Something is coming.

Her eyes have turned to mine.

'You don't understand,' she whispers to me, lowering the phone. For the briefest of moments it dangles at the end of her fingers, as if trying to cling on to her and then tumbles away, disappearing into the void.

The air darkens and a half-formed image comes to mind – a gape-mouthed melting figure screaming in despair. Her buttocks are no longer pressing against the metal. Her arm is no longer wrapped around the wire.

13

She doesn't fight gravity. Arms and legs do not flail or clutch at the air. She's gone. Silently, dropping from view.

Everything seems to stop, as if the world has missed a heartbeat or been trapped in between the pulsations. Then everything begins moving again. Paramedics and police officers are dashing past me. People are screaming and crying. I turn away and walk back towards the barricades, wondering if this isn't part of a dream.

They are gazing at where she fell. Asking the same question, or thinking it. Why didn't I save her? Their eyes diminish me. I can't look at them.

My left leg locks and I fall onto my hands and knees, staring into a black puddle. I pick myself up again and push through the crowd, ducking beneath the barricade.

Stumbling along the side of the road, I splash through a shallow drain, swatting away raindrops. Denuded trees reach across the sky, leaning towards me accusingly. Ditches gurgle and foam. The line of vehicles is an unmoving stream. I hear motorists talking to each other. One of them yells to me.

'Did she jump? What happened? When are they going to open the road?'

I keep walking, my gaze fixed furiously ahead, moving in a kind of dream. My left arm no longer swinging. Blood hums in my ears. Perhaps it was my face that made her do it. The Parkinson's Mask, like cooling bronze. Did she see something or *not* see something?

Lurching towards the gutter, I lean over the safety rail and vomit until my stomach is empty.

There's a guy on the bridge puking his guts out, on his knees, talking to a puddle like it's listening. Breakfast. Lunch. Gone. If something round, brown and hairy comes up, I hope he swallows hard.

People are swarming across the bridge, staring over the side. They watched my angel fall. She was like a puppet whose strings had been cut, tumbling over and over, loose limbs and ligaments, naked as the day she was born.

I gave them a show; a high-wire act; a woman on the edge stepping into the void. Did you hear her mind breaking? Did you see the way the trees blurred behind her like a green waterfall? Time seemed to stop.

14

I reach into the back pocket of my jeans and draw out a steel comb, raking it through my hair, creating tiny tracks front to back, evenly spaced. I don't take my eyes off the bridge. I press my forehead to the window and watch the swooping cables turned red and blue in the flashing lights.

Droplets are darting down the outside of the glass driven by gusts that rattle the panes. It's getting dark. I wish I could see the water from here. Did she float or go straight to the bottom? How many bones were broken? Did her bowels empty the moment before she died?

The turret room is part of a Georgian house that belongs to an Arab who has gone away for the winter. A rich wanker dipped in oil. It used to be an old boarding house until he had it tarted up. It's two streets back from Avon Gorge, which I can see over the rooftops from the turret room.

I wonder who he is – the man on the bridge? He came with the tall police constable and he walked with a strange limp, one arm sawing at the air while the other didn't move from his side. A negotiator perhaps. A psychologist. Not a lover of heights.

He tried to talk her down but she wasn't listening. She was listening to me. That's the difference between a professional and a fucking amateur. I know how to open a mind. I can bend it or break it. I can close it down for the winter. I can fuck it in a thousand different ways.

I once worked with a guy called Hopper, a big redneck from Alabama, who used to puke at the sight of blood. He was a former marine and he was always telling us that the deadliest weapon in the world was a marine and his rifle. Unless he's puking, of course.

Hopper had a hard-on for films and was always quoting from Full Metal Jacket – the Gunnery Sergeant Hartman character, who bellowed at recruits, calling them maggots and scumbags and pieces of amphibian shit.

Hopper wasn't observant enough to be an interrogator. He was a bully, but that's not enough. You've got to be smart. You've got to know people – what frightens them, how they think, what they cling to when they're in trouble. You've got to watch and listen. People reveal themselves in a thousand different ways. In the clothes they wear, their shoes, their hands, their voices, the pauses and hesitations, the tics and gestures. Listen and see.

My eyes drift above the bridge to the pearl-grey clouds still crying for my angel. She did look beautiful when she fell, like a dove with a broken wing or a plump pigeon shot with an air rifle.

I used to shoot pigeons as a kid. Our neighbour, old Mr Hewitt who lived *across the fence, had a pigeon loft and used to race them. They were proper homing pigeons and he'd take them away on trips and let them go. I'd sit in my bedroom window and wait for them to come home. The silly old bastard couldn't work out why so many of them didn't make it.*

I'm going to sleep well tonight. I have silenced one whore and sent a message to the others.

To the one . . .

She'll come back just like a homing pigeon. And I'll be waiting.

2

A muddy Land Rover pulls on to the verge, skidding slightly on the loose gravel. The woman detective I met on the bridge leans across and opens the passenger door. Hinges groan in protest. I'm wet. My shoes are covered in vomit. She tells me not to worry.

Pulling back onto the road, she rips through stiff gears wrestling the Land Rover around corners. For the next few miles we sit in silence. 'I'm Detective Inspector Veronica Cray. Friends call me Ronnie.'

She pauses for a moment to see if the irony of the name registers. Ronnie and Reggie Kray were legendary East End hard men back in the sixties.

'It's Cray with a "C" not a "K",' she adds. 'My grandfather changed the spelling because he didn't want anyone thinking we were related to a family of violent psychopaths.'

'So that means you *are* related?' I ask.

'A distant cousin – something like that.'

Wipers slap hard against the bottom edge of the windscreen. The car smells vaguely of horse manure and wet hay.

'I met Ronnie once,' I tell her. 'It was just before he died. I was doing a study for the Home Office.'

'Where was he?'

'Broadmoor.'

'The psychiatric prison.'

'That's the place.'

'What was he like?'

'Old school. Well-mannered.'

'Yeah, I know the sort – very good to his mother,' she laughs. We sit in silence for another mile.

'I once heard a story that when Ronnie died the pathologist removed his brain because they were going to do experiments. The family found out and demanded the brain back. They gave it a separate funeral. I've always wondered what you do at a funeral for a brain.'

'Small coffin.'

'Shoebox.'

She drums her fingers on the steering wheel.

'It wasn't your fault, you know, back there on the bridge.'

I don't answer.

'Skinny Minnie made the decision to jump before you even stepped up to the plate. She didn't want to be saved.'

My eyes wrench to the left, out the window. Night is closing in. No views remain.

She drops me at the university, holding out her hand to shake mine. Short nails. A firm grip. We pull apart. Flat against my palm is a business card.

'My home number is on the back,' she says. 'Let's get drunk some time.'

My mobile has been turned off. There are three messages from Julianne on my voicemail. Her train from London arrived more than an hour ago. Her voice changes from angry to concerned to urgent with each new message.

I haven't seen her in three days. She's been in Rome on business with her boss, an American venture capitalist. My brilliant wife speaks four languages and has become a corporate high-flyer.

She is sitting on her suitcase working on her PDA when I pull into the pick-up zone.

'You need a ride?' I ask.

'I'm waiting for my husband,' she replies. 'He should have been

18

here an hour ago but didn't show up. Didn't call. He won't turn up now without a very good excuse.'

'Sorry.'

'That's an apology, not an excuse.'

'I should have called.'

'That's stating the obvious. It's still not an excuse.'

'How about if I offer you an explanation, a grovelling apology and a foot rub.'

'You only give me foot rubs when you want sex.'

I want to protest but she's right. Getting out of the car, I feel the cold pavement through my socks.

'Where are your shoes?'

I look down at my feet.

'They had vomit on them.'

'Someone vomited on you.'

'I did.'

'You're drenched. What happened?' Our hands are touching on the handle of the suitcase.

'A suicide. I couldn't talk her down. She jumped.'

She puts her arms around me. There is a smell about her. Something different. Wood smoke. Rich food. Wine.

'I'm so sorry, Joe. It must have been awful. Do you know anything about her?'

I shake my head.

'How did you get involved?'

'They came to the university. I wish I could have saved her.'

'You can't blame yourself. You didn't know her. You didn't know her problems.'

Dodging the oily puddles, I put her case in the boot and open the driver's door for her. She slips behind the steering wheel, adjusting her skirt. She does it automatically nowadays – takes over the driving. In profile I see an eyelash brush against her cheek as she blinks and the pink shell of her ear poking through her hair. God, she's beautiful.

I still remember the first time I laid eyes on her in a pub near Trafalgar Square. She was doing first year languages at the University of London and I was a post-grad student. She'd witnessed one of my best moments, a soapbox sermon on the evils of apartheid outside the South African Embassy. I'm sure that somewhere in the bowels of MI5 there's a transcript of that speech along with a photograph of yours truly sporting a handlebar moustache and high-waisted jeans.

After the rally we went to a pub and Julianne came up and introduced herself. I offered to buy her a drink and tried not to stare at her. She had a dark freckle on her bottom lip that was utterly mesmerising . . . it still is. My eyes are drawn to it when I speak to her and my lips are drawn to it when we kiss.

I didn't have to woo Julianne with candlelit dinners or flowers. She chose me. And by next morning, I swear this is true, we were plotting our life together over Marmite soldiers and cups of tea. I love her for so many reasons but mostly because she's *on* my side and *by* my side and because her heart is big enough for both of us. She makes me better, braver, stronger; she allows me to dream; she holds me together.

We head along the A37 towards Frome, between the hedgerows, fences and walls.

'How did the lecture go?'

'Bruno Kaufman thought it was inspired.'

'You're going to be a great teacher.'

'According to Bruno, my Parkinson's is a bonus. It creates an assumption of sincerity.'

'Don't talk like that,' she says, crossly. 'You're the most sincere man I've ever known.'

'It was a joke.'

'Well, it's not funny. This Bruno sounds cynical and sarcastic. I don't know whether I like him.'

'He can be very charming. You'll see.'

She's not convinced. I change the subject. 'So how was your trip?'

'Busy.'

She begins telling me about how her company is negotiating to buy a string of radio stations in Italy on behalf of a company in Germany. There must be something interesting about this but I turn off well before she reaches that point. After nine months, I still can't remember the names of her colleagues or her boss. Worse still, I can never *imagine* remembering them.

The car pulls into a parking space outside a house in Wellow. I decide to put on my shoes.

'I phoned Mrs Logan and told her we'd be late,' Julianne says.

'How did she sound?'

'Same as ever.'

'I'm sure she thinks we're the worst parents in the world. You're an über-career woman and I'm a . . . I'm a . . .'

'A man?'

'That'll do it.'

We both laugh.

Mrs Logan looks after Emma, our three year old, on Tuesdays and Fridays. Now that I'm lecturing at the university we need a full-time nanny. I'm interviewing on Monday.

Emma charges to the door and wraps her arms around my leg. Mrs Logan is in the hallway. Her XL T-shirt hangs straight from her breasts covering a bump of uncertainty. I can never work out if she's pregnant or fat so I keep my mouth shut.

'I'm sorry we're late,' I explain. 'An emergency. It won't happen again.'

She takes Emma's coat from a hook and thrusts her bag into my arms. The silent treatment is pretty normal. I lift Emma onto my hip. She's clutching a crayon drawing – a scribble of lines and blotches.

'For you, Daddy.'

'It's wonderful. What is it?'

'A drawing.'

'I know that. What is it a drawing of?'

'It's just a drawing.'

She has her mother's ability to state the obvious and make me look foolish.

Julianne takes her from me, giving her a cuddle. 'You've grown in four days.'

'I'm three.'

'Indeed you are.'

'Charlie?'

'She's at home, sweetheart.'

Charlie is our eldest. She's twelve going on twenty-one.

Julianne straps Emma in her car seat and I put on her favourite CD, which features four middle-aged Australian men in Teletubbie-coloured tops. She babbles from the back seat, pulling off her socks because she likes to go native.

I guess we've all gone a little native since we moved out of London. It was Julianne's idea. She said it would be less stressful for me, which is true. Cheaper houses. Good schools. More room for the girls. The usual arguments.

Our friends thought we were crazy. Somerset? You can't be serious. It's full of Aga louts and the green wellie brigade who go to Pony Club meetings and drive four-by-fours towing heated horse floats.

Charlie didn't want to leave her friends but came round when she saw the possibility of owning a horse, which is still under negotiation. So now we're living here, in the wilds of the West Country, being treated like blow-ins by locals who will never entirely trust us until four generations of O'Loughlins are buried in the village churchyard.

The cottage is lit up like a uni dormitory. Charlie is yet to equate her desire to save the planet with turning off the lights when she leaves a room. Now she's standing at the front gate with her hands on hips.

'I saw Dad on TV. Just now . . . on the news.'

'You never watch the news,' says Julianne.

'Sometimes I do. A woman jumped off a bridge.'

'Your father doesn't want to be reminded . . .'

I lift Emma from the car. She immediately wraps her arms around my neck like a koala clinging to a tree.

Charlie continues telling Julianne about the news report. Why are children so fascinated by death? Dead birds. Dead animals. Dead insects.

'How was school?' I ask, trying to change the subject.

'Good.'

'Learn anything?'

Charlie rolls her eyes. I have asked her this same question every

22

afternoon of every school day since she started kindergarten. She gave up answering long ago.

The house is suddenly filled with noise and industry. Julianne starts dinner while I bath Emma and spend ten minutes looking for her pyjamas while she runs naked in and out of Charlie's room.

I call downstairs, 'I can't find Emma's pyjamas.'

'In her top drawer.'

'I looked.'

'Under her pillow.'

'No.'

I know what's going to happen. Julianne will come all the way upstairs and discover the pyjamas sitting right in front of me. It's called 'domestic blindness'. She yells to Charlie. 'Help your father find Emma's pyjamas.'

Emma wants a bedtime story. I have to make one up involving a princess, a fairy and a talking donkey. That's what happens when you give a three-year-old creative control. I kiss her goodnight and leave her door partly open.

Supper. A glass of wine. I do the dishes. Julianne falls asleep on the sofa and apologises dreamily as I coax her upstairs and run her a bath.

These are our best nights, when we haven't seen one another for a few days; touching, brushing against each other, almost unable to wait until Charlie is in bed.

'Do you know why she jumped?' asks Julianne, slipping into the bath. I sit on the edge of the tub, trying to keep contact with her eyes. My gaze wants to drift lower to where her nipples are poking through the bubbles.

'She wouldn't talk to me.'

'She must have been very sad.'

'Yes, she must have been.'

3

Midnight. It is raining again. Water gurgles in the downpipes outside our bedroom window, sliding down the hill into a stream that has become a river and covered the causeway and stone bridge.

I used to love being awake when my girls were sleeping. It made me feel like a guardian, watching over them, keeping them safe. Tonight is different. Every time I shut my eyes I see images of a tumbling body and the ground opens up beneath me.

Julianne wakes once and slides her hand across the sheets and onto my chest, as if trying to still my heart.

'It's all right,' she whispers. 'You're here with me.'

Her eyes haven't opened. Her hand slides away.

At six in the morning I take a small white pill. My leg is twitching like a dog in the midst of a dream, chasing rabbits in its sleep. Slowly it becomes still. In Parkinson's parlance, I am now 'on'. The medication has kicked in.

It is four years since my left hand gave me the message. It wasn't written down, or typed or printed on fancy paper. It was an unconscious, random flicker of my fingers, a twitch, a ghost movement, a shadow made real. Unknown to me then, working in secret, my brain had begun divorcing my mind. It has been a long drawn-out separation with no legal argument over division

24

of assets – who gets the CD collection and Aunt Grace's antique sideboard?

The divorce began with my left hand and spread to my arm and my leg and my head. Now it feels as if my body is being owned and operated by someone else who looks like me only less familiar.

When I look at old home movies I can see the changes even two years before the diagnosis. I'm on the sidelines, watching Charlie play football. My shoulders are canted forwards, as though I'm braced against a cold wind. Is it the beginning of a stoop?

I have been through the five stages of grief and mourning. I have denied it, ranted at the unfairness, made pacts with God, crawled into a dark hole and finally accepted my fate. I have a progressive, degenerative neurological disorder. I will not use the word incurable. There *is* a cure. They just haven't found it yet. In the meantime, the divorce continues.

I wish I could tell you that I've come to terms with it now; that I'm happier than ever before; that I have embraced life, made new friends and become spiritual and fulfilled. I wish.

We have a falling-down cottage, a cat, a duck and two hamsters, Bill and Ben, who may in fact be girls. (The pet shop owner didn't seem exactly sure.)

'It's important,' I told him.

'Why?'

'I have enough women in my house.'

According to our neighbour, Mrs Nutall (if ever a name suited . . .) we also have a resident ghost, a past occupant who apparently fell down the stairs after hearing her husband had died in the Great War.

I'm always amazed by that term: The Great War. What was so great about it? Eight million soldiers died and a similar number of civilians. It's like the Great Depression. Can't we call it something else?

We live in a village called Wellow, five and a half miles from Bath Spa. It's one of those quaint, postcard-sized clusters of buildings, which barely seem big enough to hold their own history. The

25

village pub, the Fox & Badger, is two hundred years old and has a resident dwarf. How rustic is that?

We no longer have learner drivers reversing into our drive or dogs crapping on the footpath or car alarms blaring in the street. We have neighbours now. In London we had them too but pretended they didn't exist. Here they drop by to borrow garden tools and cups of flour. They even share their political opinions, which is a total anathema to anyone living in London unless you're a cab driver or a politician.

I don't know what I expected of Somerset but this will do. And if I sound sentimental, please forgive me. Mr Parkinson is to blame. Some people think sentimentality is an unearned emotion. Not mine. I pay for it every day.

The rain has eased to a drizzle. The world is wet enough. Holding a jacket over my head I open the back gate and head up the footpath. Mrs Nutall is unblocking a drain in her garden. She's wearing her hair in curlers and her feet in Wellingtons.

'Good morning,' I say.

'Drop dead.'

'Rain might be clearing.'

'Fuck off and die.'

According to Hector, the publican at the Fox & Badger, Mrs Nutall has nothing against me personally. Apparently, a previous owner of our cottage promised to marry her but ran off instead with the postmaster's wife. That was forty-five years ago and Mrs Nutall hasn't forgiven or forgotten. Whoever owns the cottage owns the blame.

Dodging the puddles, I follow the footpath to the village store, trying not to drip on the stacks of newspapers inside the door. Starting with the broadsheets, I flick through the pages, looking for a mention of what happened yesterday. There are photographs, but the story makes only a few paragraphs. Suicides make poor headlines because editors fear a contagion of copycats.

'If you're going to read 'em here I'll bring you a comfy chair and a cup of tea,' says Eric Vaile, the shopkeeper, peering up from a copy of the *Sunday Mirror* spread beneath his tattooed forearms.

'I was just looking for something,' I explain, apologetically.

'Your wallet, perhaps.'

Eric looks like he should be running a dockside pub rather than a village shop. His wife Gina, a nervous woman who flinches whenever Eric moves too suddenly, emerges from the storeroom. She's carrying a tray of soft drinks, almost buckling under the weight. Eric steps back to let her pass before planting his elbows on the counter again.

'Saw you on the TV,' he grunts. 'Could've told you she was gonna jump. I could see it coming.'

I don't answer. It won't make any difference. He's not going to stop.

'Tell me this, eh? If people are going to top themselves, why don't they have the decency to do it somewhere private, instead of blocking traffic and costing taxpayers money?'

'She was obviously very troubled,' I mumble.

'Gutless, you mean.'

'It takes a lot of courage to jump off a bridge.'

'Courage,' he scoffs.

I glance at Gina. 'And it takes even more courage to ask for help.'

She looks away.

Mid morning I call Bristol Police Headquarters and ask for Sergeant Abernathy. The rain has finally stopped. I can see a patch of blue above the tree-line and the faint traces of a rainbow.

Gravel and phlegm down the phone: 'What do you want, Professor?'

'I apologise for yesterday – leaving so suddenly. I wasn't feeling well.'

'Must be catching.'

Abernathy doesn't like me. He thinks I'm unprofessional or inept. I've met coppers like him before – warrior types who think they're separate from normal society, above it.

'We need a statement,' he says. 'There'll be an inquest.'

'You've identified her?'

'Not yet.'

There's a pause. My silence irritates him.

'In case it escaped your attention, Professor, she wasn't wearing any clothes, which means she wasn't carrying any identification.'

'Of course. I understand. It's just—.'

'What?'

'I thought somebody would have reported her missing by now. She was so well groomed: her hair, her eyebrows, her bikini-line; her fingernails were manicured. She spent time and money on herself. She's likely to have friends, a job, people who care about her.'

Abernathy must be taking notes. I can hear him scribbling. 'What else can you tell me?'

'She had a Caesarean scar, which means children. Given her age, they're probably school age by now. Primary or secondary.'

'Did she say anything to you?'

'She was talking to someone on a mobile phone – pleading with them.'

'Pleading for what?'

'I don't know.'

'And that's all she said?'

'She said I wouldn't understand.'

'Well, she got that much right.'

This case annoys Abernathy because it isn't straightforward. Until he has a name, he can't gather the required statements and hand it over to the coroner.

'When do you want me to come in?'

'Today.'

'Can't it wait?'

'If I'm working Saturday, so can you.'

Avon and Somerset Police Headquarters is in Portishead on the Severn Estuary, nine miles west of Bristol. The architects and planners were perhaps labouring under the misapprehension that if they built a police headquarters a long way from the crime-ridden pockets of inner-city Bristol, the perpetrators might relocate and join them. If we build it – they will come.

The skies have cleared, but the fields are still flooded and fence posts stick out of the brackish water like the masts of sunken ships. On the outskirts of Saltford, on the Bath Road, I see a dozen cows huddling on an island of grass surrounded by water. A broken bale of hay is scattered beneath their hooves.

Elsewhere waves of water, mud and debris are trapped against fences, trees and bridges. Thousands of farm animals have drowned and machinery lies abandoned on low ground, caked in mud like tarnished bronze sculptures.

Abernathy has a civilian secretary, a small grey woman whose clothes are more colourful than her personality. She rises grudgingly from her chair and ushers me into his office.

The sergeant, a large, freckled man, is seated at a desk. His sleeves are buttoned down and starched resolutely with a sharp crease running from his wrists to his shoulders.

He speaks in a low rumble. 'I take it you can write your own statement.' A foolscap pad is pushed towards me.

I glance down at his desk and notice a dozen manila folders and bundles of photographs. It's remarkable how much paperwork has been generated in such a short space of time. One of the files is marked 'Post Mortem'.

'Do you mind if I take a look?'

Abernathy glances at me like I'm a nosebleed and slides it over.

AVON & SOMERSET CORONER
Post-Mortem Report   No: DX-56 312
Date and time of death: 28/09/2007. 1707 hours.

Name:	*Unknown*
DOB:	*Unknown*
Sex:	*Female*
Weight:	*58.52 kgs.*
Height:	*168 cms.*
Eye colour:	*Brown*

The body is that of a well-developed, well-nourished Caucasian female. The irises are brown. The corneas are clear. The pupils are fixed and dilated.

The body is cool to the touch and there is posterior lividity and partial rigidity. There are no tattoos, deformities or amputations. The victim has a linear 5" surgical scar on her abdomen at the bikini line, indicating a prior Caesarean section.

Her right and left earlobes are pierced. Her hair is approximately sixteen inches in length, brown, with a wave. Her teeth are natural and in good condition. Her fingernails are short, neatly rounded with polish present. Pink polish is also present on her toenails.

The abdomen and back show evidence of significant soft tissue abrasions and heavy bruising caused by blunt force trauma. These markings are consistent with an impact such as a fall.

The external and internal genitalia show no evidence of sexual assault or penetration.

The facts have a stark cruelty about them. A human being with a lifetime of experiences is labelled like a piece of furniture in a catalogue. The pathologist has weighed her organs, examined her stomach contents, taken tissue samples and tested her blood. There is no privacy in death.

'What about the toxicology report?' I ask.

'It won't be ready until Monday,' he says. 'You thinking drugs?'

'It's possible.'

Abernathy is on the way to saying something and changes his mind. He takes a satellite map from a cardboard tube and unrolls it across his desk. Clifton Suspension Bridge is at the centre, flattened of its perspective until it appears to be lying on top of the water instead of seventy-five metres above it.

'This is Leigh Woods,' he says, pointing to an expanse of dark green on the western side of Avon Gorge. 'At 13.40 on Friday afternoon a man walking his dog on the Ashton Nature Reserve saw a near-naked woman in a yellow raincoat. When he approached her, the woman ran away. She was talking on a mobile and he thought it might be some sort of TV stunt.

'A second sighting was made at 15.45. A delivery driver for a dry cleaning firm saw a fully naked woman walking along Rownham Hill Road near St Mary's Road.

'A CCTV camera on the western approach of the bridge picked

her up at 16.02. She must have walked along Bridge Road from Leigh Woods.'

The details are like markers on a timeline, dividing the afternoon into gaps that can't be accounted for. Two hours and half a mile separated the first and second sightings.

The sergeant flicks through the CCTV images so quickly it appears as if the woman is moving in juddering slow motion. Raindrops have smeared the lens, blurring the edges of each print, but her nakedness couldn't be sharper.

The final photographs show her body lying on the deck of a flat bottomed boat. Albino white. Tinged with lividity around her buttocks and her flattened breasts. The only discernible colour is the red of her lipstick and the smeared letters on her stomach.

'Did you recover her mobile?'

'Lost in the river.'

'What about her shoes?'

'Jimmy Choos. Expensive but re-heeled.'

The photographs are tossed aside. The sergeant shows little sympathy for the woman. She is a problem to be solved and he wants an explanation – not for peace of mind or out of professional curiosity – but because something about the case disturbs him.

'The thing I don't understand,' he says, without looking up at me, 'is why did she go walking in the woods? If she wanted to kill herself, why not go straight to the bridge and jump off?'

'She could have been making up her mind?'

'Naked?'

He's right. It does seem bizarre. The same is true of the body art. Suicide is the ultimate act of self loathing, but it's not usually characterised by public self abuse and humiliation.

My eyes are still scanning the photographs. They come to rest on one of them. I see myself standing on the bridge. The perspective makes it look as though I'm close enough to touch her, to reach out and grab her before she falls.

Abernathy notices the same photograph. Rising from his desk, he walks to the door, opening it before I get to my feet.

'It was a bad day at the coal face, Professor. We all have them. Make your statement and you can go home.'

31

The phone on his desk is ringing. I'm still in the doorway as he answers it. I can hear only one side of the conversation.

'You're sure? When did she last see her? . . . OK . . . And she hasn't heard from her since? Right . . . Is she at home now? . . .

'Send someone to the house. Pick her up. Make sure they get a photograph. I don't want a sixteen-year-old identifying a body unless we're bloody certain it's her mother.'

My stomach drops. A daughter. Sixteen. Suicide is not a matter of self determination or free will. Someone is always left behind.

4

It takes me ten minutes to walk from the Boat House in Eastville Park to Stapleton Road. Avoiding the industrial estates and the slime-covered canal, I follow the concrete brutality of the M32 flyover.

The plastic shopping bags are cutting into my fingers. I put them down on the footpath and rest. I'm not far from home now. I have my supplies: meals in plastic trays, a six pack of beer, a slice of cheesecake in a plastic triangle – my treats for a Saturday night, purchased from a Paki grocer who keeps a shotgun under his counter, next to the porn magazines in their plastic wrappers.

The narrow streets cut in four directions, flanked by terraces and flat-fronted shops. An off-licence. A bookmakers. The Salvation Army selling second hand clothes. Posters warn against kerb crawling and urinating in public and, I love this one, putting up posters. Nobody takes a blind bit of notice. This is Bristol – city of lies, greed and corrupt politicians. The right hand always knows what the left is doing: robbing it blind. That's something my dad would say. He's always accusing people of ripping him off.

The wind and rain have stripped leaves from the trees along Fishponds Road, filling the gutters. A street sweeping machine, squat with spinning wheels, weaves between the parked cars. Shame it can't pick up the human garbage – strung-out slum kids who want me to fuck them or buy crack from them.

One of the whores is standing on the corner. A car pulls up. She negotiates, throwing her head back and laughing like a horse. A doped horse. Don't ride her, mate, you don't know where she's been.

At a café on the corner of Glen Park and Fishponds, I hang my waterproof on a hook beside the door and my hat next to it, along with my orange scarf. The place is warm and smells of boiled milk and toast. I choose a table by the window and take a moment to comb my hair, pressing the metal teeth hard against my scalp as I pull it backward from my crown to the nape of my neck.

The waitress is big-boned and almost pretty, a few years shy of being fat. Her ruffled skirt brushes against my thigh as she passes between the tables. She's wearing a plaster on her finger.

I take out my notebook and a pencil that is sharp enough to maim. I begin writing. The date comes first. Then a list of things to do.

There is a customer at a table in the corner. A woman. She's sending text messages on her mobile. If she looks at me I'll smile back.

She won't look, I think. Yes, she will. I'll give her ten seconds. Nine . . . eight . . . seven . . . six . . . five . . .

Why am I bothering? Uppity bitch. I could wipe the sneer off her face. I could stain her cheeks with mascara. I could make her question her own name.

I don't expect every woman to acknowledge me. But if I say hello to them or smile or pass the time of day, they should at least be polite enough to respond in kind.

The woman at the library, the Indian one, with hennaed hands and disappointed eyes, she always smiles. The other librarians are old and tired and treat everyone like book thieves.

The Indian woman has slender legs. She should wear short skirts and make the most of them instead of covering them up. I can only see her ankles when she crosses her legs at her desk. She does it often. I think she knows I'm watching her.

My coffee has arrived. The milk should be hotter. I will not send it back. The waitress with the almost-pretty face would be disappointed. I will tell her next time.

The list is almost finished. There are names down the left-hand column. Contacts. People of interest. I will cross each of them off as I find them.

Leaving coins on the table, I dress in my coat, my hat and my scarf. The waitress doesn't see me leave. I should have handed her the money. She would have had to look at me then.

I can't walk quickly with the shopping bags. Rain leaks into my eyes and *gurgles in the downpipes. I am here now, at the end of Bourne Lane, outside a gated forecourt, fenced off and topped with barbed wire. It was once a panel-beaters or some sort of workshop with a house attached.*

The door has three deadlocks – a Chubb Detector, a five pin Weiser and a Lips 8362C. I start at the bottom, listening to the steel pins retracting in their cylinders.

I step over the morning mail. There are no lights in the hallway. I removed the bulbs. Two floors of the house are empty. Closed off. The radiators are cold. When I signed the lease, the landlord Mr Swingler asked if I had a big family.

'No.'

'Why do you need such a big house?'

'I have big dreams,' I said.

Mr Swingler is Jewish but looks like a skinhead. He also owns a boarding house in Truro and a block of flats in St Pauls, not far from here. He asked me for references. I didn't have any.

'Do you have a job?'

'Yes.'

'No drugs. No parties. No orgies.'

He might have said 'corgis', I couldn't understand his accent, but I paid three months rent in advance, which shut him up.

Taking a torch from on top of the fridge, I return to the hall and collect the mail: a gas bill, a pizza menu, and a large white envelope with a school crest in the top left corner.

I take the envelope to the kitchen and leave it sitting on the table while I pack away the shopping and open a can of beer. Then I sit and slide my finger beneath the flap, tearing a ragged line.

The envelope contains a glossy magazine and a letter from the admissions secretary of Oldfield Girls School in Bath.

Dear Mrs Tyler,

In reference to your request for addresses, I'm afraid that we don't keep on-going records of our past students but there is an Old Girls website. You will need to contact the convenor Diane Gillespie to get a username, pin and password to access the secure section of the site containing the contact details of old girls.

I am enclosing a copy of the school yearbook for 1988 and hope it will bring back some memories.

Good luck with your search.
Yours sincerely,
Belinda Casson

The front page of the yearbook has a photograph of three smiling girls, in uniform, walking through the school gates. The school crest has a Latin quotation: 'Lux et veritas' (Light and Truth).

There are more photographs inside. I turn the pages, running my fingers over the images. Some of them are class photographs on a tiered stage. Girls at the front are seated with knees together and hands clasped on their laps. The middle row girls are standing and those at the back must be perched on an unseen bench. I study the captions, the names, the class, the year.

There she is – my beloved – the whore's whore. Second row. Fourth from the right. She had a brown bob. A round face. A half-smile. You were eighteen years old. I was still ten years away. Ten years. How many Sundays is that?

I tuck the school yearbook under my arm and get a second can of beer. Upstairs a computer hums on my desk. I type in the password and call up an online telephone directory. The screen refreshes. There were forty-eight girls in the leaving year of 1988. Forty-eight names. I won't find her today. Not today, but soon.

Maybe I'll watch the video again. I like watching one of them fall.

5

Charlie is dressed in jeans and a sweatshirt, dancing with Emma in the lounge. The music is turned up loud and she lifts Emma onto her hip and spins her round, dipping her backwards. Emma giggles and snorts with laughter.

'You be careful. You'll make her throw up.'

'Look at our new trick.'

Charlie hoists Emma onto her shoulders and leans forward, letting the youngster crawl down her back.

'Very clever. You should join the circus.'

Charlie has grown up so much in the past few months it's nice to see her acting like a kid again, playing with her sister. I don't want her to grow up too quickly. I don't want her becoming one of the girls I see roaming around Bath with pierced navels and 'I-slept-with-your-boyfriend' T-shirts.

Julianne has a theory. Sex is more explicit everywhere except in real life. She says teenage girls may dress like Paris Hilton and dance like Beyoncé but that doesn't mean they're making amateur porn videos or having sex over car bonnets. Please, God, I hope she's right.

I can already see the changes in Charlie. She is going through that monosyllabic stage where no words are wasted on her parents.

She saves them up for her friends and spends hours texting on her mobile and chatting online.

Julianne and I talked about sending her to boarding school when we moved out of London, but I wanted to kiss her good-night each evening and wake her of a morning. Julianne said I was trying to make up for the time I *didn't* spend with my own father, God's-personal-physician-in-waiting, who sent me to boarding school from the age of eight.

Maybe she's right.

Julianne has come downstairs to see what the fuss is about. She's been working in the office, translating documents and sending emails. I grab her around the waist and we dance to the music.

'I think we should practise for our dance classes,' I say.

'What do you mean?'

'They start on Tuesday. Beginners Latin – Samba and the Rhrrrrumba!'

Her face suddenly falls.

'What's wrong?'

'I can't make it.'

'Why?'

'I have to get back to London tomorrow afternoon. We're flying to Moscow first thing Monday morning.'

'We?'

'Dirk.'

'Oh, Dirk the Jerk.'

She looks at me crossly. 'You don't even know him.'

'Can't he find another translator?'

'We've been working on this deal for three months. He doesn't want to use someone new. And I don't want to hand it over to someone else. I'm sorry, I should have told you.'

'That's OK. You forgot.'

My sarcasm irritates her.

'Yes, Joe, I forgot. Don't make an issue out of it.'

There is an uncomfortable silence. A gap between songs. Charlie and Emma have stopped dancing.

Julianne blinks first. 'I'm sorry. I'll be back on Friday.'

'So I'll cancel the dancing.'

38

'You go. You'll have a great time.'

'But I've never been before.'

'It's a beginner's class. Nobody is going to expect you to be Fred Astaire.'

The dance lessons were my idea. Actually, they were suggested by my best mate, Jock, a neurologist. He sent me literature showing how Parkinson's sufferers benefit from practising their co-ordination. It was yoga or dancing lessons. Both if possible.

I told Julianne. She thought it was romantic. I saw it as a challenge.

I would throw down the gauntlet to Mr Parkinson; a duel to the death, full of pirouettes and flashing feet. May the best man win.

Emma and Charlie are dancing again. Julianne joins them, effortlessly finding the rhythm. She holds out her hand to me. I shake my head.

'Come on, Dad,' says Charlie.

Emma does a bum wiggle. It's her best move. I don't have a best move.

We dance and sing and collapse on the sofa laughing. It's a long while since Julianne has laughed like this. My left arm trembles and Emma holds it still. It's a game she plays. Holding it with both hands and then letting go to see if it trembles, before grabbing it again.

Later that evening when the girls are asleep and our horizontal waltz is over, I cuddle Julianne and grow melancholy.

'Did Charlie tell you she saw our ghost?'

'No. Where?'

'On the stairs.'

'I wish Mrs Nutall would stop putting stories in her head.'

'She's a mad old bat.'

'Is that a professional diagnosis?'

'Absolutely,' I say.

Julianne stares into space, her mind elsewhere . . . in Rome perhaps, or Moscow.

'You know I give them ice-cream all the time when you're not here,' I tell her.

'That's because you're buying their love,' she replies.

'You bet. It's for sale and I want it.'

She laughs.

'Are you happy?' I ask.

She turns her face to mine. 'That's a strange question.'

'I can't stop thinking about that woman on the bridge. Something made her unhappy.'

'And you think I'm the same?'

'It was nice to hear you laughing today.'

'It's nice to be home.'

'Nicest place to be.'

6

Monday morning. Grey. Dry. The agency is sending three candidates for me to interview. I don't think they're called nannies any more. They are carers or childcare professionals.

Julianne is on her way to Moscow, Charlie is on the bus to school and Emma is playing with her dolls' clothes in the dining room, trying to put a bonnet on Sniffy our neurotic cat. Sniffy's full name is Sniffy Toilet Roll, which is again what happens when you give a three-year-old the naming rights to family pets.

The first interview starts badly. Her name is Jackie and she's nervous. She bites her nails and touches her hair constantly as if needing reassurance that it hasn't disappeared.

Julianne's instructions were clear. I am to make sure the nanny doesn't do drugs, drink or drive too fast. Exactly how I'm supposed to find this out is beyond me.

'This is where I'm supposed to find out if you're a granny basher,' I tell Jackie.

She gives me a puzzled look. 'My granny's dead.'

'You didn't bash her, did you?'

'No.'

'Good.'

I cross her off the list.

The next candidate is twenty-four from Newcastle with a sharply pointed face, brown eyes and dark hair pulled back so tightly it raises her eyebrows. She seems to be casing the house with the view to robbing it later with her burglar boyfriend.

'What car will I be driving?' she asks.

'An Astra.'

She's not impressed. 'I can't drive a manual. I don't think I should be expected to. Will there be a TV in my room?'

'There can be.'

'How big is it?'

'I'm not sure.'

Is she talking about watching it or flogging it, I wonder. I scrub out her name. Two strikes.

At 11.00 a.m. I interview a pretty Jamaican with braided hair, looped back on itself and pinned with a large tortoiseshell clip at the back of her head. Her name is Mani, she has good references and a lovely deep voice. I like her. She has a nice smile.

Halfway through the interview, there's a sudden cry from the dining room. Emma in pain. I try to rise but my left leg locks. The effect is called *bradykinesia*, a symptom of Parkinson's, and it means that Mani reaches Emma first. The hinged lid of the toy box has trapped her fingers. Emma takes one look at the dark-skinned stranger and howls even louder.

'She hasn't been held by many black people,' I say, trying to rescue the situation. It makes things worse. 'It's not your colour. We have lots of black friends in London. Dozens of them.'

My God, I'm suggesting my three-year-old is a racist!

Emma has stopped crying. 'It's my fault. I picked her up too suddenly,' Mani says, looking at me sadly.

'She doesn't know you yet.' I explain.

'Yes.'

Mani is gathering her things.

'I'll call the agency,' I say. 'They'll let you know.'

But we both realise what's happening. She's going to take a job elsewhere. It's a shame. A misunderstanding.

After she's gone, I make Emma a sandwich and settle her for her afternoon nap. There are chores to do – washing and ironing.

I know I'm not supposed to admit such a thing, but being at home is boring. Emma is wonderful and enchanting and I love her to bits but there are only so many times I can play sock puppets or watch her stand on one leg or listen to her declare from the top of the climbing frame that she is indeed the king of the castle and I am, yet again, the dirty rascal.

Looking after young children is the most important job in the world. Believe me – it is. However, the sad, unspoken, implicit truth is that looking after young children is boring. Those guys who sit in missile silos waiting for the unthinkable to happen are doing an important job too, but you can't tell me they're not bored out of their tiny skulls and playing endless games of Solitaire and Battleships on the Pentagon computers.

The doorbell rings. Standing on the front step is a chestnut-haired teenager in low-slung black jeans, a T-shirt and tartan jacket. Ear studs like beads of mercury glisten on her earlobes.

She is clasping a shoulder bag hard to her chest, leaning forward a little. An October wind whips up an eddy of leaves at her feet.

'I wasn't expecting anyone else,' I tell her.

Her head tilts to one side, frowning.

'Are you Professor O'Loughlin?'

'Yes.'

'I'm Darcy Wheeler.'

'Come in, Darcy. We have to be quiet, Emma is sleeping.'

She follows me along the hall to the kitchen. 'You look very young. I expected somebody older.'

Again she looks at me curiously. The whites of her eyes are bloodshot and raw from the wind.

'How long have you been a childcare professional?'

'Excuse me?'

'How long have you looked after children?'

Now she looks concerned. 'I'm still at school.'

'I don't understand.'

She hugs her bag a little tighter, steeling herself. 'You talked to my mother. You were there when she fell.'

Her words shatter the quietness like a dropped tray of glasses. I see a resemblance, the shape of her face, her dark eyebrows. The woman on the bridge.

'How did you find me?'

'I read the police report.'

'How did you get here?'

'I caught the bus.'

She makes it sound so obvious but this isn't supposed to happen. Grieving daughters don't turn up on my doorstep. The police should have answered Darcy's questions and given her counselling. They should have found a family member to look after her.

'The police say it was suicide but that's impossible. Mum wouldn't . . . she couldn't, not like that.'

Her desperation trembles in her throat.

'What was your mother's name?' I ask.

'Christine.'

'Would you like a cup of tea, Darcy?'

She nods. I fill the kettle and set out the cups, giving myself a chance to work out what I'm going to say.

'Where have you been staying?' I ask.

'I'm at boarding school.'

'Does the school know where you are?'

Darcy doesn't answer. Her shoulders curve and she shrinks even more. I sit down opposite her, making sure her eyes meet mine.

'I want to know exactly how you came to be here.'

The story tumbles out. The police had interviewed her on Saturday afternoon. She was counselled by a social worker and then taken back to Hampton House, a private girls' school in Cardiff. On Sunday night she waited until lights out and unscrewed the wooden blocks on her house window, opening it far enough to slip out. Once she had dodged the security guard, she walked to Cardiff Central, and waited for the first train. She caught the 8.04 to Bath Spa and a bus to Norton St Phillips. She walked the last three miles to Wellow. The journey took most of the morning.

I notice the grass clippings in her hair and mud on her shoes. 'Where did you sleep last night?'

'In a park.'

My God, she could have frozen to death. Darcy raises the mug of tea to her lips, holding it steady with both hands. I look at her clear brown eyes, her bare neck; the thinness of her jacket and the dark bra outlined beneath her T-shirt. She is beautifully ugly in a gawky teenage way, but destined in a few years to be exceptionally beautiful and to bring no end of misery to a great number of men.

'What about your father?'

She shrugs.

'Where's he?'

'No idea. He walked out on my mum before I was born. We didn't hear from him after that.'

'Not at all?'

'Never.'

'I need to call your school.'

'I'm not going back.' The sudden steel in her voice surprises me.

'We have to tell them where you are.'

'Why? They don't care. I'm sixteen. I can do what I want.'

Her defiance has all the hallmarks of a childhood spent at boarding school. It has made her strong. Independent. Angry. Why is she here? What does she expect me to do?

'It wasn't suicide,' she says again. 'Mum hated heights. I mean really hated them.'

'When did you last talk to her?'

'On Friday morning.'

'How did she seem?'

'Normal. Happy.'

'What did you talk about?'

She stares into her mug, as if reading the contents. 'We had a fight.'

'What about?'

'It's not important.'

'Tell me anyway.'

She hesitates and shakes her head. The sadness in her eyes tells half the story. Her last words to her mother were full of anger. She wants to take them back or to have them over again.

Trying to change the subject, she opens the fridge door and begins sniffing the contents of Tupperware containers and jars. 'Got anything to eat?'

'I can make you a sandwich.'

'How about a Coke?'

'We don't have fizzy drinks in the house.'

'Really?'

'Really.'

She's found a packet of biscuits in the pantry and picks apart the plastic wrapping with her fingernails.

'Mum was supposed to phone the school on Friday afternoon. I wanted to come home for the weekend, but I needed her permission. I called her all day – on her mobile and at home. I sent her text messages – dozens of them. I couldn't get through.

'I told my housemistress something must be wrong, but she said Mum was probably just busy and I shouldn't worry, only I did worry, I worried all Friday night and Saturday morning. The housemistress said Mum had probably gone away for the weekend and forgotten to tell me, but I knew it wasn't true.

'I asked for permission to go home, but they wouldn't let me. So I ran away on Saturday afternoon and went to the house. Mum wasn't there. Her car was gone. Things were so random. That's when I called the police.'

She holds herself perfectly still.

'The police showed me a photo. I told them it must be somebody else. Mum wouldn't even go on the London Eye. Last summer we went to Paris and she panicked going up the Eiffel Tower. She hated heights.'

Darcy freezes. The packet of biscuits has broken open in her hands, spilling crumbs between her fingers. She stares at the wreckage and rocks forward, curling her knees to her chest and uttering a long unbroken sob.

The professional part of me knows to avoid physical contact but the father in me is stronger. I put my arms around her, pulling her head to my chest.

'You were there,' she whispers.

'Yes.'

46

'It wasn't suicide. She'd never leave me.'

'I'm sorry.'

'Please help me.'

'I don't know if I can, Darcy.'

'Please.'

I wish I could take her pain away. I wish I could tell her that it won't hurt like this forever or that one day she'll forget how this feels. I've heard childcare experts talk about how fast children forgive and forget. That's bullshit! Children remember. Children hold grudges. Children keep secrets. Children can sometimes seem strong because their defences have never been breached or eroded by tragedy, but they are as light and fragile as spun glass.

Emma is awake and calling out for me. I climb the stairs to her room and lower one side of her cot, lifting her into my arms. Her fine dark hair is tousled by sleep.

I hear the toilet flush downstairs. Darcy has washed her face and brushed her hair, pinning it tightly in a bun that makes her neck appear impossibly long.

'This is Emma,' I explain as she returns to the kitchen.

'Hi, gorgeous,' says Darcy, finding a smile.

Emma plays hard to get, turning her face away. Suddenly, she spies the biscuits and reaches out for one. I set her down and, surprisingly, she goes straight to Darcy and crawls onto her lap.

'She must like you,' I say.

Emma toys with the buttons of Darcy's jacket.

'I need to ask you a few more questions.'

Darcy nods.

'Was your mother upset about anything? Depressed?'

'No.'

'Was she having trouble sleeping?'

'She had pills.'

'Was she eating regularly?'

'Sure.'

'What did your mother do?'

'She's a wedding planner. She has her own company – Blissful. She and her friend Sylvia started it up. They did a wedding for Alexandra Phillips.'

47

'Who's she?'

'A celebrity. Haven't you ever seen that show about the vet who looks after animals in Africa?'

I shake my head.

'Well, she got married and Mum and Sylvia did the whole thing. It made all the magazines.'

Darcy still hasn't referred to her mother in the past tense. It's not unusual and has nothing to do with denial. Two days isn't long enough for the reality to take hold and permeate her thinking.

I still don't understand what she's doing here. I couldn't save her mother and I can't tell her any more than the police can. Christine Wheeler's final words were addressed to me but she didn't give me any clues.

'What do you want me to do?' I ask.

'Come to the house. Then you'll see.'

'See what?'

'She didn't kill herself.'

'I watched her jump, Darcy.'

'Well, something must have made her do it.' She kisses the top of Emma's head. 'She wouldn't do it like that. She wouldn't leave me.'

7

The eighteenth century cottage has gnarled and twisted wisteria climbing above the front door, reaching as high as the eaves. The adjacent garage was once a stable and is now part of the main house.

Darcy unlocks the front door and steps into the dimness of the entrance hall. She hesitates, jostling with emotions that retard her movements.

'Is something wrong?'

She shakes her head unconvincingly.

'You can stay outside if you like and look after Emma.'

She nods.

Emma is kicking up leaves on the path.

Crossing the slate floor of the entrance hall, I brush against an empty coat hook and notice an umbrella propped beneath it. There is a kitchen on the right. Through the windows I see a rear garden and a wood railing fence separating neatly pruned rose bushes from adjacent gardens. A cup and cereal bowl rest in the draining rack. The sink is dry and wiped clean. Inside the kitchen bin are vegetable scraps, curling orange peel and old teabags the colour of dog turds. The table is clear except for a small pile of bills and opened letters.

I yell over my shoulder. 'How long have you lived here?'

Darcy answers through the open door. 'Eight years. Mum had to take out a second mortgage when she started the company.'

The living room is tastefully but tiredly furnished, with an aging sofa, armchairs and a large sideboard with cat-scratched corners. There are framed photographs on the mantelpiece. Most of them show Darcy in various ballet costumes, either backstage or performing. Ballet trophies and medals are lined up in a display case, alongside more photographs.

'You're a dancer.'

'Yes.'

It should have been obvious. She has the classic dancer's body: lean and loose-limbed, with slightly out-turned feet.

My questions have brought Darcy inside.

'Is this how you found the house?'

'Yes.'

'You haven't moved anything?'

'No.'

'Or touched anything?'

She thinks about this.

'I used the phone . . . to call the police.'

'Which phone?'

'The one upstairs.'

'Why not use this one?' I motion to the handset of a cordless phone, sitting in a cradle on a side table.

'The handset was on the floor. The battery was flat.'

A small pile of women's clothes lie discarded at the base of the table – a pair of machine-distressed jeans, a top and a cardigan. I kneel down. A flash of colour peeks from beneath the sofa – not hidden but tossed away in a hurry. My fingers close around the fabric. Underwear, a bra and matching panties.

'Was your mother seeing anyone? A boyfriend?'

Darcy suppresses the urge to laugh. 'No.'

'What's so funny?'

'My mother is going to be one of those old women with a herd of cats and a wardrobe full of cardigans.' She smiles and then remembers she's speaking of a mother without a future.

'Would she have told you if she was seeing someone?'

Darcy isn't sure.

I hold up the underwear. 'Do these belong to your mother?'

She nods, frowning.

'What?'

'She was like really obsessed about stuff like that, picking up things. I wasn't allowed to borrow any of her clothes unless I hung them up or put them in the wash afterwards. "The floor is not a wardrobe," she said.'

I climb the stairs to the main bedroom. The bed is untouched, without a crease on the duvet. Bottles are lined up neatly on her dresser. Towels are folded evenly on the towel rails in the en suite.

I open the large walk-in wardrobe and step inside. I can smell Christine Wheeler. I touch her dresses, her skirts, her shirts. I put my hands in the pockets of her jackets. I find a taxi receipt, a dry cleaning tag, a pound coin, an after dinner mint. There are clothes she hasn't worn in years. Clothes she is making last the distance. Here is a woman used to having money who suddenly doesn't have enough.

An evening gown slips from a hanger and pools at my feet. I pick it up again, feeling the fabric slip between my fingers. There are racks of shoes, at least a dozen pairs, arranged in neat rows.

Darcy sits on the bed. 'Mum liked shoes. She said it was her one extravagance.'

I remember the pair of bright red Jimmy Choos that Christine was wearing on the bridge. Party shoes. There is a gap for a missing pair at the end of the lower shelf.

'Did your mother sleep naked?'

'No.'

'Did she ever wander around the house naked?'

'No.'

'Did she draw the curtains before she undressed?'

'I've never taken much notice.'

I glance out the bedroom window, which overlooks an allotment with vegetable gardens and a greenhouse guarded by an elm tree. Spider webs are woven through the branches of the trees like fine muslin. Someone could easily watch the house and not be noticed.

51

'If someone came to the door, would she have opened it or put on the security chain?'

'I don't know.'

My mind keeps going back to the clothes by the phone. Christine undressed, making no attempt to close the curtains. She didn't fold her clothes or place them on a chair. The cordless phone handset was found on the floor.

Darcy could be wrong about a boyfriend or a lover, but there's no sign of the bed being used. No condoms. No tissues. Similarly, there's no trace of an intruder. Nothing appears to be disturbed or missing. There is no sign of a search or a struggle. The place is clean. Tidy. It's not the house of someone who has given up hope or someone who doesn't want to live any more.

'Was the front door deadlocked?'

'I don't remember,' says Darcy.

'It's important. When you came home, you put the key in the door. Did you need two keys?'

'No. I don't think so.'

'Did your mother have a raincoat?'

'Yes.'

'What did it look like?'

'It was a cheap plastic thing.'

'What colour?'

'Yellow.'

'Where is it now?'

She takes me to the entrance hall – an empty coat hook tells the rest of the story. It was raining on Friday; bucketing down. She chose the raincoat but not an umbrella.

Emma is sitting at the kitchen table, attacking a piece of paper with coloured pencils. I walk past her into the lounge, trying to create my own picture of what happened on Friday. I glimpse the ordinariness of the day, a woman doing her chores, washing a cup, wiping down the sink and then the phone rang. She answered it.

She took off her clothes. She didn't draw the curtains. She walked naked from her house wearing only a plastic raincoat. She didn't double lock the door. She was in a hurry. Her handbag is still on the hallway table.

The thick glass top of the coffee table is supported on two ceramic elephants with tusks raised and flattened above their heads. Kneeling beside the table, I lower my head and peer along the smooth glass surface, noticing tiny shards of broken crayon or lipstick. This is where she wrote the word 'slut' across her torso.

There is something else on the glass, a series of opaque circles and truncated lines of lipstick. The circles are dried tears. She was crying. And the lines could be the edges of looping letters that departed from a page. Christine wrote something in lipstick. It can't have been a phone number, she could have used a pen for that. More likely it was a message or a sign.

Forty-eight hours ago I watched this woman plunge to her death. Surely it had to be suicide, yet psychologically it doesn't make sense. Everything about her actions suggested intent, yet she was a reluctant participant.

The last thing Christine Wheeler said to me was that I wouldn't understand. She was right.

8

Sylvia Furness lives in a flat in Great Pulteney Street on the first floor of a Georgian row that has probably featured in every BBC period drama since the original *Forsyte Saga*. I half expect to see horse-drawn carriages outside and women parading in hats.

Sylvia Furness isn't wearing a hat. Her short blonde hair is held off her face with a headband and she's clad in black spandex shorts, a white sports bra and a light blue T-shirt with a looping neckline. A gym membership card dangles from a bulky set of keys that must help burn calories simply by being lugged around.

'Excuse me, Mrs Furness. Do you have a moment?'

'Whatever you're selling, I'm not buying.'

'It's about Christine Wheeler.'

'I'm late for a spin class. I don't talk to the press.'

'I'm not a journalist.'

She glances past me then and notices Darcy at the top of the stairs.

With a squeak of anguish she pushes past me, wrapping her arms around the teenager, summoning tears. Darcy gives me a look that says, *I told you so*.

She didn't want to come upstairs because she knew her mother's business partner would make a fuss.

'What sort of fuss?'

'A fuss.'

The front door is reopened and we're ushered inside. Sylvia is still clutching Darcy's hand. Emma follows, suddenly quiet, with a thumb wedged in her mouth.

The flat has polished wooden floors, tasteful furniture and ceilings that seem higher than the clouds outside. There are women's touches everywhere – from the throw cushions in African prints to the dried flower arrangements.

My eyes scan the room and fall upon a birthday invitation propped beside the phone. 'Alice' is invited to a pizza and pyjama party. Her friend Angela is turning twelve.

Sylvia Furness is still holding Darcy's hand, asking questions and offering sympathy. The teenager manages to slip out of her grasp and tells Emma there's a park on the corner, behind the museum. It has swings and a slide.

'Can I take her?' asks Darcy.

She'll have you pushing her forever,' I warn.

'That's OK.'

'We'll talk when you get back,' says Sylvia who has tossed her gym bag on the sofa. She looks at her watch – a stainless steel, sporty number. She won't make her spin class. Instead she flops into an armchair, looking irritated. Her breasts don't move. I wonder if they're real. As if reading my mind she straightens her shoulders.

'Why are you so interested in Christine?'

'Darcy doesn't think it was suicide.'

'And why does that concern you?'

'I just want to be sure.'

Her eyes are full of a gentle curiosity as I explain my involvement with Christine and how Darcy came looking for me. Sylvia props her toned legs on the coffee table, showing what miles on the treadmill can do for a woman.

'You were business partners.'

'We were more than that,' she replies. 'We went to school together.'

'When did you last see Christine?'

'Friday morning. She came into the office. She had an

55

appointment with a young couple who were planning a Christmas wedding.'

'How did she seem?'

'Fine.'

'She wasn't concerned or worried about anything?'

'Not particularly. Chris wasn't the type.'

'What was she like?'

'The sweetest person. A total one-off. Sometimes I used to think she was too nice.'

'In what way?'

'She was too soft for this business. People would give her a sob story and she'd give them longer to pay or offer them discounts. Chris was a hopeless romantic. She believed in fairytales. Fairytale weddings. Fairytale marriages. It's funny when you think her own lasted less than two years. At school she had a wedding chest. I mean, what sort of person still has a wedding chest? And she used to say that each of us has a special soul mate. Our Mr Right.'

'You obviously don't agree.'

Her head swivels towards me. 'You're a psychologist. Do you really believe there is only one person for each of us in this big wide world?'

'It's a nice thought.'

'No it's not! How boring.' She laughs. 'If that's true, my soul mate had better have a six pack and a six figure salary.'

'What about your husband?'

'He's a lump of lard, but he knows how to make money.' She runs her hands along her legs. 'Why is it that married men let themselves go while their wives spend hours trying to look beautiful?'

'You don't know?'

She laughs. 'Maybe that's a discussion for another day.'

Sylvia stands and goes to the bedroom. 'Do you mind if I get changed?'

'Not at all.'

She leaves the door open and shucks off her T-shirt and bra. There are muscles on her back like flat stones beneath her skin.

Her black spandex shorts slide down her legs, but I can't see what replaces them; the bed and the angle defeat me.

Dressed in cream slacks and a cashmere sweater, she returns to the lounge, tossing her tiny shorts and bra on her gym bag.

'What were we talking about?'

'Marriage. You said Christine was a believer.'

'Head cheerleader. She cried at every wedding we planned. Complete strangers were tying the knot and her pockets were full of soggy tissues.'

'Is that why she set up Blissful?'

'It was her baby.'

'How was business?'

Sylvia smiles wryly.

'Like I said, Chris was a soft touch. People asked for dream weddings – with all the bells and whistles – then they refused to pay or delayed sending the cheque. Christine wasn't tough enough.'

'There were money problems?'

She stretches her arms above her head. 'Rain. Cancellations. Legal action. It wasn't a good season. We have to turn over fifty thousand pounds a month to break even. The average cost of a wedding is fifteen thousand. The big ones are few and far between.'

'How much were you losing?'

'Chris took out a second mortgage when we set up. Now we have an overdraft of twenty thousand and debts of more than two hundred thousand.'

Sylvia rattles off the numbers without emotion.

'You mentioned legal action.'

'A wedding in the spring was a disaster. Dodgy mayonnaise on the seafood buffet. Food poisoning. The father of the bride is a lawyer and a complete wanker. Christine offered to tear up the bill but he wants us to pay compensation.'

'You must have insurance.'

'The insurance underwriter is trying to find a loophole. We may have to go to court .'

She takes a plastic bottle of water from her gym bag and drinks, wiping her lips with her thumb and forefinger.

'If you don't mind me saying, you don't seem very concerned.'

Lowering the bottle, her eyes lock on mine.

'Chris put up most of the money. My exposure was minimal and my husband is very understanding.'

'Indulgent.'

'You could say that.'

The money problems and legal action could explain what happened on Friday. Perhaps the person on the phone to Christine Wheeler was owed money. Either that or she lost hope and couldn't see a way out.

'Was Christine the sort of person who would commit suicide?' I ask.

Sylvia shrugs. 'You know how they say the ones who talk about committing suicide are less likely to do it – well, Chris never talked about it. She was the most positive, up-beat, optimistic person I've ever met. I mean that. And she loved Darcy like there was no tomorrow. So the answer is no – I have no idea why she did it. I guess she cracked.'

'What's going to happen to the business now?'

Again she glances at her watch. 'As of an hour ago it belongs to the receivers.'

'You're wrapping it up.'

'What else can I do?'

She tucks her legs to the side in that casual effortless way all women can. I see no signs of regret or disappointment. Hard-bodied Sylvia Furness is as tough on the inside as she is on the outside.

Darcy and Emma meet me downstairs. I lift Emma onto my hip. 'Where are we going?' asks Darcy.

'To see the police.'

'You believe me.'

'I believe you.'

9

Detective Inspector Veronica Cray emerges from a barn wearing baggy jeans tucked into Wellingtons and a man's shirt with button-up pockets that sit almost horizontally upon her breasts.

'You caught me shovelling shit,' she says, leaning into the heavy door, which swings inwards on rusty hinges. She drops a plank into the bracket. I hear horses shifting in their stalls. Smell them.

'Thank you for seeing me.'

'So you wanted that drink after all,' she says, wiping her hands on her hips. 'Perfect day for it. My day off.'

She spies Darcy in the passenger seat of my car and Emma playing with the steering wheel.

'You brought the family.'

'The little girl is mine.'

'And the other one?'

'Is Christine Wheeler's daughter.'

The DI has spun to face me.

'You went looking for the daughter?'

'She found me.'

Suspicion has replaced some of her warmth and affability.

'What in glory's name are you doing, Professor?'

'Christine Wheeler didn't commit suicide.'

59

'With all due respect, I think we both should leave that to the coroner.'

'You saw her – she was terrified.'

'Of dying?'

'Of falling.'

'She was perched on the edge of a bridge, for God's sake.'

'No, you don't understand.'

I glance at Darcy who looks tired and apprehensive. She should be back at school or being looked after by her family. Does she have any family?

The detective sucks in a breath. Her entire chest expands and then she sighs. She strides towards the car and crouches next to the open driver's door, addressing Emma.

'Are you a fairy?'

Emma shakes her head.

'A princess?'

Another shake.

'Then you must be an angel. I'm pleased to meet you. I don't meet many angels in my line of work.'

'Are you a man or a woman?' asks Emma.

The DI laughs.

'I'm all woman, honey. One hundred per cent.'

She glances at Darcy. 'I'm very sorry about your mother. Is there anything I can do for you?'

'Believe me,' she says softly.

'Normally, I'm a true believer in most things but maybe you got to convince me of this. Let's get you somewhere warmer.'

I have to duck my head as I go through the door. DI Cray kicks off her Wellingtons. Rectangles of mud fall from between the treads.

She turns away from me and begins making her way along the hall.

'I'm going to take a shower, Professor. You put these girls in front of the fire. I got six different sorts of hot chocolate and I'm in the mood to share.'

Darcy and Emma haven't said a word since leaving the car. Veronica Cray can render someone speechless. She's unavoidable. Immovable. Like a rocky outcrop in a force ten gale.

I can hear the shower running. I put a kettle on the Aga stove and search through the pantry. Darcy has found a cartoon for Emma to watch on TV. I haven't fed her anything since breakfast except for biscuits and a banana.

I notice a calendar pinned to a corkboard. It is dotted with scribbled reminders of feed suppliers, farriers and horse sales. There are bills to be paid and reminder notes. Wandering into the dining room, I look for signs of a partner. There are photographs on the mantelpiece and more on the fridge of a young dark-haired man, a son perhaps.

I don't normally, knowingly search so openly for clues about a person but Veronica Cray fascinates me. It's as though she's fought a lifelong battle to be accepted for who she is. And now she's comfortable with her body, her sexuality and her life.

The bathroom door opens and she emerges, wrapped in a huge towel knotted between her breasts. She has to step around me. We both move the same way and back again. I apologise and flatten myself against the wall.

'Don't worry, Professor, I'm inflatable. Normally I'm size ten.'

She laughs. I'm the only person embarrassed.

The bedroom door closes. Ten minutes later she emerges in the kitchen wearing a pressed shirt and trousers. Her spiky hair is beaded with water.

'You breed horses.'

'I save old showjumpers from the knacker's yard.'

'What do you do with them?'

'Find them homes.'

'My daughter Charlie wants a horse.'

'How old is she?'

'Twelve.'

'I can get her one.'

The girls are drinking chocolate. DI Cray offers me something stronger, but I'm not supposed to drink any more because it affects my medication. I settle instead for coffee.

'Do you have any idea what you're doing?' she says, concerned rather than angry. 'That poor girl's mother is dead and you're dragging her around the countryside on some fool's errand.'

'She found me. She ran away from school.'

'And you should have sent her straight back there.'

'What if she's right?'

'She's not.'

'I've been to Christine Wheeler's house. I've talked to her business partner.'

'And?'

'She was having money problems, but nothing else suggests a woman on the verge of a breakdown.'

'Suicide is an impulsive act.'

'Yes, but people still choose a method that suits them, normally something they perceive as being quick and painless.'

'What's your point?'

'They don't jump off a bridge if they're afraid of heights.'

'But we both saw her jump.'

'Yes.'

'So your argument doesn't make sense. Nobody pushed her. You were nearest. Did you see anyone? Or you think she was murdered by remote control. Hypnotism? Mind control?'

'She didn't *want* to jump. She was resigned to it. She took off her clothes and put on a raincoat. She walked out of the house without deadlocking the door. She didn't leave a suicide note. She didn't tidy up her affairs or give away her possessions. None of her behaviour was typical of a woman contemplating suicide. A woman who is scared of heights doesn't choose to jump off a bridge. She doesn't do it naked. She doesn't scrawl insults on her skin. Women of her age are body conscious. They wear clothes that flatter. They care about their appearance.'

'You're making excuses, Professor. The lady jumped.'

'She was talking to someone on the phone. They could have said something to her.'

'Perhaps they gave her bad news: a death in the family or a bad diagnosis. For all you know she had an argument with a boyfriend who dumped her.'

'She didn't have a boyfriend.'

'Did the daughter tell you that?'

'Why hasn't the person on the phone come forward? If a woman threatens to jump off a bridge, surely you call the police or an ambulance.'

'He's probably married and doesn't want to get involved.'

I'm not convincing her. I have a theory and no solid evidence to support it. Theories achieve the permanence of facts by persisting and acquiring an incremental significance. So do fallacies. It doesn't make them true.

Veronica Cray is staring at my left arm which has begun to twitch, sending a shudder through my shoulder. I hold it still.

'What makes you think Mrs Wheeler was afraid of heights?'

'Darcy told me.'

'And you believe her – a teenage girl who's in shock; who's grieving; who can't understand how the most important person in her life could abandon her . . .'

'Did the police search her car?'

'It was recovered.'

That's not the same thing. She knows it.

'Where is the car now?' I ask.

'In the police lock-up.'

'Can I see it?'

'No.'

She doesn't know where I'm going with this, but whatever happens I'm creating more work for the police. I'm questioning the official investigation.

'This isn't my case, Professor. I've got *real* crimes to solve. This was a suicide. Death by gravity. We both saw it happen. Suicides aren't supposed to make sense because they're pointless. I tell you something else, most people don't leave a note. They just snap and leave everyone wondering.'

'She showed no signs—'

'Let me finish,' she barks, making it sound like an order. Embarrassment prickles beneath my skin.

'Look at you, Professor. You got an illness. Do you wake up every day thinking, Wow, isn't it great to be alive? Or some days do you look at those shaking limbs and contemplate what lies ahead and, just for a moment, a fleeting second, consider a way out?'

She leans back in her chair and stares at the ceiling. 'We all do.

63

We carry our past with us – the mistakes, the sadness. You say Christine Wheeler was an optimist. She loved her daughter. She loved her job. But you don't really know her. Maybe it was something about the weddings that got to her. All those fairytales. The white dresses and flowers; the exchanging of vows. Maybe they reminded her of her own wedding and how it didn't match up to the fantasy. Her husband walked out. She raised a child alone. I don't know. No one does.'

The DI rocks her head from side to side, stretching her neck muscles. She isn't finished.

'You're feeling guilty, I understand that. You think you should have saved her, but what happened on the bridge wasn't your fault. You did what you could. People appreciate that. But now you're making a bad situation worse. Take Darcy back to school. Go home. It's not your concern any more.'

'What if I told you I heard something,' I say.

She pauses, eyeing me suspiciously.

'On the bridge when I was trying to talk to Christine Wheeler, I thought I heard something being said to her – over the mobile.'

'What did you hear?'

'A word.'

'What?'

'Jump!'

I watch the subtle change in the detective, a little shrinking created by a single word. She glances at her large square hands and back to me, meeting my eyes without embarrassment. This is not a case she wants to carry forward.

'You *think* you heard it?'

'Yes.'

Her uncertainty is transient. Already she has rationalised the possible outcomes and weighed only the downside.

'Well, I think you should tell that to the coroner. I'm sure he'll be pleased as punch to hear it. Who knows – maybe you'll convince him, but I seriously doubt it. I don't care if God himself was on the other end of that phone, you can't *make* someone jump – not like that.'

*   *   *

On-coming headlights sweep over the inside of the car and pass into darkness.

Darcy lifts her eyes to the windscreen.

'That detective isn't going to help, is she?'

'No.'

'So you're giving up.'

'What do you expect me to do, Darcy? I'm not a policeman. I can't make them investigate.'

She turns her face away. Her shoulders rise as though protecting her ears from hearing any more. We drive in silence for another mile.

'Where are we going?'

'I'm taking you back to school.'

'No!'

The aggression in her voice surprises me. Emma flinches and looks at us from the back seat of the car.

'I'm not going back.'

'Listen, Darcy, I know you're very sure of yourself, but I don't think you fully realise what's happened. Your mother isn't coming back. And you don't suddenly become an adult simply because she's not here.'

'I'm old enough to make my own decisions.'

'You can't go home – not alone.'

'I'll stay in a hotel.'

'And how will you pay for that?'

'I have money.'

'You must have other family.'

She shakes her head.

'What about grandparents?'

'I have a shortage.'

'What does that mean?'

'I have one left and he drools. He lives in a nursing home.'

'Is there anyone else?'

'An aunt. She lives in Spain. Mum's older sister. She runs a donkey sanctuary. I think they're donkeys. I guess they could be burros. I don't know the difference. My mum said she was a poor man's Brigitte Bardot, whoever that is.'

'A film star.'

'Whatever.'

'We'll call your aunt.'

'I'm not living with donkeys.'

There must be other possibilities . . . other names. Her mother had friends. Surely one of them could look after Darcy for a few days. Darcy doesn't have their numbers. She's not even trying to be helpful.

'I could stay with you,' she says, pressing her tongue to the inside of her cheek like she's sucking a boiled sweet.

'I don't think that's a good idea.'

'Why not? Your house is big enough. You're looking for a nanny. I could help look after Emma. She likes me . . .'

'I can't let you stay.'

'Why?'

'Because you're sixteen and you should be at school.'

She reaches over the seat for her bag. 'Stop the car. Let me out here.'

'I can't do that.'

The electric window glides down.

'What are you doing?'

'I'm going to yell rape or kidnapping or whatever else it takes for you to stop the car and let me out. I'm not going back to school.'

Emma's voice interrupts from the back seat. 'No fighting.'

'Pardon?'

'No fighting.'

She looks at us sternly.

'We're not fighting, sweetheart,' I explain. 'We're having a serious talk.'

'I don't like fighting,' she announces. 'It's bad.'

Darcy laughs. Her gaze is defiant. Where does she get such confidence? How did she become so fearless?

Circling the next roundabout, I turn back.

'Where are we going now?' she asks.

'Home.'

10

If Darcy were a grieving husband or a mate, we'd go to the pub and get rolling drunk. Then we'd come staggering home, put on Sky Sports and watch some obscure ice-hockey game in Canada or that weird sport where they ski across country and shoot at targets. Men do that sort of thing. Alcohol isn't a substitute for tears. It feeds them on the inside where it's less public and the tissues don't get soggy.

Teenage girls are trickier. I know from my consulting room. They're more likely to fret, to stop eating, to become depressed or promiscuous. Darcy is a singular creature. She doesn't prattle away like Charlie and Emma. She acts so grown up; smart mouthed and sassy, but beneath the bravado is a hurt child who knows less about the world than a blind girl at an art gallery.

She took herself to bed in the spare room as soon as the dishes were packed away. I paused outside her door a few minutes ago, pressing my ear against the painted wood and thought I heard her crying. I may have imagined it.

What am I going to do? I can't investigate her mother's death. Maybe DI Cray is right and nobody will ever know the truth.

Sitting in the study, I open my palms on the desk and watch them. My left hand is shaking uncontrollably but I don't want to take any more medication today. My doses are already too high and the drugs become less effective over time. Vincent Ruiz's telephone number is on the desk blotter.

Ruiz is a former detective inspector with the London Metropolitan Police. Five years ago he arrested me on suspicion of murder after a former patient of mine had been found stabbed to death beside the Grand Union Canal in London. My name was in her diary. It's a long story. Let's call it history.

Ever since then, Ruiz has been one of those peripheral characters that drift in and out of my life, adding brightness to the beige. Before he retired, he used to invite himself to dinner, flirt with Julianne and pick my brain about his latest murder investigation. He'd tickle the girls, drink too much wine and spend the night on our sofa.

Julianne's soft spot for Ruiz is bigger than the man's liver, which says something about his drinking and her ability to attract strays.

It takes me three attempts to punch Ruiz's number on the phone. I hear it ringing.

'Hi, Vincent.'

'Hey, hey, if it isn't my favourite shrink.'

He has a voice that matches his body, hard on the inside and fleshy on the outside – gravel coated in phlegm.

'I saw you on one of those reality TV shows the other night,' he says. 'I think they call it the News at Ten. You were tossing a woman off a bridge.'

'She jumped.'

'No shit,' he laughs. 'No wonder you have all those letters after your name. How is your gorgeous wife?'

'She's in Moscow.'

'Alone?'

'With her boss.'

'Why can't I be her boss?'

'Because you know nothing about high finance and your idea of up-sizing is to buy a bigger pair of trousers.'

'That's harsh but true.'

I hear ice clinking in a glass.

'Fancy a few days in the West Country?'

'Nope. I'm allergic to sheep.'

'I need your help.'

'Say it like you mean it, baby.'

I tell him about Christine Wheeler and Darcy, describing the past twelve hours in a series of bullet points that ex-coppers regard as almost a second language. Ruiz knows how to fill in the gaps. Without my even mentioning DI Cray he predicts exactly how she reacted to my request.

'Are you sure about this?'

'As sure as I can be for now.'

'What do you need?'

'Christine Wheeler was talking to someone on her mobile before she fell. Is it possible to trace the call?'

'They recover the phone?'

'It's at the bottom of the Avon Gorge.'

'Do you know the lady's number?'

'Darcy does.'

He is silent for a moment. 'I know a guy who works for British Telecom. He's a security consultant. He was our go-to man when we were tapping phones or tracing calls – all above board, of course.'

'Of course.'

I can hear him taking notes. I can even picture the marbled notebook that he carries everywhere, bulging with business cards and scraps of paper, held together with a rubber band.

Another rattle of ice in a glass.

'So if I do come down to Somerset can I sleep with your wife?'

'No.'

'I thought country folk were supposed to be hospitable.'

'The house is sort of full. You can stay in the pub.'

'Well, that's almost as good.'

The call ends and I slip Ruiz's number into a drawer. There's a tap on the door. Charlie wanders in and slumps sideways in a perfectly good armchair, dangling her legs over the armrest.

'Hi, Dad.'

'Hi.'

'What's up?'

'Nothing much, what's up with you?'

'I got a history test tomorrow.'

'You been studying?'

'Yep. Did you know when they embalmed pharaohs in ancient Egypt they used to take out their brains through their left nostril with a hook?'

'I didn't know that.'

'Then they used to put the body on a bed of salt to dry it out.'

'Is that so?'

'Yep.'

Charlie has a question, but needs a moment to frame it. She's like that, very precise with no ums and ahs or long pauses.

'Why is she here?'

She means Darcy.

'She needed somewhere to stay.'

'Does Mum know?'

'Not yet.'

'What should I tell her if she calls?'

'Leave that to me.'

Charlie stares at her knees. She thinks about things far more deeply than I ever remember doing. Sometimes she will mull over something for days, formulating a theory or an opinion and then deliver it out of the blue, long after everyone else has stopped thinking about it or forgotten the original discussion.

'The woman on the news the other night: the one who jumped.'

'What about her?'

'It was Darcy's mum.'

'Yes.'

'Should I say something to her? I mean, I don't know whether to avoid the subject or pretend nothing's wrong.'

'If Darcy doesn't want to talk about it, she'll tell you.'

Charlie nods in agreement. 'Will there be a funeral or something like that?'

'In a few days.'

'So where is her mum now?'

'At the morgue – it's a place where they . . .'

'I know,' she answers, sounding very grown up. There's another long pause. 'Did you see Darcy's trainers?'

'What about them?'

'I want a pair just like them.'

'OK. Anything else?'

'Nope.'

Charlie tosses her ponytail over one shoulder and exits with a kick of her heels.

I am left alone. A pile of household bills and invoices has to be sorted, paid or filed. Julianne has separated her work receipts and bundled them in an envelope.

As I close the drawer I notice a partially crumpled receipt on the floor. I pick it up and flatten it on the blotter. The name of the hotel is written in elaborate script across the top. It is a room service bill for breakfast, including champagne, bacon, eggs, fruit and pastries. Julianne really went to town. She normally has just muesli or fruit salad.

I screw the bill into a ball and motion to throw it away. I don't know what stops me – a question mark: a tinge of disquiet. The sensation scrambles and disappears. It's too quiet outside. I don't want to hear myself think.

11

To pick a lock requires a supreme sense of touch and sound. First I picture the inner mechanism in my mind and project my senses within. All the senses are important – not just sound and touch. Sight to identify the make and model. Smell to tell if the lock has been lubricated recently. Taste to identify the lubricant.

Each lock has a personality. Time and weather will change its characteristics. Temperature. Humidity. Condensation. Once the pick is inside, I close my eyes. Listen. Feel. As the pick bounces up and down over the pins, I must apply a fixed amount of pressure, measuring their resistance. This requires sensitivity, dexterity, concentration and analytical thinking. It is fluid – but there are rules.

This one is a 437-rated high security lock. It has six pins, some of which are mushroom-shaped. The keyhole is paracentric, like a misshapen lightning bolt. Insurance underwriters consider it a twenty-minute pick job because of its degree of difficulty. I can open it in twenty-three seconds. It takes practise. Hours. Days. Weeks.

I can remember the first time I entered a house. It was in Osnabrück, Germany, fifty miles north of Dortmund. The house belonged to an army chaplain who was counselling my wife, visiting her while I was away. I left his dog in the freezer and the bath and the washing machine.

The second place I entered was the Special Forces Club in Knightsbridge, a few steps from the rear door of Harrods. The building had no nameplate on the door. It is a private club for current and former members of the intelligence services and the SAS. I, however, cannot become a member because I am so elite nobody has ever heard of me. I am untouchable. Unnameable.

I can walk through walls. Locks crumble in my hands. The pins are like musical keys with a different tone and timbre as the pick passes over them. Listen. That's the final note. The door opens.

I step into the flat, placing my feet carefully on the polished floorboards. My tools are wrapped and put away. A torch is now needed.

The bitch has taste, which doesn't always come with money. None of her furniture came out of a flat pack or was put together with keys. The coffee table is hammered copper and ceramic bowls are hand-painted.

I look for the phone connections. There is a cordless console in the kitchen and a cradle in the living room and another in the main bedroom.

I work my way through the rooms, opening cupboards and drawers, sketching the layout in my mind. There are letters to read, bills to peruse, phone numbers and photographs to study. Propped near the telephone is a birthday invitation.

What else can I find? Here is a bright envelope with polished paper – you are cordially invited to a hen night. A note has been scrawled across the bottom. Bring your dancing shoes.

There are three bedrooms in the flat. The smallest belongs to a child. She has a Coldplay poster on the wall alongside a Harry Potter calendar. There are photographs of horses and pony club rosettes. Her pyjamas are beneath her pillow. A crystal hangs from a hook on the windowsill. Stuffed animals spill from a box in the corner.

The main bedroom has an en suite. The vanity drawers are full of lipsticks, body scrubs, nail polish and sample packs from a dozen hotel stays and airline flights. Tucked away in the lowest drawer is a faux fur make-up bag containing a small pink vibrator and a set of handcuffs.

A change in air pressure rattles a window. The main door has opened downstairs, creating a slight vacuum in the stairwell. There are footsteps. I stand for a moment in the bedroom with an ear cocked. Keys jangle. One of them slides into the barrel of the lock. Turns.

The door opens and closes. I feel the tiny tremor under my feet and hear their voices. Coats are shrugged off and hung on hooks. A kettle is filled. There is soft laughter and the smell of food – takeaway – something Asian with coriander and coconut milk. I listen to the sound of food being spooned onto plates and eaten in front of a TV.

Afterwards the dishes are cleared away. Somebody is coming. I draw back sharply into the shadows, stepping into a wardrobe, pulling clothes around me. I breathe in the bitch's scent, her stale perfume and sweat.

As a child I used to love playing hide and seek with my brother; the ball-tightening, bladder-clenching sense of excitement, the fear of discovery. Sometimes I'd curl up and try not to breathe, but my brother always found me. He said he could hear me because I was trying too hard not to make a sound.

A shadow passes the door. I see the bitch's reflection in the tilted mirror. She goes to the toilet. Her skirt is pulled up, her tights rolled down. Her thighs are pale as candle wax. She stands and flushes, turning to face the mirror, pivoting forward over the sink to examine her face, pulling at the skin around her eyes. She talks to herself. I can't hear what she says. Her tights are tossed aside. She raises her arms and a nightdress slides over her shoulders and the hem drops to her knees.

Her daughter has gone to her room. I hear her schoolbag tossed in a corner and the sound of the shower. Later she comes to say goodnight. Air kisses. Tousled hair. Sweet dreams.

I'm alone with the bitch. There is no man of the house. He has been evicted, cast out, passed over, disenfranchised; the king is dead, long live the queen!

She has turned on the TV and watches from her bed, flicking through the channels, a bright square in her eyes. She isn't really watching. She picks up a book instead. Does she feel me here? Is there a shiver of apprehension or a sense of disquiet, like a ghost leaving footprints on her grave?

I am the voice she's going to hear when she dies. My words. I am going to ask her if she's frightened. I am going to unlock her mind. I am going to stop her heart. I am going to beat her to floor and feed on her bloody mouth.

When?

Soon.

12

My legs don't want to move this morning. It takes harsh words and willpower to swing them from the bed. I stand and pull on a dressing gown. It's after seven. Charlie should have woken me by now. She's going to be late for school. I yell out for her. Nobody answers.

The bedrooms are empty. I make my way downstairs. Two bowls of soggy cereal sit on the kitchen table. The milk has been left out of the fridge.

The phone rings. It's Julianne.

'Hello.'

There is a beat of silence. 'Hi.'

'How are you?'

'Good. How's Rome?'

'I'm in Moscow. Rome was last week.'

'Oh, that's right.'

'Are you OK?'

'Fine. Just woke up.'

'How are my beautiful girls?'

'Perfect.'

'How is it that when I'm home they're capable of being absolutely horrid but around you they're perfect?'

'I bribe them.'

'I remember. Have you found a nanny?'

'Not yet.'

'What happened?'

'I'm still interviewing. I'm looking for Mother Teresa.'

'You know she's dead.'

'How about Scarlett Johansson?'

'We're *not* having Scarlett Johansson look after our children.'

'*Now* who's being picky?'

She laughs. 'Can I talk to Emma?'

'She's not here just now.'

'Where is she?'

I look at the open door and can hear the rustle of my own breathing in the mouthpiece. 'In the garden.'

'It must have stopped raining.'

'Uh-huh. How's the trip?'

'Painful. The Russians are stalling. They want a better deal.'

I'm standing at the sink, looking out the window. The lower panes are smeared with condensation. The upper panes frame a blue sky.

'Are you sure everything is all right?' she asks. 'You're sounding very strange.'

'I'm fine. I miss you.'

'I miss you too. I've got to go. Bye.'

'Bye.'

I hear the click of the phone. As if on cue, Emma comes bounding through the back door with Darcy behind her. The teenager catches the youngster and hugs her tightly. Both are laughing.

Darcy is wearing a dress. It belongs to Julianne. She must have found it in the ironing basket. The light from the doorway paints the outline of her body within it. Teenage girls don't feel the cold.

'Where have you been?'

'We went for a walk,' she says, defensively. Emma reaches towards me with her arms and I pick her up.

'Where's Charlie?'

'On her way to school – I walked her to the bus stop.'

'You should have told me.'

'You were asleep.' She nudges me gently sideways with her hip and picks up the cereal bowl.

'You should have written a note.'

She fills the sink with hot water and suds. For the first time she notices my arm is twitching and my leg seems to spasm in sympathy. I haven't taken my morning medication.

'So what's with the shaking thing?'

'I have Parkinson's.'

'What's that?'

'It's a progressive degenerative neurological disorder.'

Darcy pushes her bra strap onto her shoulder. 'Is it contagious?'

'No. I shake. I take pills.'

'Is that it?'

'Pretty much.'

'My friend Jasmine had cancer. She had to have a bone marrow transplant. She looked cool without any hair. I don't think I could have done it. I'd rather die.'

The last sentence has the bluntness and hyperbole of youth. Only teenagers can turn pimples into catastrophes or leukaemia into a fashion dilemma.

'This afternoon I'll go and see the headmistress of your school . . .'

Darcy's mouth opens in protest. I cut her off. 'I'm going to tell her that you're spending a few days away from school – until the funeral or we decide what you want to do. She's going to ask questions and want to know who I am.'

Darcy doesn't answer. Instead she turns back to the sink and continues washing a plate.

My arm trembles. I need to shower and change. I'm on the stairs when I hear her final remark.

'Don't forget to take your pills.'

Ruiz arrives just after eleven. His early model, forest green Mercedes is splattered with mud on the fenders and lower doors. It's the sort of car they're going to outlaw when emission regulations come into force because entire Pacific atolls disappear every time he refills the tank.

He has put on weight since he retired, and let his hair grow longer, just over his ears. I can't tell if he's contented. Happiness is not a concept that I associate with Ruiz. He confronts the world like a sumo wrestler, slapping his thighs and throwing his weight around.

Rumpled and careworn as ever, he gives me a crushing hand-shake. His hands are unfailingly steady. I envy him.

'Thanks for coming,' I say.

'What are friends for?'

He says it without any irony.

Darcy is standing at the gate, looking like an elf maiden in that dress. Before I can introduce her, Ruiz mistakes her for Charlie and grabs her around the waist, spinning her round.

She fights at his arms. 'Let me go, you pervert!'

Ruiz puts her down suddenly. He looks at me.

'You said Charlie had grown.'

'Not that much.'

I don't know if he's embarrassed. How do you tell? Darcy tugs down the dress and brushes hair from her eyes.

Ruiz smiles and bows slightly. 'No offence meant, miss. I mistook you for a princess. I know a couple who live round here. They turn frogs into princes in their spare time.'

Darcy looks at me, confused, but she can recognise a compliment. The flush in her face has nothing to do with the cold. Meanwhile, Emma comes flying down the path and hurls herself into his arms. Holding her high in the air, Ruiz seems to be estimating how far he could throw her. Emma calls him Dooda. I have no idea why. It's a name she's used ever since she could talk whenever Ruiz came to visit. Her shyness around adults has never applied to him.

'We have to go,' he says. 'I might have found someone who can help us.'

Darcy looks at me. 'Can I come?'

'I need you to look after Emma. It's just for a few hours.'

Ruiz is already at the car. I pause at the passenger door and glance back at Darcy. I hardly know this girl and I'm leaving her alone with my youngest daughter. Julianne would have something to say. Maybe I won't tell her this part.

*　　*　　*

Heading west towards Bristol, we take the coast road to Portishead, along the Severn Estuary. Gulls swing and wheel above the rooftops, working against a blustery wind.

'She's a pretty thing,' says Ruiz, dangling his fingers over the steering wheel. 'Is she staying with you?'

'For a few days.'

'What does Julianne say?'

'I haven't told her yet.'

Nothing changes on his face. 'Do you think Darcy is telling you everything – about the mother?'

'I don't think she's lying.' We both know it's not the same thing.

I tell him the details of Friday, describing Christine Wheeler's last moments on the bridge; and how her clothes were found lying on the floor of her house, beside the phone; and how she wrote some sort of sign in lipstick while leaning on the coffee table.

'Was she seeing anyone?'

'No.'

'Any money problems?'

'Yes, but she didn't seem to be too worried.'

'So you think someone threatened her?'

'Yes.'

'How?'

'I don't know. Blackmail, intimidation . . . She was terrified.'

'Why didn't she call the police?'

'Maybe she couldn't.'

We turn off into a new business park full of metal and glass office buildings. The bitumen roads are starkly grey against the newly planted garden beds.

Ruiz turns into a car park. The only sign on the building is a plaque beside a buzzer: *Fastnet Telecommunications*. The receptionist is barely twenty with a pencil skirt, a white blouse and even whiter teeth. Not even the sight of Ruiz interrupts her winning smile.

'We're here to see Oliver Rabb,' he says.

'Please take a seat.'

Ruiz prefers to stand. There are posters on the walls of beautiful young people, chatting on designer phones that obviously bring them great happiness, wealth and hot dates.

'Imagine if mobiles had been invented earlier,' says Ruiz. 'Custer could have called up the cavalry.'

'And Paul Revere would have saved himself a long ride.'

'Nelson could have sent a text from Trafalgar.'

'Saying what?'

'I won't be home for dinner.'

The receptionist is back. We are taken to a room lined with screens and shelves full of software manuals. It has that new computer smell of moulded plastic, solvents and adhesives.

'What does this Oliver Rabb do?' I ask.

'He's a telecommunications engineer – the best, according to my mate at BT. Some guys fix phones. He fixes satellites.'

'Can he trace Christine Wheeler's last call?'

'That's what we're going to ask him.'

Oliver Rabb almost sneaks up on us, appearing suddenly through a second door. Tall and bald, with big hands and a stoop, he seems to present the top of his head as he bows and shakes our hands. A study of tics and eccentricities, he is the sort of man who regards a bow tie and braces as practical rather than a fashion statement.

'Ask away, ask away,' he says.

'We're looking for calls made to a mobile number,' replies Ruiz.

'Is this investigation official?'

'We're assisting the police.'

I wonder if Ruiz is so good at lying because he's met so many liars.

Oliver has logged onto the computer and is running through a series of password protocols. He types Christine Wheeler's mobile number. 'It's amazing how much you can tell about a person by looking at their phone records,' he says, scanning the screen. 'A few years ago a guy at the Massachusetts Institute of Technology did a PhD project where he gave out a hundred free mobile phones to students and employees. Over nine months he monitored these phones and logged over 350,000 hours of data. He wasn't listening to the actual calls. He only wanted the numbers, the duration, the time of day and location.

'By the time he finished he knew much more than that. He

knew how long each person slept, what time they woke, when they went to work, where they shopped, their best friends, favourite restaurants, nightclubs, hangouts and holiday destinations. He could tell which of them were co-workers or lovers. And he could predict what people would do next with eighty-five per cent accuracy.'

Ruiz looks over his shoulder at me. 'That sounds like your territory, Professor. How often do you get it right?'

'I deal with the deviations, not the averages.'

'Touché.'

The screen refreshes with details of Christine Wheeler's account and phone usage.

'These are her call logs for the past month.'

'What about Friday afternoon?'

'Where was she?'

'The Clifton Suspension Bridge – about five.'

Oliver starts a new search. A sea of numbers appears on the screen. The flashing cursor seems to be reading them. The search comes up with nothing.

'That doesn't make sense,' I say. 'She was talking on a mobile when she jumped.'

'Maybe she was talking to herself,' replies Oliver.

'No. There was another voice.'

'Then she must have had another phone.'

My mind trips over the possibilities. Where did she get a second mobile? Why change phones?

'Could the data be wrong?' asks Ruiz.

Oliver bristles at the suggestion. 'Computers in my experience are more reliable than people.' His fingers stroke the top of the monitor as if worried that its feelings might have been hurt.

'Explain to me again how the system works,' I ask.

The question seems to please him.

'A mobile phone is basically a sophisticated radio, not much different to a walkie-talkie, but while a walkie-talkie can transmit perhaps a mile and a CB radio about five miles, the range of a mobile phone is huge because it can hop between transmission towers without losing the signal.'

He holds out his hand. 'Show me your phone.'

I hand it to him.

'Every mobile handset identifies itself in two ways. The Mobile Identification Number (MIN) is assigned by the service provider and is similar to a landline with a three-digit area code and a seven-digit phone number. The Electronic Serial Number (ESN) is a 32-bit binary number assigned by the manufacturer and can never be changed.

'When you receive a call on your mobile, the message travels through the telephone network until it reaches a base station close to your phone.'

'A base station?'

'A phone tower. You might have seen them on top of buildings or mountains. The tower sends out radio waves that are detected by your handset. It also assigns a channel so you're not suddenly on a party line.'

Oliver's fingers are still tapping at keys. 'Every call that is placed or received leaves a digital record. It's like a trail of breadcrumbs.'

He points to a flashing red triangle on the screen.

'According to the call log, the last time Mrs Wheeler's mobile received a call was at 12.26 on Friday afternoon. The call was routed through a tower in Upper Bristol Road. It's on the Albion Buildings.'

'That's less than a mile from her house,' I say.

'Most likely the closest tower.'

Ruiz is peering over his shoulder. 'Can we see who called her?'

'Another mobile.'

'Who owns it?'

'You need a warrant for that sort of information.'

'I won't tell,' replies Ruiz, sounding like a schoolboy about to sneak a kiss behind the bike shed.

'When did the call end?' I ask.

Oliver turns back to the screen and calls up a new map, covered in numbers. 'That's interesting. The signal strength started to change. She must have been moving.'

'How do you know?'

'These red triangles are the locations of mobile phone towers.

In built up areas they're usually about two miles apart, but in the country there can be twenty miles between them.

'As you move further away from one tower the signal strength diminishes. The next base station – the tower you're moving towards – notices the signal strengthening. The two base stations coordinate and switch your call to the new tower. It happens so quickly we rarely notice it.'

'So Christine Wheeler was still talking on her mobile when she left her house?'

'Looks like it.'

'Can you tell where she went?'

'Given enough time. Breadcrumbs, remember? It might take a few days.'

Ruiz has suddenly become interested in the technology, pulling up a chair and staring at the screen.

'There are three missing hours. Perhaps we can find out where Christine Wheeler went.'

'As long as she kept the phone with her,' replies Oliver. 'Whenever a mobile is turned on it transmits a signal, a "ping", looking for base stations within range. It may find more than one but will latch onto the strongest signal. The "ping" is actually a very short message lasting less than a quarter of a second, but it contains the MIN and ESN of the handset: the digital fingerprint. The base station stores the information.'

'So you can track any mobile,' I say.

'As long as it's turned on.'

'How close can you get? Can you pinpoint the exact location?'

'No. It's not like a GPS. The nearest tower could be miles away. Sometimes it's possible to triangulate the signal from three or more towers and get a better fix.'

'How accurate?'

'Down to a street: certainly not a building.' He chuckles at my incredulity. 'It's not something your friendly service provider likes to advertise.'

'And neither do the police,' adds Ruiz, who has started taking notes, boxing off details with doodled circles.

We know Christine Wheeler finished up at the Clifton

Suspension Bridge on Friday afternoon. At some point she stopped using her mobile and picked up another. When did it happen and why?

Oliver pushes his chair away from the desk and rolls across the room to a second computer. His fingers flick at the keyboard.

'I'm searching the base stations in the area. If we work backwards from five o'clock, we may find Mrs Wheeler's mobile.'

He points to the screen. 'There are three base stations nearby. The closest is on Sion Hill, at the bottom of Queen Victoria Avenue. The tower is on the roof of the Princes' Building. The next closest is two hundred yards away on the roof of Clifton Library.'

He types Christine Wheeler's number into the search engine. The screen refreshes.

'There!' He points to a triangle on the screen. 'She was in the area at 3.20 p.m.'

'Talking to the same caller?'

'It appears so. The call ends at 3.26.'

Ruiz and I look at each other. 'How did she get another mobile?' he asks.

'Either someone gave it to her or she had it with her. Darcy didn't mention a second phone.'

Oliver is listening in. He's slowly being drawn into the search. 'Why are you so interested in this woman?'

'She jumped off the Clifton Suspension Bridge.'

He exhales slowly, making his face look even more skull-like.

'There must be some way of tracing the conversation on the bridge,' says Ruiz.

'Not without a number,' replies Oliver. 'There were eight thousand calls going through the nearest base stations every fifteen minutes. Unless we can narrow the search down . . .'

'What about duration? Christine Wheeler was perched on the edge of the bridge for an hour. She was on the phone the whole time.'

'Calls aren't logged by length,' he explains. 'It could take me days to separate them.'

I have another idea. 'How many of the calls ended precisely at 5.07 p.m.?'

'Why?'

'That's when she jumped.'

Oliver turns back to the keyboard, typing in parameters for a new search. The screen becomes a stream of numbers that flash by so quickly they blur into a waterfall of black and white.

'That's amazing,' he says, pointing to the screen. 'There's a call that ended at precisely 5.07 p.m. It lasted more than ninety minutes.'

His fingers are tracing the details when they suddenly stop.

'What's wrong?' I ask.

'That's strange,' he replies. 'Mrs Wheeler was talking to another mobile which was routed through the same base station.'

'Which means what?'

'It means whoever was taking to her was either on the bridge or looking at it.'

13

There are girls playing hockey on the field. Blue-pleated skirts swirl and dip against muddy knees, pigtails bounce and sticks clack together. The word budding comes to mind. I have always liked how it sounds. It reminds me of my childhood and the girls I wanted to fuck.

The sports mistress is refereeing, her voice as shrill as a whistle. She yells at them not to bunch up and to pass and to run.

'Do keep up, Alice. Get involved.'

I know of some of the girls' names. Louise has the long brown hair, Shelly the sunshine smile and poor Alice hasn't hit the ball once since the game began.

A group of adolescent boys are watching from beneath a yew tree. They are sizing up the girls and poking fun at them.

Every time I look at the girls I imagine my Chloe. She's younger. Six now. I missed her last birthday. She's good at ball games. She could catch by the time she was four.

I built her a basketball hoop. It was lower than regulation height so she could reach. We used to go one-on-one and I always let her win. In the beginning she could hardly sink a basket but as she grew stronger and her aim improved, she landed maybe two shots in every three.

The hockey game is over. The girls are running indoors to change. Shelly with the sunshine smile runs across to flirt with the boys and is shepherded away by the sports mistress.

I squeeze my fingers around a chalky stone and begin scratching letters on *the stone capping on the wall. The powder sinks deep into the cracks. I trace the letters again.*

CHLOE

I draw a heart around the name, punctured by a cupid's arrow with a triangular point and a splayed tail. Then I close my eyes and make a wish, willing it to be so.

My eyelids flutter open. I blink twice. The sports mistress is there, holding a hockey stick over her shoulder with the colourful towelling grip squeezed in her fist.

Her lips part: 'Get lost, creep – or I'll call the police!'

14

There are moments, I know them well, when Mr Parkinson refuses to lie down and take his medicine like a man. He plays cruel tricks on me and embarrasses me in public.

There are thousands of involuntary processes in the body that we cannot control. We cannot stop our hearts from beating or our skin from sweating or our pupils dilating. Other movements are voluntary and these are abandoning me. My limbs, my jaw, my face, will sometimes tremble or twitch or become fixed. Without warning, my face will lock into a mask, leaving me unable to smile in welcome or to show sadness or concern. What good will I be as a clinical psychologist if I lose my ability to express emotion?

'You're giving me the stare again,' says Ruiz.

'Sorry.' I look away.

'We should go home,' he says gently.

'Not yet.'

We're sitting outside a Starbucks, braving the chill because Ruiz refuses to be seen inside such a place and thinks we should have gone to a pub instead.

'I want an espresso, not a pint,' I told him.

To which he countered, 'Do you *try* to sound like a hairdresser?'

'Drink your coffee.'

His hands are buried in the pockets of his overcoat. It's the same rumpled coat he was wearing when I first met him – five years ago. He interrupted a talk that I was giving to prostitutes in London. I was trying to help them stay safe on the streets. Ruiz was trying to solve a murder.

I liked him. Men who take too much care of themselves and their clothes can appear vain and over-ambitious but Ruiz had long ago stopped caring about what other people thought of him. He was like a big dark vague piece of furniture, smelling of tobacco and wet tweed.

Another thing that struck me was how he could stare into the distance even when sitting in a room. It was as though he could see beyond walls to a place where things were clearer or better or easier on the eye.

'You know what I can't understand about this case?' he says.

'What's that?'

'Why didn't someone stop her? A naked woman walks out of her house, gets in a car, drives fifteen miles and climbs over a safety rail on a bridge and nobody stops her. Can you explain that?'

'It's called the bystander effect.'

'It's called apathy,' he grunts.

'No.'

I tell him the story of Kitty Genovese, a New York waitress who was attacked outside her apartment building in the mid-sixties. Forty neighbours heard her cries for help or watched her being stabbed but none of them called the police or tried to help her. The attack lasted thirty-two minutes. She escaped twice but each time her assailant caught her and stabbed her again.

The caller who eventually raised the alarm phoned a friend first to ask what he should do. Then he went next door and asked a neighbour to make the call because 'he didn't want to get involved.' Kitty Genovese died only two minutes after the police arrived.

The crime caused a massive outpouring of anger and disbelief in America and abroad. People blamed overcrowding, urbanisation and poverty for creating a generation of city dwellers with the morals and behaviour of rats in cages.

Once the hysteria died down and proper studies were done, psychologists identified the bystander effect. If a group of people witness an emergency they look to each other to react, expecting someone else to take the lead. They are lulled into inaction by a pluralistic ignorance.

Dozens of people must have seen Christine Wheeler on Friday afternoon – motorists, passengers, pedestrians, toll collectors, people walking their dogs in Leigh Woods – and they each expected someone else to get involved and help her.

Ruiz grunts sceptically. 'Don't you just love people?'

He closes his eyes and exhales slowly as if trying to warm the world. 'Where to now?' he asks.

'I want to see Leigh Woods.'

'Why?'

'It might help me understand.'

We emerge out of Junction 19 and take back roads towards Clifton, winding between playing fields, farms and streams that are brackish and sullen as the floodwaters recede. Small sections of the blacktop are dry for the first time in weeks.

Pill Road becomes Abbots Leigh Road and the gorge drops dramatically away on our left behind the trees. According to local legend it was created by two giant brothers, Vincent and Goram, who carved it with a single pickaxe. The giants died and their bodies floated down the Avon River to form islands in the Bristol Channel.

Ruiz likes the legend (and the names). Maybe it appeals to his sense of the absurd.

A sandstone arch marks the entrance to Leigh Woods. The narrow access road, flanked by trees, leads to a small car park, a dead end. This is where they found Christine Wheeler's car, parked amongst the fallen leaves. It is not a place that she would necessarily know about unless she were given directions or had been here before.

Thirty yards from the car park is a signpost pointing out several walking trails. The red trail takes an hour and covers two miles to the edge of Paradise Bottom with views over the gorge. The purple trail is shorter but takes in Stokeleigh Camp, an iron-age hill fort.

Ruiz walks ahead of me, pausing occasionally for me to catch up. I'm not wearing the right shoes for this. Neither was Christine Wheeler. How naked and exposed she must have felt. How cold and frightened. She walked this path in high heels. She stumbled and fell. She tore her skin on brambles. Someone was issuing instructions to her, leading her away from the car park.

Fallen leaves are piled like snowdrifts along the ditches and the breeze shakes droplets from the branches. This is ancient woodland and I can smell it in the damp earth, rotting boles and mould: a cavalcade of reeks. Occasionally, between the trees I glimpse a railing fence that marks the boundary. Above and beyond it there are roofs of houses.

During the Troubles in Ireland, the IRA would often bury arms caches in open countryside, using line of sight between three landmarks to hide the weapons in the middle of fields with nothing on the surface to mark the spot. British patrols searching for these caches learned to how to study the landscape, picking out features that caught the eye. It might be a different coloured tree, or a mound of stones or a leaning fencepost.

In a sense I'm doing the same thing – looking for reference points or psychological markers that could indicate Christine Wheeler's last walk. I take out my mobile and check the signal strength. Three bars. Strong enough.

'She took this path.'

'What makes you so sure?' asks Ruiz.

'It has less cover. He wanted to be able to see her. And he wanted *her* to be seen.'

'Why?'

'I'm not sure yet.'

Most crimes are a coincidence – a juxtaposition of circumstances. A few minutes or a few yards one way or the other and the crime may not have happened. This one was different. Whoever did this knew Christine Wheeler's phone numbers and where she lived. He told her to come here. He chose what shoes she wore.

How? How did you know her?

91

You must have seen her somewhere before. Perhaps she was wearing the red shoes.

Why bring her here?

You wanted her to be seen, but this is too open, too public. Someone could have stopped her or called the police. Even on a miserable day like Friday there were people on the walking trails. If you truly wanted to isolate her you could have chosen almost anywhere. Somewhere private, where you had more time.

And rather than kill her privately, you made it very public. You told her to walk onto the bridge and climb over the railing. That sort of control is mind-boggling. Unbelievable.

Christine didn't fight back. There were no skin cells under her fingernails or defence bruises. You didn't need ligatures to subdue her or physical force. Nobody saw you with Christine Wheeler in her car. None of the witnesses mention someone with her. You must have been waiting for her; somewhere you felt safe – a hiding place.

Ruiz has paused to wait for me. I walk past him and leave the footpath, climbing up a small slope. At the top of the ridge there is a knoll formed by three trees. The view of Avon Gorge is uninterrupted. I kneel on the grass, feeling the wetness of the earth soak through to my trousers and the elbows of my coat. The path is visible for a hundred yards in either direction. It's a good hiding place, a place for innocent courting or illicit stalking.

A sudden burst of sunshine breaks through the scurrying clouds. Ruiz has followed me up the slope.

'Someone uses this place to watch people,' I explain. 'See how the grass is crushed. Somebody lay on their stomach with their elbows here.'

Even as I utter the words my gaze is snagged by a piece of yellow plastic caught in a mesh of brambles a dozen yards away. Rising to my feet, I close the gap, leaning between thorny branches until my fingers close around the plastic raincoat.

Ruiz lets out a long whistling breath. 'You're a freak. You know that.'

The engine is running. The heater at full blast. I'm trying to dry my trousers.

'We should call the police,' I say.

'And say what?' counters Ruiz.

'Tell them about the raincoat.'

'It changes nothing. They already *know* she was in the woods. People saw her. They saw her jump.'

'But they could search the woods, seal it off.'

I can picture dozens of uniformed officers doing a fingertip search and police dogs following a scent.

'You know how much rain we've had since Friday. There won't be anything left to find.'

He takes a tin of boiled sweets from his jacket pocket and offers me one. The rocklike sweet rattles against his teeth as he sucks.

'What about her mobile phone?'

'It's in the river.'

'The first one – the one she took from home.'

'It wouldn't tell us anything we don't know already.'

I know Ruiz thinks I'm reading too much into this or that I'm looking for some sort of closure. It's not true. There is only one natural convincing closure – the one none of us can avoid. The one Christine Wheeler collided with at seventy-five miles per hour. I just want the truth for Darcy's sake.

'You said she had money problems. I've known loan sharks to get pretty heavy.'

'This is a step up from breaking legs.'

'Maybe they pushed her so hard that she cracked.'

I stare at my left hand where my thumb and forefinger are 'pill-rolling'. This is how the tremors start, a rhythmic back and forth of two digits at three beats per second. If I concentrate hard on my thumb, willing it to stop moving, I can halt the tremor momentarily.

Clumsily, I try to hide my hand in my pocket. I know what Ruiz is going to say.

'One more stop-off,' I argue. 'Then we'll go home.'

15

The police vehicle lock-up in Bristol is near Bedminster Railway Station, hidden behind soot-stained walls and barbed wire fences. The ground shakes each time a train rattles past or brakes hard at a platform.

The place smells of grease, transmission fluid and sump oil. A mechanic peers through the dirt-stained glass of an office and lowers a teacup to a saucer. Dressed in orange overalls and a checked shirt he meets us at the door, bracing one arm on the frame as if waiting to hear a password.

'Sorry to disturb you,' says Ruiz.

'Is that what you're gonna do?'

The mechanic makes a show of wiping his hands on a rag.

'A car was towed here from Clifton a few days ago. A blue Renault Laguna. It belonged to a woman who jumped from the suspension bridge.'

'You here to pick it up?'

'We're here to look at it.'

This answer doesn't seem very palatable. He swirls it around his mouth for a moment and spits it into the rag. Glancing sideways at me, he contemplates whether I could possibly be a policeman.

'You waiting to see a badge, son?' says Ruiz.

94

He nods absently, no longer so sure of himself.

'I'm retired,' continues Ruiz. 'I was a detective inspector with the London Metropolitan Police. You're going to humour me today and you know why? Because all I want to do is look inside a car that isn't the subject of a criminal investigation and is only here until a member of the deceased's family comes and picks it up.'

'I suppose that's OK.'

'Say it like you mean it, son.'

'Yeah, sure, it's over there.'

The blue Renault is parked along the north wall of the workshop beside a crumpled wreck that must have taken at least one life. I open the driver's door of the Renault and let my eyes adjust to the darkness inside. The interior light isn't strong enough to chase away the shadows. I don't know what I'm looking for.

There is nothing in the glove compartment or beneath the seats. I search the pockets in the doors. There are tissues, moisturiser, make-up and loose change. Bunched beneath the seat is a rag for wiping the windscreen and a de-icing tool.

Ruiz has popped the boot. It's empty except for the spare tyre, a tool kit and a fire extinguisher.

Going back to the driver's door, I sit in the seat and close my eyes trying to imagine a wet Friday afternoon with rain streaking the windscreen. Christine Wheeler drove fifteen miles from her home, naked beneath a raincoat. The demister worked overtime, the heater as well. Did she open the window to call for help?

My eyes are drawn to the right where the glass has been smudged by fingerprints and something else. I need more light.

I yell to Ruiz. 'I need a torch!'

'What you got?'

I point to the markings.

The mechanic fetches an electric lantern with a bulb in a metal cage. The power cord is draped over his shoulder. Giant shadows slide across the brick walls and soak away as the light moves.

Holding the lantern on the opposite side of the glass, I can just make out the faintest of lines. It's like seeing a child's finger drawings on a misty window after the rain has gone. These lines weren't drawn by a child. They were transferred from something pressed against the glass.

Ruiz looks at the mechanic. 'You smoke?'

'Yeah.'

'I want a cigarette.'

'You're not supposed to smoke in here.'

'Humour me.'

I look at Ruiz mystified. I've seen him give up smoking at least twice, but never take it up on the spur of the moment.

I follow them to the office. Ruiz lights a cigarette and draws in deeply, staring at the ceiling as he exhales.

'Here, have one too,' he says, offering me one.

'I don't smoke.'

'Just do it.'

The mechanic lights up. Meanwhile, Ruiz picks squashed cigarette butts from the tin ashtray and begins crushing the grey ash into a powder.

'You got a candle?'

The mechanic searches the drawers until he finds one. Lighting it, Ruiz drips wax into the centre of a saucer and pushes the base of the candle into the melted wax until it stands upright. Then he takes a coffee cup and rolls it sideways over the flame, turning the surface black with soot.

'It's an old trick,' he explains, 'taught to me by a guy called George Noonan, who talks to dead people. He's a pathologist.'

Ruiz begins scraping soot from the mug into the growing pile of ash and gently mixing them together with the point of a pencil.

'Now we need a brush. Something soft. Fine.'

Christine Wheeler had a small bag of make-up in the glove compartment of the car. Retrieving it, I tip the contents onto the desk – a lipstick, mascara, eyeliner and a polished steel compact holding blusher and a brush.

Ruiz picks up the brush gently as though it might crumble between his thumb and forefinger. 'This should do. Bring the lantern.'

Returning to the Renault, he sits in the driver's seat with the door propped open and the lantern on the opposite side of the window. Careful not to breathe too heavily, he gently begins

96

'painting' the mixture of soot and ash onto the inside of the glass. Most of it falls from the brush and dusts his shoes, but just enough of it clings to the faint markings on the interior window. As if by magic, symbols begin to form and then turn into words.

HELP ME

Thunder crumples the air above us, rolling together continuously. Something rattles deep inside me. Christine Wheeler wrote a sign in lipstick and pressed it against the inside of her car window, hoping somebody would notice. Nobody did.

Arc lights balance on tripods at the centre of the garage, the square heads facing inwards creating a blaze of white that renders the eyes useless for the shadows beyond. Crime scene investigators are moving inside the brightness. Their white overalls seem to glow from within.

The car is being disassembled. Seats, carpets, windows, panels and lining are being removed, vacuumed, dusted, sifted, scraped and picked over like the carcass of a metal beast. Every sweet wrapper, fibre, piece of lint and smudged print will be photographed, sampled and logged.

Fingerprint brushes dance across the hard surfaces, leaving behind a layer of black or silver powder that is finer than Ruiz's homemade version. Magnetic wands skim through the air, picking out details invisible to the human eye.

The head of the CSI team is a thickset Brummie who looks like a white jellybean in his overalls. He seems to be holding a master class for a group of trainees: talking about the 'transient physical evidence' and 'maintaining the integrity of the crime scene'.

'What exactly are we looking for, sir?' a trainee asks.

'Evidence, son, we're looking for evidence.'

'Evidence of what?'

'The past.' He smooths his latex gloves across his palms. 'It might only be five days old but it's still history.'

Outside the light is fading and the temperature is dropping. DI Veronica Cray is standing in the main doorway to the garage, an archway of blackened bricks beneath the railway viaduct. A train rumbles above her head.

She lights a cigarette and inserts the dead match in the book behind the others. It creates a thoughtful pause as she issues instructions to her second in command.

'I want to know how many people have touched this car since it was found. I want every one of them fingerprinted and discounted.'

The sergeant has steel-rimmed glasses and a flat-top haircut. 'What exactly are we investigating, boss?'

'A suspicious death. The Wheeler house is also a crime scene. I want it sealed off and guarded. You might also want to find a decent curry house.'

'Are you hungry, boss?'

'Not me, sergeant, but you're going to be here all night.'

Ruiz is sitting in his Merc with the door open and his eyes closed. I wonder if he finds it hard stepping back from a case like this, now that he's retired. Surely old instincts must come into play, the desire to solve the crime and restore order. He once told me that the trick with investigating violent crimes was to focus on a suspect, not the victim. I'm the opposite. By knowing the victim I know the suspect.

A murderer isn't always uniform in his actions. Circumstances and events will alter what he says and does. So will the victim. How did she react under pressure? What did she say?

Christine Wheeler doesn't strike me as the sort of woman who was sexually provocative or likely to draw attention to herself through her appearance and mannerisms. She wore conservative clothes, rarely went out and tended to be self-effacing. Different women present different levels of vulnerability and risk. I need to know these things. By knowing Christine, I am a step closer to knowing whoever killed her.

DI Cray is beside me now, staring into the grease pit.

'Tell me, Professor, do you always talk your way into police lock-ups and contaminate important evidence?'

'No, DI.'

She blows smoke and sniffs twice, glancing across the forecourt to where Ruiz is dozing.

'Who's your dance partner?'

'Vincent Ruiz.'

She blinks at me. 'You're shitting me.'

'I shit you not.'

'How in glory's name do you know Vincent Ruiz?'

'He once arrested me.'

'I can see how that might be tempting.'

She hasn't taken her eyes off Ruiz.

'You couldn't leave this alone.'

'It wasn't suicide.'

'We both saw her jump.'

'She didn't do it willingly.'

'I didn't see anyone holding a gun to her head. I didn't see a hand reach out and push her.'

'A woman like Christine Wheeler doesn't suddenly decide to take off her clothes and walk out the door holding a sign that says, "HELP ME".'

The DI stifles a belch as though something I've said has disagreed with her. 'OK. Let's assume for a moment that you're right. If Mrs Wheeler was being threatened, why didn't she phone some-body or drive to the nearest police station?'

'Perhaps she couldn't.'

'You think he was in the car with her?'

'Not if she held up a sign.'

'So he must have been listening.'

'Yes.'

'And I suppose he *talked* her to her death?'

I don't answer. Ruiz has climbed out of the Merc and is stretching, rolling his shoulders in lazy circles. He wanders over. The two of them size each other up like roosters in a henhouse.

'DI Cray, this is Vincent Ruiz.'

'I've heard a lot about you,' she says, shaking his hand.

'Don't believe half of it.'

'I don't.'

He glances at her feet. 'Are they men's shoes?'

'Yep. You got a problem with that?'

'Not at all. What size you take?'

'Why?'

'I might be your size.'

'You're not big enough.'

'Are we talking shoes or something else?'

She smiles. 'Aren't you just as cute as French knickers.'

Then she turns to me. 'I want you in my office first thing in the morning.'

'I've already given a statement.'

'That's just the beginning. You're going to help me understand this because right now it's beyond my fucking comprehension.'

16

'What happened to you?'

'I knelt down in the mud.'

'Oh.'

Darcy is in the doorway, regarding me with a brief, disarming concern. I take off my shoes and leave them on the back step. Sugar and cinnamon scent the air. Emma is standing on a chair in the kitchen with a wooden spoon in her hand and a chocolate goatee.

'Don't play in the mud, Daddy. You'll get dirty,' she says seriously, before announcing, 'I'm making biscuits.'

'I can see that.'

She's wearing an oversized apron that reaches her ankles. A pyramid of unwashed dishes sits in the sink.

Darcy brushes past me and joins Emma. There is a bond between them. I almost feel like I'm intruding.

'Where's Charlie?'

'Upstairs doing her homework.'

'I'm sorry I took so long. Have you all eaten?'

'I cooked spaghetti.'

Emma nods, pronouncing it 'pagetti'.

'You had a few phone calls,' says Darcy. 'I took messages. Mr Hamilton the kitchen fitter said he could come next Tuesday. And they're going to deliver your firewood on Monday.'

I sit down at the kitchen table and, with great ceremony, sample one of Emma's biscuits, which are proclaimed to be the best ever baked. The cottage should be a mess but it's not. Apart from the kitchen, the place is spotless. Darcy has cleaned up. She even straightened the office and replaced a light bulb in the utilities room that hasn't worked since we moved in.

I ask her to sit down.

'The police are going to investigate your mother's death.'

Her eyes cloud momentarily.

'They believe me.'

'Yes. I need to ask you some more questions about your mother. What sort of person was she? What were her routines? Was she open and trusting, or careful and reserved? If someone threatened her would she react aggressively or be shocked into silence?'

'Why do you need to know that?'

'When I know her, I know more about him.'

'Him?'

'The last person to speak to her.'

'The person who killed her.'

Her own statement seems to shrink her. A tiny speck of flour clings to her brow above her right eyebrow.

'You mentioned an argument with your mother: what was it about?'

Darcy shrugs. 'I wanted to go to the National Ballet School. I wasn't supposed to audition but I forged Mum's signature on the application and caught a train to London by myself. I thought that if I could win a place she'd change her mind.'

'What happened?'

'Only twenty-five dancers are chosen every year. Hundreds apply. When the letter came confirming my place, Mum read it and threw it in the bin. She went to her bedroom and locked the door.'

'Why?'

'The fees are twelve thousand pounds a year. We couldn't afford them.'

'But she was already paying school fees . . .'

'I'm on an academic scholarship. If I leave the school, I lose

102

the money.' Darcy picks at her fingernails, scratching flour from the cuticles. 'Mum's business wasn't doing so well. She borrowed a lot of money and couldn't pay it back. I wasn't supposed to know but I heard her arguing with Sylvia. That's why I wanted to leave school, to get a job and save money. I thought I could go to ballet school next year.' She drops her voice to a whisper. 'That's what we argued about. When Mum sent me the pointe shoes, I thought she must have changed her mind.'

'The pointe shoes? I don't understand.'

'They're for ballet.'

'I know what they are.'

'Someone sent me a pair. A package came. The caretaker found it at the school gates on Saturday morning. It was addressed to me. Inside were pointe shoes – Gaynor Mindens. They're really expensive.'

'How expensive?'

'Eighty quid a pair.'

Her hands are bunched in the pocket of the apron. 'I thought Mum had sent them. I tried to call her, but couldn't get through.'

She closes her eyes and takes a deep breath.

'I wish she were here.'

'I know.'

'I hate her for it.'

'Don't do that.'

She turns her face away and brushes past me as she stands. I can hear her on the stairs. Closing the bedroom door. Falling on the bed. The rest is imagined.

17

The supermarket aisles are deserted. She shops at night because her days are too busy and weekends are for long lie-ins and trips to the gym rather than household chores. She is buying a leg of lamb. Brussels sprouts. Potatoes. Sour cream. For a dinner party perhaps, or a romantic dinner.

I glance past the cash registers to the newsstand. Alice is reading a music magazine and sucking on a lollipop. She's wearing her school uniform: a blue skirt, white blouse and dark blue jumper.

Her mother calls to her. Alice puts the magazine back on the rack and begins helping her pack the groceries in bags. I follow them through a different checkout and out into the car park where she loads the shopping into the boot of a sleek VW Golf convertible.

Alice is told to wait in the car. Her mother skips across the parking lot, head up, hips swinging. She pauses at a crossing and waits for the lights to change. I stay on the opposite side of the street and follow her along the pavement past brightly lit shops and cafés until she reaches a drycleaner's and pushes open the door.

A young Asian girl smiles from behind the counter. Another customer follows her inside. A man. She knows him. They brush cheeks, left and right. His hand lingers on her waist. She has an admirer. I can't see his face but he's tall and smartly dressed.

They're standing close. She laughs and throws her shoulders back. She's flirting with him. I should warn him. I should tell him to skip the foreplay. Don't bother with marriage and the messy divorce. Buy the bitch a house and give her the keys – it'll be cheaper in the long run.

I am watching her from the far side of the road, standing near a tourist map. The lights from a nearby restaurant illuminate my lower half leaving my face in shadow. A kitchen hand has come outside to have a cigarette. She pulls the packet from her apron pocket and glances over the cupped flame.

'Are you lost?' she asks me, turning her head away as she exhales.

'No.'

'Waiting for someone?'

'Might be.'

Her short blonde hair is pinned behind her ears. She has darker eyebrows, her true colour.

She follows my gaze and sees who I'm looking at.

'You interested in her?'

'I thought I recognised her.'

'She looks pretty cosy already. You might be too late.'

She turns her head again and blows smoke away.

'What's your name?'

'Gideon.'

'I'm Cheryl. You want a coffee?'

'No.'

'I can get you one.'

'It's all right.'

'Suit yourself.' She crushes the cigarette underfoot.

I look back at the drycleaner's. The woman is still flirting. They're saying goodbye. She rises on her toes and kisses his cheek, closer to his lips this time. Lingering. Then she walks to the door, swinging her hips a little. A dozen garments in plastic sleeves are draped over her left shoulder.

She crosses the road again, towards me this time. Six steps and she'll be here. She doesn't raise her eyes. She walks straight past me as though I don't exist or I'm invisible. Maybe that's it – I'm fading away.

Sometimes I wake at night and worry that I might have disappeared in my sleep. That's what happens when nobody cares about you. Bit by bit you *begin to disappear until people can look right through your chest and your head like you're made of glass.*

It's not about love; it's about being forgotten. We only exist if others think about us. It is like that tree that falls in the forest with nobody around to hear it. Who the fuck cares except the birds?

18

I once had a patient who was convinced that his head was full of seawater and a crab lived inside. When I asked him what happened to his brain he told me that aliens had sucked it out with a drinking straw.

'It is better this way,' he insisted. 'Now there's more room for the crab.'

I tell this story to my students and get a laugh. Fresher's Week is over. They're looking healthier. Thirty-two of them have turned up for the tutorial in a brutally modern and ugly room, with low ceilings and walls of fibreboard bolted between painted girders.

On a table in front of me is a large glass jar covered in a white sheet. My surprise. I know they're wondering what I'm going to show them. I have kept them waiting long enough.

Taking the corners of the fabric, I flick my wrists. The cloth billows and falls, revealing a human brain suspended in formalin.

'This is Brenda,' I explain. 'I don't know if that's her real name but I know she was forty-eight when she died.'

Putting on rubber gloves, I lift the rubbery grey organ in my cupped hands. It drips on the table. 'Does anyone want to come down and hold her?'

Nobody moves.

'I have more gloves.'

Still there are no takers.

'Every religion and belief system in history has claimed there is an inner force within each of us – a soul, a conscience, the Holy Spirit. Nobody knows where this inner force resides. It could be in the big toe or the earlobe or the nipple.'

Guffaws and giggles confirm they're listening.

'Most people would opt for perhaps the heart or the mind as logical locations. Your guess is as good as mine. Scientists have mapped every part of the human body using X-rays, ultrasounds, MRIs and CAT scans. People have been sliced, diced, weighed, dissected, prodded and probed for four hundred years and, as yet, nobody has discovered a secret compartment or mysterious black spot or magical inner force or brilliant light shining within us. They have found no genie in a bottle, no ghost in the machine, no tiny little person madly pedalling a bicycle.

'So what are we to draw from this? Are we simply flesh and blood, neurons and nerves, a brilliant machine? Or is there a spirit within us that we cannot see or understand?'

A hand is raised. A question! It's Nancy Ewers – the reporter from the student newspaper.

'What about our sense of self?' she asks. 'Surely that makes us more than machines.'

'Perhaps. Do you think we're born with this sense of self, our sense of ego, our unique personalities?'

'Yes.'

'You may be right. I want you to consider another possibility. What if our consciousness, our sense of self, stems from our experiences – our thoughts, feelings and memories? Rather than being born with a blueprint we are a product of our lives and a reflection of how other people see us. We are lit from *without*, rather than within.'

Nancy pouts and sinks back into her seat. People are scribbling furiously around her. I have no idea why. It won't be in the exam.

Bruno Kaufman intercepts me as I leave the tutorial.

'Listen, old boy, thought I could interest you in lunch.'

'I'm meeting someone.'

'Is she beautiful?'

I picture Ruiz and tell him no. Bruno falls into step beside me. 'Terrible business on the bridge last week, absolutely dreadful.'

'Yes.'

'Such a nice woman.'

'You *knew* her?'

'My ex-wife went to school with Christine.'

'I didn't know you'd been married.'

'Yes. Maureen has taken it quite hard, poor old thing. Shock to her system.'

'I'm sorry. When did she last see Christine?'

'I could ask her, I suppose.' He hesitates.

'Is that a problem?'

'It would mean calling her.'

'You don't communicate?'

'Story of our marriage, old boy. It was like a Pinter play: full of profound silences.'

We descend the covered stairs and cross the square.

'Of course all that's changed now,' says Bruno. 'She's been calling me every day, wanting to talk.'

'She's upset.'

'I suppose so,' he ponders. 'Oddly enough, I quite enjoy her calls. I divorced the woman eight years ago, yet find myself living and dying by her opinion of me. What do you make of that?'

'Sounds like love.'

'Oh, heavens no! Friendship maybe.'

'So you're saying you'd rather snuggle up to a post-grad student half your age?'

'That's romance. I try not to confuse the two.'

I leave Bruno at the bottom of the stairs, outside the psychology department. Ruiz is waiting at his car, reading a newspaper.

'What's happening in the world?' I ask.

'Usual death and destruction. Some kid in America just shot up a high school. That's what happens when you sell automatic weapons at the school canteen.'

Ruiz hands me a takeaway coffee from a tray resting on the seat.

'How was your room at the Fox & Badger?'

'Too close to the bar.'

'Noisy, huh?'

'Too tempting. I got to meet some of the locals. You have a dwarf.'

'Nigel.'

'I thought he was taking the piss when he said his name was Nigel. He wanted to take me outside and fight me.'

'He does that all the time.'

'Does anyone ever hit him?'

'He's a dwarf!'

'He's still an annoying little fuck.'

I have an appointment to see Veronica Cray at Trinity Road Police Station in Bristol.

'Are you sure you want me to come?' asks Ruiz.

'Why not?'

'Job's done. You got what you wanted.'

'You can't go back to London – not yet. You've only just arrived. You haven't even seen Bath. You can't come to the West Country and not see Bath. It's like going to LA and not sleeping with Paris Hilton.'

'I can pass on both of those.'

'What about Julianne? She's coming home this afternoon. She'll want to see you.'

'That's more tempting. How is she?'

'Good.'

'How long has she been away?'

'Since Monday. It seems like longer.'

'It always does.'

Trinity Road Police Station is an inward looking building without any windows on the lower floors. Like a bunker built for a siege, it is the perfect expression of modern law enforcement with CCTV cameras on every corner and spikes on the walls. Someone has daubed graffiti on the brickwork: *Stop Killer Cops: End State Terrorism.*

Opposite the station, the Holy Trinity Church is boarded up and deserted. An old woman shelters beneath the portico, dressed in black and bent like a burnt matchstick.

We wait downstairs for someone to arrive. A metal security door opens. A tall black man has to almost duck his head to get through. My first assumption is the wrong one. He's not being released from custody. He belongs here.

'I'm Detective Constable Abbott,' he says, 'but you can call me Monk. Every other bastard does.'

His hands are the size of boxing gloves. I feel ten years old again.

'Does everyone have a nickname around here?' asks Ruiz.

'Most of us do.'

'What about the DI?'

'We call her boss.'

'Is that it?'

'We like our jobs.'

Veronica Cray's office is a box within this box, furnished with a simple pine desk and a few filing cabinets. The walls are covered with photographs of unsolved cases and uncaught suspects. While other people fill drawers and diaries with their unfinished business, the DI turns it into wallpaper.

She is dressed in black, with breakfast in progress. A sweet bun and a cup of tea rest upon the paperwork.

She takes a final mouthful and gathers her notes.

'I got a briefing. You can listen.'

The incident room is clean, modern and open plan, broken only by moveable partitions and whiteboards. A photograph has been taped to the top of one of them. Christine Wheeler's name appears alongside.

The assembled detectives are mostly men who stand as DI Cray enters. A dozen officers have been assigned to the investigation, which hasn't yet been classified as a murder inquiry. Unless the taskforce can produce a motive or a suspect within five days, the powers that be are going to toss this one to the coroner to decide.

DI Cray licks sugar from her fingers and begins.

'At 5.07 p.m. last Friday afternoon, this woman jumped to her death from Clifton Suspension Bridge. Our first priority is to piece together the final hours of her life. I want to know where she went, who she spoke to and what she saw.

'I also want interviews with her neighbours, friends and business associates. She was a wedding planner. The business was in financial trouble. Talk to the usual suspects – loan sharks and money lenders – see if they knew her.'

She outlines the timeline of events, beginning on Friday morning. Christine Wheeler spent two hours in her office at Blissful and then went home. At 11.54 she received a call on her landline that came from a public phone box in Clifton at the corner of Westfield Place and Sion Lane, overlooking the Clifton Suspension Bridge.

'This call lasted thirty-four minutes. It may have been someone she knew. Perhaps she arranged to meet them.

'The landline call ended just after her mobile phone began ringing. One call may have produced the other.'

DI Cray signals an officer working an overhead projector. A map covering Bristol and Bath is beamed onto the white board behind her. 'Telecommunications engineers are triangulating signals from Christine Wheeler's mobile and plotting the likely route she took on Friday when she drove from her house to Leigh Woods.

'We have the two positive eyewitness sightings. Those witnesses have to be reinterviewed. I also want the names of everyone else who was in Leigh Woods on Friday afternoon. I want their reasons for being there and their home addresses.'

'It was raining, ma'am,' offers one of the detectives.

'This is Bristol – it's always bloody raining. And don't call me ma'am.'

She focuses on the only woman among the detectives. 'Alfie.'

'Yes, boss.'

'I want you go through the Sex Offenders' Register. Get me a list of every known pervert living within five miles of Leigh Woods. I want them graded by the seriousness of the offence and when they were last charged or released from prison.'

'Yes, boss.'

The DI shifts her gaze. 'Jones and McAvoy, I want you to go through the CCTV footage. There are four cameras on the bridge.'

'What time period?' one of them asks.

'From midday until six p.m. Six hours, four cameras, do the maths.'

'What exactly are we looking for, boss?'

'Take down every vehicle number. Run them through the Automatic Number Plate Recognition software. See if any of them come up as stolen and cross-check the names with Alfie. We may get lucky.'

'You're talking about more than a thousand cars.'

'Then you'd better get started.' She turns to another detective who is dressed in a short-sleeved jacket and jeans. She calls him 'Safari Roy' – another nickname. It suits him.

'Check out the business partner, Sylvia Furness. The company accounts. Find out who the major creditors are and if any of them were getting heavy.'

She mentions the food poisoning incident. The father of a bride wants compensation and is threatening to sue. Safari Roy makes a note to check it out.

DI Cray throws a file into the lap of another detective. 'That's a list of every sexual assault or complaint of indecent behaviour on Leigh Woods over the past two years, including nude sunbathing and flashing. I want you to find every one of them. Ask them what they were doing on Friday afternoon. Take D.J. and Curly with you.'

'You think it's sexual, boss?' asks Curly.

'The woman was naked with "slut" written on her torso.'

'What about her mobile?' asks Alfie.

'Still missing. Monk will be handling the search of Leigh Woods. Those of you who haven't got assignments will be going with him. You're going to knock on doors and talk to the locals. I want to know if anyone has been acting strangely or if anything unusual happened in the past few weeks. Did a sparrow fart? Did a bear shit in the wood? You get the picture.'

A new face appears at the briefing, a senior officer in uniform with polished buttons and a cap tucked beneath his left arm.

The detectives find their feet quickly.

'Carry on, carry on,' he says in a pretend-I'm-not-here sort of way. DI Cray makes the introductions. Assistant Chief Constable Fowler is short and broad-shouldered with a bulletproof hand-shake and the air of a battlefield general trying to gee up his troops. He focuses his attention on me.

'A professor of what?' he asks.

'Psychology, sir.'

'You're a psychologist.' He makes it sound like a disease. 'Where are you from?'

'I was born in Wales. My mother is Welsh.'

'Ever heard the definition of a Welsh rarebit, Professor?'

'No, sir.'

'A Cardiff virgin.'

He looks around the room, waiting for the laughter. In due course, it arrives. Satisfied, he takes a seat and places his hat on a desk with his leather gloves inside.

DI Cray continues with the briefing, but is immediately interrupted.

'Why isn't this a suicide?' asks Fowler.

She turns to him. 'We are looking at it again, sir. The victim wrote a sign asking for help.'

'I thought most suicides *were* a cry for help.'

The DI hesitates. 'We believe whoever was speaking to Mrs Wheeler on the phone told her to jump.'

'Somebody *told* her to jump and she did – just like that?'

'We believe she may have been threatened or intimidated.'

Fowler nods and smiles but something about the mannerism is vaguely patronising. He turns to me. 'This is your opinion is it, Professor? How exactly was this woman threatened or intimidated into committing suicide?'

'I don't know.'

'You don't know?'

I can feel my jaw tightening and my face becoming fixed. Bullies have this effect on me. I become a different person around them.

'So you think there's a psycho out there telling women to jump off bridges?'

'No, not a psycho; I have seen no evidence of mental illness.'

'Excuse me?'

'I don't find it helpful when people use labels such as psycho or nutcase. It can allow a perpetrator to excuse his actions or construct a defence of insanity or diminished responsibility.'

114

Fowler's face is stiffer than shirt cardboard. His eyes are fixed on mine.

'We have certain protocols around here, Professor O'Loughlin, and one of them requires that senior officers be addressed as "sir" or by their correct title. It is a matter of *respect*. I think *I've* earned it.'

'Yes, sir, my mistake.'

For a brief moment his self-control threatens to break but now it's restored. He stands, taking his hat and gloves, and leaves the incident room. Nobody has moved.

I look at Veronica Cray, who lowers her head. I've disappointed her.

The briefing is over. Detectives disperse.

On our way to the stairs, I apologise to the DI.

'Don't worry about it.'

'I hope I haven't made an enemy.'

'The man swallows a bullshit pill every morning.'

'He's a former military man,' I say.

'How do you know that?'

'He carries his hat under his left arm, so his right arm is free to salute.'

The DI shakes her head. 'How do you know shit like that?'

'Because he's a freak,' answers Ruiz.

I follow him outside. An unmarked police car is idling in the loading zone. The driver, a female constable, opens the passenger doors. Veronica Cray and Monk are both heading off to Leigh Woods.

I wish them luck.

'Do you believe in luck, Professor?'

'No.'

'Good. Neither do I.'

19

Julianne is on the 15.40 Great Western service from Paddington.
It's an easy drive at this time of day, with most of the traffic
coming the other way.

Emma is strapped in her booster seat and Darcy is sitting beside
me, with her knees drawn up and her arms wrapped around them.
She takes up so little space when she concertinas her body like
that.

'What's your wife like?' she asks.

'She's wonderful.'

'Do you love her?'

'What sort of question is that?'

'It's just a question.'

'Well, the answer is yes.'

'You have to say that, I suppose,' she says, sounding very world-
weary. 'How long have you been married?'

'Sixteen years.'

'Have you ever had an affair?'

'I don't think that's any of your business.'

She shrugs and stares out the window. 'I don't think it's normal
being faithful to one person for a whole lifetime. Who's to say you
won't stop loving someone or meet someone you love more?'

'You sound very wise. Have you ever been in love?'

She tosses her head dismissively. 'I'm not going to fall in love. I've seen how it turns out.'

'Sometimes we don't have a choice.'

'We *always* have a choice.'

She rests her chin on her knees and I notice the purple polish on her fingernails.

'What does your wife do?'

'Call her Julianne. She's an interpreter.'

'Is she away a lot?'

'More so lately.'

'And you stay home?'

'I work part-time at the university.'

'Is that because of the shaking business.'

'Yes, I suppose it is.'

'You don't look sick – if that makes you feel better – apart from the shaking, I mean. You look OK.'

I laugh at her. 'Well, thank you very much.'

Julianne steps off the train and her eyes magically widen when she sees the flowers.

'Who's the lucky girl?'

'I'm making up for what happened last time.'

'You had a reason.'

I kiss her. She goes for a swift peck. My lips linger. She hooks her arm through mine. I pull her suitcase behind us.

'How are the girls?' she asks.

'Great.'

'Now what's this about the nanny? You were very coy on the phone. Did you find someone?'

'Not exactly.'

'What does that mean?'

'I started the interviews.'

'And?'

'Something came up.'

She stops now. Turns. Concerned.

'Where's Emma?'

'In the car.'

'Who's with her?'

'Darcy.'

I try to keep moving and talking at the same time. Her suitcase wheels rattle over the cobblestones. Having rehearsed the story in my head, it should sound perfectly natural, but as it comes out of my mouth the logic grows more and more tenuous.

'Have you gone completely mad?' she says.

'Shush.'

'Don't shush me, Joe.'

'You don't understand.'

'Yes, I think I do. What you're telling me is that our baby is being looked after by a teenager whose mother was murdered.'

'It's complicated.'

'And she's living in our house.'

'She's a good kid. She's great with Emma.'

'I don't care. She has no training, no references. She should be at school.'

'Shush.'

'I said don't shush me.'

'She's here.'

Her eyes snap up. Darcy is standing beside the car, rhythmically chewing gum. Emma is balancing on the bumper bar, perched between her arms.

'Darcy, this is Julianne. Julianne, this is Darcy.'

Julianne gives her a fixed larger-than-life smile. 'Hello.'

Darcy raises her hand a few inches in a nervous wave. 'Did you have a nice trip?'

'Yes. Thank you.' Julianne takes Emma from her. 'I'm sorry about your mother, Darcy. It's an awful thing.'

'What happened?' asks Emma.

'Nothing to concern you, sweetheart.'

We drive in silence. The only person talking is Emma, who asks and fields all the questions. Darcy has withdrawn into a bubble of silence and uncertainty. I don't know what's wrong with Julianne. It's not like her to be so unwelcoming and intractable.

At the cottage Charlie comes running outside to greet us. She's

118

bursting with news for Julianne, most of it about Darcy, which she can't tell because Darcy is standing next to her.

I carry the bags inside where Julianne moves from room to room, as though making an inspection. Maybe she expects to find the place a mess, with unwashed laundry, unmade beds and dirty dishes in the sink. Instead it's spotless. For some reason this deepens her funk. She drinks two glasses of wine over dinner – a casserole prepared by Darcy – but instead of relaxing, her lips tighten into narrow lines and her comments become sharp and accusatory.

'I'll give Emma a bath,' Julianne says, turning towards the stairs. Darcy's eyes meet mine, framing a question.

After the dishwasher is packed, I go up and find Julianne sitting on our bed. Her suitcase is open. She is sorting clothes. Why is she so annoyed at Darcy being here? It's almost an ownership issue: a marking out of her territory or a defence of an existing claim. But that's ridiculous. Darcy isn't a threat.

I notice a bundle of black lace in her case. Lingerie. A camisole and knickers.

'When did you buy these?'

'Last week in Rome.'

'You didn't show me.'

'I forgot.'

I drape the straps of the camisole over my forefingers. 'I bet they look even better when you're wearing them. Perhaps you can show me later.'

She takes the lingerie from me and tosses it in the washing basket. Who did she wear it for? Something snags in my chest – the same niggling sense of disquiet that I felt when I found the hotel receipt for a champagne breakfast.

Julianne doesn't wear sexy lingerie. She says it's uncomfortable and impractical. Whenever I've bought her something flimsy for Valentine's Day she's only worn it the once. She prefers her Marks & Spencer briefs, high cut, size twelve, black or white. What made her change her mind?

She bought the lingerie in Rome and took it to Moscow. I want to ask her why but I don't know how to frame the question without it sounding jealous or worse.

119

The moment passes. Julianne turns away. Tiredness shows in her movements, her small steps and the slope of her shoulders.

I don't accept the premise that there's no smoke without fire, nor am I a believer in portents or auguries, but I cannot shake the discomfiting sense that a space is opening up between us. I want to put it down to tiredness. I tell myself that Julianne has been travelling a lot, being pulled in too many directions, taking on too much.

A month ago on her birthday I planned to cook her a special meal. I drove into Bristol and bought seafood at the fish markets. She phoned just after six to say that she was still in London. There was some sort of crisis, a missing funds transfer. She wouldn't be home.

'Where are you going to stay?'

'In a hotel; the company will pay.'

'You don't have any clothes.'

'I'll make do.'

'It's your birthday.'

'I'm sorry. I'll make it up to you.'

I ate a dozen oysters and threw the rest of the meal in the bin. Then I walked up the hill to the Fox & Badger and had three pints with Nigel and a Dutch tourist who knew more about the area than anyone in the bar.

There have been other moments. (I won't call them signs.) Julianne was due to fly back from Madrid one Friday and I tried to call her mobile but couldn't get through. I called her office instead. A secretary told me that Mrs O'Loughlin had been in London all day, having flown in the previous night.

When I finally found Julianne, she apologised, saying she'd meant to call me. I asked about the flights and she said I must have been mistaken. I have no reason to doubt her. We have been married for sixteen years and I can't remember a single moment or event that caused me to question her commitment. At the same time, she's still a mystery. When people ask me why I became a psychologist, I say, 'Because of Julianne. I wanted to know what she was really thinking.' It didn't work. I still have no idea.

I watch her sorting through her clothes, aggressively opening drawers and pulling hangers from the rack.

'Why are you so angry?'

She shakes her head.

'Talk to me.'

The suitcase is slammed shut. 'Do you have any idea what you're doing, Joe? Just because you couldn't save that woman on the bridge, we're looking after her daughter.'

'No.'

'Well, why is she here?'

'She had nowhere else to go. Her house is a crime scene. Her mother is dead . . .'

'Murdered?'

'Yes.'

'And the police haven't caught the killer?'

'Not yet.'

'You know nothing about this girl or her family. Does she even realise her mother is dead? She doesn't look grief-stricken.'

'You're not being fair.'

'Well, tell me, is she psychologically stable? You're the expert. Is she going to flip out and hurt my baby?'

'She would never hurt Emma.'

'And you base that upon . . . ?'

'Twenty years experience as a psychologist.'

The last sentence is delivered with my own version of cold certainty. Julianne stops. When it comes to personality readings, I'm rarely wrong and she knows it.

Sitting on the bed, she tucks a pillow behind her and leans against the wall, playing the tasselled cord of her dressing gown. I crawl across the bed towards her.

'Stop,' she says, holding up her hand like a policeman directing traffic. 'Don't come any closer.'

I sit on my side of the bed. We can stare at each other in the mirror. It's like watching a scene from a TV sitcom.

'When I go away I don't want things to change, Joe. I want to come home and find everything as I left it. I know that sounds selfish but I don't want to miss anything.'

'What do you mean?'

'Remember when you taught Emma to pedal her tricycle?'

'Sure.'

'She was so excited. It was all she wanted to talk about. You shared that moment with her. I missed it.'

'That's going to happen sometimes.'

'I know and I don't like it.' She leans sideways resting her head on my shoulder. 'What if I miss seeing Emma lose her first tooth or Charlie going on her first date? I don't want things to change when I go away, Joe. I know it's irrational and selfish and impossible. I want you to keep them exactly the same until I get home, so I can be here too.'

Julianne runs a finger along the side of my thigh. 'I know your job is about helping people. And I know that mentally ill people are often stigmatised, but I don't want Charlie and Emma exposed to damaged people and their damaged minds.'

'I would never . . .'

'I know, I know, but remember last time.'

'Last time?'

'You know what I mean.'

She's talking about one of my former patients who tried to destroy me by taking away everything I loved – Julianne, Charlie, my career, my life.

'This is completely different,' I say.

'I'm just warning you. I don't want your work in this house.'

'Darcy isn't a danger. She's a good kid.'

'She's doesn't look like a kid,' she says, turning to face me. The corners of her mouth are turned down. It is neither a smile nor an invitation to kiss. 'Do you think she's pretty?'

'Only until *you* stepped off the train.'

Three a.m. The girls are asleep. I slip out of bed and close the office door before turning on the lamp. I could blame my medication again, but too many thoughts are tripping over each other in my mind.

This time I'm not thinking about Christine Wheeler or Darcy or reliving that moment on the bridge. My concerns are more personal. I keep reflecting on the lingerie and the hotel receipt. One thought leads to another. The late night phone calls when Julianne closes the office door. The overnight stays in London. The sudden changes in her diary that have kept her away from home . . .

I hate the clichés about marriages having ups and downs and changing over time. Julianne is a better person than I am. She is stronger emotionally and has more invested in holding this family together. Here's another cliché – there's a third person in our marriage. His name is Mr Parkinson and he took up residence four years ago.

The hotel receipt is pressed between the pages of a book. The Hotel Excelsior. Julianne said it was a short walk from the Spanish Steps and the Trevi Fountain. I dial the number. A woman answers, the night manager. She sounds young and tired. It's four a.m. in Rome.

'I want to query an invoice,' I whisper, cupping my hand over the phone.

'Yes, sir. When did you stay here, sir?'

'No, it's not for me. It's for an employee.'

I think of a cover story. I'm an accountant calling from London. I'm doing an audit. I give her Julianne's name and the dates of her stay.

'Mrs O'Loughlin settled her account in full. She paid with her credit card.'

'She was travelling with a business colleague.'

'The name?'

Dirk. What is his last name? I can't remember.

'I just wanted to ask about a room service charge for breakfast . . . with champagne.'

'Is Mrs O'Loughlin querying her bill?' she asks.

'Could there be a mistake?'

'The room charges were shown to Mrs O'Loughlin when she settled her account.'

'Under the circumstances, it seems rather a lot for one person. I mean, look at the order: bacon and eggs, smoked salmon, pancakes, pastries, strawberries, and champagne.'

'Yes, sir, I have the details of the order.'

'It's a lot for one person.'

'Yes, sir.'

She doesn't seem to understand my point.

'Who signed for it?'

'Someone signed the docket when breakfast was delivered to the room.'

'So you can't tell me if Mrs O'Loughlin signed for it?'

'Is she disputing the bill, sir?'

I lie. 'She has no recollection of ordering that amount of food.'

There is a pause. 'Would you like me to fax a copy of the signature, sir?'

'Is it legible?'

'I don't know, sir.'

Another phone is ringing in the background. The night manager is alone on the desk. She suggests I call later in the morning and talk to the hotel manager.

'I'm sure he will be happy to reimburse Mrs O'Loughlin. The charges will be refunded to her credit card.'

I recognise the danger. Julianne will see the refund on her card statement.

'No, it's fine. Don't bother.'

'But if Mrs O'Loughlin feels she has been overcharged—.'

'She may have been mistaken. I'm sorry to have troubled you.'

20

A dozen women have taken over a corner of the bar, pushing chairs and tables together on the edge of the dance floor. The bitch is dancing, grinding her hips like a pole dancer, her face flushed from laughter and too much wine. I know what she's thinking. She's thinking every man in the place is looking at her, desiring her, but her face is too hard and her body even harder.

Mercifully, it's not youthful innocence that I am after. It is not purity. I want to wade in filth. I want to see the cracks in her make-up and stretch marks on her stomach. I want to see her body swing.

Someone shrieks with laughter. The middle-aged bride-to-be is so drunk she can barely stand. I think her name is Cathy and she's late to the altar or going around for a second time. She bumps into some guy at a table, spilling his pint, and then apologises with all the sincerity of a whore's kiss. Pity the poor bastard putting his prick in that!

Alice walks to the jukebox and studies the song titles beneath the glass. What sort of mother brings her pre-teen daughter to a hen night? She should be at home in bed. Instead she's sulking, plump and sedentary, eating crisps and drinking lemonade.

'You don't like dancing?' I ask.

Alice shakes her head.

'Must be pretty boring if you don't dance.'

She shrugs.

'Your name is Alice, right?'

'How did you know that?'

'I heard your mother say it. It's a nice name. "Will you walk a little faster?" said a whiting to a snail, "There's a porpoise close behind us and he's treading on my tail. See how eagerly the lobsters and the turtles all advance! They are waiting on the shingle – will you come and join the dance? Will you, won't you, will you, won't you, will you join the dance?"'

'That's from Alice in Wonderland,' she says.

'Yes it is.'

'My dad used to read that to me.'

'Curiouser and curiouser. Where's your dad now?'

'Not here.'

'Is he away on business?'

'He travels a lot.'

Her mum is being spun across the dance floor, sending her dress twirling and knickers flashing.

'Your mum is having a good time.'

Alice rolls her eyes. 'She's embarrassing.'

'All parents are embarrassing.'

She looks at me more closely. 'Why are you wearing sunglasses?'

'So I won't be recognised.'

'Who are hiding from?'

'Why do you think I'm hiding? I might be famous.'

'Are you?'

'I'm incognito.'

'What does that mean?'

'In disguise.'

'It's not a very good disguise.'

'Thanks very much.'

She shrugs.

'What sort of music do you like, Alice? Wait! Don't tell me. I think you're a Coldplay fan?'

Her eyes widen. 'How did you know?'

'You're obviously a girl of very good taste.'

This time she smiles.

'Chris Martin is a mate of mine,' I say.

'No way.'

'Yeah.'

'The lead singer of Coldplay – you know him?'

'Sure.'

'What's he like?'

'A good guy: not conceited.'

'What's that mean?'

'Big headed. Up himself.'

'Yeah, well, she's a cow.'

'Gwyneth is OK.'

'My friend Shelly says Gwyneth Paltrow is a wannabe Madonna. Shelly shouldn't talk 'cos she told Danny Green that I thought he was fit only I never said that. As if! I don't fancy him at all.'

Someone stands in the open doorway and lights a cigarette. She screws up her nose. 'People shouldn't smoke. It causes gangrene. My dad smokes and my two uncles. I tried it once and puked over my mum's leather seats.'

'She must have been impressed.'

'Shelly made me do it.'

'I wouldn't listen to Shelly so much.'

'She's my best friend. She's prettier than I am.'

'I don't think she is.'

'How would you know? You've never seen her.'

'I just find it hard to believe that anyone could be prettier than you are.'

Alice frowns sceptically and changes the subject.

'What's the difference between a boyfriend and a husband?' she asks.

'Why?'

'It's a joke. I heard someone say it.'

'I don't know. What's the difference between a boyfriend and a husband?'

'Forty-five minutes.'

I smile.

'OK. Now explain it to me,' she says.

'That's how long a wedding ceremony lasts. The difference between a boyfriend and a husband is forty-five minutes.'

'Oh. I thought it was going to be rude. Now tell me a joke?'

'I'm not very good at remembering jokes.'

She's disappointed.

'Do you really know Chris Martin?'

'Sure. He has a house in London.'

'You been there?'

'Yep.'

'You're so lucky.'

She has a small almond-shaped birthmark on her neck below her right ear. Lower still, a gold chain with a horseshoe pendant sways back and forth as she rocks on her heels.

'You like horses?'

'I have one. A chestnut mare called Sally.'

'How tall is she?'

'Fifteen hands.'

'That's a good size. How often do you ride?'

'Every weekend. I have lessons every Monday after school.'

'Lessons. Where do you have those?'

'Clack Mill Stables. Mrs Lehane is my riding teacher.'

'You like her.'

'Sure.'

Another shriek of laughter echoes across the bar. Two men have joined the hen party. One of them has his arm around her mum's waist and a pint glass in his other hand. He whispers something in her ear. She nods her head.

'I wish I could go home,' says Alice, looking miserable.

'I'd take you if I could,' I say, 'but your mum wouldn't allow it.'

Alice nods. 'I'm not even supposed to talk to strangers.'

'I'm not a stranger. I know all about you. I know you like Coldplay and you have a horse called Sally and you live in Bath.'

She laughs. 'How do you know where I live? I didn't tell you that.'

'Yes you did.'

She shakes her head adamantly.

'Well, your mother must have mentioned it.'

'Do you know her?'

'Maybe.'

Her lemonade is finished. I offer to buy her another one but she refuses. The wet cold from the open doorway makes her shiver.

'I must go, Alice. It's been nice meeting you.'

She nods.

I smile but my eyes are focused on the dance floor where her mother clinging to her new male friend who bends her backwards and nuzzles her neck. I bet she smells like overripe fruit. She'll bruise easily. She'll break quickly. I can taste the juice already.

21

The phone is ringing in my sleep. Julianne reaches across me and lifts the handset from its cradle.

'Do you know what time it is?' she says angrily. 'It's not even five o'clock. You've woken the whole house.'

I manage to pry the handset from her fingers. Veronica Cray is on the line.

'Rise and shine, Professor, I'm sending a car.'

'What's wrong?'

'We have a development.'

Julianne has rolled over, pulling the duvet resolutely under her chin. She pretends to be asleep. I begin dressing and struggle to button my shirt and tie my shoes. Eventually, she sits up, tugging at the front panels of my shirt and drawing me closer. I can smell the soft sourness of her sleepy breath.

'Don't wear your corduroy trousers.'

'What's wrong with corduroy?'

'We don't have enough time for me to tell you what's wrong with corduroy. Trust me on this one.'

She unscrews my pill bottles and fetches me a glass of water. I feel decrepit and grateful. Melancholy.

'I thought it would be different,' she whispers, more to herself than to me.

'What do you mean?'

'When we moved out of London – I thought things would be different. No detectives or police cars or you thinking about terrible crimes.'

'They need my help.'

'You *want* to help them.'

'We'll talk later,' I say, bending to kiss her. She turns her cheek and pulls the bedclothes around her.

Monk and Safari Roy are waiting for me outside. Monk opens the car door for me and Roy guns the car around the turning circle outside the church, spraying gravel and mud across the grass. God knows what the neighbours will think.

Monk is so tall his knees seem to concertina against the dashboard. The radio chatters. Neither detective seems ready to tell me where we're going.

Half an hour later we pull up in the shadow of Bristol City football ground, where three brutally ugly tower blocks rise above Victorian terraces, prefabricated factories and a car yard. A police bus is parked on the corner. A dozen officers are sitting inside, some of them wearing body armour. Veronica Cray raises her head from a car bonnet where a map has been spread across the cooling metal. Oliver Rabb is alongside her, bending low, as if embarrassed by his height or her lack of it.

'Sorry if I caused any marital disharmony,' the DI says, disingenuously.

'That's OK.'

'Oliver here has been a busy boy.' She indicates a reference point on the map. 'At 19.00 hours last night Christine Wheeler's mobile began "ping"ing a tower about four hundred yards from here. It's the same phone she left home with on Friday afternoon but it hasn't transmitted since the signal went dead in Leigh Woods and she began using a second mobile.'

'Someone made a call?' I ask.

'Ordered a pizza. It was delivered to the flat belonging to Patrick Fuller – an ex-soldier. He was discharged from the army for being "temperamentally unsuitable".'

'What does that mean?'

She shrugs. 'Your area not mine. Fuller was wounded by a road-side bomb in southern Afghanistan a year or so back. Two of his platoon died. A nurse at a military hospital in Germany accused him of feeling her up. The army discharged him.'

I glance at the grey concrete tower blocks, which are like islands against a brightening sky.

The DI is still talking.

'Four months ago Fuller lost his licence for DUI after testing positive for cocaine. Wife walked out on him around that time, taking their two kids.'

'How old is he?'

'Thirty-two.'

'Does he know Christine Wheeler?'

'Unknown.'

'So what happens now?'

'We arrest him.'

The tower block has internal stairs and a lift serving all floors. The service entrance smells of disembowelled bin bags, cat piss and wet newspapers. Patrick Fuller lives on the fourth floor.

I watch as a dozen officers in body armour climb the stairs. Four more use the lift. Their movements are choreographed by months of training yet it still seems overblown and unnecessary when considering the suspect has no history of violence.

Maybe this is the future – a legacy of 9/11 and the London train bombings. Police no longer knock on doors and politely ask suspects to accompany them to the station. Instead they dress up in body armour and break the doors down with battering rams. Privacy and personal freedom are less important than public safety. I understand the arguments but I miss the old days.

The lead officer has reached the flat and presses his ear against the door. He turns and nods. Veronica Cray nods back. A battering ram swings in a short arc. The door disappears. The arrest party suddenly stops. A snarling pit bull terrier lunges at the closest officer, who rocks back and stumbles. All fangs and fury, the pit bull hurls itself at his throat but is held back.

A man in baggy trousers and a sweatshirt has hold of the dog's collar. He looks older than twenty-eight, with pale eyes and wispy blonde hair combed straight back. Screaming accusations at the police, he tells them to fuck off and leave him alone. The dog scrabbles on its hind legs, trying to wrench itself free. Guns are drawn. Someone or something is going to get shot.

I'm watching from the stairwell. Officers have retreated halfway along the corridor. Another group are twelve feet on the far side of the door.

Fuller can't get away. Everyone should settle down.

'Don't let them shoot him,' I say.

Veronica Cray looks at me derisively. 'If I wanted to shoot him, I'd do it myself.'

'Let me talk to him.'

'Leave this to us.'

Ignoring her, I push through shoulders. Fuller is twelve feet away, still screaming above the snarling and frothing of his dog.

'Listen to me, Patrick,' I shout. He hesitates, sizing me up. His face is working relentlessly, writhing in anger and accusation. 'My name is Joe.'

'Fuck off, Mr Joe.'

'What seems to be the problem?'

'No problem, if they leave me alone.'

I take another step and the dog lunges.

'I'll let him go.'

'I'm staying right here.'

I lean against the wall and look at the concrete floor which is stained with oily black discs of flattened chewing gum. Taking out my mobile, I slide it open and flick through the menu options, looking through old text messages. The pit bull feels less threatened when I don't make eye contact. There is a lull that allows everybody to take a deep breath.

Out of the corner of my eye I can see the guns still raised.

'They're going to shoot you, Patrick, or shoot your dog.'

'I've done nothing wrong. Tell them to go away.'

His accent is more educated than I expected. 'They won't do that. It's gone too far.'

'They broke my fucking door.'

'OK, maybe they should have knocked first. We can talk about that later.'

The pit bull lunges again. Fuller wrenches it back. The animal hacks and coughs.

'You ever watched those American real life crime shows, Patrick? The ones where TV helicopters and news crews film police car chases and people getting arrested.'

'I don't watch much TV.'

'OK, but you know the shows I mean. Remember O.J. Simpson and the Ford Bronco? We all watched it: news helicopters beaming pictures around the world as O.J. drove along the freeway.

'You know what always struck me as stupid about that scene. It's the same with a lot of getaways. Guys keep trying to run with a string of police cars behind them and a chopper in the air and news crews filming the whole thing. Even when they crash the car, they jump out and leg it over barricades and wire fences and garden walls. It's ridiculous because they're not going to get away – not with all those people chasing them. And the only thing they're doing is making themselves look guilty as sin.'

'O.J. wasn't found guilty.'

'You're right. A dozen people on a jury couldn't decide, but the rest of us did. O.J. looked guilty. He sounded guilty. Most people think he is.'

Patrick is watching me closely now. His features have stopped writhing. The dog has gone quiet.

'You look like a pretty clever guy, Patrick. And I don't think a clever guy like you would make that sort of mistake. You'd say: "Hey, officers, what's all the fuss? Sure I'll answer your questions. Let me just call my lawyer."'

There's a hint of a smile. 'I don't know any lawyers.'

'I can get you one.'

'Can you get me Johnny Cochran?'

'I'll get you his distant cousin, Frank.'

This earns a proper smile. I slip my phone back in my pocket.

'I fought for this country,' says Patrick. 'I saw mates die. You know what that's like?'

'No.'

'Tell me why I should put up with shit like this.'

'It's the system, Patrick.'

'Fuck the system.'

'Most of the time it works.'

'Not for me.'

I straighten up and open my hands in a show of submission.

'It's up to you. If I walk back down the corridor, they're going to shoot your dog or they're going to shoot you. Alternatively, you go back to your flat, lock the dog in a bedroom and come on out, hands raised. Nobody gets hurt.'

He contemplates this for a few more moments and pulls hard on the collar, wrenching the animal's head around and pulling it inside. A minute later he emerges. The police close in.

Within moments Patrick is forced to his knees, then his stomach, with his hands dragged behind his back. A dog handler has gone inside with a long pole and noose. The pit bull thrashes in the air as he brings it outside.

'Not the dog,' whispers Patrick. 'Don't hurt my dog.'

22

A police interrogation is a performance with three acts. The first introduces the characters; the second provides the conflict and the third the resolution.

This interrogation has been different. For the past hour Veronica Cray has been trying to make sense of Patrick Fuller's rambling answers and bizarre rationalisations. He denies being in Leigh Woods. He denies seeing Christine Wheeler. He denies being discharged from the army. He seems ready to deny his own history. At the same time he can suddenly, inexplicably, become absorbed in a single fact and focus on it, ignoring everything else.

I watch from behind the one-way glass, feeling like a voyeur. The interview suite is new, refurbished in pastel colours with padded chairs and seaside prints on the walls. Patrick stalks the four corners with his head down and hands at his sides as though he's lost his bus fare. DI Cray asks him to sit down. He does but only for a moment. Each new question sets him in motion again.

He reaches for his back pocket, looking for something – a comb perhaps. It's no longer there. Then he runs his fingers through his hair, combing it back. He has a scar on his left hand, an 'x' that stretches from the base of his thumb and smallest finger to either edge of his wrist.

A lawyer from Legal Services has been summoned to advise

him. Middle-aged and business-like, she tucks her briefcase between her knees and sits with a large foolscap pad beneath her clasped hands. Patrick doesn't seem impressed. He wanted a man.

'Please instruct your client to sit down,' demands Veronica Cray.

'I'm trying,' she says.

'And tell him to stop pissing about.'

'He is co-operating.'

'That's an interesting interpretation of it.'

The two women don't like each other. Perhaps there's a history. The DI produces a sealed plastic evidence bag.

'I'm going to ask you again, Mr Fuller, have you seen this phone before?'

'No.'

'It was recovered from your flat.'

'Then it must be mine.'

'Where did you get it?'

'Finders keepers.'

'Are you saying you found it?'

'I can't remember.'

'Where were you on Friday afternoon?'

'I went to the beach.'

'It was raining.'

He shakes his head.

'Was anyone with you?'

'My children.'

'You were looking after your children.'

'Jessica collected shells in her bucket and George made a sandcastle. George can't swim but Jessica is learning. They paddled.'

'How old are your children?'

'Jessica is six and I think George is four.'

'You don't seem sure?'

'Of course, I'm sure.'

The DI tries to pin him down on the details, asking what time he arrived at the beach, what time they left and who they might have seen. Fuller describes a typical outing on a summer's day, buying ice-cream, sitting on the shingles and queuing for donkey rides.

It is a persuasive performance, yet impossible to believe. A dozen counties had flood warnings on Friday. There were gales along the Atlantic Coast and in the Severn.

Veronica Cray is becoming frustrated. It would be easier if Fuller said nothing at all – at least she could unpack the evidence logically and build a wall of facts to hold him. Instead his excuses are constantly changing and forcing her to backtrack.

The phenomenon is not so strange to me. I have seen it in my consulting room – patients who construct elaborate conceits and fictions, unwilling to be tied down.

The interview is suspended. There is silence in the anteroom. Monk and Roy exchange glances and lip-bitten smiles, taking perverse pleasure in seeing their boss fail. I doubt if it happens very often.

DI Cray hurls a clipboard against a wall. Papers flutter to the floor.

'I don't think he's being consciously deceitful,' I say. 'He's trying to be helpful.'

'The guy is madder than a clown's dick.'

'It could be that he *can't* remember.'

'What a load of shite!'

I stand awkwardly before her. Monk studies the polished toes of his shoes. Safari Roy examines his thumbnail. Fuller has been taken downstairs to a holding cell.

A brain injury could explain his behaviour. He was wounded in Afghanistan. A roadside bomb. The only way to be certain is to get his medical records or to give him a psych evaluation.

'Let me talk to him.'

There is a beat of silence. 'What good is that to us?'

'I'll tell you if he's a legitimate suspect.'

'He's already a suspect. He had Christine Wheeler's phone.'

'I want to treat Fuller like a patient. No recordings. No videos. Off the record.'

Anger ripples across Veronica Cray's shoulders. Monk and Roy give me a pitying look, as though I'm a condemned man. The DI begins listing reasons why I'm not allowed in the interview suite. If Patrick Fuller is charged with murder, he could use my interview as a loophole and try to escape prosecution because due process wasn't followed.

'What if we call it a psychological evaluation?'

'Fuller would have to agree.'

'I'll talk to his lawyer.'

Fuller's Legal Aid solicitor listens to my arguments and we agree on the rules of engagement. Nothing her client says can be used against him unless he agrees to be interviewed on the record.

Patrick is brought upstairs again. I watch from the darkness of the observation room as he walks carefully across the interview suite, turns and retraces his steps, trying to put his feet on exactly the same squares of carpet. He hesitates. He has forgotten how many steps it is to get back to where he started. Closing his eyes, he tries to picture his steps. Then he moves again.

I open the door and startle him. For a moment I am too much to fathom. Then he remembers me. His concern is replaced by a series of small covert grimaces, as though he's fine-tuning his facial muscles until he's happy with the face he shows the world.

The Legal Aid solicitor follows me into the room and takes a seat in the corner.

'Hello, Patrick.'

'My dog.'

'Your dog is being looked after.'

'What did you see on the floor a minute ago?'

'Nothing.'

'You didn't want to step on something.'

'The mousetraps.'

'Who put the mousetraps on the floor?'

He looks at me hopefully. 'You can see them?'

'How many can *you* see?'

He points, counting. 'Twelve, thirteen . . .'

'I'm a psychologist, Patrick. Have you ever talked to someone like me before?'

He nods.

'After you were wounded?'

'Yes.'

'Do you have nightmares?'

'Sometimes.'

'What are your nightmares about?'

'Blood.' He takes a seat and stands again almost immediately.

'Blood?'

'First I see Leon's body, lying on top of me. His eyes have rolled back in his head. There's blood everywhere. I know he's dead. I have to push him off me. Spike is trapped underneath the chassis of the troop carrier, pinned by his legs. No way we can lift it off him. Bullets are bouncing off the metal like raindrops and we're scrambling for cover.

'Spike is screaming his head off because his legs are crushed and the carrier is on fire. And we all know that when the flames reach the arsenal the whole thing's going to blow.'

Patrick is breathing in rapid, truncated gasps and his forehead is beaded with sweat.

'Is that what happened in real life, Patrick?'

He doesn't answer.

'Where is Spike now?'

'He's dead.'

'Did he die in the contact?'

Patrick nods.

'How did he die?'

'He was shot.'

'Who shot him?'

He whispers. 'I did.'

His lawyer wants to intervene. I raise my hand slightly, wanting just a moment more.

'Why did you shoot Spike?'

'A bullet had hit him in the chest, but he was still screaming. The flames had reached his legs. We couldn't get him out. We were pinned down. We were ordered to pull back. He screamed out to me. He was begging . . . dying.'

Patrick's facial muscles are twisting in anguish. He covers his face with his hands and peers at me through the splayed fingers.

'It's OK,' I tell him. 'Just relax.' I pour him a cup of water.

He reaches forward and needs two hands to raise the cup to

his lips. His eyes are watching me as he drinks. Then he notices my left hand. My thumb and forefinger are pill rolling again. It's a detail he seems to register and store away.

'I'm going to ask you some questions, Patrick. It's not a test, but I just need you to concentrate.'

He nods.

'What day is today?'

'Friday.'

'What is the date?'

'The sixteenth.'

'Actually it's the fifth. What month?'

'August.'

'What makes you say that?'

'It's hot outside.'

'You're not dressed for a hot day.'

He looks at his clothes, almost surprised. I then notice his eyes lift and move slightly to focus on something behind me. I keep talking to him about the weather and turn my head far enough to see the wall at my back. A framed print is hanging beside the mirror – a beachside scene with children playing on the shingles and paddling. There is a Ferris wheel in the background and an ice-cream barrow.

Patrick constructed his entire alibi from a single scene. The picture helped him fill in the details that he couldn't remember about last Friday. That's why he was so sure it was a hot day and that he took his children to the beach.

Patrick has a problem with his contextual memory. He retains snippets of autobiographical information, but cannot anchor them to a specific time or place. The memories drift loose. Images collide. That's why he tells rambling stories and avoids eye contact. He sees mousetraps on the floor.

Reality is under constant review in his head. When a question comes along that he feels he should be able to answer, he looks for clues and creates a new script to fit them. The photograph on the wall gave him a framework and he spun a story around it, ignoring anomalies such as the rain or the time of year.

If Patrick were a patient, I'd make an appointment schedule and ask to see his medical records. I might even organise a brain scan, which would probably show a right hemisphere brain injury – some sort of haemorrhage. At the very least he is suffering from post-traumatic stress. That's why he confabulates and invents, constructing fantastic stories to explain things that he can't remember. He does it inadvertently. Automatically.

'Patrick,' I say gently, 'if you don't remember what happened last Friday, just tell me. I won't think you foolish. Everybody forgets things. A phone was found in your house that belonged to a woman who was at Leigh Woods.'

He looks at me blankly. I know the memory is there. He just can't access the information.

'She was naked,' I say. 'She was wearing a yellow raincoat and high heel shoes.'

His eyes stop wandering and rest on mine. 'Her shoes were red.'

'Yes.'

It's as though the wheels of a fruit machine have lined up inside his head. The scattered fragments of memory and emotion are falling into place.

'You saw her?'

He hesitates. This time it will be a genuine lie. I don't give him the opportunity.

'She was on the path.'

He nods.

'Was she with anyone?'

He shakes his head.

'What was she doing?'

'Walking.'

'Did you speak to her?'

'No.'

Did you follow her?'

He nods. 'That's all I did.'

'How did you get her phone?'

'I found it.'

'Where?'

141

'She left it in her car.'

'So you took it?'

'It was unlocked,' he mumbles, unable to think of an excuse. 'I was worried about her. I thought she might be in trouble.'

'Then why didn't you call the police.'

'I-I-I didn't have a phone.'

'You had *hers*.'

His face is a riot of tics and grimaces. He is on his feet, pacing back and forth, no longer avoiding the mousetraps. He says something. I don't catch it. I ask him to say it again.

'The battery was flat. I had to buy a charger. It cost me ten quid.'

He looks at me hopefully. 'Do you think they'll give me a refund?'

'I don't know.'

'I only used it a few times.'

'Listen to me, Patrick. Focus on me. The woman in the park, did you talk to her?'

His face is twisting again.

'What did she say, Patrick? It's important.'

'Nothing.'

'Don't shake your head, Patrick. What did she say?'

He shrugs, looking around the room, trying to find another picture to help him.

'I don't want you to make it up, Patrick. If you don't remember, just tell me. But it's really important. Think hard.'

'She asked about her daughter. She wanted to know if I'd seen her.'

'Did she say why?'

He shakes his head.

'Is that all she said?'

'Yeah.'

'What happened then?'

He shrugs. 'She ran away.'

'Did you follow her?'

'No.'

'Did she have a phone with her, Patrick? Was she talking to someone?'

'Maybe. I don't know. I couldn't hear.'

I carry on with the questioning, trying to build a framework of truths. Without warning, Patrick stops and gazes at the floor. Raising one foot, he steps over a 'mousetrap'. I've lost him again. He's somewhere else.

'Maybe we should give him a break,' says the lawyer.

Outside the interview room, I sit down with the detectives and explain why I think Patrick confabulates and invents stories.

'So he's brain damaged,' says Safari Roy, trying to paraphrase my clinical descriptions.

'Doesn't make him innocent,' adds Monk.

'Is this a permanent condition?' asks Veronica Cray.

'I don't know. Patrick retains kernels of information but he can't anchor them to a specific time or place. His memories drift loose. If you show him a photograph and prove to him that he was in Leigh Woods, he will accept it. But that doesn't mean he *remembers* being there.'

'Which means he could still be our man.'

'That's very unlikely. You heard him. His head is crowded with snatches of conversations, images, his wife, his children, things that happened before he was injured. These things are bouncing around in his head without any sense or order. He can function. He can hold down a simple job. But whenever his memory fails him, he makes something up.'

'So we won't get a statement,' says the DI, dismissively. 'We don't need one. He admitted to being at the scene. He had her phone.'

'He didn't make her jump.'

DI Cray cuts me off. 'With all due respect, Professor, I know you're good at what you do but you have no idea *what* this man is capable of.'

'You can think I'm wrong, but that's no reason to quit thinking. I'm giving my opinion. You're making a mistake.'

With an air of finality the DI straightens a stack of papers and begins issuing instructions. She wants the manager of the mobile phone shop and his assistant brought to the station.

'Patrick locked her car,' I say.

Veronica Cray stops in mid-sentence. 'What does that have to do with anything?'

'It just strikes me as an odd thing for a killer to do.'

'Did you ask him why?'

'He said he didn't want anyone stealing it.'

23

Little Alice is riding her chestnut mare. Her hair is braided into a single plait that bounces up and down on her back as she rises and falls in the saddle, doing long slow circles of the enclosure.

Three other students are mounted and have joined the class, all wearing jodhpurs, riding boots and riding helmets. The instructor, Mrs Lehane, has big hips and messy blonde hair. She reminds me of a CO's wife I met in Germany, who was more intimidating than her husband.

I can smell the horses. Never trust animals that are bigger than you are, that's my motto. Horses may look intelligent and placid in photographs but in real life, up close, they ripple and snort. And those big, soft, wet eyes are hiding a secret. Come the revolution four legs will rule the world.

A couple of the parents have stayed to watch their children ride. Others are chatting in the parking area. Alice has nobody to watch her except for me. Don't worry, snowflake, I'm looking at you. Sit up straight. Trot, trot, trot . . .

I punch the numbers on the mobile and hit the green button. A woman answers.

'Is that Sylvia Furness?'

'Yes.'

'The mother of Alice?'

'Yes. Who's calling?'

'I'm the good Samaritan who's looking after your daughter.'

'What do you mean?'

'She had a fall from her horse. Twisted her knee quite badly. But it's OK now, I've kissed it better.'

There's a sharp intake of breath. 'Who are you? Where's my daughter?'

'She's right here, Sylvia, lying on the bed.'

'What do you mean?'

'She was muddy after her fall. Her jodhpurs were filthy. I popped them in the washing machine and gave Alice a bath. She has such lovely skin. What conditioner do you use on her hair? It's very soft.'

'I-I-I don't know which one.'

'And she has such a pretty birthmark on her neck. It's shaped like an almond. I'm going to kiss it.'

'No! Don't touch her!'

Pain and confusion strangle her words. Fear. Panic. She's going through them all now. Emotional overload.

'Where's Mrs Lehane?' she asks.

'With the rest of the class.'

'Let me speak to Alice.'

'She can't speak.'

'Why?'

'She has masking tape across her mouth. But don't worry, Sylvia, she can hear you. Let me put the phone down next to her ear. You can tell her how much you love her.'

A groan. 'Please, let her go.'

'But we're having fun together. She's such a sweet little thing. I'm looking after her. Little girls need looking after. Where's Alice's daddy?'

'He's not here.'

'Little girls need a father.'

'He's away on business.'

'Why do you act like such a whore when he's away?'

'I don't.'

'Alice thinks you do.'

'No.'

'She's growing up. Budding.'

'Please, don't touch her.'

'She's very brave. She didn't cry at all when I cut her clothes off. Now she's a little embarrassed about being naked but I told her not to worry. I

146

couldn't put her muddy clothes back on. You really should invest in a bra for her. I think she's ready . . . I mean, she will be twelve in May.'

She is begging me now, sobbing into the phone.

'I know all about Alice. She likes Coldplay. Her horse is called Sally. She has a picture of her father on her bedside table. Her best friend's name is Shelly. She likes a boy at school called Danny Green. She's a little young to have a boyfriend but it won't be long before she's giving blowjobs in the back row at the cinema and spreading her legs all over town. I'm going to break her in.'

'No, please. She's just a——.'

'Virgin, I know, I've checked.'

Sylvia is hyperventilating.

'Calm down,' I tell her. 'Take a deep breath. Alice needs you to listen to me.'

'What do you want?'

'I want you to help me make her a woman.'

'No. No.'

'Listen to me, Sylvia. Don't interrupt.'

'Please, let her go.'

'What did I tell you?'

'Please.'

I slam the phone into my fist. 'You hear that, Sylvia. That's the sound of my fist hitting Alice's face. I'm going to hit her again, every time you interrupt me.'

'No. Please. I'm sorry.'

She falls silent.

'That's good, Sylvia. Much better. I'm going to let you say hello to Alice now. She can hear you. What do you want to say to her?'

She sobs: 'Baby, it's Mummy. It's OK. Don't be scared. I'm going to help you. I'm . . . I'm . . .'

'Tell her to relax.'

'Just relax.'

'Tell her to co-operate.'

'Do as the man says.'

'That's very good, Sylvia. She's much calmer. Now I can begin. You can help me. Which hole shall I fuck first?'

She wails down the line. 'Please, don't touch her. Please no. Take her outside. Leave her in the street. I won't call the police.'

147

'Why would I want to do that?'

'She's only a baby.'

'In some countries they marry girls off when they're her age. They also circumcise them and sew their cunts shut.'

A groan rattles deep inside her.

'Take me. You can have me.'

'Why would I want you when I have little Alice? She's young. You're old. She's clean. You're a slut.'

'Please take me.'

'Can you hear her breathing? I am resting my head on her chest. Her heart is going, "Pitter patter, pitter patter".'

'Take me, please. I'll do anything you want.'

'Oh, be careful what you say, Sylvia. Will you really take her place?'

'Yes.'

'Could you . . . would you . . . ?'

'Yes.'

'How do I know that I can trust you?'

'You can. Please. Let her go.'

A second mobile is cradled in my hand. I dial a new number. I can hear it ringing in the background. Sylvia covers the mouthpiece and answers her mobile, whispering urgently, 'Help me! Please! Call the police. He has my daughter.'

I pronounce each syllable: 'Syl-vee-a. Guess who this is?'

She groans in despair.

'Alice gave me your mobile number. It was a test. You failed. I can't trust you any more. Sylvia, I'm going to hang up now. You won't see Alice again.'

She wails. 'No! No! No! I'm sorry. Please. It was a mistake. It won't happen again.'

'I'm putting the phone next to Alice's ear again. Tell her you're sorry. I was going to rape her and send her back. Now you'll never see her again.'

'Please don't hurt her.'

'Oh, look at that! You've made her cry.'

'Anything. I'll do anything.'

'I'm lying on top of her, Sylvia. Relax, little one. Don't be frightened. It's Mummy's fault. She couldn't be trusted.'

'No, no, no, please . . .'

'Open your thighs, little one. This is going to hurt. And when I'm finished

I'm going to bury you so deep Mummy will never find you. The worms will. Your body will taste so sweet to those worms.'

'Take me! Take me!' Sylvia screams. 'Don't touch her. Don't hurt my baby.'

'Say you're sorry, Sylvia. And then say goodbye.'

'No. Listen. I'll do anything. Don't hurt her. Take me instead.'

'Are you worthy, Sylvia? You have to prove to me that you're worthy of taking her place.'

'How?'

'Take off your clothes.'

'What?'

'Alice is naked. I want you to be naked. Take off your clothes. Oh, look! Alice is nodding her head. She wants you to help her.'

'Can I talk to her again?'

'OK. She's listening.'

'Baby, can you hear me? It's OK. Don't be scared. Mummy is going to come and get you. I promise. I love you.'

'That was very touching, Sylvia. Are you naked, yet?'

'Yes.'

'Walk to the window and open the curtains.'

'Why?'

'I can see everywhere, Sylvia. I can tell you all about your bedroom and your wardrobe, the clothes on the hangers, your shoes . . .'

'Who are you?'

'I'm the man who's going to fuck your daughter to death if you don't do exactly as I say.'

'I just want to know your name.'

'No you don't. You want to make a connection. You want to develop a bond between us because you think I'll be less likely to hurt Alice. Don't play mind games with me, Sylvia. I'm a professional. I'm a mind-fuck expert. I do this for a living. I did it for my country.'

'What does that mean?'

'It means I know what you're thinking. I know all about you. I know where you live. I know what friends you have. I'm going to give you another test, Sylvia. Remember what happened last time. I know one of your friends: her name is Helen Chambers.'

'What about Helen?'

'I want you to tell me where she is.'

'I don't know. I haven't seen her in years.'

'Liar!'

'No, it's true. She sent me an email a few weeks ago.'

'What did it say?'

'She-she-she said she was coming home. She wanted to meet up.'

'Syl-vee-a, don't lie to me.'

'I'm not.'

'YOU'RE A FUCKING LIAR!'

'No.'

'Are you naked yet?'

Tearfully, 'Yes.'

'You haven't opened the curtains.'

'Yes I have.'

'That's good. Now go to your wardrobe. I want you to find your black boots. The ones with the pointy toes and fuck-me heels. You know the pair. I want you to put them on.'

I hear her looking for them. I imagine her on her knees, scrabbling on the floor.

'I can't find them.'

'You can.'

'I have to put the phone down.'

'No. If you put the phone down, Alice dies. It's very simple.'

'I'm trying.'

'You're taking too long. I am going to take the blindfold off Alice. Do you know what that means? She can recognise me. I'll have to kill her. I'm undoing the knot. When she opens her eyes, she dies.'

'I found them! They're here!'

'Put them on.'

'I have to put the phone down to zip them up.'

'No you don't.'

'It's not poss—'

'Do you think I'm stupid, Sylvia? Do you think I haven't done this before? There are dead girls up and down this country. You read about them in the newspapers and see their pictures on the TV. Missing teenagers. Their bodies never found. I did that! It was me! Don't fuck with me, Sylvia.'

'I won't. You will let Alice go. I mean, if I do what you say, you'll let her go?'

150

'One or two get spared, but only if someone is willing to take their place. Are you willing, Sylvia? Don't disappoint me. Don't disappoint Alice. Either you do it for me or she does it for me.'

'Yes.'

I direct her to the bathroom. In the second drawer of the vanity there is a lipstick. Glossy. Pink.

'Look at yourself in the mirror, Sylvia. What do you see?'

'I don't know.'

'Oh, come on. What do you see?'

'Me.'

'A slut. Wear the lipstick for me. Make yourself beautiful.'

'I can't do it.'

'You do it for me or she does it for me.'

'All right.'

'Now in the bottom drawer – there's a pink bag – take it with you.'

'I can't see a pink bag. It's not here.'

'Yes it is. Don't lie to me again.'

'I won't.'

'Are you ready?'

'Yes.'

I tell her to walk to the front door of the flat, to take her car keys and the pink bag.

'Open the door, Sylvia. Take one step at a time.'

'And you'll let Alice go.'

'If you do as I say.'

'You won't hurt her.'

'I'll keep her safe. Look at that – Alice is nodding. She's happy. She's waiting for you.'

Sylvia is downstairs. She opens the main door. I tell her not to look at anyone or signal anyone. She says the street is empty.

'Now, walk to your car. Get in. Plug in the hands free. You have to talk and drive.'

'I don't have one.'

'Don't lie to me, Sylvia. There's one in the glove compartment.'

'Where am I going?'

'You're coming to me. I'm going to give you directions. Don't take any wrong turns. Don't flash your lights or sound your horn. I'll know. Don't disappoint

151

me. Go straight ahead, through the roundabout and turn right into Sydney Road.'

'Why are you doing this? What have we done to you?'

'Don't even get me started.'

'I've done nothing wrong. Alice has done nothing.'

'You're all the same.'

'No, we're not. I'm not like you say—'

'I've watched you, Sylvia. I've seen what you're like. Tell me where you are.'

'Passing the museum.'

'Turn into Warminster Road. Stay on it until I tell you.'

Sylvia changes her tactics, trying to find a way through to me. 'I can be very good to you,' she says, hesitatingly. 'I'm very good in bed. I can do things. Whatever you want.'

'I know you can. How many times have you cheated on your husband?'

'I don't cheat—'

'Liar!'

'I'm telling the truth.'

'I want you to slap yourself, Sylvia.'

She doesn't understand.

'Slap yourself on the face . . . as punishment.'

I give her a moment to obey. I hear nothing. I whack the phone against my fist. 'You hear that, Sylvia. Alice took your punishment again. Her lip is bleeding. Don't blame me, little one, it's Mummy's fault.'

Sylvia screams at me to stop but I've heard enough of her mewling, pathetic pesthole excuses. I slam the phone into my fist again and again.

She sobs. 'Please don't hurt her. Please. I'm coming.'

'Alice is such a sweet thing. I have tasted her tears. They're like sugar water. Has she had her period yet?'

'She's only eleven.'

'I can make her bleed. I can make her bleed from places that you can't even imagine.'

'No. I'm coming. Where's Alice?'

'She's waiting for you.'

'Let me talk to her?'

'She can hear you.'

'I love you, baby.'

'How much do you love her? Will you take her place?'

'Yes.'

'Come to me, Sylvia. She's waiting. Come and take her home.'

24

The tree is an ogre with outstretched arms. A body hangs beneath it, suspended from a branch, motionless, white. Not white. Naked. Hooded.

Behind the branches, across the valley a monochrome landscape is slowly emerging from the darkness. Fields divided by hedges and patches of evergreen scrub. Twisting trails of beech trees that follow the streams. The sun is hiding behind a bruised sky. Nosegays and primroses and daffodils are beneath the ground. Colours might not exist.

The wide metal gate has been sealed off with blue and white police tape. Spotlights have been set up around an adjacent barn. The weathered wood seems to be whitewashed by the brightness.

More police tape seals off the farm track. Vehicle tyre prints are being photographed and cast in plaster. At the end of the track is a narrow lane, blocked in both directions by police cars and vans.

The police have erected makeshift barriers and a checkpoint. I have to give my name to a constable with a clipboard. Picking my way along the track, avoiding the puddles, I reach the barn and can look across a ploughed field to where the body is hanging.

Duckboards cover the rest of the journey, white plastic stepping-stones, leading to the base of the tree, fifty feet away. The blades of a plough have created a teardrop shape around the trunk. The furrowed earth is dusted with frost.

Veronica Cray is standing beside the body, looking like an executioner. A naked woman, hanging by one arm, is suspended from a branch by a set of handcuffs. Her left wrist is raw and bleeding beneath the locked metal band. A white pillowcase encases her head, bunching on her shoulders. Her toes barely touch the earth.

Lying on the ground at her feet is a mobile phone. The battery is dead. She's wearing knee-length leather boots. One of the heels has broken off. The other is embedded in mud. A flashgun fires in rapid bursts, creating the illusion that the body is moving like a stop-motion animation puppet.

The same Geordie pathologist who examined Christine Wheeler's car at the lock-up is working again, issuing instructions to the photographer. For the next few hours at least the scene belongs to the evidence gatherers.

Ruiz is already here, slapping his arms against the cold. I woke him at the pub and told him to meet me.

'You interrupted a great dream,' he says. 'I was in bed with your wife.'

'Was I there?'

'If I ever have *that* dream, we can no longer be friends.'

Both of us listen as the pathologist briefs Veronica Cray. The unofficial cause of death is exposure.

'Hypostasis indicates that this is where she died. Upright. There are no obvious signs of sexual assault or defence wounds. But I'll know more when I get her to the lab.'

'What about time of death?' she asks.

'Rigor mortis has set in. A body normally loses a degree of temperature every hour but it dropped below freezing last night. She could have been dead for twenty-four hours, perhaps longer.'

The pathologist scrawls his signature on a clipboard and goes back to his staff. The DI motions me to follow her. We pick our way across the duckboards to the tree.

Today I have my walking stick – a sign that my medication is having less effect. It is a nice stick, made of polished walnut with a metal tip. I'm less self-conscious about using it nowadays. Either that or I'm more frightened of my leg locking up and sending me over.

The photographer is shooting close-ups of the woman's fingers. Her nails are slim and painted. Her nakedness is marbled with lividity and I can smell the sweet sourness of her perfume and urine.

'You know who this is?'

I shake my head.

The DI gently rolls the hood upwards, bunching the fabric in her fists. Sylvia Furness is staring at me, her head hanging forward, twisted to one side by the weight of her body. Her ash blonde hair is matted into curls and is darker at her temples.

'Her daughter, Alice, reported her missing late Monday afternoon. Alice was dropped home after a horse-riding lesson and found the front door open. No sign of her mother. Clothes lying on the floor. A missing persons report was filed on Tuesday morning.'

'Who discovered her body?' I ask.

She motions over my shoulder towards a farmer who is sitting in the front seat of a farm truck. 'Last night he thought he heard foxes. He came out early to take a look. He found Sylvia Furness's car parked in the barn. Then he saw the body.'

Veronica Cray lets the hood fall and cover Sylvia's face. The death scene has a surreal, abstract, achingly theatrical sensibility; a whiff of sawdust and face paint, as if somehow it has been laid out like this for someone to find.

'Where is Alice now?'

'Being looked after by her grandparents.'

'What about her father?'

'He's flying back from Switzerland. He's been away on business.'

DI Cray plunges her hands into the pockets of her overcoat.

'This make any sense to you?'

'Not yet.'

'There's no sign of a struggle or defence injuries. She hasn't been raped or tortured. She froze to death, for glory's sake.'

I know she's thinking about Christine Wheeler. The similarities are impossible to ignore, yet for every one of them I could find an equally compelling difference. Sometimes in mathematics, randomness itself becomes a pattern.

She's also contemplating whether Patrick Fuller could have been involved. He was released from custody on Sunday morning having been charged with stealing Christine Wheeler's mobile.

Uniformed officers have gathered beside the farm shed, waiting to begin a fingertip search of the field. Veronica Cray makes her way towards them, leaving me standing beside the body.

Nine days ago I glimpsed Sylvia Furness through an open door as she undressed in her flat. Her muscles were sculptured from hours in the gym. Now death has turned the sculpture to stone.

Stepping across the duckboards, I reach the perimeter of the roped area and begin walking up the slope towards the oak ridge. My polished cane is useless in the mud. I tuck it under one arm.

The sky has a porcelain quality as the sun fights to break through the high white clouds. The last of the mist has burned off and the valley has fully materialised, revealing humpback bridges and cows dotting the pastures.

I reach the fence and try to scramble over it. My leg locks and I fall into a ditch full of knee-high grass and muddy water. At least it was a soft landing.

Turning back, I scrutinize the scene, watching as the SOCOs lift Sylvia's body down from the tree and lay it upon a plastic sheet. Nature is a cruel, heartless observer. No matter how terrible the act or disaster, the trees, rocks and clouds are unmoved. Perhaps that is why mankind is destined to chop down the last tree and catch the last fish and shoot the last bird. If nature can be so dispassionate about our fate, why should we care about nature?

Sylvia Furness froze to death. She had a mobile phone, but didn't call for help. He kept her talking until the battery ran out. Either that or he was here, taunting her with it.

This was a piece of twisted sadistic theatre, but what was the artist trying to say? He gained pleasure from her pain; he revelled in his power over Sylvia, but why did he leave her body so obviously on display? Is it a message or a warning?

There he is again, the man who knows Johnny Cochran's distant cousin; the one who tried to talk to my fallen angel. He's a regular corpse chaser, isn't he? The grim reaper.

I watch him cross the field, ruining his shoes. Then he falls over the fence into the ditch. What a clown!

I've known my share of shrinks, doctor-major types who administer mental enemas, trying to get soldiers to bring their nightmares into daylight like some steaming pile of crap. Most of them were bullshit artists, who made me feel like I was doing them a favour by telling them things. Instead of asking questions, they sat and listened – or pretended to.

It's like that old joke about two shrinks meeting at a university reunion and one looks old and haggard while the other is bright-eyed and youthful. The older-looking one says, 'How do you do it? I listen to other people's problems all day, every day, year after year, and it's turned me into an old man. What's your secret?'

The younger-looking one replies, 'Who listens?'

A guy I know called Felini, my first CO in Afghanistan, used to have nightmares. We called him Felini because he said his family came from Sicily and he had an uncle in the Mafia. I don't know his real name. We weren't supposed to know.

Felini had been in Afghanistan for twelve years. At first he fought alongside Osama Bin Laden against the Soviets and then finished up fighting against him. In between times he reported to the CIA and DEA monitoring opium production.

He was the first westerner into Mazar-e-Sharif after the Taliban captured the city in 1998. He told me what he saw. The Taliban had gone through the streets, strafing everything that moved with machine guns. Then they went from house to house, rounding up Hazaras, before locking them in steel shipping containers in the broiling sun. They baked to death or suffocated. Others were thrown alive into wells before the tops were bulldozed over. No wonder Felini had nightmares.

Strangely, none of that changed how he felt about the Talibs. He respected them.

'The Talibs knew they were never going to win over the locals,' he told me. 'So they taught them a lesson. Each time they lost a village and won it back again, they were more savage than before. Payback can be a bitch, but it's what you have to do,' he said. 'Forget about winning hearts and minds. You rip out their hearts and break open their minds.'

Felini was the best interrogator I've ever seen. There was no part of the body he couldn't hurt. Nothing he couldn't find out. His other theory was

about Islam. He said that for four thousand years the guy who carried the
biggest stick had been in charge and been respected in the Middle East. It's
the only language the Arabs understand – Sunni, Shiite, Kurdish, Wahhabi,
Ismaili, Kufi – makes no fucking difference.

Enough of the nostalgia. They're taking the bitch's body down.

A bird flies out of the trees in a clatter of wings. It startles me. I brace my hands against the top strand of wire, feeling the cold radiate from the metal.

On the lower reaches of the field, dozens of police officers are shuffling forward in a long unbroken line. Clouds of condensed vapour billow from their faces. As I watch the strange procession, a realisation washes over me, a sense that I'm not alone. Peering into the trees, I scan the deeper shadows. On the periphery of my vision I notice a movement. A man is crouched behind a fallen tree, trying not to be seen. He is wearing a woollen hat and something dark is covering his face.

Without even realising it, I am moving towards him.

He hears a sound. Turning, he tucks something into a bag and then scrambles to his feet and begins to run. I yell at him to stop. He carries on, crashing through the undergrowth. Big, slow and shiny faced, he can't stay ahead of me. I close the gap and he stops suddenly. Unable to slow down, I hurtle into him, knocking him to the ground.

I scramble to my knees and raise my walking stick, holding it above my head like an axe.

'Don't move!'

'Christ, mate, ease up.'

'Who are you?'

'I'm a photographer. I work for a press agency.'

He sits up. I look at his bag. The contents have spilled across the sodden leaves. A camera and flash, long lenses, filters, a notebook . . .

'If anything's broken you're fucking paying,' he says, examining the camera.

My shouts have summoned Monk who vaults the fence with far more proficiency than I did.

159

'Shit!' he says, 'Cooper.'

'Morning, Monk.'

'Detective Constable Abbott to you.' Monk hauls him to his feet. 'This is a crime scene and private property. You're trespassing.'

'Fuck off.'

'Offensive language – that's another charge.'

'Gimme a break.'

'The film.'

'I don't have any film. It's digital.'

'Then give me the bloody memory card.'

'People have got a right to see these pictures,' says Cooper. 'It's in the public interest.'

'Yeah, sure, woman hanging from a tree; big public interest story.'

I leave the two of them arguing. Monk is going to prevail. He's six-foot four. Nature wins again.

I climb a gate and follow the road to where police cars have blocked off the lane. DI Cray is standing beside a mobile canteen, stirring sugar into tea. She stares at my trousers.

'I fell down.'

She shakes her head and pauses to watch the white body bag being carried past us on a stretcher and loaded into a waiting Home Office van.

'What makes someone like Sylvia Furness take off her clothes, walk out of her flat and come here?'

'I think he used the daughter.'

'But she was at a riding school.'

'Remember what Fuller said? When he met Christine Wheeler on the path last Friday, she asked about her daughter.'

'Darcy was at school.'

'Exactly. But what if Christine didn't know that? What if he convinced her otherwise?'

DI Cray draws breath and runs her hand across her scalp. Her short hair flattens and springs back again. I catch her staring at me as though I'm a strange artefact that she has stumbled across and can't name.

Off to my right I hear the sounds of a commotion, several

people shouting at once. Reporters and news crews have crossed the police tape and are charging up the farm track. At least a dozen uniforms and plainclothes converge on them, forming a barricade.

One reporter pivots and ducks under the line. A detective tackles him from behind and they both finish up in the mud.

Veronica Cray utters a knowing sigh and tips out her tea.

'It's feeding time.'

Moments later she disappears into the throng. I can barely see the top of her head. She orders them to step back . . . further still. I can see her now. The TV lights have bleached her face whiter than a full moon.

'My name is Detective Inspector Veronica Cray. At 7.55 this morning the body of a woman was found at this location. Early indications suggest the death is suspicious. We will not be releasing her name until her next of kin have been informed.'

Each time she pauses, a dozen flashguns fire and the questions come almost as quickly.

'Who found the body?'

'Is it true she was naked?'

'Was she sexually assaulted?'

Some of them are answered, others parried. The DI looks directly at the cameras and maintains a calm, businesslike demeanour, keeping her answers short and to the point.

There are angry objections when she ends the impromptu press conference. Already pushing through their shoulders, she reaches my side and pulls me towards a waiting car.

'I have no illusions about my work, Professor. My job is pretty straightforward most of the time. Your average murderer is drunk, angry and stupid. He's white, in his late twenties, with a low IQ and a history of violence. And gets into a pub brawl or gets sick of his wife's nagging and puts a claw hammer in the back of her head. I can understand that sort of homicide.'

By inference she's saying this case is different.

'I've heard stories about you. They say you can tell things about people; understand them; read them like tealeaves in a cup.'

'I make clinical judgements.'

161

'Whatever you want to call it, you seem to be good at this sort of thing. Details are important to you. You like finding patterns to them. I want you to find a pattern for me. I want to know who did this. I want to know why he did it and how he did it. And I want to stop the sick fuck from doing it again.'

25

The house is quiet. Strains of classical music drift along the hall. The dining table has been pushed back against the wall. A lone chair remains in the centre of the room.

Darcy is dressed in trackies rolled low onto her hips and a green midriff top which shows the paleness of her shoulders and stomach. Her chestnut hair is pinned tightly into a bun.

She balances one leg on the back of a chair with her toes pointed and leans forward until her forehead touches her knee. The outlines of her shoulder blades are like stunted wings beneath her skin.

She holds the pose for a minute and rises again, drawing her arm above her head as if painting the air. Every movement has an economy of effort, the dip of a shoulder or extension of a hand. Nothing is forced or wasted. She is barely a woman, yet she moves with such grace and confidence.

Sitting on the floor, she stretches her legs wide apart and leans forward until her chin touches the floor. Her teenage body, extremely stretched and open, looks athletic and beautiful rather than vulgar.

Her eyes open.

'Aren't you cold?' I ask.

'No.'

'How often do you practise?'

'I should do it twice a day.'

'You're very good.'

She laughs. 'Do you know anything about ballet?'

'No.'

'They say I have a dancer's body,' she says. 'Long legs and a short torso.' She stands and turns side-on. 'Even when my legs are straight the knee is bent slightly backwards, you see that? It creates a better line when I'm on *pointe*.' She rises onto her toes. 'I can also flex my feet forward to be vertical from knee to toe. Can you see?'

'Yes. You're very graceful.'

She laughs. 'I'm bow-legged and duck-footed.'

'I used to have a patient who was a ballerina.'

'Why were you seeing her?'

'She was anorexic.'

Darcy nods sadly. 'Some girls have to starve themselves. I didn't have a period until I was fifteen. I also have curvature of the spine, partially dislocated vertebrae and stress fractures in my neck.'

'Why do you do it?'

She shakes her head. 'You wouldn't understand.'

She turns her toes outward.

'This is a *pas de chat*. I leap off my left leg starting from a *plié* and raise my right leg into a *retiré*. In mid-air I raise my left leg into a *retiré* as well so that my legs form a diamond shape in the air. You see? That's what the four cygnets do when they dance in *Swan Lake*. Their arms are interlaced and they do sixteen *pas de chats*.'

An abiding sense of lightness makes her float through each jump.

'Can you help me practise my *pas de deux*?'

'What's that?'

'Come here. I'll show you.'

She takes my hands and puts them on her waist. I feel as though my fingertips could reach right around her and touch in the small of her back.

'A little lower,' she says. 'That's it.'

'I don't know what I'm doing.'

'It doesn't matter. Nobody watches the man in a *pas de deux*. They're too busy watching the ballerina.'

'What do I do?'

'Hold me as I jump.'

Effortlessly, she takes off. If anything it feels as though I'm holding her down rather than up. Her bare skin slides beneath my fingers.

She does it half a dozen times. 'You can let go of me now,' she says, giving me a teasing smile.

'Perhaps you don't like ballet. I can do other dances.' Reaching up, she unpins her hair and lets it tumble over her eyes. Then she grinds her hips in a long slow circle, squatting with her knees apart, running her hands along her thighs and over her crotch.

It is shamelessly provocative. I force myself to look away.

'You shouldn't dance like that.'

'Why not?'

'It's not something you should do in front of a stranger.'

'But you're not a stranger.'

She's making fun of me now. Adolescent girls are the most complicated life forms in the known universe. It astonishes me how they manage to be so discomfiting. With little more than a glance or a flash of skin or a dismissive smirk, they can make a man feel ancient, meddlesome and vaguely lecherous.

'I need to talk to you.'

'What about?'

'Your mother.'

'I thought you'd asked me everything already.'

'Not yet.'

'Can I keep stretching?'

'Of course.'

She sits on the floor again, pushing her legs wide apart.

'Did you talk to anyone about your mother – in the past month? Was there someone who asked questions about her or about you?'

She shrugs. 'I don't think so. I can't remember. What's wrong? What's happened?'

'There's been another death. The police are going to want to interview you again.'

Darcy stops stretching and her eyes meet mine. They're no longer bright with energy or amusement.

'Who?'

'Sylvia Furness. I'm sorry.'

A slight noise catches in Darcy's throat. She holds her hands to her mouth as if trying to stop the sound from escaping.

'Did you ever meet Alice?' I ask.

'Yes.'

'Did you know her well?'

She shakes her head.

I don't have enough information to explain to Darcy what happened today or ten days ago. Her mother and Sylvia Furness were in business together but what else did they share? The man who killed them knew things about them. He chose them for a reason.

This is a search that must go backwards rather than forwards. Address books. Diaries. Wallets. Emails. Letters. Telephone messages. The movements of both victims have to be traced – where they went, who they spoke to, what shops they visited, where they had their hair done. What friends do they have in common? Were they members of the same gym? Did they share a doctor or a drycleaner or a palm reader? And this is important: where did they buy their shoes?

A key rattles in the lock. Julianne, Charlie and Emma come bustling into the hallway with polished paper shopping bags and red cheeks from the cold. Charlie is in her school uniform. Emma is wearing new boots that look too big for her but she'll grow into them before winter is over.

Julianne looks at Darcy. 'Are you dressed for dancing or double pneumonia?'

'I've been practicing.'

She turns to me. 'And what have you been doing?'

'He's been helping me,' says Darcy.

Julianne gives me one of her impenetrable looks; the same look that makes our children confess immediately to wrongdoing and

166

sends unwelcome Seventh Day Adventists jostling for the front gate.

I sit Emma on the table and unzip her boots.

'Where did you go this morning?' asks Julianne.

'I had a call from the police.'

There is something in my tone that makes her turn and fix her gaze on mine. No words are spoken, but she knows there has been another death. Darcy tickles Emma under the arms. Julianne glances at her and then back to me. Again, no words are exchanged.

Perhaps this is what happens when two people have been married for sixteen years: it gets so that they know what the other is thinking. It's also what happens when you're married to someone as intuitive and perceptive as Julianne. I have made a career out of studying human behaviour but like most in my profession I'm lousy at psychoanalysing myself. I have a wife for that. She's good. Better than any therapist. Scarier.

'Can you take me into town?' Darcy asks me. 'I need a few things.'

'You should have asked me to get them,' answers Julianne.

'I didn't think.'

A sudden tight smile covers Julianne's annoyance. Darcy goes upstairs to change.

Julianne begins unpacking groceries. 'She can't stay here indefinitely, Joe.'

'I called her aunt in Spain today and left a message for her. I'm also talking to her headmistress.'

Julianne nods, only partially satisfied. 'Well, tomorrow I'm interviewing more nannies. If I find someone we'll need the spare room. Darcy has to go.'

She opens the fridge door and arranges eggs in a tray.

'Tell me what happened this morning.'

'Another woman is dead.'

'Who is it?'

'Christine Wheeler's business partner.'

Julianne is speechless. Stunned. She stares at the grapefruit in her hand, trying to decide if she was putting it in the fridge or taking it out. She doesn't want to hear any more. Details matter

167

to me but not to her. She closes the fridge and steps around me, taking her silent verdict upstairs.

I wish I could make her understand that I didn't choose to get involved in this. I didn't choose to watch Christine Wheeler jump to her death or have her daughter turn up on my doorstep. Julianne used to love my sense of fairness and compassion and my hatred of hypocrisy. Now she treats me like I have no other role to play except to raise my children, perform a handful of lectures and wait for Mr Parkinson to steal what he hasn't already taken.

Even when Ruiz came to dinner last night she took a long while to relax.

'I'm surprised at you, Vincent,' she told him. 'I thought *you* would have talked Joe out of this.'

'Out of what?'

'This nonsense.' She looked at him over her wine glass. 'I thought you retired. Why aren't you playing golf?'

'I have actually hired a hitman to bump me off if I ever leave the house wearing tartan trousers.'

'Not a golfer.'

'No.'

'What about bowling or driving a caravan around the country?'

Ruiz laughed nervously and looked at me as though he no longer envied my life.

'I hope you never retire, Professor.'

From upstairs there are raised voices. Julianne is shouting at Darcy.

'What are you doing? Get away from my things.'

'Ow! You're hurting me.'

I take the stairs two at a time and find them in our bedroom. Julianne is gripping Darcy's forearm, squeezing it hard to stop her getting away. The teenager is bent over, cupping something against her stomach as if hiding it.

'What's wrong?'

'I caught her going through my things,' says Julianne. I look at the dresser. The drawers are open.

'No, I wasn't,' says Darcy.

'What were you doing?'

'Nothing.'

'It doesn't look like nothing,' I say. 'What were you looking for?'

She blushes. I haven't seen her blush before.

She straightens and moves her arms. A small dark crimson stain is visible in the crotch of her track pants.

'My period started. I looked in the bathroom, but I couldn't find any pads.'

Julianne looks mortified. She lets go of Darcy and tries to apologise.

'I am so sorry. You should have said something. You could have asked me.'

Ignoring my inertia, she takes Darcy by the hand and leads her to the en-suite. As the door closes, Julianne's eyes connect with mine. Normally so poised and unflappable, she has become a different person around Darcy and she blames me.

26

I was thirty-one years old when I understood what it was like to watch someone die. A Pashtun taxi driver, with psoriasis on his joints, expired as I watched. We had made him stand for five days until his feet swelled to the size of footballs and the shackles cut into his ankles. He didn't sleep. He didn't eat.

This is an approved 'stress and duress position'. It's in the manual. Look it up. SK 46/34.

His name was Hamad Mowhoush and he'd been arrested at a checkpoint in southern Afghanistan after a roadside bomb killed two Royal Marines and wounded three others, including a mate of mine.

We put a sleeping bag over Hamad's head and bound it with wire. Then we rolled him back and forth and sat on his chest. That's when his heart gave out.

Some folks claim torture isn't an effective way to get reliable information because the strong defy pain and the weak will say anything to make it stop. They're right. Most of the time, it's pointless, but if you act quickly and combine the shock of capture with the fear of torture, it's amazing how often the mind unlocks and all sorts of secrets tumble out.

We weren't allowed to call the detainees POWs. They were PUCs (persons under control). The military loves acronyms. Another one is HCI (Highly Coercive Interrogation). That's what I was trained to do.

When I first saw Hamad someone had sandbagged and zip-tied him. Felini gave him to me. 'Fuck a PUC,' he said, grinning. 'We can smoke him later.'

To 'fuck a PUC' meant to beat him up. To 'smoke' them meant using a stress position. Felini used to make them stand in the sun in hundred degree heat with their arms outstretched, holding up five-gallon jerry cans.

We added some of our own touches. Sometimes we doused them in water, rolled them in dirt and beat them with chem lights until they glowed in the dark.

We buried Hamad's body in lime. I couldn't sleep for days afterwards. I kept imagining his body slowly bloating and the gas escaping from his chest, making it seem like he was still breathing. I still think about him sometimes. I wake at night, with a weight on my chest and imagine lying in the ground with the lime burning my skin.

I'm not scared of dying. I know there's something worse than than lying underground, worse than being smoked, or fucked over with chem lights. It happened to me on Thursday May 17, just after midnight. That's when I last saw Chloe. She was sitting in the passenger seat of a car, still in her pyjamas, being stolen from me.

That was twenty-nine Sundays ago.

Ten things I remember about my daughter:

1) The paleness of her skin.
2) Yellow shorts.
3) A homemade Father's Day card with two stick figures, one large and one small, holding hands.
4) Telling her about Jack and the Beanstalk, but leaving out the bit about the giant wanting to grind Jack's bones to make his bread.
5) The time she tripped over and opened up a cut above her eye that needed two and a half stitches. (Is there such a thing as a half-stitch? Perhaps I made this up to impress her.)
6) Watching her play an Indian squaw in a primary school production of Peter Pan.
7) Taking her to see a European cup tie in Munich, even though I missed the only goal while retrieving the Maltesers she dropped beneath her seat.
8) Walking along the seafront at St Mawes on our last holiday together.
9) Teaching her to ride a bicycle without training wheels.
10) Putting down her pet duck when a fox broke into the pen and ripped off its wing

The phone is ringing. I open my eyes. Heavy curtains and blackout blinds make the room almost totally dark. I reach for the telephone.

'Yeah.'

'Is that Gideon Tyler?' *The accent is pure Belfast.*

'Who wants to know?'

'Royal Mail.'

'How did you get this number?'

'It was inside a package.'

'What package?'

'You posted a package to a Chloe Tyler seven weeks ago. We were unable to deliver it. The address you provided appears to be out-of-date or incorrect.'

'Who are you?'

'This is the National Return Letter Centre. We handle undeliverable mail.'

'Can you try another address?'

'What address, sir?'

'You must have records . . . on computer. Type in the name Chloe Tyler, see what comes up. Or you could try Chloe Chambers.'

'We don't have such a capability, sir. Where should we return the parcel?'

'I don't want it returned. I want it delivered.'

'That has not been possible, sir. What action would you like us to take?'

'I paid the fucking postage. You deliver it.'

'Please don't swear, sir. We have permission to hang up on customers who use abusive language.'

'Fuck off!'

I slam the handset down. It bounces on the cradle and settles again. The phone rings again. At least I didn't break it.

My father is calling. He wants to know when I'm coming to see him.

'I'll come tomorrow.'

'What time?'

'Afternoon.'

'What time in the afternoon?'

'What does it matter — you never go anywhere.'

'I might go to bingo.'

'Then I'll come in the morning.'

27

Alice Furness has three aunts, two uncles, two grandparents and a great grandfather who all seem to be competing to show the most compassion. Alice can't take a step without one of them jumping to her side and asking her how she feels, if she's hungry, or what they can get for her?

Ruiz and I are made to wait in the living room. The large semi-detached house on the outskirts of Bristol belongs to Sylvia's sister, Gloria, who seems to be holding the clan together. She's in the kitchen, discussing with other family members whether we should be allowed to interview Alice.

The great grandfather isn't taking part. He's sitting in an armchair, staring at us. His name is Henry and he's older than Methuselah (one of my mother's sayings).

'Gloria,' Henry bellows, frowning towards the kitchen.

His daughter appears. 'What is it, Dad?'

'These fellas want to interview our Alice.'

'We know that, Dad, that's what we're discussing.'

'Well, hurry up then. Don't keep them waiting.'

Gloria smiles apologetically and goes back to the kitchen.

Sylvia Furness must have been the youngest sister. Her older siblings have entered that long, uncertain period of middle age where years are not a faithful measure of life. Their husbands are less vocal or interested – I can see them through the French doors in the back garden, smoking and discussing men's business.

The debate in the kitchen is getting heated. I can hear servings of pop psychology and clichés. They're protective of Alice, which I understand, but she's already talked to the detectives.

Agreement is reached. One aunt will sit with Alice during the interview – a thin woman in a dark skirt and cardigan. Her name is Denise and like a magician she produces a never-ending supply of tissues from the sleeve of her cardigan.

Alice has to be coaxed from a computer screen. She is a sullen-faced pre-teen, with a down-turned mouth and apple cheeks that owe more to her diet than her bone structure. Dressed in jeans and a rugby jumper, her arms are folded around a bundle of white fur – a rabbit with long pink-fringed ears that lie flat along its body.

'Hello, Alice.'

She doesn't acknowledge me. Instead she asks for a cup of tea and a biscuit. Denise obeys without hesitation.

'When is your father due to arrive?' I ask.

She shrugs.

'You must miss him. Does he go away often?'

'Yes.'

'What does he do?'

'He's a drug dealer.'

Denise draws a sharp breath. 'That's not very nice, dear.'

Alice corrects herself. 'He works for a drug company.' She sniffs at her aunt. 'It's just a joke, you know.'

'Very funny,' says Ruiz.

Alice narrows her eyes, unsure of whether to trust him.

'Tell me about Monday afternoon,' I say.

'I came home and Mum wasn't here. She didn't leave a note. I waited for a while, but then I got hungry.'

'What did you do then?'

'I called Auntie Gloria.'

'Who had a key to the flat?'

'Mum and me.'

'Anyone else?'

'No.'

Ruiz is fidgeting. 'Did your mother ever invite men home?'

She giggles. 'You mean boyfriends?'

'I mean male friends.'

'Well, she liked Mr Pelicos, my English teacher. We call him "the Pelican" because he has a big nose. And Eddie from the video shop comes round after work sometimes. He brings DVDs. I'm not allowed to watch them. He and Mum use the TV in her bedroom.'

Denise tries to shush her. 'My sister was happily married. I don't think you should be asking Alice questions like that.'

She produces another tissue from her sleeve.

The rabbit has crawled up Alice's front and tries to burrow beneath her chin. She giggles. The smile transforms her.

'Does he have a name?' I ask.

'Not yet.'

'He must be new.'

'Yes. I found him.'

'Where?'

'In a box outside our flat.'

'When was that?'

'On Monday.'

'When you came home from your riding lesson?'

She nods.

'Tell me exactly what you found.'

She sighs. 'The door was unlocked. There was a box on the mat. Mum wasn't home.'

'Was there a note with the box?'

'Just my name written on the side.'

'Do you know who left it for you?'

Alice shakes her head.

'Did you ever talk to anyone about wanting a rabbit?'

'No. I thought it was from my dad. He always talks about white rabbits and Alice in Wonderland.'

'But it wasn't from your dad.'

A shake of the head – her ponytail sways.

'Who else might send you a rabbit?'

She shrugs.

'It's really important, Alice. Have you talked to anyone about your mum or about rabbits or Alice in Wonderland? It could be someone your mum knew or a stranger. Someone who found a reason to talk to you.'

She grows defensive. 'How am I supposed to remember? I talk to people all the time.'

'This is someone you *will* remember. Think hard.'

Her tea is getting cold. She strokes the rabbit's ears, trying to make them stand upright.

'Maybe there was somebody.'

'Who?'

'A man. He said he was incognito. I didn't know what that meant.'

'Where did you meet him?'

'I was out with Mum.'

Alice talks about going to a party with Sylvia to celebrate one of her mother's friends getting married. She was standing next to the jukebox when a man came up to her. He was wearing sunglasses. They talked about music and horses and he offered to buy her another lemonade. He quoted from Alice in Wonderland.

'How did he know your name?'

'I told him.'

'Had you ever seen him before?'

'No.'

'Did he know your mother's name?'

'I don't know. He knew where we lived.'

'How?'

'I don't know. I didn't tell him, he just knew.'

Taking her over the story again and again, I build up layers of detail, putting sinew and flesh on the bones. I don't want her paraphrasing or skipping sections. I need her to remember his exact words.

He was my height with thin fair hair, older than her mother, younger than me. Alice can't remember what he was wearing and didn't notice any tattoos or rings or distinguishing features apart from his sunglasses.

She yawns. The conversation has begun to bore her.

'Did he talk to your mother?' asks Ruiz.

'No. That was the other one.'

'The other one?'

'The man who drove us home.'

Ruiz elicits another description, this one of a younger man, early thirties, curly hair and an earring. He was dancing with her mother and offered to take them home.

Her aunt interrupts again. 'Is this really necessary? Poor Alice has told the police everything.'

Alice suddenly holds her rabbit at arm's length. There's a wet patch on her jeans.

'Oooh, he peed on me! How gross!'

'You squeezed him too hard,' says her aunt.

'No I didn't.'

'You shouldn't handle him so much.'

'He's *my* rabbit.'

The animal is dumped on the kitchen table. Alice wants to change her clothes. I've failed to instil any sense of urgency into her and she's sick of talking. Staring at me reproachfully, she gives the impression that it's somehow my fault – her mother's death, the stain on her jeans, the general upheaval in her life.

Everyone deals with grief differently and Alice is hurting in places I can't even imagine. I have spent more than twenty years studying human behaviour, treating patients and listening to their doubts and fears, but no amount of experience or knowledge of psychology will ever allow me to feel what someone else feels. I can witness the same tragedy or survive the same disaster, but my feelings, like hers, will be unique and forever private.

It's cold but not painfully so. Bare trees, savagely pruned around the power lines, are etched against a lavender sky. Ruiz shoves his hands deep in his pockets and walks away from the house. He rocks slightly on his right leg, which has never fully recovered from an old gunshot wound.

I fall into step alongside him, struggling to keep up. Somebody sent ballet shoes to Darcy after her mother died – with no note or return address. The same person is likely to have left the rabbit for Alice. Are they calling cards or condolence gifts?

'You got a fix on this guy yet?' asks Ruiz.

'Not yet.'

'I'll bet you twenty quid it's an ex-boyfriend or a lover.'

'Of both women?'

'Maybe he blames one of them for breaking up the relationship with the other.'

'And you base this theory upon?'

'My gut.'

'Are you sure it's not wind?'

'We could make a wager.'

'I'm not a betting man.'

We've reached the car. Ruiz leans on the door. 'Let's say you're right and he targets the daughters – how does he do it? Darcy was at school. Alice was riding her horse. They weren't in any danger.'

I don't have an easy explanation. It requires a leap of the imagination: a tumble into darkness.

'How does he *prove* a lie like that?' asks Ruiz.

'He has to know things about the daughters – not just their names and ages, but intimate details. He could have been in their houses, found reasons to meet them, watched them.'

'Surely a mother would phone the school or the riding centre. You don't just *believe* someone who claims to have your daughter.'

'That's where you're wrong. You *never* hang up. Yes, you want to check. You want to phone the police. You want to scream for help. But what you never, ever do is hang up the phone. You *can't* take the risk that he's right. You don't *want* to take that risk.'

'So what do you do?'

'You keep talking. You do exactly what he says. You stay on the phone and you keep asking for proof and you pray, over and over, that you're wrong.'

Ruiz rocks back on his heels and looks at me with a kind of repulsive wonderment.

Passers-by are stepping round us on the footpath, glancing with disapproval and curiosity.

178

'And this is your theory?'

'It fits the details.'

I expected him to argue with me. I thought it would be too great a leap to contemplate someone stepping off a bridge or chaining herself to a tree on the basis of any sort of belief or rational fear.

Instead he clears his throat.

'I once knew a man in Northern Ireland who drove a truck full of explosives into an army barracks because the IRA was holding his wife and two children hostage. They killed his youngest by slitting her throat in front of him.'

'What happened?'

'Twelve soldiers died in the blast . . . so did the husband.'

'And what about his family?'

'The IRA let them go.'

Both of us fall silent. Some conversations don't need a final word.

28

Charlie is in the front garden, kicking a football against the fence. She's wearing her football boots and her old strip from the Camden Tigers.

'What's up?'

'Nothing.'

The ball cannons harder off the wall. Thump. Thump. Thump.

'You practicing for the big trial?' I ask.

'Nope.'

'Why not?'

She catches the ball in two hands and looks at me now, giving me her mother's stare.

'Because the trial was today and you were supposed to take me, so I've missed it. Thanks a lot, Dad. Special effort.'

She drops the ball and volleys it so hard it almost takes off my head as it ricochets past me.

'I'll make it up to you,' I say, trying to apologise. 'I'll talk to the coach. They'll give you another trial.'

'Don't worry about it. I don't want any favours,' she says. Could she be any more like her mother?

Julianne is in the kitchen. A towel is wrapped like a turban over her freshly washed hair. It makes her walk with rolling hips like an African woman carrying a clay pot on her head.

'I've upset Charlie.'

'Yes.'

'You should have called.'

'I tried. Your phone was turned off.'

'Why couldn't you take her?'

She snaps: 'Because I had to interview nannies – because you didn't find one.'

'I'm sorry.'

'Don't apologise to *me*.' She glances out the window to Charlie. 'And by the way – I don't think it's just about the football trial.'

'What do you mean?'

She chooses her words carefully. 'You and Charlie are always doing things together, running errands, going for walks, but ever since Darcy arrived you've been too busy. I think she may be a little jealous.'

'Of Darcy?'

'She thinks you've forgotten her.'

'But I haven't.'

'She's also having a few problems at school. There's a boy who keeps picking on her.'

'She's being bullied?'

'I don't know if it's that serious.'

'We should talk to the school.'

'She wants to try to sort it out herself.'

'How?'

'In her own way.'

I can still hear the football being kicked against the wall. I hate the idea that Charlie feels neglected. And I hate even more that Julianne has learned these things while I missed them. I'm at home all the time. I'm the go-to parent, the primary carer, and I haven't been paying attention.

Julianne unwraps the towel, letting wet curls tumble over her face. She pats them dry between her palms and the soft weave of the fabric.

'I had a phone call from Darcy's aunt,' she says. 'She's flying from Spain for the funeral.'

'That's good.'

181

'She wants to take Darcy back to Spain with her.'

'What does Darcy say?'

'She doesn't know. Her aunt wants to tell her face-to-face.'

'She won't be happy.'

Julianne arches an eyebrow tellingly. 'That's not our responsibility.'

'You treat Darcy like she's done something wrong,' I say.

'And you treat her like she's your daughter.'

'That's unfair.'

'Explain fairness to Charlie.'

'You can be a real bitch sometimes.'

The statement is laden with more anger and import than either of us expect. A hurt helplessness floods Julianne's eyes but she refuses to let me witness her unhappiness. She takes her towel and her tenderness, carrying both upstairs. I listen to her footsteps on the stairs and tell myself she's being unreasonable. She'll understand eventually.

Raising a knuckle, I tap gently on the door of the guestroom.

After what seems an age the door opens. Darcy is barefoot in three-quarter length leggings and a T-shirt. Her hair is out and over her shoulders.

Without looking at me, she goes back to the bed and sits on the mussed sheets with her knees drawn up and her arms wrapped around them. The curtains are closed and shadows gather in the corners of the room.

For the first time I notice her feet. Her toes are misshapen and covered in calluses, blisters and raw skin. The littlest toe is curled under the others as if hiding and the biggest is bloated with a discoloured nail.

'They're ugly,' she says, covering her feet with a pillow.

'What happened to them?'

'I'm a dancer, remember? One of my old ballet teachers used to say that pointe shoes were the last instruments of torture that were still legal.'

Moving a magazine, I take a seat on a corner of the bed. There's nowhere else to sit.

'I wanted to talk about pointe shoes,' I say.

She laughs. 'You're a bit old for ballet.'

'The package that was left for you at school – tell me about it.'

She describes a shoebox wrapped in brown paper with no note, just her name written in capital letters.

'Other than your mum, is there anyone else who would have sent you a gift like that?'

She shakes her head.

'This is very important, Darcy. I need you to think back over the past few weeks. Did you talk to or meet anyone new? Was there anyone who asked questions about your mother?'

'I was at school.'

'OK, but you must have had weekends. Did you go shopping? Did you leave the school for anything?'

'I went to London for the auditions.'

'Did you talk to anyone?'

'The teachers and other dancers . . .'

'What about on the train?'

Her mouth opens and closes. Her forehead creases.

'There was this one guy . . . he sat down opposite me.'

'And you talked to him?'

'Not right away.' She pushes her fringe back behind her ears. 'He seemed to fall asleep. I went to the buffet car and when I came back he asked me if I was a dancer. He said he could tell from the way I walked – splayfooted, you know. It seemed weird that he knew so much about ballet.'

'What did he look like?'

She shrugs. 'Ordinary.'

'How old?'

'Not as old as you. He wore sunglasses, like Bono. I think he was a bit of a try-hard.'

'A try-hard.'

'One of those old guys who try to look cool.'

'Was he flirting with you?'

She shrugs. 'Maybe. I don't know.'

'Would you recognise him again?'

'I guess.'

She describes him. It might be the same man Alice spoke to, but his hair was darker and longer and he wore different clothes.

'I want to try something,' I tell her. 'Lie down and close your eyes.'

'Why?'

'Don't worry – nothing's going to happen – you just have to close your eyes and think about that day. Try to picture it. Imagine you're back there, stepping onto the train, finding a seat, putting your bag in the overhead rack.'

Her eyes close.

'Can you see it?'

She nods.

'Describe the train carriage for me. Where were you sitting in relation to the doors?'

'Three rows from the rear, facing forwards.'

I ask her what she was wearing. Where she put her bag. Who else was in the carriage.

'There was a little girl sitting in front of me, peering between the seats. I played peek-a-boo with her.'

'Who else do you remember?'

'A guy in a suit. He was talking too loudly on his mobile.' She pauses. 'And a backpacker with a maple leaf on his rucksack.'

I ask her to focus on the man who sat opposite her. What was he wearing?

'I don't remember. A shirt, I think.'

'What colour was it?'

'Blue with a collar.'

'Did it have anything written on it?'

'No.'

I move on to his face. His eyes. His hair. His ears. Feature by feature, she begins to describe him in small ways. His hands. His fingers. His forearms. He wore a silver wristwatch, but no rings.

'When did you first see him?'

'When he sat down.'

'Are you sure? I want you to go further back. When you caught the train in Cardiff, who was on the platform?'

'A few people. The backpacker was there. I bought a bottle of water. I knew the girl in the kiosk. She'd bleached her hair since I saw her last.'

I take her back further. 'When you bought your ticket, was there a queue?'

'Um . . . yes.'

'Who was in the queue?'

'I don't remember.'

'Picture the ticket window. Look at the faces. Who can you see?'

Her brow furrows and her head rocks from side to side on the pillow. Suddenly, her eyes open. 'The man from the train.'

'Where?'

'At the top of the stairs near the ticket machine.'

'The same man?'

'Yes.'

'You're sure?'

'I'm sure.'

She sits up and rubs her hands along her upper arms as if suddenly cold.

'Did I do something wrong?' she asks.

'No.'

'Why do you want to know about him?'

'It may be nothing.'

She wraps the duvet around her shoulders before leaning her back against the wall. Her gaze drifts over me awkwardly.

'Do you ever get the feeling that something terrible is about to happen?' she asks. 'Something dreadful that you can't change because you don't know what it is.'

'I don't know. Maybe. Why do you ask?'

'That's how I felt on that Friday – when I couldn't get through to Mum. I knew something was wrong.' She drops her head and looks at her knees. 'That night I said a prayer for her, but I left it too late, didn't I? Nobody heard me.'

29

DI Cray has organised for six boxes to be delivered to the cottage. They must be back in the incident room by morning. A courier will collect them just after midnight.

Inside the boxes are witness statements, timelines, phone wheels and crime scene photographs relating to both murders. I managed to get them into the house without Julianne noticing.

Closing the study door, I turn the key and take a seat before opening the first box. My mouth is dry but I can't blame my medication. Stacked in boxes around my feet is evidence of two lives and two deaths. Nothing will bring these women back and nothing can harm their feelings any more, yet I feel like an uninvited guest sorting through their underwear. Photographs. Statements. Timelines. Videos. Versions of the past.

They say once is an event, twice is a coincidence and three times is a pattern. I have only two crimes to consider. Two victims. Christine Wheeler and Sylvia Furness were the same age. They went to school together. Both were mothers of young daughters. I try to imagine each of their lives, the places they went, the people they met and the events they experienced.

Already, in the space of forty-eight hours, detectives have pieced together a biographical history of Sylvia Furness (nee Ferguson). She was born in 1972, grew up in Bath and went to

Oldfield School for Girls. Her father worked as a haulage contractor and her mother a nurse. Sylvia went to university in Leeds but dropped out in her second year to go travelling. She worked on charter boats in the Caribbean where she met her future husband, Richard Furness, in St Lucia in the West Indies. He had taken a year off from university and was transferring yachts for rich Europeans. They married in 1994. Alice came along a year later. Richard Furness graduated from Bristol University and has worked for two major pharmaceutical companies.

Sylvia was a party girl who loved to socialise and go dancing. Christine couldn't have been more different. Quiet, unadventurous, hardworking and reliable, she didn't have boyfriends or an active social life.

One interesting point was that Sylvia took self-defence classes. Karate. In this case, it didn't help her fight back. There were no defence wounds on her body. She submitted. The pillowcase that hooded her head was a popular high street brand. The handcuffs belonged to the husband – purchased from a sex shop in Amsterdam – 'to spice up their sex life.'

How did the killer know about the handcuffs? He must have been inside Sylvia's flat, invited or otherwise. She didn't report any burglaries or break-ins. Maybe Ruiz is right and it's a former a lover or boyfriend.

Wondering out loud, I begin talking to him, trying to under-stand how a predator like this one thinks and feels. 'You knew so much about them – about their houses, their movements, their daughters, their shoes . . . Did you tell them what to wear?'

There's a knock on the study door. I turn the key and open it a crack.

It's Julianne. 'What's going on?'

'Nothing.'

'I heard you talking to someone.'

'Myself.'

She tries to peer under my arm to the desk. I block her view. 'Why is the door locked?'

'There are things I don't want the girls to see.'

187

Her eyes suddenly narrow. 'You're doing it, aren't you. You're bringing this poison into our house.'

'It's just for tonight.'

She shakes her head. Her voice is flat. 'I hate secrets. I know most people have them, but I hate them.'

She turns away. I see her bare feet beneath her dressing gown, disappearing along the hall. *What about your secrets*, I feel like saying, but she's gone and the question remains unspoken. Closing the door, I turn the key.

The second box contains crime scene photographs, beginning with long distance shots and narrowing down to the minutia of individual body parts. Halfway through the albums my constitution fails. I get up, recheck the door, and stand at the window, looking through the bare branches of the cherry trees to the churchyard.

I have two hours before the courier arrives. Taking a notebook, I place a photograph of Christine Wheeler and Sylvia Furness side-by-side on my desk. Not an image of them naked, but a normal, head and shoulders shot. Then I create a more confronting collage, using images from each crime scene.

Those of Sylvia stand out more because of the hood covering her head. Her feet could barely touch the ground. She had to stand on her tiptoes. Within minutes her legs must have been in agony. As she grew exhausted, her heels dropped and her handcuffed wrist took the full weight of her body. More pain.

The hood, nakedness and stress position are elements redolent of torture or execution. The more I stare at the photographs, the more familiar they seem. These are images from a different sort of theatre – one of conflict and war.

Abu Ghraib prison in Iraq became synonymous with torture and physical abuse. Pictures were beamed around the world of hooded prisoners, naked and leashed, being taunted and humiliated. Some were kept in stress positions, standing on tiptoes with arms outstretched, or pulled painfully behind them. Sleep deprivation, humiliation, extreme heat or cold, hunger and thirst, these are the hallmarks of interrogation and torture.

It took six hours to break Christine Wheeler. How long did

he have with Sylvia Furness? She went missing on Monday afternoon; she was found on Wednesday morning – a window of thirty-six hours. She was dead for two-thirds of that time. Normally, it takes days to brainwash a person, to pick apart their defences. Whoever did this, managed to break Sylvia within twelve hours. That's incredible.

This wasn't bloodlust. He didn't lash out with his fists or his feet. He didn't batter these women into submission. There were no marks on their bodies that indicated beatings or violence or any sort of physical assault. He used words. Where does a person gain this type of skill? It takes practice. Rehearsal. Training.

Dividing the page of a notebook, I write the heading *Things I Know* and begin writing points.

These were deliberate, relaxed, almost euphoric crimes, expressions of a corrupt lust. He chose what each victim wore and didn't wear. He knew what they each had in their wardrobe. What make-up they wore. When they'd be home alone. The shoes were important to him.

I think out loud again. 'Why these women? What did they do to you? Did they ignore you? Laugh at you? Leave you behind?

'Sylvia Furness would not have submitted easily. She was no innocent. You must have worn her down, marched her to the tree, your voice in her ear, saying what? It takes enormous skill to control somebody to this degree – to unlock a woman's mind. You've done this before.

'I have met minds like yours. I have seen what sexual sadists can do. These women represented something or someone you despised. They were symbolic as well as precise targets – that's why they were so unalike. They were actors, cast in your drama because they had a particular look or were the right age or because of some other factor.

'What are the elements of your fantasy? Public humiliation is a feature. You wanted them to be found. You made these women strip naked and parade. Sylvia's body was hung like a piece of meat. Christine scrawled "slut" on her stomach.

'The first crime scene didn't make sense. It was too public and exposed. Why didn't you choose somewhere private – an empty

189

house or isolated farm building? You *wanted* Christine to be seen. It was part of the deviant theatre.

'You did this for gratification. It might not have begun as your motive, but that's what it's become. At some point in your fantasy, sexual desire has become messed with anger and the need to dominate. You have learned to eroticise pain and torture. You have fantasised about it – taken women in your dreams and humiliated, punished, and broken them. Degraded. Devalued. Destroyed.

'You are fastidious. You take notes. You find out everything you can about them by watching their houses and their movements. You know when they leave for work, when they get home, when the lights go off at night.

'I don't know the exact details of your planning, therefore I don't know how closely you followed the strategy, but you were willing to take risks. What if Christine Wheeler had been rescued on the bridge or if Sylvia Furness had been found before the cold stopped her heart, they could have identified you.

'It doesn't make sense . . . unless . . . unless. They never saw your face! You whispered in their ears, you told them what to do and they obeyed, but they didn't see your face.'

Pushing the notebook aside, I lean back and close my eyes, drained, tired, trembling.

It is late. The house is silent. Above my head, the light fitting has captured dead moths in the bowl of frosted glass. Inside there is a light bulb, a fragile glass shell, and inside that is a glowing filament. People often use light bulbs to represent ideas. Not me. My ideas begin as pencil marks on a white page, soft abstract outlines. Slowly the lines grow clearer and acquire light and shade, depth and clarity.

I have never met the man who killed Christine Wheeler and Sylvia Furness, but suddenly I feel as though he has sprung from within my mind, flesh and blood, with a voice that echoes in my ears. He is no longer a figment, no longer a mystery, no longer part of my imagining. I have *seen* his mind.

30

The door barely opens. His grizzled face is peering at me.

'You're late.'

'I had a job.'

'It's Sunday.'

'I still have to work.'

He turns and shuffles a few paces down the hall, broken slippers flapping at his heels.

'What sort of job?'

'I had to change some locks.'

'Get paid?'

'That's the idea.'

'I need some money.'

'What about your pension?'

'Gone.'

'What do you spend it on?'

'Champagne and fucking caviar.'

He's wearing a pyjama shirt, threadbare at the elbows and tucked into high waisted trousers that bulge over his stomach and have no room at all at his crotch. Maybe your penis drops off when you reach a certain age.

We're in the living room. The place smells of old farts and cooking fat. The only two pieces of furniture that matter are an armchair and the television.

I take out my wallet. He tries to look over my hands to see how much I'm carrying. I give him forty quid.

Hitching up his trousers, he sinks into the chair, filling the depressions that are moulded to the shape of his arse. His head cocks forward, chin to chest, and his eyes focus on the television, his life support system.

'You gonna watch the game, Pop?' I ask.

'Which one?'

'Everton and Liverpool.'

He shakes his head.

'I bought cable so you could see the big derby games.'

He grunts. 'Man shouldn't have to pay to watch football. It's like paying to drink water. I won't do that.'

'I'm paying.'

'Makes no difference.'

The only colour in the room is coming from the screen and it paints a bright square in his eyes.

'You going out later?'

'Nah.'

'I thought you said you had bingo.'

'Don't play bingo no more. Them cheating cunts said I couldn't come back.'

'Why?'

'Cos I caught 'em rigging things.'

'How do you rig bingo?'

'I'm one bloody number short every fucking time. One number. Cheating cunts!'

I'm still holding a bag of groceries. I take them to the kitchen and offer to fix him something to eat. I've bought a tin of ham, baked beans and eggs.

Dirty dishes are stacked in the sink. A cockroach crawls to the top of a cup and looks at me as if I'm trespassing. It scrambles away as I scrape plates into a pedal bin and turn on the tap. The gas water heater rumbles and coughs as a blue flame ignites along the burners.

'You should never have left the army,' he shouts. 'The army treat you like family.'

Yeah, some family!

He launches into a bullshit spiel about mateship and camaraderie, when the truth is he never fought in a war. He missed out on the Falklands because he couldn't swim.

192

I smile to myself. It's not really true. He was medically unfit. He got his hand caught in the breech of a 155 mm cannon and broke most of his fingers. The old bastard is still bitter about it. Fuck knows why. Who in their right mind wanted to fight a war over a few rocks in the South Atlantic?

He's still whining, yelling over the sound of the TV.

'That's the problems with soldiers today. They're soft. They're pampered. Feather pillows. Gourmet food . . .'

I'm frying pieces of ham and breaking eggs into the spaces between the slices. The beans won't take long to heat in the microwave.

Pop changes the subject. 'How's my granddaughter?'

'Good.'

'How come you never bring her to see me?'

'She doesn't live with me, Pop.'

'Yeah, but that judge gave you—.'

'Don't matter what the judge said. She doesn't live with me.'

'But you see her, right? You talk to her.'

'Yeah. Sure.' *I lie.*

'So why don't you bring her round? I want to see her.'

I look around the kitchen. 'She doesn't want to come.'

'Why not?'

'I don't know.'

He grunts.

'I guess she's at school now.'

'Yeah.'

'What school?'

I don't answer him.

'Probably some fancy private school like her mother went to. She was always too good for the likes of you. Couldn't stand her father. Thought his shit didn't smell. Drove a different car every year.'

'They were company cars.'

'Yeah, well, he looked down his nose at you.'

'No he didn't.'

'Fucking did. We weren't his type. Golf clubs, skiing holidays . . . He paid for that posh wedding.' *He pauses and gets excited.* 'Maybe you should apply for alimony, you know. Take her to court. Get your share.'

'I don't want her money.'

'Give it to me.'

'No.'

'Why not? I deserve something.'

'I got you this place.'

'Yeah, a fucking palace!'

He shuffles into the kitchen and sits down. I dish up the food. He smothers everything in brown sauce. Doesn't say thank you. Doesn't wait for me.

I wonder when he looks in the mirror if he sees what other people see: a useless bladder of piss and wind. That's what I see. The man has no right to lecture me. He's a foul-mouthed, whining, skid-mark on the world and I wish sometimes that he'd just die or at least get even.

I don't know why I bother coming to visit him. When I remember what he did to me, it's all I can do not to spit in his face. He won't remember. He'll say I'm making it up.

His beltings were never as bad as the long, drawn out prelude to them. I was sent to the stairs, where I had to drop my trousers and put my arms through the railings, crossing them and gripping my wrists. I'd stand there waiting and waiting, with my forehead pressed against the wood.

The first sound I heard was the swishing of the flex as it curled through the air a split-second before it landed. He used an old toaster cord with the plug still attached, which he gripped in his fist.

I'll tell you the strange thing about them beatings. They taught me how to split my mind in two. I didn't leave home at sixteen. I left home years earlier when I was hanging on those railings. I left home when that cord whipped through the air and sank into my skin.

I used to fantasise about what I'd do to him when I was big enough and strong enough. I didn't have much of an imagination back then. I thought of punching him or kicking him in the head. It's different now. I can imagine a thousand ways to cause him pain. I can imagine him begging to die. He might even think he was already dead. That's happened to me before. An Algerian terrorist, captured fighting for the Talibs in the mountains north of Gardeyz, asked me if he was in hell.

'Not yet,' I said. 'But it's going to seem like a holiday camp when you get there.'

Pop pushes his plate away and rubs a hand over his jaw, giving me a quick sly look. A gin bottle appears from the cupboard below the sink. He pours a glass, with the air of a man who is putting something over on the world.

194

'You want one?'

'No.'

I look around, seeking a distraction, an excuse to leave.

'You got to be somewhere?' he asks.

'Yeah.'

'You only just got here.'

'There's a job.'

'Fixing more locks.'

'Yeah.'

He snorts in disgust. 'You must be cock-deep in cash.'

Then he launches into another speech, complaining about his life and telling me I'm useless and selfish and a fucking disappointment.

I look at his neck. I could break it easily enough. Two hands, thumbs in the right place, and he stops talking . . . and breathing. No different to killing a rabbit.

On he goes, blah, blah, blah, his mouth opening and closing, filling the world with shit. Maybe the Algerian was right about hell.

31

A shadow fills the glass panels of the door. It opens. Veronica Cray turns and sways down the hallway.

'You seen the Sunday papers, Professor?'

'No.'

'Sylvia Furness is all over them – page one, page three, page five . . . Monk just called. There are two dozen reporters outside Trinity Road.'

I follow her to the kitchen. She moves to the stove and begins pushing pots and pans around the hotplates. A spill of sunlight from the window highlights flecks of silver at the roots of her hair.

'This is a tabloid editor's wet dream. Two victims – white, attractive, middle-class women. Mothers. Both naked. Business partners. One of them jumps off a bridge and the other is left hanging from a tree like a side of beef. You should read some of the theories they're coming up with – love triangles, lesbian affairs, jilted lovers.'

She opens the fridge and retrieves a carton of eggs, butter, rashers of bacon and a tomato. I'm still standing.

'Sit down. I'm going to make *you* breakfast.' She makes it sound like I'm on the menu.

'That's really not necessary.'

'For you maybe – I've been up since five. You want coffee or tea?'

'Coffee.'

Breaking eggs into a bowl, she begins whisking them into a liquid froth, every movement practised and precise. I take a seat, listening to her talk. A dozen different newspapers are open on the table. Sylvia Furness is smiling from the pages of each one of them.

The investigation is focusing on the wedding planning business, Blissful, now in receivership. The unpaid bills and final demands had built up over two years, but Christine Wheeler had kept the bailiffs at bay by periodically injecting cash, most of it borrowed against her house. Legal action over a food poisoning scare proved to be the final straw. She defaulted on two loans. The carrion began circling.

Police artists are due to sit down with Darcy and Alice. They're going to be interviewed separately to see if their recollections can help create identikit images of the man they spoke to in the days before their mothers died.

Physically the girls described him as being roughly the same height and build, but Darcy remembered him having dark hair, while Alice was sure that he was fair. Appearances can be altered, of course, but eyewitness descriptions are notoriously fickle. Very few people can remember more than a handful of descriptors: sex, age, height, hair colour and race. This isn't enough to draw up a truly accurate identikit and a poor one does more harm than good.

The detective scoops bacon from the frying pan and halves the scrambled eggs, tipping them onto thick slices of toast.

'You want Tabasco on your eggs?'

'Sure.'

She pours the coffee, adds milk.

The task force is following up a dozen other leads. A traffic camera on Warminster Road picked up Sylvia Furness's car at 16.08 on Monday. An unidentified silver van followed her through the traffic lights. A week earlier, a similar looking van crossed the Clifton Suspension Bridge twenty minutes before Christine Wheeler climbed the safety fence. Same make. Same model. Neither CCTV camera picked up a full number plate.

Sylvia Furness received a call at home at four-fifteen on Monday afternoon. It was made from a mobile phone that was purchased two months ago at a high street outlet in south London, using a dodgy ID. A second handset, purchased on the same day, was used to call Sylvia's mobile at 16.42. It was the same MO as with Christine Wheeler. One call overlapped the other. The caller passed Sylvia from her landline to her mobile, possibly ensuring that he didn't break contact with her.

DI Cray eats quickly, refilling her plate. The coffee must burn her throat as she washes down every mouthful. She wipes her lips with a paper napkin.

'Forensics came up with something interesting. Semen stains from two different men on her bed-sheets.'

'Does the husband know?'

'Seems they had an arrangement – an open marriage.'

Whenever I hear that term I think of a small delicate craft floating on an ocean of shit. The DI senses my disillusionment and chuckles.

'Don't tell me you're a romantic, Professor.'

'I guess I am. What about you?'

'Most women are – even a woman like me.'

She makes it sound like a statement of intent. I use it as an opening.

'I noticed photographs of a young man. Is he your son?'

'Yes.'

'Where is he now?'

'Grown up. He lives in London. They all seem to go to London eventually – like turtles returning to the same beach.'

'You miss him?'

'Does Dolly Parton sleep on her back?

I want to pause and study this mental picture, but carry on. 'Where's his father?'

'What is this – twenty questions?'

'I'm interested.'

'You're nosy.'

'Curious, that's all.'

'Yeah, well, I'm not one of your bloody patients.' She says it with unexpected anger and then looks slightly self-conscious. 'You want to know, I was married for eight months. They were the longest years of my life. And my son is the only good thing that came out of them.'

She takes my plate from the table and dumps the cutlery into the sink. The tap is turned on and she scrubs the dishes as though cleaning away more than scrambled eggs.

'Do you have a problem with psychologists?' I ask.

'No.'

'Maybe it's me?'

'No offence, Professor, but a century ago people didn't need shrinks to get by. They didn't need therapy, Prozac, self-help manuals or the fucking "Secret". They just got on with their lives.'

'A century ago people only lived to be forty-five.'

'So you're saying that living longer makes us unhappier?'

'It gives us more time to be unhappy. Our expectations have changed. Survival isn't enough. We want fulfilment.'

She doesn't answer, but it's not a sign of consensus. Instead her demeanour suggests an episode in her past, a family history, or a visit to a psychologist or psychiatrist.

'Is it because you're gay?' I ask.

'You got a problem with it?'

'No.'

'Gertrude Stein told Hemingway that the reason he had a problem with accepting homosexuality was because the male homosexual act was ugly and repugnant whereas with women it is the opposite.'

'I try not to judge people on their sexuality.'

'But you *do* judge them, every day in your consulting room.'

'I no longer have a clinical practice, but when I did I tried to help people.'

'Have you ever had a patient who didn't want to be gay?'

'Yes.'

'Did you try to fix them?'

'There was nothing to fix. I can't change someone's sexuality. I help them come to terms with who they are. I help them cope with their own nature.'

The DI dries her hands and sits down again, reaching for her cigarettes. Lights one.

'You finish the psychological profile?'

I nod. The crunch of wheels on gravel signals an arrival outside. Safari Roy has come to take her to Trinity Road.

'I got a morning briefing. You should come.'

Roy knocks on the door and comes inside. He dips his head in greeting.

'You ready, boss?'

'Yeah. The Prof is coming with us.'

Roy looks at me. 'Always room.'

The incident room is busier and noisier than before. There are more detectives and civilian support staff, inputting data and cross-referencing the details of each crime. This is now an official murder investigation with task force status.

Sylvia Furness has her own whiteboard, alongside Christine Wheeler's. Thick black lines are drawn between family members, colleagues and mutual friends.

The taskforce has been split into two teams. One team has already devoted hundreds of hours to tracking down every person who was in Leigh Woods, locating vehicles, checking alibis and studying CCTV cameras.

It has also focused on Christine Wheeler's debts and dealings with a local loan shark called Tony Naughton, whose name appeared in her phone records. Naughton has been questioned but has an alibi for Friday October 5. Half a dozen drinkers say he was in a pub from early afternoon until closing time. The same half-dozen who give him an alibi every time he's pulled in by the police.

I listen as Veronica Cray brings everyone up to speed on the previous twenty-four hours.

'Whoever killed Sylvia Furness *knew* about the handcuffs which means we could be looking at a former boyfriend, a lover, or someone who had access to the house. A tradesman, a cleaner, a friend . . .'

'What about the husband?' asks Monk.

200

'He was in Geneva, shacked up with his twenty-six-year-old secretary.'

'He could have hired someone.'

She nods. 'We're looking at his phone records and emails.'

She hands out tasks and then glances quickly at me. 'Professor O'Loughlin has drawn up a psychological profile. I'll hand over to him.'

My notes are written on a page, tucked into my jacket pocket. I keep taking them out and glancing at them as if cribbing for a test. I consciously lift my feet and avoid shuffling as I move to the front of the gathering. It's one those tricks I've had to learn since Mr Parkinson arrived. I don't stand with my feet close together and I try not to pivot when I turn quickly.

'The man you are looking for is a fully-fledged sexual sadist,' I announce, pausing for a moment to look at their faces. 'He didn't just want to kill these women, he wanted to destroy them physically and mentally; to take bright, vibrant, intelligent women and strip away every last vestige of hope and faith and humanity.

'You are looking for a male in the same age range as his victims or older. His planning, confidence and degree of control indicate maturity and experience.'

'He has an above average IQ with high verbal intelligence and good social skills. He will come across as pleasant and confident, almost deceptively charming. For this reason his friends, work-mates or drinking buddies are likely to have no idea of his sadistic nature.

'His formal education won't match his intelligence. He gets bored easily and is likely to have dropped out of school or university.

'His organisational skills and methodology suggest military training, but he has reached a point where he won't take orders unless he respects the person giving them. For this reason, he is likely to be self-employed or work alone. The timings of the killings suggest that he may work flexible hours, nights or weekends.

'He is likely to be a local, someone who knows the roads, distances and street names. He directed both victims by phone.

He knew where they lived, their phone numbers and when they'd be alone. This took planning and research.

'He will live alone or with an elderly parent. He needs the freedom to come and go, without having to answer questions from a wife or partner. He may have been married in the past and his hatred towards women could stem from this or another failed relationship or a problem in his childhood with his mother.

'This man is forensically aware. Apart from the mobile phone he gave to Christine Wheeler, he left nothing behind. And he uses concealing behaviour – buying different handsets under false names, choosing different call boxes and staying on the move.

'His victims were targeted. The question we have to answer is why and how. They were friends and business partners. They went to school together. They shared dozens of mutual friends and perhaps a hundred acquaintances. They lived in the same city, went to the same hairdresser and used the same drycleaning service. Find out why he chose them and we move a step closer to finding him.'

I pause and glance down at my notes, making sure I haven't left anything out. My left forefinger has begun twitching but my voice is strong. I bob gently on my toes and begin pacing and talking at the same time. Their eyes move with me.

'I think our perpetrator convinced each woman that they had no choice but to co-operate or their daughters would suffer. This suggests that he is supremely confident verbally but I think there is a question mark over his physical confidence. He didn't over-power these women with brute force. He used his voice to intimidate and control. He may lack the courage for a face-to-face confrontation.'

'He's a coward,' says Monk.

'Or he's not physically strong.'

DI Cray wants more practical information. 'What are the chances that he's an old boyfriend or spurned lover?'

'I don't think so.'

'Why?'

'If either victim had escaped or been rescued they could have identified an old boyfriend or lover. I doubt if he'd take this risk. There's another issue. Would these women have followed his commands so completely if they knew him? The unknown voice is more frightening; more intimidating . . .'

Someone coughs. I pause, wondering if it's a signal. There are muffled comments.

'This leads me to another point,' I say. 'He might not physically have touched them.'

Nobody reacts. Monk speaks first. 'What do you mean?'

'The victims might not have *seen* him.'

'But Sylvia Furness was handcuffed to a tree.'

'She could have done that to herself.'

'What about the hood?'

'She could have done that too.'

I explain the evidence. The field was muddy. Only one set of footprints was found beneath the tree. There was no evidence of sexual assault or defence wounds. No other tyre tracks led to the field.

'I'm not saying that he didn't visit the scene in advance – he chose it very carefully. I also think he was nearby – the mobile signals indicate as much – but I don't think she saw him. I don't think he touched her – not physically.'

'He fucked with her mind,' says Safari Roy.

I nod.

There are whistling sighs and grunts of scepticism. This is beyond their comprehension.

'Why? What's the motive?' asks the DI.

'Revenge. Anger. Sexual gratification.'

'What – we take our pick?'

'It's all of them. This man is a sexual sadist. It's not about killing women. It's more personal than that. He humiliates them. He destroys them psychologically because he hates what they represent. He may have had issues with his own mother or an ex-wife or a former girlfriend. You might even find that his first victim sparked his resentment.'

'You mean Christine Wheeler?' says Monk.

'No. She wasn't the first.'

Silence. Disbelief.

'There are more?' asks the DI.

'Almost certainly.'

'When? Where?'

'Answer that question and you'll find him. The man who did this has been working towards this moment – rehearsing and refining his techniques. He's an expert.'

Veronica Cray looks away, gazing silently out the window, staring so hard I wonder if she wants to escape outside and disappear into someone else's life. I knew this would be the most difficult point to get across. Even experienced police officers and mental health workers struggle with the reality that someone could experience intense pleasure and exhilaration from torturing and killing another human being.

Suddenly, everyone is talking at once. I'm bombarded with questions, opinions and arguments. Some of the detectives appear almost eager, excited by the hunt. Perhaps I have the wrong mindset but nothing about murder exhilarates or energises me.

Solving crime is a vocation for these men and women. It is a longing to restore moral order to a fractured world: a means of exploring questions of innocence and guilt, justice and punishment. For me the only truly important person is the victim who triggers everything. Without him or her none of us would be here.

The briefing is over. DI Cray escorts me downstairs.

'If you're right about this man, he's going to kill again, isn't he?'

'At some point.'

'Can we slow him down?'

'You might be able to communicate with him.'

'How's that?'

'He's not looking to engage the police in some sort of cat and mouse game but he will be reading the newspapers, listening to radio and watching TV. He's plugged in, which means you *can* send him a message.'

'What would we say?'

'Say you want to understand him. The media are putting labels on him that are less than flattering. Let him correct the misunderstandings. Don't demean. Don't antagonise. He wants respect.'

'And where does that get us?'

'If you can get him to call, it means that you have dictated an outcome. It's one small step. The first.'

'Who delivers the message?'

'It has to be one face. It can't be a woman. It must be a man.'

The DI raises her chin slightly as if something on the horizon has caught her attention.

'What about you?'

'Not me.'

'Why not?'

'I'm not a detective.'

'Makes no difference. You *know* this man. You know how he thinks.'

I'm standing in the foyer as she lists all the arguments without giving me a chance to rebut. A police car accelerates out of the rear gates, the bleat-bleeping siren drowning out my protests.

'So that's decided then. You script a statement. I'll set up a press conference.'

The electronic doors unlock. I step outside. The sound of the siren has faded and left behind a feeling of change and of loss. Putting down my head, I swing my arms and legs, aware that she's still watching me.

32

There are flowers everywhere – propped against the railing fence and the trunks of trees. A photograph of Christine Wheeler is wedged in a clear plastic sleeve at the centre of the largest wreath.

Darcy is wearing one of Julianne's dresses and a black winter coat that almost touches the ground as she walks. She stands in a circle on the opposite side of the grave, beside her aunt – who arrived this morning from Spain – and her grandfather who sits in a wheelchair with a tartan blanket over his knees.

Her aunt is a tall woman who stands squarely as though addressing a golf ball instead of a person. The breeze is playing havoc with her hair, flattening it on one side of her head.

I've been to funerals before but this one is wrong. The mourners are too young. They're Christine's old school friends and mates from university. Some had nothing appropriate to wear in their wardrobe and have chosen muted greys rather than black. They don't know what to say so they stand in clusters, whispering and glancing sorrowfully at Darcy.

Alice Furness peeks out from beside her aunt Gloria. Her father, home from Geneva, is dressed in a black suit and talking on a mobile. His eyes meet mine and then his gaze drifts to the right and he reaches out and puts a hand on Alice's shoulder. He has to bury *his* wife next. I can't imagine what it would be like to lose Julianne. I don't want to imagine it.

On the opposite side of the cemetery, gathered on a ridge, TV crews and photographers have taken up positions behind a barricade of traffic cones and police tape. Uniformed officers are keeping them away from mourners.

Safari Roy and Monk stand shoulder to shoulder, looking like pallbearers. DI Cray is standing separately. She has brought a wreath of flowers, which she rests on the mound of dark brown earth that is covered by a carpet of artificial grass.

A hearse murmurs through the gates. The curved road is lower than the surrounding grass and I can't see the tyres turning. It gives the impression that the vehicle is floating towards us.

Julianne's shoulder brushes mine and her right hand takes my left hand – the one that trembles. She holds it still, as though keeping my secret.

Ruiz joins us. I haven't seen him since yesterday.

'Where you been?'

'An errand.'

'Care to elaborate?'

He glances across at Darcy. 'I've been looking for her father.'

'Seriously?'

'Yeah.'

'Did *she* ask you?'

'Nope.'

'She's never met him!'

'Never met mine either,' he shrugs. 'Still thought he might like to know. If he turns out to be an axe-murderer I won't give Darcy his address.'

The coffin has been placed in a cradle over the grave. Flowers are piled high on the polished wood. Darcy is crying openly. Her aunt doesn't seem interested. Another woman wraps an arm around Darcy's shoulder. Wretched and red-eyed, she's wearing a black coat over a long grey skirt.

Suddenly, I recognise the man next to her – Bruno Kaufman. It must be his ex-wife, Maureen. Bruno mentioned that she went to school with Christine, which means she also went to school with

Sylvia. My God, she's lost two friends in just over a week. No wonder she looks so desolate.

Bruno raises a finger towards me in a casual salute.

The vicar is ready to start. His voice, thick with cold, is too clogged to carry far. I find my mind drifting further, over the gravestones and lawns, beyond the trees and the machinery shed to where a gravedigger sits watching. He peels an egg, dropping the pieces of shell into a brown paper bag.

Ashes to ashes, dust to dust . . . if God don't get you, the devil must. Have you ever noticed how cemeteries smell like compost heaps? They've sprinkled blood and bone on the roses. It gets right up my nose.

The mourners are in black like crows around road kill. I can feel their sadness, but it doesn't feel sad enough. I know true sadness. It's the sound of a child opening birthday presents without me; wearing clothes that I paid for. That is sadness.

The shrink is here; he's like one of those B-grade celebrities who would turn up for the opening of an envelope. This time he's brought along his wife who is far too hot for the likes of him. Perhaps his shake makes foreplay interesting.

Who else is here? The dyke detective and her keystone cops. Darcy, the ballet dancer, is being stoic and brave. We passed briefly at the gates and she gave me the briefest look of recognition, as though she couldn't remember if she knew me. Then she noticed the wheelbarrow and my overalls and discounted the possibility.

The minister is telling the mourners that death is just the beginning of a journey. It's a fairytale echoed down the ages. Chests are shaking. Tears are falling. The ground is soggy enough. Why does death come as such a shock to people? Surely it's the most fundamental truth. We live. We die. You take this egg. If it had been fertilised and kept warm it might have been a baby chick. Instead it was dropped in boiling water and became a snack.

Heads are lowered in silent prayer. Coats flap against knees as a breeze picks up. The branches groan above my head like the stomachs of dead souls.

I have to go now. I have places to be . . . locks to pick . . . minds to open.

*   *   *

208

The service is over. We walk across the lawn and find the path. A warm wet smell rises from the flowerbeds and overhead, etched against a pearl grey sky, migratory birds fly in formation, heading south.

Bruno Kaufman takes my arm. I introduce him to Julianne. He bows theatrically.

'Where has Joseph been hiding you?' he asks.

'Nowhere in particular,' she replies, happy to let Bruno flirt with her.

Mourners are stepping round us. Darcy is with some of her mother's friends, who seem to want to squeeze her hand and stroke her hair. Her aunt is wheeling her grandfather along the path, complaining about the slope.

'The police are everywhere, old boy,' says Bruno, glancing at Monk and Safari Roy. 'They stand out like purple cows.'

'I've never seen a purple cow.'

'Madison, Wisconsin, has lots of colourful cows,' he says. 'Not real ones. Statues. They're a tourist attraction.'

He begins telling a story about his tenure at the University of Wisconsin. A wind lifts his fringe and makes it hover, defying gravity. Bruno is directing the story to Julianne. I glance past him and notice Maureen.

'We haven't met,' I tell her. 'I'm very sorry about Christine and Sylvia. I know they were friends of yours.'

'Old friends and good ones,' she says, her breath condensing as she exhales.

'How are you doing?'

'I'm fine.' She blows her nose on a tissue. 'I'm scared.'

'What are you scared of?'

'My two best friends are dead. That scares me. The police have come to my house, interviewed me; that scares me. I jump at loud noises, I deadlock the doors, I look in the rear mirror when I'm driving . . . that scares me, too.'

The soggy tissue is slipped into the pocket of her coat. A new one is retrieved from a small plastic packet. Her hands are shaking.

'When did you see them last?'

'A fortnight ago. We had a reunion.'

209

'What sort of reunion?'

'It was just the four of us – the old gang from Oldfield. We were at school together.'

'Bruno mentioned it.'

'We arranged to meet at our favourite pub. Helen organised it.'

'Helen?'

'Another friend: Helen Chambers.' She casts her eye around the cemetery. 'I thought she would be here. It's odd. Helen organised the reunion; she was the reason we were getting together. None of us had seen her in years, but she didn't show up.'

'Why?'

'I still don't know. She didn't call or email.'

'You haven't heard from her at all?'

She shakes her head and sniffles. 'It's pretty typical of Helen. She is famous for being late and for getting lost in her own back-yard.' She glances past me. 'I mean it seriously. They had to send out search parties.'

'Where did she live?'

'Her father has a country house with a big back yard, so perhaps I shouldn't tease her.'

'You haven't seen her in how long?'

'Seven years. Nearly eight.'

'Where has she been?'

'She married and moved to Northern Ireland and then to Germany. Chris and Sylvie were her bridesmaids. I was supposed to be the maid of honour but Bruno and I were living in America and couldn't get back for the wedding. I videoed a good luck message.'

Maureen's eyes seem to shimmer. 'We all promised to stay in touch, but Helen just seemed to drift away. I sent her cards every birthday and Christmas. The odd letter came back out of the blue but didn't say much. Weeks turned to months and then to years. We lost touch. It was sad.'

'And then she contacted you?'

'Six months ago she sent us all an email – Christine, Sylvie and me – saying that she'd left her husband. She was going on a holiday with her daughter – "to clear her head" – and then she was coming home.

'Then about a month ago she sent another email saying she was back and we should get together. She chose the place: the Garrick's Head in Bath. Do you know it?'

I nod.

'We used to go there all the time – before we all married and had kids. We'd have a few drinks and a laugh; and sometimes kick on to a nightclub. Sylvie loved to dance.'

Maureen's hands have stopped shaking, but the calm never comes. She talks as though some rejected life has come back to claim her. A lost friend. A voice from the past.

'When I heard about Christine committing suicide I didn't believe it, not for a minute. She'd never kill herself like that. Never leave Darcy.'

'Tell me about Sylvia?'

Maureen gives me a sad smile. 'She was a wild one, but not in a bad way. She worried me sometimes. She was a crash or crash-through sort of girl, who took so many risks. Thankfully, she married someone like Richard who was very forgiving.'

Her eyes are liquid, but her mascara is still in place.

'You know what I loved most about Sylvie?'

I shake my head.

'Her voice. I miss hearing her laugh.' She glances across the cemetery. The sun shines on a glitter of green grass. 'I miss both of them. I miss knowing I'll see them again. I keep thinking they're going to phone or text me or turn up for a coffee . . .'

Another silence, longer this time. She lifts her head, frowning. 'Who would do such a thing?'

'I don't know.'

'Bruno says you're helping the police.'

'As much as I can.'

She looks towards Bruno, who is explaining to Julianne that the first fossil records of the rose date back 35 million years and Sapho wrote 'Ode to a Rose' in 600 B.C. calling it the queen of flowers.

'How does he know stuff like that?' I ask.

'He says the same about you.'

She looks at him fondly. 'I used to love him, then I hated him, and now I'm caught between the two. He's not a bad man, you know.'

'I know.'

33

Cars are parked in the driveway and on the footpath outside the Wheeler house. Darcy is welcoming the mourners, taking coats and handbags. She looks at me as if I'm coming to rescue her.

'When can we leave?' she whispers.

'You're doing great.'

'I don't think I can handle much more of this.' More guests are arriving. The sitting room and dining rooms are crowded. Julianne takes hold of my left hand as we skirt the clusters of mourners, weaving between outstretched cups of tea and plates of sandwiches and cakes.

Ruiz has found a beer.

'So you want to hear about Darcy's father?' he asks.

'Have you found him?'

'Getting closer. His name wasn't on her birth certificate, but I got confirmation of the marriage. Parish records. Wonderful things.'

Julianne gives him a hug. 'Can't we talk about something else?'

'You mean like pensions,' Ruiz says playfully, 'or maybe mergers and acquisitions.'

'Very funny.'

She punches him playfully. Ruiz takes another swig of beer, enjoying himself. I leave them talking and go looking for Darcy's aunt. She's directing traffic in the kitchen, waving plates of sand-wiches through one door and collecting empty dishes through another. The benches are covered with food and the air is thick with the smell of cakes and tea.

Kerry Wheeler is a big woman with a Spanish suntan and heavy jewellery. The expanse of skin below her neck is mottled and lipstick has smeared in the corners of her mouth.

'Call me Kerry,' she says, pouring boiling water into a teapot. The steam has flattened her perm and she tries to make it bounce again by flicking it with her fingers.

'Can we talk?' I ask.

'Sure. I'm dying for a fag.'

She pulls a packet of cigarettes from her handbag and a large glass of white wine from a hiding place behind the biscuit jars. She takes them outside, down three steps, to the garden.

'You want one?'

'I don't smoke.'

She lights up.

'I hear you're famous.'

'No.'

She exhales and watches the smoke dissipate. I notice the purple veins on the back of her ankles and raw skin where her high heels have been rubbing.

'Couldn't wait for that funeral to end,' she says. 'Felt cold enough to snow. Crazy weather. I'm not used to it any more. Too long in the sun.'

'About Darcy.'

'Yeah. I meant to say, thanks for looking after her. It won't be necessary any more.'

'You're going back to Spain.'

'Day after tomorrow.'

'Have you told Darcy?'

'Going to.'

'When?'

'I just buried my sister. That was my first priority.'

She pulls her jacket closer around her chest; sucks on the ciga-rette. 'I didn't ask for this, you know.'

214

'Ask for what?'

'Darcy.' The wine glass clinks against her teeth. 'Kids are difficult. Selfish. That's why I don't have any.' She looks at me. 'You got children?'

'Yes.'

'So you know what I mean.'

'Not really.' I speak softly. 'Darcy wants to go to ballet school in London.'

'And who's going to pay for that?'

'I think she plans to sell this place.'

'This place!' The big woman laughs. Her teeth are yellow and dotted with fillings. 'Bank owns "this place". Just like the bank owns the car. Bank owns the furniture. Bank owns the friggin' lot.'

She belches into her fist and flicks the cigarette butt into the garden where it bounces and sparks. 'My sister – the big shot businesswoman – writes a will when there's nothing to bloody give away. And even if there is something left when I sell this place, young missy is too young to inherit. I'm her legal guardian. Says so in the will.'

'I think you should talk to Darcy about Spain. She won't want to go.'

'Not her decision.'

She rubs her heels as if trying to restore blood flow to her feet.

'I still think you should talk to her.'

A ravelled silence and a sigh. 'I appreciate your concern, Mr O'Loughlin.'

'Call me Joe.'

'Well, Joe, we all have to make compromises. Darcy needs someone to look after her. I'm the only family she's got.'

I can feel myself getting annoyed. Angry. I shake my head and press my hands tighter into my jacket pockets.

'You think I'm wrong,' she says.

'Yes.'

'That's another advantage of being my age – I don't have to give a shit.'

As soon as I enter the house Julianne senses something is wrong. She looks at me questioningly. My left arm is trembling.

215

'You ready to go?' she asks.

'Let me talk to Darcy first.'

'To say goodbye.'

It's a statement, not a question.

I look in the lounge and the dining room, the front hallway and then upstairs. Darcy is in her bedroom, sitting at the window, staring at the garden.

'You hiding?'

'Yep,' she says.

The room is full of music posters and stuffed toys. It's a time capsule from Darcy's childhood, which seems incredibly distant. I notice scraps of torn paper on the floor and a pile of condolence cards stacked haphazardly on the bed. Someone has opened them quickly, without care.

'You've been reading cards.'

'No. I found them like this.'

'When?'

'Just now – when I got home.'

'Who opened them?'

She shrugs but senses the edge in my voice. I ask if the house was locked, who had keys, where did she find the cards and envelopes . . .

'They were on the bed.'

'Are any of them missing?'

'I can't tell.'

I glance out the window at a line of poplar saplings that ends on the corner. I see a silver van moving slowly along the street, searching for a house number.

'Can we go now?'

'Not this time.'

'What do you mean?'

'You're going to stay here with your aunt.'

'But she's going back to Spain.'

'She wants you to go with her.'

'No! No!' Darcy looks at me accusingly.

'I can't. I won't. What about my ballet scholarship? I won a place.'

'Spain can be like a holiday.'

'A holiday! I can't suddenly stop dancing and take it up again. I've never been to Spain. I don't know anyone there.'

'You have your aunt.'

'Who hates me.'

'No she doesn't.'

'Talk to her.'

'I have.'

'Did I do something wrong?'

'Of course not.'

Her bottom lip is trembling. Suddenly, she throws herself against me, wrapping her arms around my chest.

'Let me come home with you.'

'I can't do that, Darcy.'

'Please. Please.'

'I can't, I'm sorry.'

What happens next is not so much unplanned as unimagined. Some leaps can only be made in the space between the head and the heart. Darcy raises her face and presses her lips to mine. Her breath. Her tongue. Inexperienced, exploring, she tastes of potato chips and cola. I try to pull back. Her hand grips my hair. She pushes her hips against mine, offering her body.

My head is filled with seven visions of crazy. Taking hold of her hands, I gently ease her away and hold her there. She blinks at me desperately.

Her coat is unbuttoned. One side of her blouse has fallen off her shoulder, exposing a bra strap.

'I love you.'

'Don't say that.'

'But I do. I love you more than *she* does.'

She steps away, freeing her hands, letting her coat fall from her shoulders, pulling her top down, exposing her bra.

'Don't you want me? I'm not a child!' Her voice sounds different.

'Please, Darcy.'

'Let me stay with you.'

'I can't.'

She shakes her head, bites her lip, trying not to cry. She

understands everything. The stakes have changed completely. I can never take her into my home – not now – not after what she has offered me. Her tears are not meant to blackmail me emotionally or to make me change my mind. They're just tears.

'Please leave,' she says. 'I want to be alone.'

I close the door, lean against it. I can still taste her in my mouth and feel her trembling. The sensation is one of fear: fear of discovery, fear of what she did and how much I am to blame. My area of supposed expertise is in human behaviour but sometimes I am astonished by how profoundly ignorant I am. How can someone be a psychologist yet know so little about the subject? The mind is too complex, too unpredictable, an ocean of uncertainty. And I have no option but to tread water or to swim for a distant shore.

Julianne is at the bottom of the stairs. 'Is everything OK?' she asks. Can she see something in my eyes?

'There's been a break-in. I have to call the police.'

'Now?'

'You go home. I should stay.'

'How will you get home?'

'Ruiz is still here.'

She stands on tiptoes and gently kisses my lips. Then she leans back and looks into my eyes.

'Are you sure you're OK?'

'I'm fine.'

An hour later and police have replaced mourners. The cards and envelopes have been bagged and taken to the lab. The doors and windows checked for any signs of forced entry. Nothing has been taken.

There is no reason for me to be here and every reason for me to leave. I keep thinking of Darcy's kiss and her awkwardness. It embarrassed us both but she is of an age where rejection can crush. I live with discomfit every day, in the tremble of a hand or a sudden frozen fall.

I keep thinking about what Maureen said about the reunion and losing two of her best friends. Perhaps the murders had nothing to do with a business failing or Christine Wheeler owing money to loan sharks. It was more personal than that. Why would someone open condolence cards? What were they looking for?

Darcy is still upstairs. Her aunt is talking to police in the kitchen. Outside I let my eyes adjust to the darkness. Ruiz is waiting in his car. The heater blasts warm air onto the windscreen.

'I need another favour.'

'You got any of those left?'

'One.'

'I must have lost count.'

'I need you to look for someone. Her name is Helen Chambers.'

'Haven't you got enough women in your life?'

'She went to school with Christine Wheeler and Sylvia Furness. They were supposed to meet up a fortnight ago. She didn't show.'

'Last known address?'

'Her folks live somewhere near Frome. A big country house.'

'Shouldn't be hard to find.'

The car swings from the parking space and the glare of approaching headlights stings my eyes. Ruiz turns up the music. Sinatra is crooning about a lady who never flirts with strangers or blows on another guy's dice.

It is after midnight when I get home. The cottage is dark. Above and behind it, a church steeple is black against a purple sky. I close the door gently and take my shoes off. Climb the stairs.

Emma is spreadeagled on top of her duvet. I fold her legs beneath it and tuck it beneath her chin. She doesn't stir. Charlie's door is open a few inches. Her lava lamp casts a pink glow over the room. I can see her lying on her side with her hand close to her mouth.

Julianne is asleep. I undress in the bathroom and brush my teeth before sliding alongside her. She turns and wraps her arms and legs around me, pressing her breasts against my back.

'It's late,' she whispers.

'Sorry.'

'How is Darcy?'

'She's with her aunt.'

Her hand seeks me out, with resolute determination; making a ring with her thumb and finger. She bends and takes me in her mouth. And when I'm ready she rolls on top, straddling my waist, trapping me beneath her.

Her thighs are open. She slides backwards, taking me inside her, inhaling sharply. She guides my hands to her breasts. Her nipples are hard. I don't have to move. I watch her rise and descend, inch-by-inch, accepting my surrender, seeking her own release and summoning mine.

It doesn't feel like make-up sex or new-beginning sex. It's like a quiet sigh drawing colour from the embers. Afterwards Julianne rests her head on my chest and I listen to her fall asleep.

An hour passes. I slide her head onto her pillow and slip out of bed, tiptoeing to the study. Closing the door before turning on the light, I look for the hotel receipt from Rome. Taking it from between the pages of a notebook, I rip it into small pieces that flutter into the wastepaper bin.

34

I can understand why a man might lavish affection on a machine instead of a human being. Machines are more reliable. Turn the key, flick a switch, step on the gas and they do the business when it counts.

I have never owned a sports car — never desired one — but I have one now. It belongs to a futures trader who lives in one of the luxury apartments overlooking Queen Square. You can't steal a Ferrari F430 Spider off the street — not without disabling the alarm, ripping the guts out of the steering lock and circumventing the engine immobiliser. It's far easier to steal the keys of the rich bastard who owns it. He left them on the radiator cover, just inside his front door, next to the secure parking key and his leather driving gloves.

The one thing I can't get around is the 'vehicle tracking system'. Once he reports the car missing I'll have to say goodbye to my wet dream on wheels.

Steering the Spider through the streets on a Monday morning, I watch the reactions it produces, the looks of admiration, awe and envy. It doesn't even have to be moving to draw the eye.

A lot of guys I knew in the army were obsessed with cars. The poor bastards spent their careers rumbling along at sixty k's an hour in an armoured personnel carrier or a Challenger, with six forward gears and two reverse. So on their own time they went for something with more finesse and speed. Sports cars. Some of them were in hock up their eyeballs but they didn't care. It was all about living the dream.

I park the Spider in a quiet street. The dew-slimed footpath is beginning to dry and sunlight filters through the branches of plane trees. I take a map and spread it out on the bonnet. The engine is ticking as it cools.

I wait. He'll be along soon. Here he comes now, shuffling through the leaves, dressed in a blazer and dark grey trousers.

He's seen the Ferrari. He pauses and studies the lines. His hand is drawn towards it, wanting to touch the gleaming paintwork and run a finger over its curves.

'Nice wheels,' he says.

'Oughta be.'

'Yours?'

'I'm holding the keys.'

He does a slow circuit of the Spider. His schoolbag hangs off one shoulder.

'How fast?' he asks.

I fold the map in half. 'Let's just say I could be a quarter of a mile from here in twelve seconds.'

'That's if you weren't lost.' He grins.

'Yeah, wise-arse, maybe you could help me with that.'

He crouches and peers inside the tinted driver's window.

'Where you going?'

'Beacon Hill. Seymour Road.'

'Beacon Hill isn't far. I'm heading that way.'

'Walking?'

'Catching the bus.'

I show him the map. He points to his school and shows me the route. I can smell toothpaste on his breath and glimpse a younger version of myself, ripe with potential, ready to take on the world.

'Can I take a look inside?' he asks.

'Sure.'

He opens the door.

'Get behind the wheel.'

Dropping his schoolbag in the gutter, he slides into the seat, gripping the steering wheel with both hands and settling himself. Any minute he's going to start making revving noises.

'This is awesome.'

'You could say that.'

'What's her top speed?'

'A hundred and ninety-three miles an hour. She has a 4.3 litre V8 483 horsepower engine with 343 pounds of torque.'

'What's the most you've had her up to?'

'You're not a copper, are you?'

'No.' He laughs.

'Hundred and eighty.'

'No shit.'

'She was purring like a kitten. But the real rush is the acceleration. She does nought to sixty in 4.1 seconds. Like shit off a shovel.'

I've hooked him now. It's more than curiosity. It's red-blooded male longing. It's like the sex dream a boy has before he's tasted a woman. It's speed. It's an engine. It's love at first sight.

'How much did it cost?' he whispers.

'Didn't your mum ever tell you it's rude to ask a question like that?'

'Yeah, but she drives a Ford Astra.'

I smile. 'Not really a car person, huh?'

'No.'

'When do you get your licence?'

'Nine months.'

'You going to get a car?'

'I don't think Mum can afford one. Maybe my dad could help.'

His fingers close around the gearstick. With one hand still on the wheel, he peers through the windscreen and imagines taking the corners.

'What time's your bus?' I ask.

He looks at his watch. 'Shit!'

'Don't worry. I'll give you a lift.'

'Really?'

'Yeah. Get in. Buckle up.'

35

It's after nine. I lie in bed staring at the ceiling. Downstairs I hear footsteps, laughter and the sound of nursery rhymes. It's like tuning into my favourite radio soap and listening to another instalment of life in the O'Loughlin household.

I lumber downstairs, teeth brushed, face washed and body medicated. There's laughter from the sitting room. I listen at the door. Julianne is interviewing nannies. Emma seems to be asking most of the questions.

Ruiz is in the kitchen, eating toast and reading my morning paper.

'Morning,' I say.

'Morning.'

'Don't they feed you at the pub?'

'It doesn't have the ambience of this place.'

I pour myself a cup of coffee and take a seat opposite him.

'I found Helen Chambers' family. They live on the Daubeney Estate, outside Westbury. It's about thirty miles from here. I tried to call and got an answering machine. Helen Chambers isn't listed on the voter rolls or telephone directories.'

He senses I'm only half-listening.

'What's up?'

'Nothing.'

He goes back to reading the paper. I take a sip of coffee.

'Do you ever have nightmares?' I ask. 'I mean, you dealt with some pretty terrible things – murders, rapes, missing children – don't they ever come back to you, the memories?'

'No.'

'What about Catherine McBride?' She was a former patient of mine. That's how I first met Ruiz, he was investigating her murder.

'What about her?'

'I still see her in my dreams sometimes. Now I'm seeing Christine Wheeler.'

Ruiz folds the newspaper in half and half again. 'Does she talk to you?'

'No, nothing like that.'

'But you're seeing dead people?'

'You make it sound crazy.'

He slaps me hard across the side of my head with the newspaper.

'What was that for?'

'It's a wake up call.'

'Why?'

'You once told me that a doctor is no good to a patient if he dies of the disease. Don't go soft in the head. You're supposed to be the sane one.'

The Daubeney Estate is two miles north of Westbury on the borders of Somerset and Wiltshire. The rolling countryside is dotted with small farms and swollen lakes and dams from the recent rain.

Ruiz is driving his Merc. The suspension is so soft it's like a waterbed on wheels.

'What do we know about the family?' I ask.

'Bryan and Claudia Chambers. He owns a construction company that does a lot of big money contracts in the Gulf. The Daubeney Estate used to be one of the biggest landholdings in the country until it was broken up and sold in the 1980s. The Chambers own the manor house and eleven acres.'

'What about Helen?'

'She's an only child. She left Oldfield Girls School in Bath in

1988 – same years as Christine Wheeler and Sylvia Furness. She went Bristol University; studied economics and married eight years ago. Since then she's lived abroad.'

He raises his forefinger from the steering wheel. 'This is the place.'

We pull into an opening guarded by a ten-foot-high iron gate hinged on stone pillars. On either side, a perimeter wall stretches through the trees. It is topped with broken bottles that sprout from the concrete like jagged flowers.

The gate has an intercom box. I press a button and wait. A voice answers.

'Who is it?'

'Is that Mr Chambers?'

'No.'

'Is he at home?'

'He's not available.'

'Is Helen Chambers at home?'

'You trying to be funny, pal?' He has a Welsh accent.

I glance at Ruiz who shrugs.

'I'm Joseph O'Loughlin. It's important that I speak to a member of the family.'

'I'll need more information than that.'

'It's a police matter. It concerns their daughter.'

There is a pause. Maybe he's seeking instructions.

The voice comes back: 'Who are you with?'

I dip my head and look through the windscreen. A CCTV camera is perched on a metal pole twenty feet above the gate. He's watching us.

Ruiz leans across me, 'I'm a retired detective inspector. I formerly worked for the London Metropolitan Police.'

'Retired?'

'You heard me.'

'I'm sorry. Mr and Mrs Chambers are both unavailable.'

'When is the best time to speak to them?' I ask.

'Write a letter.'

'I'd prefer to leave a note.'

The gate stays firmly closed. Ruiz walks around the Merc and

226

stretches. The camera pivots and follows every move. He hoists himself onto a fallen tree, peering over the wall.

'Can you see the house?' I ask.

'No.' He looks left and right. 'Now there's an interesting thing.'

'What?'

'Motion sensors, and more cameras. I know the rich get nervous – come the revolution and all that – but this is complete overkill. What does this guy have to hide?'

Boots sound on gravel. A man appears on the far side of the gate, walking towards us. Dressed like a gardener in jeans, a checked shirt and oilskin coat, he has a dog with him; a massive German Shepherd with a black and tan coat.

'Get away from the wall,' he demands.

Ruiz swings himself down and makes eye contact with me.

'Great day,' I say.

'Yes, it is,' says the man with the dog. We both know we're lying.

Ruiz has moved to my side of the car. He drops his hand behind his back and holds down the intercom button, leaving it there.

The German Shepherd is watching me as if deciding which leg to eat first. His handler is more concerned with Ruiz and what sort of physical threat he might pose.

Ruiz takes his finger off the intercom.

A woman's voice answers: 'Yes, who is it?'

'Mrs Chambers?' Ruiz replies.

'Yes.'

'I'm sorry, but your gardener said you weren't home. He was obviously mistaken. My name is Vincent Ruiz. I'm a former detective inspector with the London Metropolitan Police. Is it possible to have a few moments of your time?'

'What is this about?'

'It concerns two of your daughter's friends – Christine Wheeler and Sylvia Furness. Do you remember them?'

'Yes, I do.'

'Have you seen the newspapers?'

'No. Why? What's happened?'

Ruiz glances at me. She doesn't know.

'I'm afraid they're dead, Mrs Chambers.'

227

Silence. Static.

'You should really talk to Skipper,' she says, her voice straining.

Is she talking about the gardener or the dog?

'I'm talking to Skipper right now,' says Ruiz. 'He's come down to the gate to meet us. He's a very charming chap. Must be a dab hand with the roses.'

She is knocked off guard. 'He doesn't know daffodils from dogwood.'

'Me neither,' says Ruiz. 'Can we come in? It's important.'

The gate lets out a hollow click and swings inwards. Skipper has to step back. He's not happy.

Ruiz slides behind the wheel and drives past him, raising his hand in a half-salute before spinning wheels in the gravel.

'He doesn't look much like a gardener,' I say.

'He's ex-military,' says Ruiz. 'See how he stands. He doesn't advertise his strengths. He keeps them under wraps until he needs them.'

The gables and roofline appear through the trees. Ruiz slows over a grated gate and pulls up in front of the main house. The large double door must be four inches thick. One side opens. Claudia Chambers peers from within. A slender, still pretty woman in her late fifties, she's dressed in a cashmere cardigan and khaki slacks.

'Thank you for seeing us,' I say, making the introductions.

She doesn't offer her hand. Instead she leads us through a marble foyer to a large sitting room full of oriental rugs and matching Chesterfield sofas. Bookshelves fill the alcoves on either side of a large fireplace that is set but not burning. There are photographs on the mantelpiece and side tables showing a child's passage through life from birth to toddler to girlhood. A first lost tooth, first day at school, first snowman, first bicycle – a lifetime of firsts.

'Your daughter?' I ask.

'Our granddaughter,' she replies.

She motions to the sofa, wanting us to sit down.

'Can I get you something? Tea perhaps.'

'Thank you,' says Ruiz, answering for both of us.

As if by magic, a plump woman in uniform appears at the door.

228

There must be a hidden bell at Claudia's feet, beneath the rug or tucked down the side of the sofa.

Claudia issues instructions and the maid disappears. She turns back to us and takes a seat on the sofa opposite, tucking her hands in her lap. Everything about her demeanour is closed off and defensive.

'Poor Christine and Sylvia. Was it some sort of accident?'

'No, we don't believe so.'

'What happened?'

'They were murdered.'

She blinks. Grief is like a moist sheen over her pupils. It's as much emotion as she's going to show.

'Christine jumped off the Clifton Suspension Bridge,' I say. 'We believe she was coerced.'

'Coerced?'

'She was forced to jump,' explains Ruiz.

Claudia shakes her head fiercely, as if trying to clear the information from her ears.

'Sylvia died of exposure. She was found handcuffed to a tree.'

'Who would do such a thing?' asks Claudia, a little less sure of the world.

'You haven't seen the TV or the newspapers?'

'I don't follow the news. It depresses me.'

'When did you last see Christine and Sylvia?'

'Not since Helen's wedding; they were bridesmaids.' She counts on her fingertips. 'Eight years. Goodness, has it really been that long.'

'Did your daughter keep in touch with them?'

'I don't know. Helen went overseas with her husband. She didn't get home very often.'

The maid has returned with a tray. The teapot and china cups seem too delicate to hold boiling water. Claudia pours, almost willing her hands to be steady.

'Do you have milk or sugar?'

'Milk.'

'Straight from the pot,' says Ruiz.

She stirs without letting the teaspoon touch the edges of her cup. Her thoughts seem to drift away for a moment before returning to the room.

A car sounds outside – tyres on gravel. Moments later the front door slams opens and hurried footsteps cross the foyer. Bryan Chambers makes the sort of entrance that befits a man his size, bursting into the room, hell bent on hitting someone.

'Who the fuck are you?' he bellows. 'What are you doing in my house?'

Balding, with big hands and a thick neck, his head is shaped like a hard hat and glistens with sweat.

Ruiz is on his feet. I take longer to find mine.

'It's all right, dear,' says Claudia. 'Something awful has happened to Christine and Sylvia.'

Bryan Chambers isn't satisfied. 'Who sent you?'

'Excuse me?'

'Who sent you here? These women have nothing to do with us.'

It's obvious he knows about Christine and Sylvia. Why didn't he tell his wife?

'Calm down, dear,' Claudia says.

'Just be quiet.' he barks. 'Leave this to me.'

Skipper has followed him into the room, moving behind our backs. There is something in his right hand, which is tucked inside his jacket.

Ruiz turns to face him. 'We don't want to upset anyone. We just want to know about Helen.'

Bryan Chambers scoffs. 'Don't play games with me! He sent you, didn't he?'

I look at Ruiz. 'I don't know what you're talking about. We're helping the police investigate two murders. Both victims were friends of your daughter.'

Chambers switches his attention to Ruiz. 'You a police officer?'

'Used to be.'

'What's that mean?'

'I'm retired.'

'So you're a private detective?'

'No.'

'So none of this is fucking official.'

'We just want to speak to your daughter, Helen.'

He claps his hands together and laughs indignantly. 'Well, that just takes the biscuit!'

Ruiz is growing annoyed. 'Maybe you should do like your wife suggests and calm down, Mr Chambers.'

'Are you trying to intimidate me?'

'No, sir, we're just trying to get some answers.'

'What's my Helen got to do with it?'

'Four weeks ago she sent emails to Christine Wheeler, Sylvia Furness and another school friend, Maureen Bracken. She arranged to meet them at a pub in Bath on the 21st of September, a Friday night. The others turned up but Helen didn't. They didn't hear from her. We were hoping to find out why.'

Bryan Chambers gapes at me incredulously. The manic glimmer in his gaze has been replaced by a fever of uncertainty.

'What you are suggesting is impossible,' he says. 'My daughter couldn't have sent any emails.'

'Why?'

'She died three months ago; she and my granddaughter drowned in Greece.'

Suddenly the room isn't big enough to hide the awkwardness of the moment. The air has become cloying and harsh. Ruiz looks at me, unable to respond.

'I'm so sorry,' I tell them. I don't know what else to say. 'We had no idea.'

Bryan Chambers isn't interested in apologies or explanations.

'They died in a ferry accident,' says Mrs Chambers, still sitting upright on the edge of the sofa. 'It sank in a storm.'

I remember the story. It was late in the summer, a freak storm in the Aegean. Ships were damaged and yachts destroyed. Some of the holiday resorts had to be evacuated and a passenger ferry sank off one of the islands. Dozens of tourists were rescued. Passengers died.

I glance around the room, looking at the photographs. The Chambers have created a shrine to their dead granddaughter.

'Please leave now,' says Bryan Chambers.

Skipper emphasises the demand, by holding open the door. I'm still looking at the images of a blonde-haired, clear-skinned grand-daughter, missing a front tooth, holding a balloon, blowing out birthday candles . . .

'We're very sorry to have troubled you,' I say. 'And for your loss.'

Ruiz dips his head. 'Thank you for the tea, ma'am.'

Neither Bryan nor Claudia respond.

Skipper escorts us outside and stands sentry at the door, still with his right hand inside his oilskin jacket. Bryan Chambers appears beside him.

Ruiz has started the Merc. My door is open. I turn back.

'Mr Chambers, who did you think sent us?'

'Goodbye,' he says.

'Is someone threatening you?'

'Drive carefully.'

36

We emerge out of the wooded drive and swing right, taking the back road as far as Trowbridge. The Merc floats over the dips. Sinatra has been turned down.

'That's one fucking crazy family,' mutters Ruiz. 'The wheels are spinning but the hamster's dead. Did you see Chambers' face? I thought he was having a heart attack.'

'He's frightened of something.'

'What? World War III?'

Ruiz begins listing the security measures – the cameras, motion sensors and alarms. Skipper could have come straight from SAS central casting.

'A guy like that earns five grand a week as a bodyguard in Baghdad – what's he doing here?'

'Wiltshire is safer.'

'Maybe Chambers has been doing business with the wrong sort of people. That's the problem with those big corporations – it's like Friday night at the movies. Someone is always trying to get a handful of tit or a finger in the pie.'

'Colourful analogy.'

'Think so?'

'My daughters are never going to the cinema.'

'Just you wait.'

We take the A363 through Bradford-on-Avon and skirt the top of Bathampton Down. We crest a hill. Bath Spa is there before us, nestled sedately in a valley. A billboard announces: *Your Dream Retirement Lies Just Ahead*. Ruiz thinks it sums up Bath, which has that sulphurous reek of old age and money.

I can't get a single question out of my head: how did a dead woman send emails organising a night out with friends? Someone sent the messages. Whoever sent the messages must have had access to Helen Chambers' computer or her login details. Either that or they stole her identity and set up a new account. If so, why? It makes no sense. What possible interest would someone have in getting four old friends together?

It could have been the killer. He may have drawn them together and then followed them home. It certainly would explain how he scoped his victims – learning where they lived and worked, discovering the rhythm of their lives. It still doesn't explain how Helen Chambers is linked to this.

'We have to talk Maureen Bracken,' I say. 'She's the only person who turned up at that reunion who's still alive.'

Ruiz doesn't say a word but I know he's thinking the same thing. Someone has to warn her.

Oldfield School is set amid trees and muddy sporting fields, over-looking the Avon Valley. A sign in the car park tells all visitors to report to the office.

A lone student is sitting in reception, swinging her legs beneath a plastic chair. She is dressed in a blue skirt, white blouse and dark blue jumper with a swan motif. She glances up briefly and resumes her wait.

A school secretary appears behind a sliding glass window. Behind her a colour-coded timetable covers the wall; a feat of logic and organisation that encompasses 850 students, thirty-four classrooms and fifteen subjects. Running a school is like being an air traffic controller without a radar screen.

The secretary runs her finger down the timetable, tapping the board twice. 'Mrs Bracken is teaching English in the annex. Room 2b.' She glances at the clock. 'It's almost lunchtime. You can wait

234

for her in the corridor or in the staffroom. It's up the stairs – to the right. Jacquie will show you.'

The schoolgirl raises her head and looks relieved. Judgement for whatever she's done has been postponed.

'This way,' she says, pushing through the doors and quickly climbing the stairs, pausing at the landing for us to catch up. A noticeboard advertises a design competition, photography class and Oldfield's anti-bullying policy.

'So what did you do?' asks Ruiz.

Jacquie glances at him sheepishly. 'Got kicked out of class.'

'What for?'

'You're not one of the governors, are you?'

'Do I look like a school governor?'

'No,' she admits. 'I accused my drama teacher of raging mediocrity.'

Ruiz laughs. 'Not just any mediocrity then?'

'No.'

A bell rings. Bodies fill the corridors, flooding around us. There are peals of laughter and cries of, 'Don't run! Don't run!'

Jacquie has reached the classroom. She knocks on the door. 'Visitors to see you, miss.'

'Thank you.'

Maureen Bracken is wearing a knee-length dark green dress with a brown leather belt and court shoes that show off her solid calves. Her hair is pinned back and minimal make-up colours her lips and eyelids.

'What's wrong?' she asks immediately. Her fingers are spotted with black marker pen.

'It might be nothing,' I say, trying to reassure her.

Ruiz has picked up a toy from her desk – a fluffy animal stuck on the end of a pen.

'Confiscated,' she explains. 'You should see my collection.'

She straightens a stack of essays and tucks them inside a folder. I look around. 'You're teaching at your old school.'

'Who would have thought?' she says. 'I was a complete tearaway at school. Not as bad as Sylvie, mind you. That's why they were always trying to separate us.'

235

She's nervous. It makes her want to talk. I let her carry on, knowing she'll run out of steam.

'My careers advisor told me I'd become an out-of-work actress who waited tables. I did have one teacher, Mr Halliday – he taught me English – who said I should consider teaching. My parents are still laughing.'

She glances at Ruiz and back to me, growing more anxious.

'You mentioned that Helen Chambers sent you an email organising the reunion.'

She nods.

'It must have come from someone else.'

'Why?'

'Helen died three months ago.'

The folder slides from Maureen's fingers and essay papers spill across the floor. She curses and bends, trying to gather them together. Her hands are shaking.

'How?' she whispers.

'She drowned. It was a ferry accident in Greece. Her daughter was with her. We spoke to her parents this morning.'

'Oh, those poor, poor people . . . poor Helen.'

I'm on the floor beside her, collecting the scattered papers, bundling them haphazardly back into the folder. Something has changed in Maureen, a hollowness that echoes in her heartbeat. She's suddenly in a dark place, listening to a dull repeated rhythm in her head.

'But if Helen died three months ago – how did she . . . I mean . . . she . . .'

'Someone else must have sent the email.'

'Who?'

'We were hoping you might know.'

She shakes her head, sticky-eyed and wavering, as if suddenly unable to recognise her surroundings or to remember where she's supposed to be next.

'It's lunchtime,' I tell her.

'Oh, right.'

'Can I see the email?'

She nods. 'Come to the staff room. There's a computer.'

We follow her along the corridor and up another set of stairs. Chatter and laughter flood through the windows from outside, filling even the quietest corners.

Two students are waiting outside the staffroom. They want an extension on an English assignment. Maureen is too preoccupied to listen to their excuses. She gives them until Monday and sends them on their way.

The staffroom is almost completely deserted except for a fossil of a man, motionless in his chair with his eyes closed. I think he's sleeping until I notice the ear jacks. He doesn't stir as Maureen sits at a computer and logs on with her username and password. She opens her email messages and searches backward through the dates.

The message from Helen Chambers is headed: *Guess who's back in town?* It was sent on September 16 and copied to Christine Wheeler and Sylvia Furness.

> *Hi gang,*
>
> *It's me. I'm back in the country and looking forward to seeing you all. How about we get together this Friday at the Garrick's Head? Champagne and chips all round – just like the old days.*
>
> *I can't believe it's been eight years. I hope you're all fatter and frumpier than I am – (that means you too, Sylvie.) I might even get my legs waxed for the occasion.*
>
> *Be there or be square. The Garrick's Head. 7.30 p.m. Friday. I can't wait.*
>
> *Love Helen*

'Does it sound like her?' I ask.

'Yes.'

'Anything strange about it?'

Maureen shakes her head. 'We used to go to the Garrick's Head all the time. In our last year at Oakfield Helen was the only one of us who had a car. She used to drive us all home.'

The message came through a web-based server. It's easy to create an account and get a password and username.

'You mentioned that she emailed you earlier.'

Again she searches for Helen's name. The previous message arrived on May 29.

Dear Mo, it begins. It must be Maureen's nickname.

Long time no see . . . or hear. Sorry I'm such a slack correspondent, but I have my reasons. Things have been tough these last few years – with lots of changes and challenges. The big news is that I've left my husband. It's a long sad story, which I won't go into now, suffice to say that things didn't work out for us. For a long while I've been terribly lost but now I'm almost out of the woods.

For the next few months I'm taking a holiday with my beautiful daughter Chloe. We're going to clear our heads and have some adventures, which are long overdue.

Stay tuned. I'll let you know when I'm coming home. We'll get together at the Garrick's Head and have a night out with the old gang. Do they still do champagne and chips?

I miss you and Sylvie and Christine. I'm sorry you haven't heard from me in so long. I'll explain it all later.

Lots of love to all,
Helen.

I read both messages again. The language and neat construction are similar, along with casual tone and use of short sentences. Nothing stands out as being forced or fabricated yet Helen Chambers wasn't alive to write the second email.

She wrote of being 'out of the woods' referring I assume to her marriage.

'Was there anything else?' I ask. 'Letters, postcards, phone calls . . .'

Maureen shakes her head.

'What was Helen like?' I ask.

She smiles. 'Adorable.'

'I need a little more than that.'

'I know, I'm sorry.' Colour is returned to her cheeks. She glances at her colleague, who still hasn't stirred in his chair.

'Helen was the sensible one. She was the last one of us to have a boyfriend. Sylvie spent years trying to hook her up with different guys, but Helen didn't feel any pressure. Sometimes I felt sorry for her.'

'Why's that?'

'She always said her father wanted a son and she could never quite match up to his expectations. She did have a brother, but he died when Helen was young. Some sort of accident with a tractor.'

Maureen turns in a worn swivel chair and crosses her legs. I ask her again how she and Helen lost touch. Her lips tighten and jerk at the corners.

'It just seemed to happen. I don't think her husband liked us very much. Sylvia thought he was jealous of how close we all were.'

'Do you remember his name?'

'Gideon.'

'Did you ever meet him?'

'Once. Helen and Gideon came back from Northern Ireland for her father's sixtieth birthday party. People were invited for the whole weekend, but Helen and Gideon left on Saturday at lunchtime. Something happened. I don't know what.

'Gideon was quite strange. Very secretive. Apparently he only invited one person to their wedding – his father – who got hideously drunk and embarrassed him.'

'What does this Gideon do?'

'He's something or other in the military, but none of us ever saw him in uniform. We used to joke that he was some sort of spy, like in *Spooks*, you know the TV programme? Helen sent this one letter to Christine that had red ink stamped across the flap saying it had been scanned and opened for security reasons.'

'Where was the letter posted?'

'Germany. After Helen married they were stationed in Northern Ireland and later they went to Germany.'

Another teacher has turned up at the staffroom. She nods to us, curious about our presence, and collects a mobile phone from a desk drawer, taking it outside to make a call.

Maureen gives her head a clearing shake. 'Poor Mr and Mrs Chambers.'

'Did you know them well?'

'Not really. Mr Chambers was big and loud. I remember this one particular day when he tried to squeeze into a pair of breeches and boots to go hunting. God, he looked a sight. I felt more sorry for the horse than I did for the fox.' She smiles. 'How are they?'

'Sad.'

'They also seem frightened,' adds Ruiz, who is gazing out the window at the playground. 'Can you think of a reason?'

Maureen shakes her head and her brown eyes gaze hard into mine. Another question is hovering on her lips.

'Do you know why? I mean, whoever did this to Chris and Sylvie, what did he want?'

'I don't know.'

'Will he stop now, do you think?'

Ruiz turns away from the window. 'Do you have any children, Maureen?'

'A son.'

'How old is he?'

'Sixteen. Why?'

She knows the answer but anxiety makes her ask the question anyway.

'Is there anywhere you could stay for a few days?' I ask.

Fear catches alight in her eyes. 'I could ask Bruno if he could put us up.'

'That might be a good idea.'

My mobile is vibrating in my pocket. It's Veronica Cray.

'I tried you at home, Professor. Your wife didn't know where you were.'

'How can I help you, DI?'

'I'm looking for Darcy Wheeler.'

'She's with her aunt.'

'Not any more – she ran away last night. Packed a bag and took some of her mother's jewellery. I thought she might try to reach you? She seems to like you.'

Saliva turns to dust in my mouth.

'I don't think she'll do that.'

Veronica Cray doesn't ask why. I'm not going to tell her.

'You talked to her yesterday after the funeral. How did she seem?'

'She was upset. Her aunt wants her to live in Spain.'

'Worse things in life.'

'Not to Darcy.'

'So she didn't say anything . . . confide?'

'No.' Guilt seems to thicken the word until I can barely spit it out. 'What are you going to do?' I ask.

'Figured I might leave it a day or two. See what happens.'

'She's only sixteen.'

'Old enough to find her way home.'

I'm about to argue. She's not about to listen. For DI Cray this is an added complication, one that she doesn't need. Darcy hasn't been kidnapped and she's not a threat to herself or a danger to the public. Missing Persons won't break any records looking for a teenage runaway. In the meantime, there's a press briefing organised for three o'clock this afternoon. I'm supposed to make a statement and appeal directly to the killer.

The call ends and I relay the news to Ruiz, who is driving.

'She'll turn up,' he says, sounding like he's seen it a dozen times before. Maybe he has. It doesn't make me feel any better. I call Darcy's mobile and get a recorded message:

'Hi, this is me. I'm unavailable. Leave me a message after the beep. Make it short and sweet – just like me . . .'

It beeps.

'Hey, it's Joe. Call me . . .' What else am I going to say? 'I just want to know if you're OK. People are worried. I'm worried. So call me, OK? Please.'

Ruiz is listening.

I punch another number. Julianne answers.

'The police are trying to find you,' she says.

'I know. Darcy has run away.'

The silence is meant to be neutral but she's caught between concern and exasperation.

'Do they know where she's gone?'

'No.'

'Is there anything I can do?'

'Darcy may call or come to the house. Keep your eye out for her.'

'I'll ask around the village.'

'Good idea.'

'When are you coming home?'

'Soon. I have to go to a press briefing.'

'Will it be over then?'

'Soon.'

Julianne wants me to say yes. 'I found a nanny. She's Australian.'

'Well, I won't hold that against her.'

'She starts tomorrow.'

'That's good.'

She hangs on, expecting me to say something more. The silence says otherwise.

'Have you taken your pills?'

'Yes.'

'I have to go.'

'OK.'

She hangs up.

37

The conference room at Trinity Road police station is a stark, windowless place, with vinyl chairs and strip lighting. Every seat is taken and most of the side walls are supporting shoulders.

The national newspapers have rolled out their gun reporters rather than rely on West-Country stringers. I recognise some of them – Luckett from the *Telegraph*, Montgomery from *The Times* and Pearson from the *Daily Mail*. Some of them know me.

I watch from a side door. Monk is directing the camera crews, trying to stop any arguments. He gives me a nod. DI Cray goes first, wearing a charcoal jacket and white shirt. I follow her onto a slightly raised platform where a long table faces the media. Microphones and recording equipment have been taped to the front edge, showing station bandwidths and logos.

The TV lights are turned on and flashguns fire. The DI pours a glass of water for herself, giving the reporters time to settle.

'Ladies and gentlemen, thank you for coming,' she says, addressing the audience rather than the cameras. 'This is a briefing, not a press conference. I will be reading a statement of the facts and then handing over to Professor Joseph O'Loughlin. There will be a limited opportunity to ask questions at the end of the briefing.

'As you're aware, a task force has been set up to investigate the murder of Sylvia Furness. A second suspicious death has been added to this investigation – that of Christine Wheeler, who jumped from the Clifton Suspension Bridge a week ago last Friday.'

An image of Christine Wheeler is projected onto a screen behind the DI's head. It's a holiday snap, taken at a water park. Christine's hair is wet and she's posing in a sarong and T-shirt.

There are murmurs of astonishment from the ranks. Many in the room saw Christine Wheeler die. How did such an obvious suicide suddenly become a murder victim?

Meanwhile, the facts are being presented – age, height, hair colour, single status and her career as a wedding planner. Soon the details shift to the day of her death. Christine's last journey is outlined, the phone calls and her walk through Leigh Woods wearing only a raincoat and high-heel shoes. CCTV images from the bridge are flashed onto the screen.

The reporters are growing restless. They want an explanation but DI Cray won't be rushed. She is listing details of the phone calls. Certain facts are withheld. There is no mention of the ballet shoes that were delivered to Darcy's school or the pet rabbit left on Alice Furness's doorstep. These are things that only the killer could know which means they can be used to filter out genuine callers from the hoaxers.

DI Cray has finished. She introduces me. I flip through my notes and clear my throat.

'Sometimes in my work I come across individuals who fascinate me and appal me in equal measure. The man who committed these crimes fascinates and appals me. He is intelligent, articulate, manipulative, sadistic, cruel and pitiless. He didn't lash out with his fists. He destroyed these women by preying on their worst fears. I want to understand why. I want to understand his motives and why he chose these women.

'If he's listening now or if he watches on TV or if he reads about it in the newspapers, I'd really like him to get in contact with me. I want him to help me understand.'

There is a hubbub at the back of the room. I pause. Veronica Cray stiffens in alarm. I follow her gaze. Assistant Chief Constable

Fowler is pushing his way through the crowded doorway. Heads turn. His arrival has become an event.

There are no spare chairs in the room except at the main table. For a fleeting moment the Assistant Chief Constable considers his options and then continues along the central aisle until he reaches the front of the room. Placing his hat on the table, leather gloves tucked inside, he takes a seat.

'Carry on,' he says gruffly.

I hesitate . . . look at Cray . . . back at my notes.

Someone calls out a question. Two more follow. I try to ignore them. Montgomery, the man from *The Times*, is on his feet.

'You said he preyed on their worst fears. Exactly what do you mean? I saw footage of Christine Wheeler on the Clifton Suspension Bridge. She jumped. Nobody pushed her.'

'She was threatened.'

'How was she threatened?'

'Let me finish, then I'll take questions.'

More reporters are standing, unwilling to wait. DI Cray tries to intervene, but Fowler beats her to the microphone, calling for quiet.

'This is a formal briefing, not a free-for-all,' he booms. 'You'll ask your questions one at a time or you'll get nothing at all.'

The reporters resume their seats. 'That's better,' says Fowler, who peers at the assembly like a disappointed schoolmaster, itching to use the cane.

A hand is raised. It belongs to Montgomery. 'How did he threaten her, sir?'

The question is directed at Fowler, who pulls the nearest microphone even closer.

'We are investigating the possibility that this man intimidates and manipulates women by targeting their daughters. There has been speculation that he threatens the daughters to make the mother co-operate.'

This drops a depth charge in the room and thirty hands shoot skyward. Fowler points to another reporter. The briefing has turned into a question and answer session.

'Are the daughters harmed?'

'No, the daughters aren't touched, but these women were made to believe otherwise.'

'How?'

'We don't know at this stage.'

DI Cray is furious. The tension at the table is obvious. Pearson from the *Daily Mail* senses an opportunity.

'Assistant Chief Constable, we've heard Professor O'Loughlin say that he wants to "understand" the killer. Is that your desire?'

Fowler leans forward. 'No.' He leans back.

'Do you agree with the Professor's assessment?'

He leans forward. 'No.'

'Why's that, sir?'

'Professor O'Loughlin's services are not materially important to this investigation.'

'So you can see no benefit in his offender profile?'

'None whatsoever.'

'Well, why is he here?'

'That's not a question I'm going to answer.'

Raised hands are slowly being lowered. The reporters are happy to let Pearson prod the Assistant Chief Constable, looking for a raw nerve. Veronica Cray tries to interrupt but Fowler won't surrender the microphone.

Pearson doesn't let up. 'Professor O'Loughlin has said that he's fascinated by the killer – are you also fascinated, Assistant Chief Constable?'

'No.'

'He said he wants the killer to call him, don't you think that's important?'

Fowler snaps. 'I don't give a toss what the Professor wants. You people, the media watch too much TV. You think murders are solved by shrinks and scientists and psychics. Bollocks! Murders are solved by good, solid, old-fashioned detective work – by knocking on doors, by interviewing witnesses and by taking statements.'

Ropes of spit are landing on the microphones as Fowler stabs his finger at Pearson, punctuating each of his points.

'What the police don't need in this investigation is some

university professor who has never made an arrest or ridden in a police car or confronted a violent criminal telling us how to do our job. And it doesn't take a degree in psychology to know we're dealing with a pervert and a coward, who targets the weak and the vulnerable because he can't get a woman, or hold on to one, or because he wasn't breastfed as a baby . . .

'The profile Professor O'Loughlin has drawn up doesn't pass the so-what test in my opinion. Yes, we're looking for a local man, aged thirty to fifty who works shifts and hates women. Fairly bloody obvious, I would have thought. No science in that.

'The Professor wants us to show this man respect. He wants to reach out to him with the hand of compassion and understanding. Not on my watch. This perpetrator is a scumbag and he'll get all the respect he wants in prison because that's where he's going.'

Every set of eyes in the room is focused on me. I'm under attack but what can I do? DI Cray takes hold of my forearm. She doesn't want me responding.

Questions are still being shouted:

'How does he threaten the daughters?'

'Were the women raped?'

'Is it true that he tortured them?'

'How were they tortured?'

Fowler ignores them. Donning his hat, he straightens it, sliding a palm across the brim. Then he slaps his gloves from one palm to the other and marches down the central aisle as if leaving the parade ground.

Flashguns are firing. Questions continue:

'Will he kill again?'

'Why did he choose these women?'

'Do you think he knew them?'

Veronica Cray cups her hand over the microphone and whispers in my ear. I nod and stand to leave, angry and embarrassed. There are howls of protest. It's become a blood sport, not a briefing.

DI Cray turns slowly and fixes the room with a fierce stare. It's a statement in itself. The press briefing is over.

38

Veronica Cray rocks along the corridor like a ship's captain leaving the bridge of her sinking vessel, retiring to her quarters while others lower the lifeboats.

'That was a complete fucking disaster.'

'It could have been worse,' I murmur, still stunned by the vitriol of Fowler's attack.

'How exactly could it have been any worse?'

'At least we warned people to be careful.'

Phones are ringing in the incident room. I have no idea what sorts of calls are being generated or what filters are in place to weed out genuine information.

Many of the detectives are trying hard not to look at me. News of my public humiliation has reached them already. Most have adopted homebound expressions, biding their time before they can put on their coats and leave.

DI Cray shuts her office door. I sit before her. Ignoring the NO SMOKING sign, she lights up and opens the window a crack. Aiming a remote control, she turns on a small TV tucked in one corner on a filing cabinet. She finds a news channel and mutes the sound.

I know what she's going to do. She's going to punish herself by watching the press briefing being broadcast.

'Want a drink?'

'No thank you.'

She reaches inside an umbrella stand and takes out a bottle of Scotch. A coffee mug doubles as a glass. I watch her pour and then return the bottle to its hiding place.

'I have an ethical question, professor,' she says, swilling the Scotch like mouthwash. 'A tabloid reporter and an assistant chief constable are trapped in a burning car and you can only save one. Who do you save?'

'I don't know.'

'There's only one true dilemma – whether you go to lunch or to a movie.'

She doesn't laugh. She's being serious.

A file is sitting on her desk decorated with a yellow Post-it note. It contains printouts from the Police National Computer. The database has been trawled for similar crimes. She hands me the cover sheet.

In Bristol two drug dealers tortured a prostitute who they accused of being a police informant. They nailed her to a tree and sexually assaulted her with a bottle.

A stevedore in Felixstowe came home to find his wife in bed with their next-door neighbour. He tied the neighbour to a chair and tortured him with his wife's curling irons.

Two German business partners fell out over the division of profits and one of them fled to Manchester. He was found dead in a hotel room with his arms stretched across the top of a table and his fingers severed.

'That's it,' she says, lighting one cigarette off another. 'No mobile phones, no daughters, no threats. We got sweet FA.'

For the first time I notice the shadows beneath her eyes and creases in the contours of her face. How much sleep has she had in the past ten days?

'You're looking for the obvious answer,' I say.

'What does that mean?'

'If you see a man in the street, dressed in a white coat with a stethoscope around his neck, straight away you think he's a doctor. And then you extrapolate. He probably has a nice car, a nice house, a trophy wife; he likes to holiday in France, she prefers Italy. They ski every year.'

'What's your point?'

'What are the odds that you're wrong about him – one in twenty, one in fifty? He might *not* be a doctor. He could be a food inspector or a lab technician, who happened to pick up a stethoscope that someone dropped. He might be on his way to a fancy dress party. We make assumptions and normally they're right, but sometimes they're wrong. That's when we have to think laterally, outside the square. The obvious solution, the easiest solution, is normally the best one – but not always. Not this time.'

Veronica Cray looks at me steadily with a formless smile, waiting.

'I don't think the murders have anything to do with the wedding planning business,' I say. 'I think you should look at another angle.'

I tell her about the reunion of old school friends at the Garrick's Head a week before Christine Wheeler died. Sylvia Furness was also there. It was organised by email, but the person who supposedly sent the invitations drowned three months ago in a ferry tragedy in Greece. Whoever sent the email set up an account in her name or had access to her password and username.

'So we're looking at family, friends, her husband . . .'

'I'd look at her husband first. They were separated. His name is Gideon Tyler. He might be stationed with British Forces in Germany.'

The DI wants to know more. I describe our visit to Stoneleigh Manor, where Bryan and Claudia Chambers were living like prisoners behind security cameras, motion sensors and jagged glass.

'Gideon Tyler knew both victims. They were bridesmaids at Helen Chambers' wedding.'

'What do you know about this ferry accident?'

'Only what I read at the time.'

The detective blinks at me slowly as if she's stared too long at a single object.

'OK, so we're dealing with one offender. He was either invited inside their houses or he broke in. He knew things about their wardrobes, their make-up, Sylvia's handcuffs. He knew their telephone numbers and what cars they drove. He orchestrated to meet their daughters earlier to obtain information. Are we agreed on this?'

'So far.'

'And the same man broke into the Wheelers' house and opened the condolence cards.'

'A reasonable assumption.'

'He was looking for something.'

'Or searching for someone.'

'His next victim?'

'I wouldn't automatically jump to that conclusion, but it's certainly a possibility.'

The detective's face betrays nothing. Emotion would be out of place like a birthmark or a nervous tic.

'This Maureen Bracken, is she at risk?'

'Quite possibly.'

'Well, I can't put her under guard unless there's a specific threat against her or hard evidence that she's a high probability target.'

I don't have any hard evidence. It's only supposition. A theory.

The DI glances at her TV and aims the remote. A news bulletin is beginning. Images from the press briefing flash across the screen. I'm not going to watch it. Being there was embarrassing enough.

Outside the day has disappeared. Everything about my clothes and my thoughts has a soiled wrapper feel to it. I'm tired. Tired of talking. Tired of people. Tired of wishing things made sense.

Christine Wheeler and Sylvia Furness grew tired. It was as if their killer pressed a fast forward button and stole years from their lives, decades of experiences both good and bad. He used up their energy, their fight, their will to live; then he watched them die.

Julianne was right. The dead remain dead, no matter what happens. I understand that intellectually but not in the hollow space that echoes in my chest. The heart has reasons that reason cannot understand.

39

The school yearbook is open beneath my fingers, displaying her class photograph. Friends are behind her and beside her. Some of them haven't changed at all since 1988. Others have grown fat and dyed their hair. And just one or two have blossomed like late flowering roses amid the weeds.

Surprisingly, many have stayed in the area. Married. Had children. Divorced. Separated. One died of breast cancer. One lives in New Zealand. Two live with each other.

The TV is on. I flick through the channels but there's nothing to watch. A rolling banner catches my attention. It says something about a manhunt for a double killer.

A pretty, plastic woman is reading the news with her eyes focused slightly to the left where an autocue must be rolling. She crosses to a reporter who talks to camera, nodding sagely with all the sincerity of a doctor holding a needle behind his back.

Then the scene changes to a conference room. The dyke detective and the shrink are side-by-side like Laurel and Hardy. Laverne and Shirley. Torvill and Dean. One of the great show-business partnerships is born.

They're talking to reporters. Most of the questions are being answered by a senior policeman who has a bug up his arse about something. I turn up the sound.

' . . . we're dealing with a pervert and a coward, who targets the weak and vulnerable because he can't get a woman or hold on to one, or because he wasn't breastfed as a baby.'

'The profile Professor O'Loughlin has drawn up doesn't pass the so-what test in my opinion. Yes, we're looking for a local man, aged thirty to fifty who works shifts and hates women. Fairly bloody obvious, I would have thought. No science in that.

'The Professor wants us to show this man respect. He wants to reach out to him with the hand of compassion and understanding. Not on my watch. This perpetrator is a scumbag and he'll get all the respect he wants in prison because that's where he's going . . .'

The media circus ends in uproar. The plastic woman moves on to another story.

Who are these people? They have no idea of who they're dealing with and what I'm capable of. They think it's a game. They think I'm a fucking amateur.

I can walk through walls.

I can unlock people's minds.

I can listen to the pins fall into place and the tumblers turn.

Click . . . click . . . click . . .

40

I wake in the folds of a duvet holding a pillow. I missed seeing
Julianne wake and get dressed. I like seeing her slip out of bed in
the half-light and the cold, lifting her nightdress over her head.
My eyes are drawn to her small brown nipples and the dimple in
the small of her back, just above the elastic of her knickers.

This morning she is already downstairs, making breakfast for
the girls. Other sounds drift from outside – a tractor in the lane,
a dog barking, Mrs Nutall calling to her cats. Opening the curtains,
I assess the day. Blue sky. Distant clouds.

A man is standing in the churchyard, looking at the gravestones.
I can just make him out through the branches, wiping his eyes
and holding a small vase of flowers. Perhaps he lost a wife or a
mother or a father. It could be an anniversary or a birthday. He
bends and digs a small hollow, resting the vase inside and pressing
earth around it.

Sometimes I wonder if I should take the girls to a church service.
I'm not particularly religious but I'd like them to have a sense of
the unknown. I don't want them to be too obsessed with truth
and certainty.

I get changed and make my way downstairs. Charlie is in the
kitchen wearing her school uniform. Soft strands of her hair have
pulled out of her ponytail, framing her face.

'Is this bacon for me?' I ask, picking up a rasher.

'It's not mine. I don't eat bacon,' says Charlie.

'Since when?'

'Since forever.'

Forever seems to have been redefined since I was at school.

'Why?'

'I'm a vegetarian. My friend Ashley says we shouldn't be killing defenceless animals to satisfy our lust for leather shoes and bacon sandwiches.'

'How old is Ashley?'

'Thirteen.'

'And what does her father do?'

'He's a capitalist.'

'Do you know what that is?'

'Not exactly.'

'If you don't eat meat, how will you get iron?'

'Spinach.'

'You hate spinach.'

'Broccoli.'

'Ditto.'

'Four of the five food groups will be enough.'

'There are five?'

'Don't be so sarcastic, Dad.'

Julianne has taken Emma to get the morning papers. I make myself a coffee and put slices of bread in the toaster. The phone rings.

'Hello?'

There's no answer. I hear the soft whoosh of traffic; brakes are applied, vehicles slow and stop. There must be an intersection nearby or a set of traffic lights.

'Hello? Can you hear me?'

Nothing.

'Is that you, Darcy?'

There's still no answer. I imagine I can hear her breathing. The traffic lights have changed again. Vehicles move off.

'Just talk to me, Darcy, tell me you're OK.'

The line goes dead. I press my finger to the receiver button and

255

let it go. I dial Darcy's mobile. I get the same recorded message as before.

I wait for the beep.

'Darcy. Next time talk to me.'

I hang up. Charlie has been listening.

'Why did she run away?'

'Who told you she ran away?'

'Mum.'

'Darcy doesn't want to live in Spain with her aunt.'

'Where else will she live?'

I don't answer. I'm making myself a bacon sandwich.

'She could live with us,' says Charlie.

'I thought you didn't like her.'

She shrugs and pours herself a glass of orange juice. 'She was OK, I guess. She had some great clothes.'

'That's all?'

'Well, no, not the only thing. I sort of feel sorry for her – about what happened to her mum.'

Julianne appears through the back door with Emma. 'Who do you feel sorry for?'

'Darcy.'

Julianne looks at me. 'Have you heard from her?'

I shake my head.

Wearing a simple dress and cardigan she looks happier, younger, more relaxed. Emma ducks in and out between her legs. Julianne holds down the hem as a modesty precaution.

'Can you drop Charlie at school? She's missed the bus.'

'Sure.'

'The new nanny will be here in fifteen minutes.'

'The Australian.'

'You make her sound like a convict.'

'I have nothing against Australians but if she mentions the cricket she'll have to leave.'

She rolls her eyes. 'I was thinking that maybe – now that Imogen has arrived – we could go for dinner tonight. It could be an "us date".'

'An "us date". Mmmmm.' I grab Emma and haul her onto my

lap. 'Well, I might be available. I will have to check my busy schedule. But if I do say yes, I don't want you getting any funny ideas.'

'Me? Never. Although I may wear my black lingerie.'

Charlie covers her ears. 'I know what you guys are talking about and it's sooooo gross.'

'What's gross?' asks Emma.

'Never mind,' we chorus.

Julianne and I used to have regular 'us dates' – nights set aside with a babysitter booked. The first time I arranged one I made a point of bringing flowers and knocking on the front door. Julianne thought it was so sweet she wanted to take me straight up to the bedroom and skip dinner.

The phone rings again. I'm surprised at how quickly I pick it up. Everyone is staring at me.

'Hello?'

Again there is no answer.

'Is that you, Darcy?'

A male voice answers. 'Is Julianne there?'

'Who's calling?'

'Dirk.'

Disappointment morphs into irritation. 'Did you call earlier?'

'Excuse me?'

'Did you call about ten minutes ago?'

He doesn't answer the question. 'Is Julianne there or not?'

She pulls the phone from my hand and takes it upstairs to the study. I watch her through the stair rails as she closes the door.

The nanny arrives. She is everything I imagined: freckled, photogenic and blighted by a singsong Australian accent that makes her sound like she's asking a question all the time. Her name is Imogen and she is rather large across the beam. I know that's an incredibly sexist description but I'm not just talking about 24oz Porterhouse big, I'm talking huge.

According to Julianne, Imogen was definitely the most qualified candidate for the job. She has loads of experience, interviewed well and will do extra babysitting if required. None of these factors are the main reason Julianne hired her. Imogen isn't competition. She's not the least bit threatening unless she accidentally sat on somebody.

I carry her two suitcases upstairs. She says the room is awesome. The house is also awesome, so is the TV and my aging Escort. Collectively, everything is 'absolutely awesome.'

Julianne is still on the phone. There must be some sort of problem at work. Either that or she and Dirk are having phone sex.

I've never met Dirk. I can't even remember his surname – yet I dislike him with an irrational zeal. I hate the sound of his voice. I hate that he buys my wife gifts; that he travels with her, that he calls her at home on a day off. Mostly, I hate the way she laughs so easily for him.

When Julianne was pregnant with Charlie and going through the tired, tearful, 'I feel fat' stage, I tried to find ways of cheering her up. I booked us a holiday in Jamaica. She vomited the entire flight. A minibus picked us up from the airport and drove us to the resort, which was lovely and tropical, teeming with bougainvillea and hibiscus. We changed and headed for the beach. A naked black man walked past us. Butt-naked. Dangling. Next came a nude woman, textile free, wearing a blossom in her hair. Julianne looked at me strangely, her pregnancy bursting from her sarong.

Finally, a smiling young Jamaican man in staff whites pointed to my trunks.

'Clothes off, mon.'

'Pardon?'

'This is a nekkid beach.'

'Uhhhhh?'

Suddenly the slogan from the brochure came back to me: 'Be Wicked for a Week'. And the penny dropped. I had booked my heavily pregnant wife on a week-long package holiday at a nudist resort where 'sex on the beach' wasn't just the name of a cocktail.

Julianne should have killed me. Instead she laughed. She laughed so hard I thought her waters might break and our first child would be delivered by a Jamaican called 'Tripod' wearing nothing but sun-block. She hasn't laughed like that for a long while.

After dropping Charlie at school, I detour to Bath Library. It's on the first floor of the Podium Centre in Northgate Street, up an escalator and through twin glass doors. The librarians are boxed behind a counter on the right.

'During the summer there was a ferry disaster in Greece,' I say to one of them. She's been changing an ink cartridge in a printer and two of her fingertips are stained black.

'I remember,' she says. 'I was on holiday in Turkey. There were storms. Our campsite was flooded.'

She starts telling me the story, which features wet sleeping bags, near pneumonia, and spending two nights in a laundry block. Not surprisingly, she remembers the date. It was the last week in July.

I ask to see the newspaper files, choosing the the *Guardian* and a local paper, the *Western Daily Press*. She'll bring them out to me, she says.

I take a desk in a quiet corner and wait for the bound volumes to be delivered. She has to push them on a trolley. I help her lift the first one onto the desk.

'What are you after?' she asks, smiling absently.

'I don't know yet.'

'Well, good luck.'

I turn the pages delicately, scanning the headlines. It doesn't take long to find what I'm looking for.

FOURTEEN DEAD IN GREEK FERRY DISASTER

A rescue operation is under way in the Aegean Sea for survivors from a Greek ferry that sank in gale force winds off the island of Patmos.

The Greek Coast Guard says fourteen people have been confirmed dead and eight people are missing after the *Argo Hellas* sank eleven miles north-east of Patmos Harbour. More than forty passengers – most of them foreign holidaymakers – were plucked from the water by local fishing boats and

259

pleasure craft. Survivors were taken to a health centre on Patmos, many suffering from cuts, bruises and the effects of hypothermia. Eight seriously injured passengers have been airlifted to hospitals in Athens.

An English hotelier helping in the rescue, Nick Barton, said those on board the ferry included UK citizens, Germans, Italians, Australians and local Greeks.

The eighteen-year-old ferry sank just after 2130 (1830 GMT) only fifteen minutes after leaving the port of Patmos. According to survivors it was swamped by the huge seas and sank so quickly that many had no time to don lifejackets before they jumped from the side.

The heavy seas and high winds have hampered the search for more survivors. Throughout the night Greek aircraft dropped flares in the sea and a helicopter from the Royal Navy's HMS Invincible assisted with the search.

Turning the pages, I follow the story as it unfolds. The ferry sank on 24 July during a storm that caused widespread destruction across the Aegean. A container ship ran aground on the island of Skiros and further south a Maltese tanker broke in two and sank in the Sea of Crete.

Survivors of the ferry tragedy told their stories to reporters. In the final moments before the *Argo Hellas* sank, passengers were hanging from the railings and jumping overboard. Some were trapped inside as the ferry went down.

Forty-one people survived the tragedy and seventeen were confirmed dead. After two days a change in the weather allowed Greek naval divers to recover three more bodies from the wreck but six people were still missing including an American, an elderly French woman, two Greeks and a British mother and daughter. This must have been Helen and Chloe, but their names aren't mentioned for several more days.

A follow up story in the *Western Daily Press* reported that Bryan Chambers was flying to Greece to look for his daughter and granddaughter. Describing him as a Wiltshire businessman, it said he was 'praying for a miracle' and preparing to mount his own search, if the official one failed to find Helen and Chloe.

A further story on Tuesday July 31 said that Mr Chambers had hired a light plane and was combing the beaches and rocky coves of the islands and Turkish coast. The story included a photograph of mother and daughter, who were travelling under Helen's married name. The holiday snap shows them sitting on a rock wall with fishing boats in the background. Helen is wearing a sarong and Jackie O sunglasses while Chloe is dressed in white shorts, sandals and a pink top with shoestring straps.

A week after the sinking, the search for survivors was officially called off and Helen and Chloe were labelled as missing presumed dead. The newspapers took increasingly less interest in the story. The only other reference to mother and daughter concerned a prayer vigil held at a NATO base in Germany where they'd been living. The maritime investigation took evidence from survivors, but the findings could be years away.

My mobile is vibrating silently. No phones are allowed in the library. I step outside the main doors. Press green.

Bruno Kaufman booms in my ear: 'Listen, old boy, I know you're happily married and chief cheerleader for the institution but did you *really* have to tell my ex-wife she should move in with me?'

'It's just for a few days, Bruno.'

'Yes, but it will seem like much longer.'

'Maureen is lovely. Why did you let her go?'

'She drove me away. Well, to be more precise she drove *at me*. I had to jump out of the way. She was behind the wheel of a Range Rover.'

'Why did she do that?'

'She caught me with one of my researchers.'

'A student?'

'A post grad student,' he corrects me, as if resenting the suggestion that he would cheat on his wife with anything less.

'I didn't know you had a son.'

'Yes. Jackson. His mother spoils him. I bribe him. We're your average dysfunctional family. Do you really think Maureen is in danger?'

'It's a precaution.'

261

'I've never seen her this scared.'

'Look after her.'

'Don't worry, old boy. She'll be safe with me.'

The call ends. The mobile vibrates again. This time it's Ruiz. He has something he wants to show me. We arrange to meet at the Fox & Badger. I'm to buy him lunch because it's my turn. I don't know when it became 'my turn' but I'm pleased he's here.

Dropping the car at home, I walk up the hill to the pub. Ruiz has taken a table in the corner, where the ceiling seems to sag. Horse tackle is festooned from the exposed beams.

'It's your shout,' he says, handing me an empty pint glass.

I go to the bar, where half a dozen flushed and lumpy regulars fill the stools, including Nigel the dwarf, whose feet swing back and forth, two feet above the floor.

I nod. They nod back. This passes as a long conversation in this part of Somerset.

Hector the publican pulls a pint of Guinness, letting it rest while he gets me a lemon squash. I set down the fresh pint in front of Ruiz. He watches the bubbles rise, perhaps saying a small prayer to the God of fermentation.

'Here's to drinkin' with bow-legged women.' He raises his glass and half a pint disappears.

'You ever considered the possibility that you might be an alcoholic?'

'Nope. Alcoholics go to meetings,' he replies. 'I don't go to meetings.' He sets down his glass and looks at my squash. 'You're just jealous because you have to drink that lolly water.'

He opens his notebook. It's the same battered marbled collection of curling pages that he always carries, held together with a rubber band.

'I decided to do a little research into Bryan Chambers. Mate in the DTI – Department of Trade and Industry – ran his name through the computer. Chambers came up clean: no fines, no lawsuits, no dodgy contracts: the man's clean . . .'

He sounds disappointed.

'So I decided to run his name through the Police National Computer through a friend of a friend . . .'

'Who shall remain nameless?'

'Exactly. He's called Nameless. Well, Nameless came back to me this morning. Six months ago Chambers took out a protection order against Gideon Tyler.'

'His son-in-law?'

'Yep. Tyler isn't allowed to go within half a mile of the house or Chambers' office. He can't phone, email, text or drive past the front gate.'

'Why?'

'That's the next thing.' He pulls out a fresh page. 'I ran a check on Gideon Tyler. I mean, we know nothing about this guy except his name – which must have got him kicked from one end of the schoolyard to the other, by the way.'

'We know he's military.'

'Right. So I called the MOD – Ministry of Defence. I talked to the personnel department but as soon as I mentioned Gideon Tyler's name they clammed up tighter than a virgin on a prison visit.'

'Why?'

'I don't know. Either they're protecting him or embarrassed by him.'

'Or both.'

Ruiz leans back in his chair and arches his back, stretching his arms behind his head. I can hear his vertebrae separating.

'Then I had Nameless run a check on Gideon Tyler.' He has a manila folder on the chair next to him. He opens it and produces several pages. I recognise the top one as a police incident report. It's dated May 22, 2007. Attached is a summary of facts.

I scan the details. Gideon Tyler was named in a complaint, accused of harassment and of making threatening phone calls to Bryan and Claudia Chambers. Among the list of allegations is a claim that Tyler broke into Stonebridge Manor and searched the house while they slept. He rifled filing cabinets, bureaus and took copies of telephone records, bank statements and emails. It was also alleged that he somehow unlocked a reinforced gun-safe and took a shotgun. Mr and Mrs Chambers woke the next morning and found the loaded weapon lying on the bed between them.

I turn the page, looking for an outcome. There isn't one.

'What happened?'

'Nothing.'

'What do you mean?'

'Tyler was never charged. Insufficient evidence.'

'What about fingerprints, fibres, anything?'

'Nope.'

'This says he made threatening phone calls.'

'Untraceable.'

No wonder the Chambers were so paranoid when we visited.

I look at the date of the police report. Helen Tyler and Chloe were still alive when Tyler allegedly harassed her family. He must have been looking for them.

'What do we know about the separation?' asks Ruiz.

'Nothing except for the email that Helen sent to her friends. She must have run away from Tyler . . . and he wasn't happy about it.'

'You think he's good for this.'

'Maybe.'

'Why would he want to kill his wife's friends?'

'To punish her.'

'But she's dead!'

'It might not matter. He's angry. He feels cheated. Helen took away his daughter. She hid from him. Now he wants to lash out and punish anyone close to her.'

I look again at the police report. Detectives interviewed Gideon Tyler. He must have had an alibi. According to Maureen, he was stationed in Germany. When did he come back to Britain?

'Is there an address for him?' I ask.

'I got a last known and the name of his solicitor. You want to pay him a visit?'

I shake my head. 'The police should handle this one. I'll talk to Veronica Cray.'

41

The window has four panes, dividing the bedroom into quarters. She is naked, fresh from the shower, with her hair wrapped in a pink turban and cheeks flushed.

Nice legs, nice tits, nice body – the full package with all the accessories. Man could have a lot of fun playing with a woman like that.

Unwrapping the towel, she bends forward, letting her dark hair drape over her face and her breasts swing. She dries the damp locks and tosses her head back.

Next she raises each foot in turn, drying between her toes. Then comes moisturiser, massaged into her skin, starting at her ankles and moving up. This is better than porn. Come on, baby, a little higher . . . show me what you got . . .

Something makes her turn towards the window. Her eyes are staring directly into mine, but she cannot see me. Instead she studies her reflection, turning one way and then the other, running her hands over her stomach, her buttocks and her thighs, looking for stretch marks or signs of age.

Sitting at a mirrored vanity with her back to me, she uses a hairdryer and some contraption to straighten her hair. I can see her reflection. She pulls faces and studies every line and crease on her face, stretching, plucking and poking. More creams and serums are applied.

Watching a woman dress is far sexier than seeing her undress. It's a dance without the music; a bedroom ballet, with every movement so practised and easy. This isn't some poxy whore stripping in a seedy bar or sex club. She's a real woman with a real figure. A pair of knickers slides up her legs, over her thighs. White. Maybe they've got a blue trim. I can't tell from here. Her arms slide into the straps of a matching bra, lifting and separating her breasts. She adjusts the under-wire, making it comfortable.

What will she wear? She holds a dress against her body . . . a second . . . a third. It's decided. She sits on the bed and rolls tights over her right foot and ankle and up her leg. She leans back on the bed and pulls the opaque black fabric over her thighs and her buttocks.

Standing again, she shimmies into the dress, letting the fabric fall to just below her knees. She's almost ready. A turn to the left, checking out her reflection in the window, then a turn to the right.

Her watch is sitting on the windowsill. She picks it up and slips it onto her wrist, checking out the time. Then she glances out the window at the fading light. The first star is out. Make a wish, my angel. Don't tell anyone what you wish for.

42

The restaurant is on the river. There is a view across the water to factories and warehouses, reclaimed and renovated into apartments. Julianne has ordered wine.

'Do you want to taste?' she asks, knowing I miss it. I take a sip from her glass. The sauvignon detonates sweetly on my palate, cold and sharp, making me yearn for more. I slide the glass back towards her, touching her fingers, and think of the last person to share a bottle of wine with her. Was it Dirk? I wonder if he loved the sound of her voice, which is capable of rendering so many languages beautiful.

Julianne raises her eyes sideways a moment to look at me.

'Would you marry me again if you had your time over?'

'Of course I would, I love you.'

She looks away, towards the river, which is painted the colours of navigation lights. I can see her face reflected in the glass.

'Where did the question come from?'

'Nowhere really,' she replies. 'I just I wondered if you regretted not waiting a little longer. You were only twenty-five.'

'And *you* were twenty-two. It made no difference.'

She takes another sip of wine and becomes aware of my concern. Smiling, she reaches across the table and squeezes my hand. 'Don't look so worried. I'm just feeling old, that's all. Sometimes I look in the mirror and wish I was younger. Then I feel guilty because I have so much more to be thankful for.'

'You're not old. You're beautiful.'

'You always say that.'

'Because it's true.'

She shakes her head helplessly. 'I know I shouldn't be so vain and self-obsessed. You're the one who has every right to be self-conscious and feel resentful.'

'I don't resent anything. I have you. I have the girls. That's enough.'

She looks at me knowingly. 'If it's enough why did you throw yourself into this murder investigation?'

'I was asked.'

'You could have said no.'

'I saw a chance to help.'

'Oh, come on, Joe, you wanted a challenge. You were bored. You didn't like being at home with Emma. At least be honest about it.'

I reach for my glass of water. My hand trembles.

Julianne's voice softens. 'I know what you're like, Joe. You're trying to save Darcy's mother all over again but that's not possible. She's gone.'

'I can stop it happening to someone else.'

'Maybe you can. You're a good man. You care about people. You care about Darcy. I love that about you. But you have to understand why I'm frightened. I don't want you involved – not after last time. You've done your bit. You've given your time. Let someone else help the police from now on.'

I watch her eyes pool with emotion and feel a desperate desire to make her happy.

'I didn't ask to become involved. It just happened,' I say.

'By accident.'

'Exactly. And sometimes we can't ignore accidents. We can't drive by without stopping or pretend we haven't seen them. We have to stop. We call for an ambulance. We try to help . . .'

'And then we leave it to the experts.'

'What if I *am* one of the experts?'

Julianne frowns and her lips tighten. 'I may have to go to Italy next week,' she announces suddenly.

'Why?'

'The TV station deal has hit a snag. One of the institutional shareholders is holding out. Unless we get ninety per cent approval the deal falls over.'

'When will you leave?'

'Monday.'

'You'll go with Dirk.'

'Yes.' She opens the menu. 'Imogen is here now. She'll help you look after Emma.'

'What's Dirk like?'

She doesn't look up from the menu. 'A force of nature.'

'What does that mean?'

'He's very full on. Some people find him abrasive and opinionated. I think he's an acquired taste.'

'Have you acquired the taste?'

'I understand him better than most people. He's very good at his job.'

'Is he married?'

She laughs. 'No.'

'What's so funny?'

'The thought of Dirk being married.'

I can hear her tights scrape as she crosses her legs. Her eyes are no longer focused on the menu. She's somewhere else. It strikes me how different she's grown since she started working, how disengaged. In the midst of a conversation she can suddenly seem to be a thousand miles away.

'I'd like to meet your workmates,' I say.

Her eyes come back to me. 'Really?'

'You sound surprised.'

'I *am* surprised. You've never shown any interest.'

'I'm sorry.'

'Well, there's an office party next Saturday – our tenth anniversary. I didn't think you wanted to go.'

'Why?'

'I told you about it weeks ago.'

'I don't remember.'

'Exactly.'

'I do want to go. It'll be fun.'

'Are you sure?'

'Yes. We can get a hotel room. Make a weekend of it.'

My foot find hers beneath the table, less gently than I'd hoped. She flinches as though I've tried to kick her. I apologise and feel my heart vibrating. Only it's not my heart. It's my phone.

I hold my hand against the pocket, wishing I'd turned it off. Julianne takes a sip of wine and ponders my dilemma. 'Aren't you going to answer it?'

'I'm sorry.'

Her shrug is not ambivalent or open to interpretation. I know what she's thinking. I flip open the handset. DI Cray's number is on the screen.

'Yes.'

'Where are you?'

'At a restaurant.'

'What's the address? I'm sending a car.'

'Why?'

'Maureen Bracken has been missing since six o'clock this evening. Her ex-husband found the front door wide open. Her car is gone. Her mobile is engaged.'

My heart swells and wedges in my throat.

'Where's her son?'

'Home. He was late getting back from football training. Someone stole his mobile phone. When he went back to look, he got locked in the changing rooms.'

My surging stare goes straight through Julianne. DI Cray is still talking.

'Oliver Rabb is trying to get a fix on the mobile. It's still transmitting.'

'Where's Bruno?'

'I told him to stay at the house in case his ex-wife calls. There's an officer with him. Ten minutes, Professor. Be waiting outside.'

The call ends. I look at Julianne. Her face doesn't begin to hint at what's on her mind.

I tell her that I have to leave. I tell her why. Without a word she stands and gathers her coat. We haven't ordered. We haven't eaten. She signals for the bill and pays for the wine.

I follow her across the restaurant, her hips swinging fluidly beneath her dress, articulating more in a few paces than most people manage in an hour of conversation. I walk her to the car. She gets in. There's no kiss goodbye. Her face is an unknowable combination of disappointment and disconnection. I want to go after her, to win back the moment, but it's too late.

43

Fears and imaginings. They begin as a tiny ceaseless tremor inside me, a buzzing blade that gnaws at the soft wet tissue opening up great cavities that are still not large enough for my lungs to expand.

I have talked to Bruno. He is a different man. Diminished. It is after midnight. Maureen is still missing. Her mobile phone has stopped transmitting. Oliver Rabb has traced the dying signal to a phone tower on the southern edge of Victoria Park in Bath. Police are searching the surrounding streets.

Coincidences and small occurrences keep adding themselves to this story, complicating the picture instead of making it clearer. The emails. The reunion. Gideon Tyler. I have no clear evidence he is behind this. Ruiz has gone to his last known address. There's nobody home.

Veronica Cray has made two official requests to the MOD for information. So far silence. We have no idea if Tyler is still serving in the army or if he's resigned his commission. When did he leave Germany? How long has he been home? What's he been doing?

Maureen's car is found just after 5.00 a.m., parked in Queen Street near the gates to Victoria Park. Two standing lions watch over the vehicle from stone plinths. The headlights are on. The driver's door is open. Maureen's mobile is resting on the seat. The battery is dead.

Victoria Park covers fifty-seven acres and has seven entrances. I look through the railing fences into the gloom. The sky is purple black, an hour before dawn and the air is freezing. We could have a thousand officers turning over every leaf and still not find Maureen.

Instead we have two dozen officers wearing reflective vests and carrying torches. The dog squad will be here by seven. A helicopter sweeps above us, tethered by a beam of light to the ground.

We move off in pairs. Monk is with me. His long legs are made for crossing open ground in the dark; and his voice is like a foghorn. I hold a torch in one hand and my walking stick in the other, watching the beam of light reflect off wet grass and the trees, turning them silver.

Staying on the gravel path until we pass the tennis courts and the pitch & putt, we then veer right climbing the slope. On the high side of the park, the Palladian style terraces of the Royal Crescent are etched against the sky. Lights are coming on. People have heard the helicopter.

Two dozen torches are moving between the trees like bloated fireflies, unable to lift off. At the same time the park lights are like balls of yellow blurred by the pre-dawn mist.

Monk is carrying a radio. He stops suddenly and raises it to his ear. The message is punctuated by static. I catch only a few words. Maureen's name is mentioned and something about a gun.

'Come on, Professor,' says Monk, grabbing my arm.

'What is it?'

'She's alive.'

Half-running and half-hobbling, I struggle to keep up with him. We head west along Royal Avenue towards the fishpond and the adventure playground. I know this area of Victoria Park. I have been here with Charlie and Emma, watching hot air balloons lift off on twilight flights.

The old Victorian bandstand appears from the darkness like an enormous cake mould cut in half and plonked near the pond. Low hanging branches reach across the gaps in the trees.

I see her then. Maureen. Naked. Kneeling at the base of the bandstand with her arms spread wide in a classic stress position. Her arms must be in agony – growing heavier by the moment.

Clasped tightly in her left fist is a pistol, adding to the weight. She's wearing a black eye mask – the sort they give out on long-distance airline flights.

A torch beam hits my face. I raise my hand to shield my eyes. Safari Roy lowers the beam.

'I've called ARG.'

I look at Monk for an explanation.

'The Armed Response Group,' he says.

'I don't think she's going to shoot anyone.'

'It's protocol. She has a firearm.'

'Has she made any threat?'

Roy looks at me incredulously. 'Well, that gun looks fairly fucking threatening. Every time we get close she waves it around.'

I peer across the open ground. Maureen is kneeling with her head tilted forward. Apart from the mask over her eyes, there is something else around her head. She's wearing headphones.

'She can't hear you,' I say.

'What do you mean?'

'Look at the headphones. They're probably attached to a mobile. She's talking to someone.'

Roy sucks air through his teeth.

It's happening again. He's isolating her.

DI Cray arrives, breathing hard. The cuffs of her trousers are wet and she's wearing a woollen ski hat which makes her face look completely round. 'Where in fuck's name did she get a gun?'

Nobody answers. A fat duck, startled by the noise, takes off from the weeds that fringe the pond. For a moment it seems to walk on the water before gaining height and lifting its undercarriage.

Maureen must be freezing. How long has she been out here? Her car engine was cold and the headlights had almost drained the battery. She was last seen twelve hours ago. He's had all this time to break her . . . to fill her mind with terrible thoughts, to drip poison in her ear.

Where is he? Watching. Police should seal off the park and set up roadblocks. No. Once he sees officers begin to fan out to search for him, he'll probably make Maureen do something with the gun. We have to move quietly – from the outside in.

274

First we have to terminate the call. There must be some way to isolate the nearest phone tower and close it down. Terrorists use mobile phones to detonate bombs. Surely there's a black out switch to freeze communications if a bomb threat is made.

Maureen hasn't moved. The mask makes her eyes look like black hollows. Her arms are shaking uncontrollably. The pistol is too heavy to hold aloft. A puddle of darkness stains the concrete at her feet.

Somehow I have to break the spell he's cast over her. A thought loop is running in Maureen's head. It's similar to those experienced by obsessive compulsives who must wash their hands a certain number of times or check the locks or turn off the lights in a certain order. He has put these thoughts in her mind – now she can't let them go. I have to disrupt this loop, but how? She can't hear me or see me.

The darkness is receding. The wind has died. I can hear sirens in the distance. The Armed Response Group. They're coming with guns.

Maureen's arms are dropping. They're too heavy. Maybe if the police rushed her, they could disarm her before she fired.

Veronica Cray is signalling her officers to stay back. She doesn't want casualties. I catch her attention. 'Let me talk to her.'

'She can't hear you.'

'Let me try.'

'Wait for the ARG.'

'She can't hold that gun up much longer.'

'That's good.'

'No. He'll make her do something before then.'

She glances at Monk. 'Get him a bulletproof vest.'

'Yes, boss.'

The vest is fetched from one of the cars. The buckles are loosened and then tightened around my chest. Monk embraces me like a tango dancer. The vest is lighter than I imagined, but still bulky. I pause a moment. The sky has turned to turquoise and watery mauve. Picking up my walking stick and a trauma blanket, I move towards Maureen, watching the pistol in her right hand.

Stopping about fifteen yards away, I say her name. She doesn't react. The headphones have separated her from her surroundings. I can just make out the wire running down her chest to a mobile phone resting between her knees.

I say her name again, louder this time. The gun swings towards me – too far to the left and then to the right. He's telling her where to aim.

I move to the left. The gun follows me. If I were suddenly to throw myself at her, she might not have time to react. Perhaps I could wrestle the gun away.

This is stupid. Foolish. I can hear Julianne's voice. Arguing. 'Why are you the one who charges into danger?' she says. 'Why can't you be the one who runs the other way, shouting for help?'

I'm at the steps now. Raising my walking stick, I smash it down hard on the handrail. The crack reverberates through the park, magnified by the fading darkness. Maureen flinches. She's heard the sound.

I smash the handrail again once, twice, three times, diverting her attention from the voice in her ears. She shakes her head. Her left arm bends and her fingers lift the mask from her eyes. She blinks at me, trying to focus. Her eyes are streaked with tears. The barrel of the gun hasn't moved. She doesn't *want* to shoot me.

I motion for Maureen to take off the headphones. She shakes her head. I raise a finger and mouth the words, 'One minute.'

Another refusal. She's listening to him, not me.

I take a step towards her. The gun steadies. I wonder how effective these vests are. Will they stop a bullet from this range?

Maureen nods to nobody and reaches for the headphones, lifting a cup away from her left ear. He told her to do it. He *wants* her to hear me.

'Do you remember me, Maureen?'

A quick nod of the head.

'Do you know where you are?'

Another nod.

'I understand what's happening, Maureen. Somebody is talking to you. You can hear him now.' Hair has fallen over her eyes. 'He says that he has someone . . . someone close to you. Your son.'

Heartbroken assent.

'It's not true, Maureen. He doesn't have Jackson. He's lying to you.'

She shakes her head.

'Listen to me. Jackson is at home with Bruno. He's safe. Remember what happened to Christine and Sylvia? The same thing. He told Christine that he had Darcy and Sylvia that he had Alice, but it wasn't true. Darcy and Alice were fine. They were never in danger.'

She wants to believe me.

'I know he's very convincing, Maureen. He knows things about you, doesn't he?'

She nods.

'And he knows things about Jackson. Where he goes to school. What he looks like.'

Maureen sobs, 'He was late getting home . . . I waited . . . I called Jackson's phone.'

'Someone stole it.'

'I heard him screaming.'

'It was a trick. Jackson was locked in the changing rooms at football practice. But he's out now. He's safe.'

I'm trying not to stare at the barrel of the gun. The pieces are together now. He must have stolen Jackson's mobile and locked him in the changing rooms. His cries for help were recorded and played down the line to Maureen.

She heard her son screaming. It was enough to convince her. It would have convinced most people. It would have convinced me.

The barrel of the pistol is all over the place, painting the air. Maureen's right forefinger is curled around the trigger. Her hands are freezing. Even if she wanted to uncurl her finger she probably couldn't.

In the periphery of my vision I see dark shapes crouching between the trees and shrubs. The Armed Response Group. They have rifles.

'Listen to me, Maureen. You can talk to Jackson. Put down the gun and we'll phone him right now.' I take out my mobile. 'I'll call Bruno. He'll put Jackson on the line.'

I can feel the change in her. She's listening. She wants to believe me . . . to hope. Then just as suddenly, in a half-breath, her eyes widen and she drops the cup of the headphone over her ear.

I yell at her, 'NO. DON'T LISTEN TO HIM.'

Her eyes flicker. The barrel of the pistol is doing figure eight patterns. She's just as likely to miss me as hit me.

'JACKSON'S SAFE! I PROMISE YOU.'

A switch has clicked off in her head. She's no longer listening to me. Her second hand is now gripping the pistol, holding it steady. She's going to do it. She's going to pull the trigger. Please don't shoot me, Maureen.

I lunge towards her. My left leg locks and carries me down. At the same moment the air explodes and Maureen's body jerks. A red mist sprays across my eyes. I blink it away. She slumps forward, collapsing over her knees, face first, hips in the air, as if subjugating herself to the new day.

The mobile clatters onto the concrete. The pistol follows, bouncing end over end and sliding to a stop beneath my chin.

Something inside me has opened; a black vacuum that is flooded with rage. I pick up the handset and scream, 'YOU SICK, SICK FUCK!'

The insult echoes back at me. Silence. Punctuated by the sound of someone breathing. Calmly. Quietly.

People are running towards me. A police officer dressed in body armour crouches a dozen feet away, his rifle pointed at me.

'Put the gun down, sir.'

My ears are still ringing. I look at the pistol in my hand.

'Sir, put down the gun.'

44

The sun is up, hidden behind grey clouds that seem low enough to have been painted by hand. White plastic sheets, strung between pillars, are shielding where Maureen Bracken fell.

She's alive. The bullet entered beneath her right collarbone and exited six inches below her right shoulder, near the middle of her back. The police marksman had aimed to wound, not to kill.

Surgeons are waiting to operate at the Bristol Royal Infirmary. Maureen is en route in an ambulance, escorted by two police cars. Meanwhile officers are scouring Victoria Park. The entrances have been sealed off and the perimeter fences are being patrolled.

Two cordons – inner and outer – create concentric circles around the bandstand, limiting access and allowing the forensic teams to safeguard the crime scene. I watch them working, while sitting on the steps with a silver trauma blanket wrapped around my shoulders. The blood on my face has dried into brittle scabs that flake off on my fingertips.

Veronica Cray joins me. I clench my left fist and open it again. It doesn't stop the shaking.

'How are you?'

'Fine.'

'You don't look fine. I can have someone drop you home.'

'I'll stay for a while.'

The DI muses a moment, gazing at the duck pond where the branches of a willow tree droop into the foam-scummed water. A search warrant is being sought for Gideon Tyler's last known address, this time with renewed urgency. Detectives are interviewing neighbours and looking for family links. Every aspect of his life will be documented and cross-checked.

'You think he's good for this?'

'Yes.'

'What would he hope to achieve by murdering his wife's friends?'

'He's a sexual sadist. He doesn't need any other reason.'

'But you think he has one?'

'Yes.'

'The break-in at the Chambers house, the phone calls and threats, all began when Helen left him and went into hiding with Chloe. Gideon was trying to find them.'

'OK, I can understand that, but now they're dead.'

'Maybe Gideon is so angry and bitter he's going to destroy anyone close to Helen. Like I said, sexual sadists don't need to look for any other reasons. They're driven by a whole different set of impulses.'

I press my face in my hands. I'm tired. My mind is tired. Yet it cannot stop working. Somebody broke into Christine Wheeler's house and opened the condolence cards. They were looking for a name or address.

'There is another explanation,' I say. 'It's possible Gideon doesn't believe they're dead. He may think Helen's family and friends are hiding her or have information about her whereabouts.'

'So he tortures them?'

'And when that doesn't work, he kills them in the hope he can force Helen out of hiding.'

Veronica Cray doesn't seem shocked or surprised. Divorced and separated couples often do terrible things to each other. They fight over their children, kidnap them and sometimes worse. Helen Chambers spent eight years married to Gideon Tyler. Even in death she can't escape him.

'I'll have Monk take you home.'

'I want to see Tyler's house.'

280

'Why?'

'It could help me.'

The air in the car has a musty, used-up feel, smelling of sweat and artificial warmth. We follow Bath Road into Bristol, hurtling forward between the traffic lights.

I lean back on the greasy cloth seat, staring out the window. Nothing about the streets is familiar. Not the gasworks, girdled in steel, or the underside of railway bridges or the cement grey high rise.

From the main road we turn off and descend abruptly into a wilderness full of crumbling terraces, factories, drug dens, rubbish bins, barricaded shops, stray cats and women who give blowjobs in cars.

Gideon Tyler lives just off Fishponds Road in the shadow of the M32. The dwelling is an old smash repair workshop with an asphalt forecourt fenced off and topped with barbed wire. Plastic bags are trapped against the chain link fence and pigeons circle the forecourt like prisoners in an exercise yard.

The landlord, Mr Swingler, has arrived with the keys. He looks like an ancient skinhead in Doc Martens, jeans and a tight T-shirt. There are four locks. Mr Swingler has only one key. The police tell him to stand back.

A snub-nosed battering ram swings once . . . twice . . . three times. Hinges splinter and the front door gives away. The police go first, crouching and spinning from room to room.

'Clear.'

'Clear.'

'Clear.'

I have to wait outside with Mr Swingler. The landlord looks at me. 'How much you press?'

'Pardon?'

'How much you bench press?'

'No idea.'

'I lift two hundred and forty pounds. How old you think I am?'

'I don't know.'

'Eighty.' He flexes a bicep. 'Pretty good, eh?'

281

Any moment he's going to challenge me to an arm wrestle.

The ground floor has been cleared. Monk says I can come inside. The place smells of dog and damp newspapers. Someone has been using the fireplace to burn papers.

The kitchen benches are clean and the cupboards tidy. Plates and cups are lined up on a shelf, equal distance apart. The pantry is the same. Staples like rice and lentils are kept in tin airtight containers, alongside canned vegetables and long life milk. These are supplies for a siege or a disaster.

Upstairs the bed has been stripped. The linen is washed and folded on the mattress, ready for inspection. The bathroom has been scrubbed, scoured and bleached. I have visions of Gideon cleaning between the tiles with his toothbrush.

Every house, every wardrobe, every shopping basket says something about a person. This one is no different. It is the address of a soldier, a man to whom routines and regimens are intrinsic to living. His wardrobe contains five green shirts, six pairs of socks, one pair of black boots, one field jacket, one pair of gloves with green inserts, one poncho . . . His socks are balled with a woollen smile. His shirts have creases, evenly spaced on the front and back. They are folded rather than hung.

I can look at these details and make assumptions. Psychology is about probabilities and prospects; the statistical bell curves that can help predict human behaviour.

People are frightened of Gideon or don't want to talk about him or want to pretend that he doesn't exist. He's like one of the monsters that I 'edit out' of the bedtime stories I read to Emma because I don't want to give her nightmares.

Beware the Jabberwock . . . the jaws that bite, the claws that catch!

There is a yell from outside in the forecourt. They want a dog handler. Descending the stairs, I use the rear door and side gate to reach the workshop area. A dog is going berserk behind a metal shuttered door.

'I want to see it.'

'We should wait for the handler,' says Monk.

'Just raise the door a few inches.'

I kneel down and put my head on the ground. Monk jemmies

the roller door lock and raises it an inch and then another. The animal is hurling itself at the metal door, snarling furiously.

I catch a glimpse of its reflection in a mirror above a wash-basin, a fleeting image of tan fur and fangs.

My guts prickle. I recognise the dog. I've seen it before. It came rearing through the door of Patrick Fuller's flat, snarling and thrashing at the police arrest party, wanting to rip out their throats. What's the dog doing here?

45

A siren is shrieking abuse at passers-by as the police car weaves between traffic, flashing its headlights like grief-maddened eyes. Old people and children turn and watch. Others carry on as if oblivious to the noise.

We cross Bristol, clearing the streets; down Temple Way, past Temple Meads Station, onto York and then Coronation Road. My heart is thudding. We had Patrick Fuller in custody. I convinced Veronica Cray to let the former soldier go.

Twenty minutes accelerate past me in a blur of speed and screaming sirens. We are standing on the pavement outside Fuller's tower block. I recognise the grey concrete and streaks of rust below the window frames.

More police cars pull up around us, nose-first into the gutter. DI Cray is briefing her team. Nobody is looking at me. I'm surplus to requirements. Redundant stock.

Maureen Bracken's blood has dried on my jacket. From a distance it looks like I've started to rust, like a tin man in search of a heart. I keep my nerve. My left thumb and forefinger are pill-rolling. I hold my walking stick in my left fist to keep it steady.

I follow the police upstairs. They don't have a search warrant. Veronica Cray raises her fist and knocks.

The door opens. A young woman is framed by the darkness

behind her. She is wearing a sparkling blue midriff top, jeans and open-toed sandals. A single roll of flesh bulges over the waistband of her jeans.

Mutton. Mutton dressed as mutton. A decade ago she might have been called pretty. Now she's still dressing like a teenager, trying to relive her salad days.

It's Fuller's younger sister. She's been staying at his flat. I catch snippets of her answers but not enough to understand what happened. Veronica Cray takes her inside, leaving me in the corridor. I try to slip past the constable on the door. Taking a step to the left, he bars my way.

The door is open. I can see DI Cray sitting in an armchair talking to Tyler's sister. Roy is watching from the kitchen through a service hatch and Monk seems to be guarding the bedroom door.

The DI catches sight of me. She nods and the constable lets me pass.

'This is Cheryl,' she explains. 'Her brother Patrick is apparently a patient at the Fernwood Clinic.'

I know the place. It's a private mental hospital in Bristol.

'When was he admitted?' I ask.

'Three weeks ago.'

'Is he a full-time patient?'

'Apparently so.'

Cheryl pulls a cigarette from a crumpled packet and straightens it between her fingertips. She sits with her knees together, perched on the edge of the sofa. Nervous.

'Why is Patrick in Fernwood?' I ask her.

'Because the army fucked him up. He came home from Iraq hurt really bad. He almost died. They had to rebuild his triceps – make new ones out of other muscles stitched together. It took months before he could even lift his arm. Ever since then he's been different, not the same, you know. He has nightmares.'

She lights the cigarette. Blows a missile of smoke.

'The army didn't give a shit. They kicked him out. They said he was "temperamentally unsuitable" – what the fuck does that mean?'

'What do the doctors at Fernwood say?'

'They say Pat's suffering from post-traumatic stress. Stands to reason after what happened. The army boned him. Gave him a medal and told him to disappear.'

'Do you know someone called Gideon Tyler?'

Cheryl hesitates. 'He's a friend of Pat's. It was Gideon who got Pat into Fernwood.'

'How do they know each other?'

'They were in the army together.'

She stabs the cigarette into an ashtray and pulls out another.

'Nine days ago. A Friday. The police arrested someone at this flat.'

'Well, it weren't Pat,' she says.

'Who else could it have been?'

Cheryl rolls her tongue over her teeth, smudging lipstick on the enamel. 'Gideon, I guess.' She sucks hard on her cigarette and blinks away the smoke. 'He's been keeping an eye on the flat since Pat went into Fernwood. Best to have someone looking after the place. Them little black shits from the estate would steal your middle name if you let 'em.'

'Where do you live?' I ask.

'In Cardiff. I got a flat with my boyfriend, Gerry. I come down every couple of weeks to see Pat.'

Veronica Cray is thin-lipped, staring vexedly at the floor. 'There was a dog here. A pit bull.'

'Yeah, Capo,' replies Cheryl. 'He belongs to Pat. Gideon's looking after him.'

'Do you have a photograph of Patrick?' I ask.

'Sure. Somewhere.'

She stands and brushes her thighs where the tight denim has wrinkled. Teetering on high heels she squeezes past Monk, chest to chest, giving him a half-smile.

She begins opening drawers and wardrobe doors.

'When were you last here?' I ask.

'Ten, twelve days ago.' Ash falls from the cigarette in her mouth and smudges her jeans on the way down. 'I came down to see Pat. Gideon was here, treating the place like he owned it.'

'How so?'

'He's a weird fucker, you know. I reckon the army does it to 'em. Fucks 'em up. That Gideon's got such a temper. All I did was use his poxy mobile phone. One call. And he went completely apeshit. One sodding call.'

'You ordered a pizza,' I say.

Cheryl looks at me as though I've stolen her last cigarette. 'How did you know that?'

'Lucky guess.'

DI Cray gives me a sidelong glance.

Cheryl has found a large photo album on a top shelf.

'I told Gideon he should be in Fernwood with Patrick. I didn't hang around. I rang Gerry and he came and picked me up. He wanted to punch Gideon's lights out and probably could have done it, but I told him not to bother.'

She turns the album to face us, propping it open on her chest.

'Here's Pat. That was taken at his passing out parade. He looked dead handsome.'

Patrick Fuller is in a dress uniform, with dark brown hair shaved at the sides. Smiling at the camera with a slightly lopsided grin, he looks like he's barely out of secondary school. More importantly, he's not the man police arrested nine days ago; the one I interviewed at Trinity Road police station.

She points a bitten fingernail to another photograph. 'That's him again.'

A group of soldiers are standing and squatting at the edge of a basketball court, having finished a game. Patrick is dressed in camouflage trousers and no shirt; he crouches casually, a forearm on his knee, his muscled torso shiny with sweat.

Cheryl turns more pages. 'There should be one of Gideon here, as well.'

She can't find it. She goes back to the beginning and looks again.

'That's funny. It's gone.'

She points to a vacant square on the page. 'I'm sure it was here,' she says.

Sometimes a gap in an album says as much as any photograph would. Gideon removed it. He doesn't want his face known. It doesn't matter. I remember him. I can remember his pale grey eyes and thin lips. And I remember him pacing the floor, stepping over invisible mousetraps, his face a mass of tics and grimaces. He confabulated. He invented fantastic stories. It was a consummate performance.

I have based a career on being able to tell when someone is lying or being deliberately vague or deceptive, but Gideon Tyler played me for a sucker. His lies were almost perfect because he managed to take charge of the conversation, to distract and divert. There were no momentary gaps while he conjured up something new or added one detail too many. Not even his unconscious physiological responses held any clues; his pupil dilation, pore size, muscle tone, skin flush and his breathing were in normal parameters.

I convinced Veronica Cray to let him go. I said he couldn't possibly have made Christine Wheeler jump off the Clifton Suspension Bridge. I was wrong.

Veronica Cray is issuing instructions. Safari Roy scribbles notes, trying to keep up. She wants a list of Tyler's friends, family, army buddies and ex-girlfriends.

'Visit them. Put pressure on them. One of them must know where he is.'

She hasn't said a word to me since we left Fuller's flat. Disgrace is an odd feeling – a fluttering in my stomach. The public recriminations will come later but the private ones begin immediately. Attribution. Condemnation. Castigation.

The Fernwood Clinic is a Grade II listed building set in five acres of trees and gardens at the edge of Durdham Down. The main building was once a stately home and the access road a private driveway.

The medical director will talk to us in his office. His name is Dr Caplin and he welcomes us as if we've arrived for a hunting weekend at his private estate.

'Isn't it magnificent,' he says, gazing across the gardens from large bay windows in his office. He offers us refreshments. Takes a seat.

'I've heard about you, Professor O'Loughlin,' he says. 'Someone told me you'd moved into the area. I thought I might see your CV pass across my desk at some point.'

'I'm no longer practicing as a clinical psychologist.'

'A pity. We could use someone of your experience.'

I glance around his office. The décor is Laura Ashley meets Ikea with a touch of new technology. Dr Caplin's tie almost perfectly matches the curtains.

I know a little about the Fernwood Clinic. It's owned by a private company and specialises in looking after those wealthy enough to afford its daily fees, which are substantial.

'What sort of problems are you treating?'

'Mainly eating disorders and addictions but we do some general psychiatry.'

'We're interested in Patrick Fuller, a former soldier.'

Dr Caplin purses his lips. 'We treat a large a number of military personnel, serving soldiers and veterans,' he says. 'The Ministry of Defence is one of our biggest referrers.'

'Isn't war a wonderful thing?' mutters Veronica Cray.

Dr Caplin flinches and his hazel irises seem to fragment with anger.

'We do important work here, detective. We help people. I'm not here to comment on our Government's foreign policy or how it conducts its wars.'

'Yes, of course,' I say. 'I'm sure your work is vital. We're only interested in Patrick Fuller.'

'You intimated over the phone that Patrick had been the victim of identify theft.'

'Yes.'

'I'm sure you understand, Professor, that I can't possibly discuss details of his treatment.'

'I understand.'

'So you won't be seeking to see his records?'

'Not unless he's confessed to murder,' says the DI.

The doctor's smile has long gone. 'I don't understand. What is he supposed to have done?'

'That's what we're seeking to establish,' says the DI. 'We wish to speak to Patrick Fuller and I expect your full co-operation.'

Dr Caplin pats his hair as though checking its dimensions.

'I assure you, Detective Inspector, this hospital is a friend of the Avon & Somerset Police. I'm actually on very good terms with your Assistant Chief Constable, Mr Fowler.'

Of all the names to drop, he chooses this one. Veronica Cray doesn't bat an eyelid.

'Well, doctor, I'll be sure to pass on your best wishes to the ACC. I'm sure he'll appreciate your co-operation as much as I do.'

Dr Caplin nods, satisfied.

He takes a file from his desk. Opens it.

'Patrick Fuller is suffering from post-traumatic stress disorder and general anxiety. He's preoccupied with suicide and plagued with guilt over the loss of comrades in Iraq. Patrick is sometimes disorientated and confused. He suffers mood swings, some of them quite violent.'

'How violent?' asks the DI.

'He's not a serious management risk and his behaviour has been exemplary. We're making real progress.'

At three thousand pounds a week I should hope so.

'Why didn't the army psychiatrists pick it up?' I ask.

'Patrick wasn't a military referral.'

'But his problems are related to his military service?'

'Yes.'

'Who's paying for his treatment?'

'That's confidential information.'

'Who brought him in here?'

'A friend.'

'Gideon Tyler?'

'I don't see how that could possibly concern the police.'

Veronica Cray has heard enough. On her feet, she leans across the desk and pins Caplin with a glare that makes his eyes widen.

'I don't think you fully understand the gravity of this situation, doctor. Gideon Tyler is a suspect in a murder investigation. Patrick Fuller may be an accessory. Unless you can provide me with medical evidence that Mr Fuller is at risk of being psychologically harmed by a police interview, I'm going to ask you one last time to make him available or I'll come back with a warrant for his arrest and for yours on charges of obstructing my investigation. Not even Mr Fowler will be able to help you then.'

Dr Caplin stammers a reply, which is totally incomprehensible. All trace of smugness has disappeared. Veronica Cray is still talking.

'Professor O'Loughlin is a mental health professional. He will be present during the interview. If at any stage Patrick Fuller becomes agitated or his condition worsens, then I'm sure the Professor will safeguard his welfare.'

There is a pause. Dr Caplin picks up his phone.

'Please inform Patrick Fuller that he has visitors.'

The room is simply furnished with a single bed, a chair, a small TV on a plinth and a chest of drawers. Patrick is much smaller than I imagined from his photographs. The handsome, dark-haired soldier in dress uniform has been replaced by a pale rumpled imitation in a white vest, yellowing under his armpits, and jogging pants rolled below his hipbones which stick out like doorknobs from beneath his skin.

Scar tissue from his surgery is puckered and hardened beneath his right armpit. Patrick has lost weight. His muscles have gone and his neck is so thin that his Adam's apple looks like a cancerous lump bobbing as he swallows.

I pull up a chair and sit opposite him, filling his vision. DI Cray seems happy to stay near the door. Fernwood makes her uncomfortable.

'Hello, Patrick, my name's Joe.'

'How ya doing?'

'I'm good. How are you?'

'Getting better.'

'That's good. You like it here?'

'It's OK.'

'Have you seen Gideon Tyler?'

The question doesn't surprise him. He's so heavily medicated his moods and movements have been flattened to a physical mono-tone.

'Not since Friday.'

'How often does he come and see you?'

'Wednesdays and Fridays.'

'Today's Wednesday.'

'Guess he'll be along soon.'

His long restless fingers pinch the skin on his wrist. I see the red pressure marks left behind.

'How long have you known Gideon?'

'Since I joined the Paras. He was a real hard case. He busted my balls all the time but that's only cos I was lazy.'

'He was an officer?'

'A one-pip wonder: second Lieutenant.'

'Gideon didn't stay with the Paras.'

'Nah, he joined the green slime.'

'What's that?'

'The Army Intelligence Corp. We used to tell jokes about them.'

'What sort of jokes?'

'They're not proper soldiers, you know. They spend all day sticking maps together and using coloured pencils.'

'Is that what Gideon did?'

'Never said.'

'Surely he must have mentioned something.'

'He'd have had to kill me if he told me.' A smile. He looks at the nurse. 'When can I get a brew? Something hot and wet.'

'Soon,' says the nurse.

Patrick scratches the scarring beneath his armpit.

'Did Gideon tell you why he came back to England?' I ask.

'Nope. He's not much of a talker.'

'His wife left him.'

'So I heard.'

'Did you know her?'

'Gideon said she was a skanky whore.'

'She's dead.'

'That's good then.'

'His daughter is also dead.'

Patrick's body flinches and he rolls his tongue into his cheek.

'How does Gideon afford to pay the bills at a place like this?'

Patrick shrugs. 'He married money.'

'But now she's dead.'

He looks at me sheepishly. 'Haven't we been over this.'

'Did Gideon come to see you last Monday?'

'When was Monday?'

'Two days ago.'

'Yeah.'

'What about the Monday before?'

'Can't remember that far back. Might have been when he took me out for a meal. We went to the pub. Don't remember which one. You should check the visitor's book. Time in. Time out.'

Patrick pinches the skin on his wrists again. It's a trigger mechanism designed to stop his mind from wandering, helping him stay on message.

'Why are you so interested in Gideon?' he asks.

'We'd like to speak to him.'

'Why didn't you say so?' he takes a mobile from the pocket of his track pants. 'I'll call him.'

'That's OK. Just give me his number.'

Patrick is punching the buttons. 'You got all these questions – just ask him.'

I glance at Veronica Cray. She shakes her head.

'Hang up,' I tell Patrick, urgently.

It's too late. He hands me the mobile.

Someone answers: 'Hey, hey, how's my favourite loony?'

There's a pause. I should terminate the call. I don't.

'It's not Patrick,' I say.

There is another silence. 'How did you get his phone?'

'He gave it to me.'

There is another pause. Silence. Gideon's mind is working over-time. Then I hear him laugh. I can picture him smiling.

'Hello, Professor, you found me.'

DI Cray is running her finger across her neck. She wants me to hang up. Tyler knows he's been identified. Nobody is tracing the signal.

'How is Patrick?' asks Gideon.

'Getting better, he says. It must be expensive keeping him here.'

'Friends look after each other. It's a matter of honour.'

293

'Why did you pretend to be him?'

'The police came bursting through the door. Nobody stopped and asked me who I was. You all assumed I was Patrick.'

'And you maintained the lie.'

'I had some fun.'

Patrick is sitting on the bed, listening and smiling secretively. I stand and walk past the nurse into a corridor. Veronica Cray follows me, whispering harshly in my ear.

Gideon is still talking. He calls me Mr Joe.

'Why are you still looking for your wife?' I ask.

'She took something that belongs to me.'

'What did she take?'

'Ask her.'

'I would, but she's dead. She drowned.'

'If you say so, Mr Joe.'

'You don't believe it.'

'I know her better than you do.'

It's a rasping statement, laced with hatred.

'What were you doing with Christine Wheeler's mobile?'

'I found it.'

'That's a coincidence – finding a phone that belonged to your wife's oldest friend.'

'Truth is stranger than fiction.'

'Did you tell her to jump from the bridge?'

'I don't know what you're talking about.'

'What about Sylvia Furness?'

'Name rings a bell. Is she a TV weathergirl?'

'You made her handcuff herself to a tree and she died of exposure.'

'Good luck proving that.'

'Maureen Bracken is alive. She's going to give us your name. The police are going to find you, Gideon.'

He chuckles. 'You're full of shit, Mr Joe. So far you've mentioned a suicide, a death due to exposure and a police shooting. Nothing to do with me. You don't have a single solid, first-hand piece of evidence that links me to any of this.'

'We have Maureen Bracken.'

294

'Never met the woman. Ask her.'

'I did. She says she met you once.'

'She's lying.'

The words are sucked through his teeth as though he's nibbling on a tiny seed.

'Help me understand something, Gideon. Do you hate women?'

'Are we talking intellectually, physically or as a sub-species?'

'You're a misogynist.'

'I knew there'd be a word for it.'

He's teasing me now. He thinks he's cleverer than I am. So far he's right. I can hear a school bell in the background. Children are jostling and shouting.

'Maybe we could meet,' I say.

'Sure. We could do lunch some time.'

'How about now?'

'Sorry, I'm busy.'

'What are you doing?'

'I'm waiting for a bus.'

Air brakes sound in the silence. A diesel engine knocks and trembles.

'I have to go, Professor. It's been nice talking to you. Give my best to Patrick.'

He hangs up. I hit redial. The mobile is turned off.

I look at DI Cray and shake my head. She swings her right boot at a wastepaper bin, which thuds into the opposite wall and bounces off again. The large dent in the side of the bin makes it rock unevenly on the carpeted floor.

46

The bus door hisses open. Students pile forward, pushing between shoulders. Some of them are carrying papier mâché masks and hollowed-out pumpkins. Halloween is two weeks away.

There she is; dressed in a tartan skirt, black tights and bottle green jumper. She finds a seat halfway down the bus and drops her school bag beside her. Strands of hair have escaped from her ponytail.

I swing past her on my crutches. She doesn't look up. All the seats are taken. I stare at one of the schoolboys, rocking back on forth on my metal sticks. He moves. I sit down.

The older boys have commandeered the back seats, yelling out the windows at their mates. The ringleader has a mouthful of braces and bum fluff on his chin. He's watching the girl. She's picking at her fingernails.

The bus has started moving – stopping, dropping and picking up. The kid with the braces makes his way forward, moving past me. He leans over her seat and snatches her schoolbag. She tries to grab it back but he kicks it along the floor. She asks nicely. He laughs. She tells him to grow up.

I move behind him. My hand seems to clap him gently on the neck. It's a friendly looking gesture – fatherly – but my fingers have closed on either side of his spine. His eyeballs are bulging and his thick-soled shoes are balancing on their toes.

His mates have come down the bus. One of them tells me to let him go.

I give him a stare. They go quiet. The bus driver, a mud-coloured Sikh in a turban, is looking in the rear mirror.

'Is there a problem?' he shouts.

'I think this kid is sick,' I say. 'He needs some fresh air.'

'You want me to stop?'

'He'll get a later bus.' I look at the boy. 'Won't you?' I move my hand. His head nods up and down.

The bus pulls up. I guide the boy to the back door.

'Where's his bag?'

Somebody passes it forward.

I let him go. He drops onto a seat at the bus shelter. The door closes with a hiss. We pull away.

The girl is looking at me uncertainly. Her schoolbag is on her lap now, beneath her folded arms.

I take a seat in front of her, resting my crutches on the metal rail.

'Do you know if this bus goes past Bradford Road?' I ask.

She shakes her head.

I open a bottle of water. 'I can never read those maps they put up in the shelters.'

Still she doesn't answer.

'Isn't it amazing how we buy water in plastic bottles. When I was a kid you would have died of thirst looking for bottled water. My old man says it's a disgrace. Soon they'll be charging us for clean air.'

No response.

'I guess you're not supposed to talk to strangers.'

'No.'

'That's OK. It's good advice. It's cold today, don't you think? Especially for a Friday.'

She takes the bait. 'It's not Friday. It's Wednesday.'

'Are you sure?'

'Yes.'

I take another sip of water.

'What difference does the day make?' she asks.

'Well you see the days of the week each have a different character. Saturdays are busy. Sundays are slow. Fridays are supposed to be full of promise. Mondays . . . well we all hate Mondays.'

She smiles and looks away. For a brief moment we are complicit. I enter her mind. She enters mine.

'The guy with the braces – he a friend of yours?'

'No.'

'He gives you problems?'

'I guess.'

'You try to avoid him but he finds you?'

'We catch the same bus.'

She's beginning to get the hang of this conversation.

'You got brothers?'

'No.'

'You know how to knee someone? That's what you do – knee him right in the you-know-where.'

She blushes. Sweet.

'Want to hear a joke?' I say.

She doesn't answer.

'A woman gets on a bus with her baby and the bus driver says, "That's the ugliest baby I've ever seen." The woman is furious but pays the fare and sits down. Another passenger says, "You can't let him get away with saying that. You go back and tell him off. Here, I'll hold the monkey for you."'

I get a proper laugh this time. It's the sweetest thing you ever heard. She's a peach, a sweet, sweet peach.

'What's your name?'

She doesn't answer.

'Oh right, I forgot, you're not supposed to talk to strangers. I guess I'll have to call you Snowflake.'

She stares out the window.

'Well, this is my stop,' I say, pulling myself up. A crutch topples into the aisle. She bends and picks it up for me.

'What happened to your leg?'

'Nothing.'

'Why do you need the crutches?'

'Gets me a seat on the bus.'

Again she laughs.

'It's been nice talking to you, Snowflake.'

298

47

Maureen Bracken has tubes flowing into her and tubes flowing out. It has been two days since the shooting and a day since she woke, pale and relieved, with only a vague idea of what happened. Every few hours a nurse gives her morphine and she floats into sleep again.

She is under police guard at the Bristol Royal Infirmary – a landmark building in a city with precious few landmarks. Inside the front entrance at a welcome desk there are volunteers wearing blue and white sashes. They look like geriatric beauty queens who missed their pageant by forty years.

I mention Maureen Bracken's name. The smiles disappear. A police officer is summoned from upstairs. Ruiz and I wait in the foyer, glancing through magazines at the hospital shop.

Bruno's voice booms from an opening lift.

'Thank God, a friendly face. Come to cheer the old girl up?'

'How is she?'

'Looking better. I had no idea a bullet could make such a mess. Horrible. Missed all the important bits, that's the main thing.'

He looks genuinely relieved. We spend the next few minutes trading clichés about what the world's coming to.

'I'm just off to get some decent food,' he says. 'Can't have her eating hospital swill. Full of super-bugs.'

'It's not as bad as you think,' I say.

'No, it's worse,' says Ruiz.

'Do you think they'll mind?' asks Bruno

'I'm sure they won't.'

He waves goodbye and disappears through the automatic doors.

A detective emerges from the lift. Italian-looking with a crew cut and a pistol slung low in a holster beneath his jacket. I recognise him from briefings at Trinity Road.

He escorts us upstairs where a second officer is guarding the corridor outside Maureen Bracken's room in a secure wing of the hospital. The detectives use metal detecting wands to screen visitors and medical personnel.

The door opens. Maureen looks up from a magazine and smiles nervously. Her shoulder is bandaged and her arm held in a sling across her chest. Tubes appear and disappear beneath the bandages and bedding.

She's wearing make-up – for Bruno's sake, I suspect. And the normally featureless room has been transformed by dozens of cards, painting and drawings. A banner is draped above her bed, fringed in gold and silver. It announces: GET WELL SOON and is signed by her hundreds of students.

'You're a very popular teacher,' I say.

'They all want to come and see me,' she laughs. 'Only in school hours of course, so they can get out of classes.'

'How are you feeling?'

'Better.' She sits up a little higher. I adjust a pillow behind her back. Ruiz has stayed outside in the corridor, swapping off-colour jokes about nurses with the detectives.

'You just missed Bruno,' says Maureen.

'I saw him downstairs.'

'He's gone to buy me lunch from Mario's. I had this craving for pasta and a rocket and parmesan salad. It's like being pregnant again and having Bruno spoil me, but don't tell him I said that.'

'I won't.'

She looks at her hands. 'I'm sorry I tried to shoot you.'

'It's OK.'

Her voice cracks momentarily. 'It was horrible . . . the things he said about Jackson. I really believed him, you know. I really thought he was going to do it.'

Maureen recounts again what happened. Every parent knows what it's like to lose sight of a child in a supermarket or a playground or in a busy street. Two minutes becomes a lifetime. Two hours and you're capable of almost anything. It was worse for Maureen. She listened to her son screaming and imagined his pain and death. The caller told her that she would never see Jackson again, never find his body; never know the truth.

I tell her that I understand.

'Do you?' she asks.

'I think so.'

She shakes her head and looks down at her wounded shoulder. 'I don't think anyone can understand. I would have put that gun in my own mouth. I would have pulled the trigger. I would have done anything to save Jackson.'

I take a seat beside the bed.

'Did you recognise his voice?'

She shakes her head. 'But I know it was Gideon.'

'How?'

'He asked about Helen. He demanded to know if she'd written or called or sent me an email. I told him no. I said Helen was dead and I was sorry, but he laughed.'

'Did he say why he thinks she's alive?'

'No, but he made me believe it.'

'How?'

She stumbles, searching for words. 'He was so sure.'

Maureen looks away, seeking a distraction, no longer wanting to think about Gideon Tyler.

'Helen's mother sent me a get well message,' she says, pointing to the side table. She directs me to the right card. It features a hand-drawn orchid in pastel shades. Claudia Chambers has written:

God sometimes tests the best people because he knows they're going to pass. Our thoughts and prayers are with you. Please get well soon.

I replace the card.

Maureen has closed her eyes. Slowly her face folds in pain. The morphine is wearing off. A memory uncurls itself from inside her head and she opens her mouth.

'Mothers should always know where their children are.'

'Why do you say that?'

'It's something he said to me.'

'Gideon?'

'I thought he was goading me, but I don't know any more. Maybe it was the only thing he said that wasn't a lie.'

48

The law firm of Spencer, Rose and Davis is located in a modern office block opposite the Guildhall and alongside the Law Courts. The foyer is like a modern day citadel, towering five storeys to a convex glass roof crisscrossed with white pipes.

There is a waterfall and a pond and a waiting area with black leather sofas. Ruiz and I watch a man in a pinstriped suit come floating to the floor in one of twin glass lifts.

'See that guy's suit,' Ruiz whispers. 'It's worth more than my entire wardrobe.'

'My shoes are worth more than your entire wardrobe,' I reply.

'That's cruel.'

The pinstriped man confers with the receptionist and moves towards us, unbuttoning his jacket. There are no introductions. We are to follow.

The lift carries us upwards. The potted plants grow smaller and the koi carp become like goldfish.

We are ushered into an office where a septuagenarian lawyer is seated at a large desk that makes him appear even more shrunken. He rises an inch from his leather chair and sits again. It's either a sign of his age or how much respect he's going to give us.

'My name is Julian Spencer,' he says. 'I act for Chambers

Construction and I'm an old friend of Bryan's family. I believe that you've already met Mr Chambers.'

Bryan Chambers doesn't bother shaking hands. He is dressed in a suit that no tailor could ever make look comfortable. Some men are built to wear overalls.

'I think we got off on the wrong foot,' I say.

'You tricked your way onto my property and upset my wife.'

'I apologise if that's the case.'

Mr Spencer tries to take the edge off the moment, tut-tutting Mr Chambers like a schoolmaster.

Family friends, he said. It doesn't strike me as a natural alliance – an old money etsablishment lawyer and working-class millionaire.

The pinstriped man has stayed in the room. He stands by the window, his arms folded.

'The police are looking for Gideon Tyler,' I say.

'It's about bloody time,' says Bryan Chambers.

'Do you know where he is?'

'No.'

'When did you last speak to him?'

'I speak to him all the time. I yell at him down the phone when he calls in the middle of the night and says nothing, just stays on the line, breathing.'

'You're sure it's him.'

Chambers glares at me, as though I'm questioning his intelligence. I meet his eyes and hold them, studying his face. Big men tend to have big personalities, but a shadow has been cast over his life and he's wilting under the weight of it.

Getting to his feet, he paces the floor, flexing his fingers, closing them into fists and then opening them again.

'Tyler broke into our house – more than once – I don't know how many times. I put new locks on the doors, installed cameras, alarms, but it didn't matter, because he still made it through. He left behind messages. Warnings. Dead birds in the microwave; a gun on our bed; my wife's cat was stuffed into a toilet cistern.'

'And you reported all this to the police.'

'I had them on speed dial. They wore a path to my door, but

304

they were next to fucking useless.' He glances towards Ruiz. 'They didn't arrest him. They didn't charge him. They said there was no evidence. The calls came from different mobile phones that couldn't be traced to Tyler. There were no fingerprints or fibres, no footage on the cameras. How can that be?'

'He's careful,' answers Ruiz.

'Or they're protecting him.'

'Why?'

Bryan Chambers shrugs. 'I don't know. Makes no sense. I got six guys guarding the house now, round the clock. It's still not enough.'

'What do you mean?'

'Last night someone poisoned the lake at Stonebridge Manor,' he explains. 'We had four thousand fish – tench, roach and bream – they're all dead.'

'Tyler?'

'Who else?'

The big man has stopped pacing. The fire has gone out of him, at least for the moment.

'What does Gideon want?' I ask.

Julian Spencer answers for him. 'Mr Tyler hasn't made this clear. At first he wanted to find his wife and daughter.'

'This was before the ferry accident.'

'Yes. He didn't accept the marriage was over and he came looking for Helen and Chloe. He accused Bryan and Claudia of hiding them.'

The lawyer produces a letter from the drawer of his desk, refreshing his memory.

'My Tyler took legal action in Germany and won a court order for joint custody of his daughter. He wanted an international warrant issued for his wife's arrest.'

'They were hiding out in Greece,' says Ruiz.

'Just so.'

'Surely, after the tragedy, Tyler stopped his harassment.'

Bryan Chambers laughs caustically and it turns into a fit of coughing. The old lawyer pours him a glass of water.

'I don't understand. Helen and Chloe are dead. Why would Tyler keep harassing you?'

Bryan Chambers slumps forward in a chair, his shoulders collapsing over his chest in a posture of abject defeat. 'I figured it was about money. Helen was going to inherit the manor one day. I thought Tyler wanted some sort of pay-off. I offered him two hundred thousand pounds if he left us alone. He wouldn't take it.'

The old lawyer tut-tuts his disapproval.

'And he hasn't asked for anything else?'

Chambers shakes his head. 'The man is a psychopath. I've given up trying to understand him. I want to crush the bastard. I want to make him pay . . .'

Julian Spencer cautions him about making threats.

'Fuck being careful! My wife is on antidepressants. She doesn't sleep any more. You see my hands?' Chambers holds them across the table. 'You want to know why they're so steady? Drugs. That's what Tyler has done to us. We're both on medication. He's made our lives a misery.'

When I first met Bryan Chambers, I thought his anger and secrecy were evidence of paranoia. I'm more sympathetic now. He has lost a daughter and granddaughter and his sanity is under threat.

'Tell me about Gideon,' I ask. 'When was the first time you met him?'

'Helen brought him home. I thought he was a cold fish.'

'Why?'

'He looked as though he knew the secrets of everyone in the room, but nobody knew his. It was obvious that he was in the military, but he wouldn't talk about the army or his work – not even to Helen.'

'Where was he based?'

'At Chicksands in Bedfordshire. It's some sort of army training place.'

'And then?'

'Northern Ireland and Germany. He was away a lot. He wouldn't tell Helen where he was going, but there were clues, she said. Afghanistan. Egypt. Morocco. Poland. Iraq . . .'

'Any idea what he was doing?'

'No.'

Ruiz has wandered across to the window, taking in the view. At the same time, he glances sidelong at the pinstriped man, sizing him up. Ruiz is more intuitive than I am. I look for telltale signals to judge a person, he *feels* it inside.

I ask Mr Chambers about his daughter's marriage. I want to know if the breakdown had been sudden or protracted. Some couples cling to nothing more than familiarity and routine, long after any real affection has gone.

'I love my daughter, Professor, but I don't profess to understand women particularly well, not even my wife,' he says, blowing his nose. 'She loves me – figure that out.'

He folds the handkerchief into quarters and returns it to his trouser pocket.

'I didn't like the way Gideon manipulated Helen. She was a different girl around him. When they married, Gideon wanted her to be blonde. She went to a hairdresser but the result was a disaster. She finished up with bright ginger hair. She was embarrassed enough, but Gideon made it worse. He poked fun at her at their wedding; belittled her in front of her friends. I hated him for that.'

'At the wedding reception, I wanted to dance with her. It's traditional – the father dancing with the bride. Gideon made Helen ask his permission first. It was her wedding day, for Christ's sake! What bride has to get permission to dance with her father on her wedding day?'

Something flashes across his face, an involuntary spasm.

'When they moved to Northern Ireland, Helen would call at least twice a week and write long letters. Then the calls and letters dried up. Gideon didn't want her communicating with us.'

'Why?'

'I don't know. He seemed to be jealous of her family and her friends. We saw less and less of Helen. When she came to visit it was never for more than a night or two before Gideon packed the car. Helen rarely smiled and she spoke in whispers but she was loyal to Gideon and wouldn't say a word against him.

'When she fell pregnant with Chloe, she told her mother not

to visit. Later we discovered that Gideon didn't want the baby. He was furious and demanded she had an abortion. Helen refused.

'I don't know for sure but I think he was jealous of his own child. Can you believe that? Funny thing is, when Chloe was born his attitude changed completely. He was besotted. Captivated. Things settled down. They were happier.

'Gideon was transferred to Osnabrück in Germany, the British Forces base. They moved into a flat provided by the army. There were lots of other wives and families in the married quarters. Helen managed to write about once a month but soon these letters stopped and she couldn't contact us without his permission.

'Every evening Gideon quizzed her about where she went, who she saw, what was said. Helen had to remember entire conversations verbatim or Gideon accused of her of lying or keeping secrets from him. She had to sneak out of the house to call her mother from a public phone because she knew any call from home or her mobile would show up on the phone bill.

'Even when Gideon went away on tours of duty, Helen had to be careful. She was sure that people were watching her and reporting back to him.

'His jealousy was like a disease. Whenever they went out socialising, Gideon would make Helen sit in a corner by herself. If another man talked to her, he'd get angry. He'd demand to know exactly what was said – word for word.'

Rocking forward in his chair Bryan Chambers clasps his hands together, as if praying he'd done something sooner to rescue his daughter.

'Gideon's behaviour became even more erratic after his last tour. I don't know what happened. According to Helen he became distant, moody, violent . . .'

'He hit her?' asks Ruiz.

'Only the once – a backhander across her face. It split Helen's lip. She threatened to leave. He apologised. He cried. He begged her to stay. She should have left him then. She should have run away. But every time she contemplated leaving, her resolve weakened.'

'What happened on his last tour?'

Chambers shrugs. 'I don't know. He was in Afghanistan. Helen said something about a friend dying and another getting badly wounded.'

'Did you ever hear the name Patrick Fuller mentioned?'

He shakes his head.

'Gideon came back and suddenly demanded that Helen have another baby, a boy. He wanted a boy that he could name after his dead friend. He flushed her birth control pills down the toilet, but Helen found ways to stop herself falling pregnant.

'Soon after that Gideon got permission to move them out of the married quarters. He rented a farmhouse about ten miles from the garrison, in the middle of nowhere. Helen didn't have a telephone or a car. She and Chloe were totally isolated. He was closing the world around them, making it shrink to fit just the three of them.

'Helen wanted to send Chloe to boarding school in England but Gideon refused. Instead she went to the garrison school. Gideon drove her every morning. From the moment Helen waved them goodbye she saw nobody. Yet every evening Gideon would quiz her about what she'd done and who she'd seen. If she stumbled or hesitated, his questions became harder.'

The big man is on his feet again, still talking.

'This one particular day, he came home and noticed tyre tracks on the driveway. He accused Helen of having had a visitor. She denied it. He claimed it was her lover. Helen pleaded with him that it wasn't true.

'He forced her head to the kitchen table and then used a knife to carve "x" into the palm of his hand. Then he squeezed his fist and the blood dripped into her eyes.'

I remember the scar on Tyler's left hand when I interviewed him at Trinity Road.

'You know the ironic thing?' says Chambers, squeezing his eyes shut. 'The tyre marks didn't belong to any visitor or lover. Gideon had forgotten that he'd driven a different vehicle home from the garrison the previous day. The tracks belonged to him.

'That night Helen waited until Gideon was asleep. She took a suitcase from beneath the stairs and woke Chloe. They didn't shut the car doors because she didn't want to make a sound. The car wouldn't start straight away, the ignition turned over and over. Helen knew the sound would wake Gideon.

'He came crashing out of the farmhouse, with one leg in a pair of trousers, hopping barefoot down the steps. The engine started. Helen put her foot down. Gideon chased them down the driveway but she didn't slow down. She took the corner onto the main road and Chloe's door flew open. My granddaughter slipped out of the seat belt. Helen grabbed her as she fell and pulled her back inside. She broke Chloe's arm, but she didn't stop. She kept driving. And she kept thinking that Gideon was following her.'

Bryan Chambers sucks in a breath. He holds it. A part of him wants to stop talking. He wishes he'd stopped ten minutes ago but the story has a momentum that won't be easily halted.

Instead of driving to Calais, Helen went in the opposite direction, towards Austria and then to Italy, stopping only to refuel. She phoned her parents from a motorway service station. Bryan Chambers offered to fly her home but she wanted to take some time to think.

Chloe had her arm set in a hospital in Milan. Bryan Chambers wired them money – enough to pay any medical bills, buy new clothes and let them travel for a few months.

'Did you see Helen at all?' I ask.

He shakes his head.

'I spoke to her on the phone . . . and to Chloe. They sent us postcards from Turkey and Crete.'

The words are thick in his throat. These memories are precious to him – last words, last letters, last photographs . . . every scrap hoarded and treasured.

'Why did none of Helen's friends know that she drowned?' asks Ruiz.

'The newspapers used her married name.'

'But there weren't any death notices or funeral notices?'

'There wasn't a funeral.'

'Why not?'

'You want to know why?' His eyes are blazing. 'Because of

310

Tyler! I was frightened that he would show up and do something to spoil the funeral. We couldn't say a proper goodbye to our daughter and our granddaughter because that psychotic bastard would have turned it into a circus.'

His chest heaves. The sudden outburst seems to have sucked the remaining fight from him.

'We had a private service,' he murmurs.

'Where?'

'In Greece.'

'Why Greece?'

'That's where we lost them. It's where they were happy. We built a memorial on a rocky headland overlooking a bay where Chloe used to go swimming.'

'A memorial,' says Ruiz. 'Where are their graves?'

'Their bodies were never recovered. The currents are so strong in that part of the Aegean. One of the navy divers found Chloe. Her life vest had snagged on the metal rungs of a ladder near the stern of the ferry. He cut the vest from her but the current ripped her away. He didn't have enough air left in his tanks to swim after her.'

'And he was sure?'

'She still had a cast on her arm. It was Chloe.'

The phone rings. The old lawyer glances at his watch. Time is measured in fifteen minute intervals – billable hours. I wonder how much he's going to charge his 'old friend' for this consultation.

I thank Mr Chambers for his time and rise slowly from my chair. The depressions left behind in the leather slowly begin to fill.

'You know I've thought about killing him,' says Bryan Chambers. Julian Spencer tries to stop him talking but is waved away. 'I asked Skipper what it would take. Who would I have to pay? I mean, you read about stuff like that all the time.'

'I'm sure Skipper has friends,' says Ruiz.

'Yes,' nods Chambers. 'I don't know whether I'd trust any of them. They'd probably wipe out half a building.'

He looks at Julian Spencer. 'Don't worry. It's just talk. Claudia

would never let me do it. She has a God she has to answer to.'
He closes his eyes for a moment and opens them, hoping the world
might have changed.

'Do you have children, Professor?'

'Two of them.'

He looks at Ruiz, who holds up two fingers.

'You never stop worrying,' says Chambers. 'You worry through
the pregnancy, the birth, the first year and every year that follows.
You worry about them catching the bus, crossing the road, riding
a bike, climbing a tree . . . You read stories in newspapers about
terrible things happening to children. It makes you frightened. It
never goes away.'

'I know.'

'And then you think how they grow up so quickly and suddenly
you don't have a say any more. You want them to find the perfect
boyfriend and the perfect husband. You want them to get their
dream job. You want to save them from every disappointment,
every broken heart, but you can't. You never stop being a parent.
You never stop worrying. If you're lucky, you're going to be around
to pick up the pieces.'

He turns away but I can see his misery reflected in the window.

'Do you have a photograph of Tyler?' I ask.

'Maybe at home. He didn't like cameras – even at the wedding.'

'How about a photograph of Helen? I haven't seen a proper
one. The newspapers had a snapshot of her in Greece taken before
the sinking.'

'It's the most recent one we had,' he explains.

'Do you have any others?'

He hesitates and glances at Julian Spencer. Then he opens his
wallet and pulls out a passport-sized print.

'When was it taken?' I ask.

'A few months ago. Helen sent it from Greece. We had to organise
a new passport for her – in her maiden name.'

'Would you mind if I borrowed this?'

'Why?'

'Sometimes it helps me to understand a crime if I have a photograph of the victim.'

'Is that what you think she is?'

'Yes. She was the first.'

Ruiz hasn't said anything since we left the lawyer's office. I'm
sure he has an opinion but he won't share it until he's ready.
Maybe it's a legacy of his former career but there's an aura of
no-place and no-time about him that releases him from the normal
rules of conversation. Saying that, he's noticeably mellowed since
he retired. The forces within him have found equilibrium and
he's made peace with whatever patron saint looks after atheists.
There's a patron saint for everything else, so why not for non-
believers?

Everything about this case has shimmered and shifted with
emotion and grief. It's been hard to focus on particular details
because I've spent so much time dealing with immediate concerns
such as Darcy, worrying what's going to happen to her. Now I want
to take a step back in the hope I can see things in some sort of
context, but it's not easy to let go from the face of a mountain.

I can understand why Bryan and Claudia Chambers were so
angry and inhospitable when we visited their estate. Gideon Tyler
has stalked them. He has followed their cars, opened their mail
and left obscene souvenirs.

The police couldn't stop the harassment, so the Chambers gave
up co-operating and took their own security measures, organising
round-the-clock protection with alarms, motion sensors, intercepts
and bodyguards. I can understand their reasoning, but not Gideon's.
Why is he still looking for Helen and Chloe, if that's what he's
doing?

There is nothing artless and spur-of-the-moment about Gideon.
He is a bully, a sadist and the control freak who has carefully and
systematically set out to destroy his wife's family and to kill each
of her friends.

It wasn't purely for pleasure – not in the beginning. He was
looking for Helen and Chloe. Now it's different. My mind goes
back to Christine Wheeler's mobile phone. Why did Gideon keep
it? Why not dispose of her mobile or leave it in Christine's car?
Instead he took it back to Patrick Fuller's flat, where Patrick's sister

unwittingly used the mobile to order a pizza. It almost brought his plans unstuck.

Gideon bought a charger. Police found the receipt. He charged the battery so he could look at the phone's memory. He thought it might lead him to Helen and Chloe. It's the same reason he broke into Christine Wheeler's house during her funeral and opened the condolence cards. He must have hoped that Helen would turn up to the funeral or at the very least send a card.

What does Gideon know that we don't? Is he delusional or in denial or does he have some insight or information that has escaped everyone else? What good is a secret if no one else knows of its existence?

Ruiz has parked the Merc in a multi-storey behind the law courts. He unlocks the door and sits behind the wheel, staring over the rooftops where gulls wheel in spirals like sheets of newspaper caught in an updraft.

'Tyler thinks his wife is still alive. Any chance he's right?'

'Next to none,' he answers. 'There was a coronial inquest and a maritime board of inquiry.'

'You got any contacts in the Greek police?'

'None.'

Ruiz is still motionless behind the wheel, his eyes closed as if listening to the slow beat of his own blood. We both know what has to be done. We need to look at the ferry sinking. There must be witness statements, a passenger manifest and photographs . . . Someone must have talked to Helen and Chloe.

'You don't believe Chambers.'

'It was one half of a sad story.'

'Who has the other half?'

'Gideon Tyler.'

49

Emma is awake, mewling and snuffling in the grip of a dream. I slip out of bed half-asleep and go to her bed, cursing the coldness of the floor and stiffness of my legs.

Her eyes are squeezed tightly shut and her head rocks from side to side. Reaching down, I put my hand on her chest. It seems to cover her entire ribcage. Her eyes open. I pick her up and hold her against me. Her heart is racing.

'It's OK, sweetheart. It was only a dream.'

'I saw a monster.'

'There are no monsters.'

'It was trying to eat you. It eated your arm and it eated one of your legs.'

'I'm fine. Look. Two arms. Two legs. Remember what I told you? There are no monsters.'

'They're just make believe.'

'Yes.'

'What if he comes back?'

'You have to dream about something else. How about this – you dream about your birthday parties, fairy bread and jelly beans.'

'Marshmallows.'

'Yes.'

'I like marshmallows. The pinks ones, not the white ones.'

'They taste the same.'

'Not to me.'

I set her down and tuck her in and kiss her on the cheek.

Julianne is in Rome. She left on Wednesday. I didn't get a chance to see her. By the time I arrived home from the Fernwood Clinic, she'd already gone.

I talked to her last night on the phone. Dirk answered her mobile when I called. He said Julianne was busy and would call back. I waited over an hour and called again. She said she didn't get my message.

'So you're working late,' I said.

'Nearly finished.'

She sounded tired. The Italians had changed their demands, she said. She and Dirk were redrafting the entire deal and approaching the major investors again. I didn't understand the details.

'Will you still be coming home tomorrow?'

'Yes.'

'Do you still want me to come to the party?'

'If you want to.' It wasn't an enthusiastic affirmative. She asked about the girls and about Imogen and Ruiz, who went back to London yesterday. I told her everything was fine.

'Listen. I have to go. Give my love to the girls.'

'I will.'

'Bye.'

Julianne hung up first. I held on, listening, as if something in the silence was going to reassure me that everything was fine and by tomorrow she'd be home and we'd have a wonderful weekend in London. Only it didn't feel OK. I kept picturing Dirk in her hotel room, answering her mobile, sharing a room service break-fast. I've never had these thoughts before, never doubted, never fretted; and now I can't tell if I'm being paranoid (because Mr Parkinson will do that to you every time) or whether my suspicions are justified.

Julianne has changed, but then so have I. When we first met, she sometimes asked me if there was something caught in her teeth or wrong with her clothes because people were staring at

316

her. She had so little sense of her own beauty that she didn't recognise the attention it garnered.

It doesn't happen so much now. She's more cautious and wary of strangers. The events of three years ago are to blame. She no longer smiles at strangers or gives money to beggars; or offers to provide directions to people who are lost.

Emma has fallen back to sleep. I tuck her elephant next to the bars of the cot and ease the door shut.

On the far side of the landing, I hear Charlie's voice.

'Is she all right?'

'She's fine. It was a nightmare. Go back to sleep.'

'Got to go to the loo.'

She's wearing baggy pyjama pants that sit low on her hips. I didn't think she'd ever have hips or a proper waist. She was straight up and down.

'Can I ask you something?' she says, standing at the bathroom door.

'Sure.'

'Darcy ran away.'

'Yes.'

'Will she come back?'

'I hope so.'

'OK.'

'OK, what?'

'Nothing. Just OK.' And then, 'Why doesn't Darcy want to live with her aunt?'

'She thinks she's old enough to look after herself.'

She nods, leaning against the doorframe. Her hair falls in an arc across one eye. 'I don't know what I'd do if Mum died.'

'Nobody is going to die. Don't be so morbid.'

She's gone. Tiptoeing back to bed, I lie awake. The ceiling seems far away. The pillow next to me is cold.

There has been no word on Gideon Tyler. Veronica Cray has called once or twice, keeping me informed. Gideon isn't listed on the voting rolls or telephone directories. He doesn't have a UK bank account or a credit card. He hasn't visited a doctor or a hospital. He didn't sign a lease or pay a bond. Mr Swingler took six months rent in advance, in cash. Some people walk softly through life, Gideon has barely left a footprint.

All we seem to know for certain is that he was born in Liverpool in 1969. His father, Eric Tyler, is a retired sheet metal worker living in Bristol. Full of gristle and bone and 'fuck-you' animosity, he abused police through the letterbox and refused to open the door unless he saw a warrant. When he was eventually interviewed he harped on about his children letting him starve.

There is another son, an older one, who runs a stationery supply company in Leicester. He claims he hasn't seen or spoken to Gideon in a decade.

Gideon joined the army at eighteen. He served in the first Gulf War and in Kosovo as a peacekeeper after the Bosnian War. According to Patrick Fuller he transferred to the Army Intelligence Corp in the mid-nineties and we know from Bryan Chambers that he trained at the Defence Intelligence and Security Centre at Chicksands in Bedfordshire.

Initially, he was stationed in Northern Ireland and later transferred to Osnabrück, Germany, as part of the NATO Immediate Reaction Force. Normally British servicemen do tours of only four years, but for some reason Gideon stayed on. Why?

Every time I contemplate what he's done and what he's capable of, I feel a rising sense of panic. Sexual sadists do not stay silent. They won't go away.

Everything about his actions has been deliberate, unperturbed and almost euphoric. He believes he is cleverer than the police, the military, the rest of humanity. Each of his crimes has been a little more perverse and theatrical than the last. He is an artist, not a butcher – that's what he's saying.

The next one will be the worst. Gideon failed to kill Maureen Bracken, which means his next victim takes on added significance. Veronica Cray and her team are tracing every one of Helen Chambers' old schoolfriends, university buddies and workmates, particularly those with children. It's a massive task. She doesn't have the personnel to guard all of them. All she can do is provide them with a mugshot of Gideon Tyler and make them aware of his methods.

These are the thoughts that follow me into sleep, sliding between shadows, echoing like someone walking behind me.

Saturday morning. There are chores to do before I leave for London. The village is having a fête.

Local shops, clubs, and community groups have set up stalls, draping their tables with bunting and gimmicky signs. There are second-hand books, homemade cakes, handicrafts, dodgy DVDs and a pile of cheap dictionaries from the mobile library.

Penny Havers, who works in a shoe-shop in Bath, has brought stacks of boxes – most of them one-size only, overly large or ridiculously small, but very cheap.

Charlie walks through the village with me. I know how this works. As soon as she sees a boy she's going to drop a dozen paces behind me and pretend to be on her own. When there are no boys, she makes me stop and look at fake jewellery and clothes she doesn't need.

Everyone is excited about the annual rugby clash between Wellow and our nearest neighbours, Norton St Philip, three miles away. It's on this afternoon on the rec behind the village hall.

Wellow is one of those villages that lay almost undiscovered until the mid-eighties, when its population swelled with commuters and sea-changers. The influx has slowed, according to the locals. Property prices have soared out of the reach of weekend visitors, who gaze in the village estate agent's window, daydreaming about owning a stone cottage with roses climbing over the door. The dream lasts as long as the M4 traffic jam getting back into London and is forgotten completely by Monday morning.

Charlie wants to get a Halloween mask: a rubbery monster with glow in the dark hair. I tell her no. Emma is already having nightmares.

There is a policeman on traffic duty outside the post office, directing cars into neighbouring fields. I think of Veronica Cray. She's in London today, knocking on doors at the MOD and Foreign Office, trying to discover why nobody wants to talk about Tyler. So far all she's managed to get is a single line statement from the

319

Chief of Defence Staff: 'Major Gideon Tyler is absent without leave from his unit.'

Ten words. It could be a cover-up. It could be denial. It could be a classic example of true British brevity. Whatever the reason, the outcome is the same – an echoing, uncomfortable, unfathomable silence.

Apart from the mugshot taken of Gideon ten days ago, under Patrick Fuller's name, there is no photograph of him that is less than a decade old. CCTV footage of him entering the UK on 19 May shows him wearing a baseball cap pulled down over his eyes.

The evidence against him is compelling, but circumstantial. He had Christine Wheeler's mobile. Alice Furness has identified him as the man she spoke to in the pub four days before her mother disappeared. Darcy is still missing but might also be able to recognise him from the train. Maureen Bracken only met Gideon once, seven years ago. She didn't remember his voice but the man who spoke to her asked about Helen Chambers.

Police haven't managed to link Gideon to any of the other mobiles used in the attacks, which had either been stolen or purchased using fake identification.

Charlie is talking to me: 'Earth to Dad, Earth to Dad. Are you reading me?'

It's her mother's line. She is looking through a rack of clothes, trying to find something dark and goth-like.

'Did you hear anything I said?'

'No. I'm sorry.'

'You're hopeless sometimes.' Again, she sounds like Julianne. 'It was about Darcy.'

'What about her?'

'Why can't she come and live with us?'

'She has her own family. And we don't have the room.'

'We could make room.'

'It doesn't work like that.'

'But her aunt hates her.'

'Who told you that?'

The hesitation is enough evidence. Charlie makes it worse by

320

turning and burrowing into an open cardboard box full of doll's clothes. She won't look at me.

'Have you talked to Darcy?'

She chooses not to answer rather than tell a lie.

'When did you talk to her?'

Charlie looks at me as though it's my fault that she can't keep a secret.

'Please, sweetheart. I've been worried. I need to know where she is.'

'In London.'

'You've talked to her?'

'Uh-huh.'

'Why didn't you tell me?'

'She told me not to. She said that you'd come looking for her. She said you'd make her go to Spain with her aunt, the one who smokes and smells like a donkey.'

I'm more relieved than angry. It's been five days since Darcy went missing and she hasn't returned any of my calls or messages. Charlie comes clean. She and Darcy have been talking most days and sending text messages. Darcy is living in London and hanging out with an older girl who used to dance with the Royal Ballet.

'I want you to call her for me.'

Charlie hesitates. 'Do I have to?'

'Yes.'

'What if she won't be my friend any more?'

'This is more important.'

Charlie takes her mobile from her jeans and punches the number.

'She's not there,' she says. 'Do you want me to leave a message?'

I think for a moment. I'll be in London four hours from now.

'Tell her to call you.'

Charlie leaves a message. Afterwards, I take the mobile from her hand and give her mine.

'We're swapping, just for today. Darcy won't answer *my* calls, but she'll answer yours.'

Charlie frowns crossly. She has the cutest twin creases above the bridge of her nose.

'If you read my text messages, I'll never talk to you again!'

50

Ruiz leans against a park bench, eating a sandwich and drinking coffee. He's watching a delivery truck trying to reverse down a narrow driveway. Someone is directing the driver, signalling left or right. A hand slaps the roller door.

'You know one of the hard things about being retired?' says Ruiz.

'What's that?'

'You never get a day off. No holidays or long weekends.'

'My heart bleeds.'

The park bench overlooks the Thames. Pale afternoon sunlight barely raises a gleam on the heavy brown water. Rowing crews and tourist launches leave white wakes that slide across the surface and wash up against the glistening mud exposed by an ebbing tide.

The old Barn Elms Water Works is across the river. South London could be another country. That's the thing about London. It's not so much a metropolis as a collection of villages. Chelsea is different from Clapham, Clapham is different from Hammersmith is different from Barnes is different from a dozen other places. The dividing line may only be as wide as a river yet the ambience changes completely once you cross from one place to the next.

Julianne is back from Rome. I wanted to meet her at Heathrow, but she said the company had sent a car and she had to go to the office. We've arranged to meet later at the hotel and go to the party together.

'You want another coffee?' asks Ruiz.

'No thanks.'

Ruiz's house is across the road. He treats the Thames like a water feature in his front garden or his own private stretch of river. This particular park bench is his outdoor furniture and he spends several hours a day here, fishing and reading the morning papers. Rumour has it that he's never actually caught a fish and this has nothing to do with the water quality of the river or the fish population. He doesn't use bait. I haven't asked if it's true. Some questions are best left unspoken.

We take our empty mugs back to the house and the kitchen. The door to the utilities room is open. Clothes spew from a dryer, light, pretty, women's things; a tartan skirt, a mauve bra and ankle socks. Something about the scene is familiar yet oddly unsettling. I don't picture Ruiz having women in his life even though he's been married three times.

'Is there something you want to share with me?' I ask.

He looks at the basket. 'I don't think they'd fit.'

'You have someone staying.'

'My daughter.'

'When did she get home?'

'A while back.' He shuts the door, trying to close off the conversation.

Ruiz's daughter Claire has been dancing in New York. Her troubled relationship with her father has been akin to global warming – a melting of the icecaps, a rise in the oceans and a refloating of the boat – none of it achieved without sceptical voices questioning the outcome.

We move to the lounge. Papers and folders relating to the sinking of the *Argo Hellas* are spread across a coffee table. Ruiz takes a seat and pulls out his battered notebook.

'I talked to the chief investigator as well as the coroner and the local police commander.' Loose pages threaten to spill out from the broken spine as he turns them. 'It was a thorough investigation. These are statements from witnesses and a transcript of the inquiry. They arrived by courier yesterday and I read them last night. Found nothing out of the ordinary.

'Three people gave evidence that Helen and Chloe Tyler were on the ferry. One of them was a navy diver who was part of the recovery team.'

Ruiz hands me his statement and waits while I read it. The diver describes recovering four bodies that day. The visibility was less than ten yards and a treacherous current made the job more difficult.

On the fifth dive of the day, he found the body of a young girl snagged on the metal rungs of a ladder near a lifeboat winch, starboard side, nearest the stern. The diver cut the straps from the girl's lifejacket, but the current ripped her body from his hands. He didn't have enough air left in his tanks to swim after her.

'He identified Chloe from a photograph,' says Ruiz. 'The girl had a cast on her arm. It matches what her grandfather said happened.'

Despite the statement, I sense that Ruiz isn't completely convinced.

'I did some checking on this diver. He's a ten-year veteran, one of the most experienced divers they have.'

'And?'

'The navy suspended him for six months last year when he failed to check gear properly and almost drowned a trainee. Word is – well, it's more a whisper – that he's a drunk.'

Ruiz hands me a second statement. It belongs to a Canadian gap-year student who said he spoke to Helen and Chloe just after the ferry sailed. They were sitting in a passenger lounge, starboard side. Chloe was seasick and the backpacker offered her a pill.

'I talked to his folks in Vancouver. They flew to Greece after the sinking and tried to talk him into coming home, but he wanted to continue. The kid is still travelling.'

'Shouldn't he have started uni by now?'

'His gap year is turning into two.'

The last statement is from a German woman, Yelena Schafer, who runs a local hotel on Patmos. She drove mother and daughter to the ferry and says she waved them off.

Ruiz tells me he put in a call to the hotel but it was closed for the winter.

'I managed to get hold of the caretaker, but this guy was all over the place like a wet dog on lino. Said he remembered Helen and Chloe. They stayed at the hotel for three weeks in June.'

'Where is Yelena Schafer now?'

'On holiday. The hotel won't reopen until the spring.'

'She might have family in Germany.'

'I'll call the caretaker again. He wasn't overly helpful.'

Ruiz has left the curtains open. Through the window I see joggers ghost past on the Thames' path and hear seagulls fighting over scraps in the ooze.

Ruiz hands me a report from the Maritime Rescue Service which lists the names of the dead, the missing and survivors. There was no official passenger manifest. The ferry was a regular island service full of tourists and locals, many of whom hopped on and off, paying for their tickets on board. Helen and Chloe most likely paid cash to avoid the paper trail left by a credit card.

Bryan Chambers said he last wired his daughter money on June 16, transferred from an account on the Isle of Man to a bank on Patmos.

What other evidence do we have that Helen and Chloe were on board the *Argo Hellas*? Luggage was found washed ashore on a beach, three miles east of the town. A large suitcase. A local fishing boat picked up a smaller bag belonging to Chloe.

Ruiz produces a hardcover book decorated with a collage of photographs cut from the pages of magazines and stuck onto the cover. The cardboard is swollen from water damage and the name-plate is illegible.

'This was among the personal effects. It's Chloe's journal.'

'How did you get it?'

'I told a few white lies. I'm supposed to deliver it to the family.'

I open the book and run my fingers over the pages, which are buckled and undulating from the dried salt. The journal is more of a scrapbook than a daily diary. It contains postcards, photographs, ticket stubs and drawings, as well as the occasional diary entry and observation. Chloe pressed flowers between the pages. Poppies. I can see where the stamens and petals have stained the paper.

The brittle pages detail their travels – mainly in the islands. Occasionally, people are mentioned: a Turkish girl Chloe befriended and a boy who showed her how to catch fish.

There is no mention of the escape from Germany, but Chloe writes of the doctor in Italy who put her arm in a cast. He was the first to sign the plaster and drew a picture of Winnie the Pooh.

Using the postcards and place references, I can make out the route Helen took. She must have sold the car or left it somewhere, before they took a bus through mountains to Yugoslavia and across the border into Greece.

Days are unaccounted for. Weeks disappear. Mother and daughter kept moving, getting further from Germany, entering Turkey and following the coast. They finally stopped running at a campground in Fethiye on the edge of the Aegean. Chloe's arm wasn't healing properly. She visited the hospital again. There were more x-rays. Consultants. She wrote a postcard to her father; drew a picture of him. It was obviously never posted.

The impression I get of Chloe is of a bright, carefree child who missed her schoolfriends in Germany and her pet cat Tinkerbell, who everyone called 'Tinkle' because that was the sound the bell on her collar made when she tried to catch birds in the garden.

The last page of the journal is dated is 22 July, two days before the *Argo Hellas* sank. Chloe was excited about her birthday. She would have turned seven in just over a fortnight.

Moving backwards through the final pages, I sense that Helen and Chloe had finally started to relax. They spent longer in Patmos than any place they'd visited in the previous two months.

I close Chloe's journal and run my fingers over the collage.

Sometimes when you look too hard at a scene it leads to a kind of blindness because the image becomes burned onto our subconscious mind and will remain unchanged even when something new happens that should draw our attention. Similarly, the desire to simplify or to see a situation as a whole can cause us to ignore details that don't fit rather than try to explain them.

'Did they include a photograph of Helen Chambers in the stuff they sent?' I ask Ruiz.

'We already have one.'

Suddenly, he senses where I'm going.

'What? You think it's a different woman?'

'No, but I want to be sure.'

He draws back, watching me. 'You're as bad as Gideon – you don't think they're dead.'

'I want to know why he thinks they're alive.'

'Because he's either deluded or in denial.'

'Or he knows something.'

Ruiz stands up, stiff-kneed and grimacing. 'If Helen and Chloe are alive, where are they?'

'Hiding.'

'How did they fake their deaths?'

'Their bodies were never found. Their luggage could have been thrown into the sea.'

'What about the statements?'

'Bryan Chambers has the money to be very persuasive.'

'It's a stretch,' says Ruiz. 'I talked to the coroner's office. Helen and Chloe are officially dead.'

'Can we ask them to fax through a photograph of Helen Chambers? I just want to be sure we're talking about the same woman.'

Veronica Cray is due to catch a train back to Bristol at six. I want to talk to her before she leaves. A minicab takes us along Fulham Palace Road, through Hammersmith and Shepherd's Bush. The cab's suspension has almost collapsed completely on the right side. Maybe there's a pedestrian lodged under the front axle.

Alongside me, Ruiz is silent. Buses shunt along the inside lane pausing to pick up queues at the bus stops. Other faces peer out from the windows or doze with their heads against the glass.

I keep going over the details of the ferry disaster. Helen and Chloe's bodies were never recovered, but that doesn't mean they survived. Gideon has no conclusive proof either way. That's what he could be searching for – proof of death or proof of life. It's not the whole answer. His crimes are too sadistic. He's enjoying this too much to stop.

Veronica Cray is waiting for us at a café near platform one. Her overcoat is unbuttoned and drapes to the ground. She and Ruiz acknowledge each other without words. The only two things they have in common are their respective careers and a shared ability to let silence speak volumes.

Seats are rearranged. Watches checked. Veronica Cray has fifteen minutes.

'The MOD wants to take over the investigation,' she announces.

'What do you mean?'

'Tyler went AWOL. They claim he's still one of theirs. They want to make the arrest.'

'What did you say?'

'I told them to fuck off. Two women are dead and this is *my* investigation. And I'm not going to back off on the say-so of some pencil dick in khakis who gets a hard-on every time a tank rolls by.'

The vitriol in her voice is in sharp contrast to the care she takes in sugaring her tea and stirring it slowly. Holding the teacup between her thumb and forefinger, she drinks half the brew, ignoring the heat. Her pale fat throat seems to have a fist inside it, moving up and down.

Setting down the cup, she begins relating what she's managed to find out about Gideon Tyler. Through a contact in the Royal Ulster Constabulary, she learned that Tyler spent four years in Belfast working for the TCG (Tasking and Co-ordination Group) in Armagh – a military intelligence body that specialised in surveillance and interrogation.

'No wonder he's so hard to find,' says Ruiz. 'These guys know how to follow someone and not be noticed. They're experts in second and third party awareness.'

'And how would you know a detail like that?' asks DI Cray.

'I worked in Belfast for a while,' says Ruiz without offering any further explanation.

The DI doesn't like being kept in the dark but carries on. 'The Department of Immigration pulled up Tyler's file. In the past six years he's made multiple trips to Pakistan, Poland, Egypt, Somalia, Afghanistan and Iraq. The length of time varies: none shorter than a week, never longer than a month.'

'Why Egypt and Somalia?' asks Ruiz. 'The British army doesn't operate there.'

'He could have been training locals,' says the DI.

'It doesn't explain the secrecy.'

'Counter intelligence.'

'Makes more sense.'

'Maureen Bracken said Christine and Sylvia used to joke about Gideon being a spook.'

I consider the list of countries he visited: Afghanistan, Iraq, Poland, Pakistan, Egypt and Somalia. He is a trained interrogator, an expert in eliciting information from suspects – POWs, detainees, terrorists . . .

The memory of Sylvia Furness, hooded and hanging from a branch, fills my head. And a second image: Maureen Bracken, kneeling, blindfolded, with her hands outstretched. Sensory deprivation, disorientation and humiliation are the tools of interrogators and torturers.

If Gideon believes Helen and Chloe are alive, it stands to reason he's also convinced people are hiding them. Bryan and Claudia Chambers, Christine Wheeler, Sylvia Furness and Maureen Bracken.

DI Cray gazes at me steadily. Ruiz sits motionless, with his eyes raised as if he's listening for an approaching train or an echo from the past.

'Let's say you're right and Tyler believes they're alive,' says Veronica Cray. 'Why is he trying to flush them out? What's the point? Helen isn't going back to him and he'll never breathe the same air as his daughter.'

'He doesn't want them back. He wants to punish his wife for having left him and he wants to see his daughter. Tyler is being driven by fear and hatred. Fear at what he's capable of and fear of never seeing his daughter again. But his hate is even stronger. It has a structure all of its own.'

'What does that mean?'

'His is a hatred that demands we step aside; it negates the rights of others, it cleanses, it poisons, it dictates his beliefs. Hate is what sustains him.'

'Who will he target next?'

'No way of telling. Helen's family are protected but she must have plenty of other friends.'

DI Cray leans hard on her knees, looking for a scrap of comfort in the polished caps of her shoes. A platform announcement ripples the air. She has to leave.

Buttoning her overcoat, she stands, says goodbye and hustles across the concourse towards her waiting train with an ogreish intensity. Ruiz watches her go and scratches his nose.

'Do you think inside Cray there's a thin woman, trying to get out?'

'Two of them.'

'You want a drink?'

I look at my watch. 'Another time. Julianne's party starts at eight. I want to buy her a present.'

'Like what?'

'Jewellery is always nice.'

'Only if you're having an affair.'

'What do you mean?'

'Expensive gifts express guilt.'

'No they don't.'

'The more expensive the jewellery, the deeper the guilt.'

'You are a *very* sad suspicious man.'

'I've been married three times. I know these things.'

Ruiz is watching me sidelong. I can feel my left hand twitching.

'Julianne's been away a lot. Travelling. I miss her. I thought I might buy her something special.'

My excuses sound too strident. I should just be quiet. I'm not going to tell Ruiz about Julianne's boss, or the room service receipt, or the lingerie or the phone calls. And I'm not going to mention

330

Darcy's kiss or Julianne's question about whether I still love her. I won't say anything – and he won't ask.

That's one of the great paradoxes of friendship between men. It's like an unspoken code: you don't start tunnelling unless you hit rock bottom.

51

The central hall of the Natural History Museum has been transformed into a prehistoric forest. Monkeys, reptiles and birds seem to scale the terracotta walls and soaring arches. A skeletal Diplodocus is lit up in green.

I am showered, neatly shaved and medicated, dressed in my finest evening attire, which hasn't had an airing for almost two years. Julianne told me to hire a tux from Moss Bros but why waste a perfectly good old one?

I arrived alone. Julianne didn't get to the hotel in time. More problems at work, she said, without elaborating. She's coming separately with Dirk and the chairman, Eugene Franklin. A hundred or more of her colleagues are here, being fed and watered by waiters, who move across the mosaic floor with silver trays of champagne. The men are dressed in black tie (far more fashionable than mine) and the women look svelte in cocktail dresses with plunging necklines, daring backs and high heels. They are professional couples, venture capitalists, bankers and accountants. In the eighties they were 'masters of the universe' now they make do with mastering corporations and conglomerates.

I should be drinking orange juice but can't find one. I guess one glass of champagne won't hurt. I don't go to many parties. Late nights and alcohol are on my list of things to avoid. Mr

Parkinson might turn up. He might seize my left arm in mid-mouthful or mid-sip and leave me frozen like one of the stuffed primates on the second floor.

Julianne should be here by now. Rising on my toes, I look for her over the heads. I see a beautiful woman at the bottom of the stairs, in a flowing silk gown that swoops in elegant folds down to the small of her back and between her breasts. For a moment I don't recognise her. It's Julianne. I haven't seen the gown before. I wish I had bought it for her.

Someone stumbles in to me, spilling her champagne.

'It's these bloody heels,' she explains, apologetically, offering me a napkin.

Tall, reed-thin and well on the way to being drunk, she dangles a champagne flute between her fingers.

'You're obviously an *other* half,' she says.

'Pardon?'

'Someone's husband,' she explains.

'How can you tell?'

'You look lost. I'm Felicity, by the way. People call me Flip.'

She offers me two fingers to shake. I'm still trying to make eye contact with Julianne.

'I'm Joe.'

'Mr Joe.'

'Joe O'Loughlin.'

Her eyes widen in surprise. 'So *you're* the mysterious husband. I thought Julianne wore a fake wedding ring.'

'Who has a fake wedding ring?' interrupts a smaller, top-heavy woman.

'Nobody. This is Julianne's husband.'

'Really?'

'Why would she wear a fake wedding ring?' I ask.

Flip plucks another glass of champagne from a passing waiter.

'To ward off unwelcome suitors, of course, but it doesn't always work. Some men see it as a challenge.'

The small woman giggles and her décolletage quakes. She's so short that I can't look at her face without feeling that I'm staring at her cleavage.

333

Julianne is talking to several men at the bottom of the stairs. They must be important because lesser mortals are hovering on the periphery, nervous about joining the conversation. A tall dark-haired man whispers something in Julianne's ear. His hand brushes her spine and rests in the small of her back.

'You must be very proud of her,' says Flip.

'Yes.'

'You live in Cornwall, don't you?'

'Somerset.'

'Julianne doesn't really strike me as a country girl.'

'Why's that?'

'She's so glamorous. I'm surprised you let her stray so far from home.'

The man talking to Julianne has made her laugh. She closes her eyes and the tip of her tongue wets the centre of her lips.

'Who's that she's with?' I ask.

'Oh, that's Dirk Cresswell. Have you met him?'

'No.'

Dirk's hand has slipped lower, trailing over the silk as it falls over Julianne's buttocks. At the same time his eyes seem to fix on the neckline of her gown.

'Perhaps you had better go and rescue her,' laughs Flip.

I'm already moving that way, squeezing between shoulders and elbows, apologising and trying not to spill my champagne. I pause and polish off the contents.

Someone has mounted the staircase and is tapping a spoon loudly against his glass, summoning quiet. He's older and authoritative. It must be the chairman, Eugene Franklin. Conversations fade. The audience is silent.

'Thank you,' he says, apologising for the interruption. 'We all know why we're here tonight.'

'To get drunk,' someone heckles.

'In due course, yes,' answers Eugene, 'but the reason you're drinking Bollinger at the company's expense is because this is our birthday. The Franklin Equity Group is ten years old.'

This raises a cheer.

'Now it's evident from some of the "bling" on display that it has been a very successful ten years and confirmation that I'm paying you all far too much money.'

Julianne laughs along with the rest of the crowd, gazing at Eugene Franklin expectantly.

'Before we enjoy ourselves too much I wish to thank a few people,' he says. 'Today we secured the biggest deal in this company's history. It is a deal that many of you have been working on for nearly five years and it will guarantee we have a very merry Christmas come bonus time.

'Now, you all know Dirk Cresswell. Like Dirk, I too was once young and handsome. I was also a ladies' man until I came to realise that there are some things more important than sex.' He pauses. 'They're called *wives*. I've had two of them.'

Someone shouts from the floor, 'Dirk's had dozens of wives – just none of his own.'

Eugene Franklin laughs along with the rest of them.

'I want to personally thank Dirk for clinching our biggest deal. And I also want to thank the woman who helped him, the beautiful, talented and (another pause) multilingual Julianne O'Loughlin.'

Amid the applause and whistles, there are nudges and winks. Dirk and Julianne are summoned onto the staircase. She steps forward like a blushing bride, accepting the praise. Glasses are raised. A toast is given.

There's no way of reaching her now. She's caught in a public lovefest. Instead, I slip backward through the crowd and linger on the edge of the party.

My mobile phone is vibrating. Charlie's mobile. I cup the phone to my ear, pressing the green button.

'Hello,' says Darcy, expecting my daughter. I can barely hear her over the noise.

'Don't hang up.'

She hesitates.

'And don't blame Charlie. I guessed.'

'I want you to stop calling me and leaving messages.'

'I just want to know you're all right.'

'I'm fine. Stop calling.' My voice mailbox is being used up. It costs me money to collect your messages.'

Turning left past the cloakroom, I find an alcove beneath a set of stone stairs.

'Just tell me where you are.'

'No.'

'Where are you living?'

'With a friend.'

'In London?'

'Do you *ever* stop asking questions?'

'I feel responsible—'

'You're not! OK? You're not responsible. I'm old enough to look after myself. I got a job. I'm earning money. I'm going to dance.'

I tell her about Gideon Tyler. He could be the man she spoke to on the train when she came to London for her audition. The police need her to look at his photograph.

She contemplates what to do. 'You won't try to trick me?'

'No.'

'And you'll stop calling me.'

'As often.'

She ponders for a little longer. 'OK. I'll call you tomorrow. I have to go back to work now.'

'Where are you working?'

'You promised.'

'OK. No questions.'

I wander back to the party, finding another drink and then another. I listen on the edges of conversations as men exchange views on the share market, the strength of the US dollar and ticket prices at Twickenham. Their wives and partners are more interested in private school fees and where they're going to ski this winter.

Julianne's arms slip around my waist.

'Where have you been?' she asks.

'Around.'

'You haven't been hiding.'

'No. Darcy called.'

Her eyes cloud momentarily, but she chases any doubts away. 'Is she all right?'

'She says so. She's in London.'

'Where is she staying?'

'I don't know.'

Julianne brushes her hands over her hips, smoothing her gown.

'I love your dress. It's stunning.'

'Thank you.'

'When did you get it?'

'In Rome.'

'You didn't tell me.'

'It was my bonus.'

'Dirk bought it for you?'

'He saw me admiring it. I didn't know he was going to buy it. He surprised me.'

'A bonus for what?'

'Pardon?'

'You said it was a bonus.'

'Oh, yes, for all the long hours. We worked so hard. I'm exhausted.'

She doesn't seem to notice how hot it's become in here and how difficult it is to breathe.

She takes my hand. 'I want you to meet Dirk. I've told him how clever you are.'

I'm being led through the crowd. Bodies simply part. Dirk and Eugene are chatting to colleagues beneath the jaws of a dinosaur that looks ready to eat them. We wait and listen. Every one of Dirk's utterances is a statement of personal principle: opinionated, loud and dogmatic. There's a lull. Julianne fills it.

'Dirk, this is Joe, my husband. Joe this is Dirk Cresswell.'

He has a fearsome grip; a finger crushing, show-me-the-whites-of-your-eyes sort of handshake. I try to match it. He smiles.

'Do you work in finance, Joe?' he asks.

I shake my head.

'Very wise. What do you do? Oh, that's right, I remember Jules mentioning that you were a shrink.'

I glance towards Julianne. Eugene Franklin has asked her something and she's no longer listening.

Dirk suddenly turns his back to me. Not completely. A shoulder.

Others in the circle are more interesting or easier to impress. I feel like a footman, standing cap in hand, waiting to be dismissed.

A waiter passes with a tray of canapés. Dirk comments on the foie gras, which isn't bad, he says, but he's had better at a little restaurant in Montparnasse, a favourite of Hemingway's.

'It tastes pretty good if you come from Somerset,' I say.

'Yes,' answers Dirk. 'Thankfully, we're not all from Somerset.'

It gets a laugh. I want to put a kink in his perfectly straight nose with my fist. He carries on talking about Paris in a voice full of privilege and bravado that cuts right through me and reminds me of everything I hate about bullies.

I drift away looking for another drink. I meet up with Flip again, who introduces me to her boyfriend, who's a dealer.

'Shares, not drugs,' he says.

I wonder how many times he's used that line.

By now I've passed from the tipsy state to being grimly drunk. I shouldn't be drinking at all, but every time I contemplate switching to mineral water, I find another champagne flute in my hand.

Just before midnight I go looking for Julianne. I'm drunk. I want to leave. She's not on the dance floor or beneath the dinosaur. I walk up the staircase and peer into dark corners. It's crazy, I know, but I keep expecting to find her with Dirk's tongue in her mouth and his hands in her dress. Surprisingly, I don't feel angry or bitter. This is the materialisation of a certainty that has been with me for weeks.

I walk outside the main doors. There she is, backed up against a stone pillar. Dirk is in front of her with one hand braced against the stone cutting off her escape.

He spies me approaching. 'Speak of the devil. Having a good time?'

'Yes, thank you.' I turn to Julianne. 'Where have you been?'

'I was looking for you. Dirk thought he saw you coming outside.'

'No.'

Dirk's hand slips down, touching her shoulder.

'Please take your hand off her,' I say, unable to recognise my own voice.

Julianne's eyes go wide.

Dirk grins. 'You seem to have the wrong end of the stick, my friend.'

Julianne tries to laugh it off. 'Come on, Joe, I think it's time to go. I'll get my coat.'

She ducks under his arm. Dirk looks at me with a mixture of pity and triumph.

'Too much champagne, my friend. It happens to the best of us.'

'I'm *not* your friend. Don't touch my wife again.'

'My apologies,' he says. 'I'm a very tactile person.' He holds up his hands as though producing the evidence. 'Sorry if there's been a misunderstanding.'

'There is no misunderstanding,' I reply. 'I know what you're doing. So does everyone else here. You want to sleep with my wife. Maybe you already have. And then you'll swagger off and brag about it to your clubster mates on golfing weekends to the Algarve or shooting weekends in Scotland.

'You're "Mr Hole in One". You're "Dead-Eye Dirk". You flirt with other men's wives and then take them to dinner at Sketch and back to a little boutique hotel in London which has matching robes and an oversized bath with a spa.

'You try to impress them by name-dropping – first names only of course: Nigella and Charles, Madonna and Guy, Victoria and David – because you think it's going to make you more attractive to these women, but underneath that sun-bed tan and sixty-quid haircut you're an overpaid glorified salesman, who can't even sell himself.'

A crowd is being sucked inwards, unable to resist a playground fight where someone has taken on the school bully. Julianne comes rushing back, pushing through onlookers, knowing something terrible is afoot. She says my name. She begs me to shut up and tugs at my arm, but it's too late.

'You see, I know your type, Dirk. I know your shabby superior smile and condescending attitude towards waiters and tradesmen and shopgirls. You use sarcasm and overweening formality to gloss over the fact that you have no real influence or power.

'So you try to make up for this by taking away what other men

339

have. You tell yourself it's the challenge that excites you; the chase, but the truth is you can't hold onto a woman for more than a few weeks because pretty quickly they work out that you're a pretentious, stuck-up, self-centred bastard and then you're fucked.'

'Please, Joe, don't say any more. Please shut up.'

'I notice things, Dirk, little details about people. Take you, for example. Your fingernails are flat and yellowing. It's a sign of an iron deficiency. Maybe your kidneys aren't working properly. If I were you I'd go easy on the Viagra for a while until I got myself checked out.'

52

By the time I reach the hotel room Julianne has locked herself in the bathroom. I tap on the door.

'Go away.'

'Please open up.'

'No.'

I press my ear to a wooden panel and imagine I hear the faint silky slithering of her gown. She might be kneeling, pressing her ear against the door, opposite mine.

'Why do you do it, Joe? Whenever I'm happy you do something to mess it up.'

I take a deep breath. 'I found a receipt from Italy. You threw it away.'

She doesn't respond.

'It was for room service. Breakfast. Champagne, bacon, eggs, pancakes . . . more food than you could ever eat.'

'You went through my receipts?'

'I found it.'

'You went through the rubbish – spying on me.'

'I wasn't spying. I know what you normally have for breakfast. Fresh fruit. Yoghurt. Bircher muesli . . .'

My certainty and loneliness are now so intense they seem

perfectly matched. I'm drunk. I'm trembling. I'm remembering the events of the night.

'I saw the way Dirk looked at you. He couldn't keep his hands off you. And I heard the snide comments and the whispers. Everyone in that room thinks he's sleeping with you.'

'And you do too! You think I'm fucking Dirk. You think I ordered breakfast after we fucked all night?'

She hasn't denied it yet. She hasn't explained.

'Why didn't you tell me about the dress?'

'He only gave it to me yesterday.'

'Was the lingerie also a bonus . . . a present from him?'

She doesn't answer. I press my ear harder to the door and wait. I hear her sigh and move away. A tap is turned on. I wait. My knees are stiff. I feel a coppery taste in my mouth, a hangover in the making.

Finally she speaks, 'I want you to think very carefully before you ask me the question, Joe.'

'What do you mean?'

'You want to know if I fucked Dirk? Ask me. But when you do, remember what's going to die. Trust. Nothing can bring it back, Joe. I want you to understand that.'

The door opens. I step back. Julianne has wrapped a white towelling robe around her and cinched it tightly at the waist. Without meeting my eyes, she walks to the bed and lies down, facing away from me. The mattress springs barely move under her weight.

Her dress is lying on the bathroom floor. I fight the urge to pick it up and run it through my fingers, to rip it into shreds and flush it away.

'I'm not going to ask,' I say.

'But you still think it. You think I've been unfaithful.'

'I'm not sure.'

She falls silent. The sadness is suffocating.

'It was a joke,' she whispers. 'We worked really late to close the deal, tying up the loose ends. I crashed. Exhausted. It was too late to call London so I emailed Eugene with the news. He didn't get the message until he arrived at the office. He told his secretary to call my hotel and order me a champagne breakfast. She didn't know what to order so he said: "Order the whole damn menu".

'I was asleep. Room service knocked on my door. There were three trolleys of food. I rang the kitchen and said there must be a mistake. They told me my company had ordered me breakfast.

'Dirk phoned from his room. Eugene had done the same thing to him. I was too tired to eat. I rolled over and went back to sleep.'

My left hand is shaking in my lap. 'Why didn't you mention it? I picked you up at the station and you didn't tell me.'

'You'd just watched a woman jump off a bridge, Joe.'

'You could have told me later.'

'It was Eugene's idea of a joke. I didn't think it was very funny. I hate seeing food go to waste.'

My tuxedo feels like a straightjacket. I look around the hotel room with its pseudo luxuries and generic furnishings. It's the sort of place that Dirk would bring another man's wife.

'I saw the way he looked at you . . . staring at your breasts, putting his hand on your back, sliding it lower. I didn't imagine that. I didn't imagine the whispers and innuendos.'

'I heard them too,' she replies. 'And I ignored them.'

'He bought you lingerie . . . and that dress.'

'So what! You think I sleep with men who buy me things. What does that make me, Joe? Is that what you think of me?'

'No.'

I sit on the bed next to her. She seems to flinch and move further away. The alcohol has hit my head, which is pounding. Through the open bathroom door, I barely recognise my own reflection.

Julianne speaks.

'Everyone knows Dirk is a sleaze. You should hear the jokes in the secretarial pool. The man puts his business card in the women's toilets like he's touting for clients. Eugene's secretary, Sally, called his bluff in the summer. In the middle of the office she unzipped Dirk's fly, grabbed his penis and said, "Is that all you've got? For someone who talks about it so much, Dirk, I thought you'd have something more substantial to back it up." You should have seen Dirk. I thought he'd swallowed his tongue.'

Devoid of emotion, her voice is a monotone, unable to raise itself an octave above disappointment or sadness.

'In the old days you would never have let a man get away with touching you like Dirk did tonight.'

'In the old days I didn't need this job.'

'He *wants* people to think he's sleeping with you.'

'Which is only a problem if people believe him.'

'Why didn't you tell me about him?'

'I did. You were never listening. Every time I mention work, you turn off. You don't care, Joe. My career isn't important to you.'

I want to deny it. I want to accuse her of changing the subject and trying to deflect blame.

'You think I choose to be away from you and the girls?' she says. 'Every night I'm away, I go to bed thinking about you. I wake up thinking about you. The only reason I don't think about you *all* the time is that I have a job to do. I *have* to work. We decided that. We chose to move out of London for the sake of the girls and for your health.'

I'm about to argue but Julianne hasn't finished.

'You don't know hard it is . . . being away from home.' She says.' Missing things. Calling and finding out that Emma has learned a skip or hop on one leg or to ride her tricycle. Finding out that Charlie has had her first period or is being bullied at school. But do you know what hurts the most? When Emma fell over the other day, when she was hurt and scared, she called for you. She wanted *your* words, *your* hugs. What sort of mother can't comfort her own child?'

'You're being too hard on yourself.' I say, reaching across the bed to hold her. She shrugs my hands away. I have lost that privilege. I must gain it back. I'm normally so good with words, but now I can't think of anything to free her from her disappointment in me, to win her heart, to be *her* boy.

Countless times I told myself there had to be an innocent explanation for the hotel receipt and the lingerie and the phone calls, but instead of believing this, I spent weeks trying to *prove* Julianne's guilt.

I stand, swaying. The curtains are open. A cold stream of headlights is edging along Kensington High Street. Above the opposite rooftops I see the glowing dome of the Royal Albert Hall.

Julianne whispers, 'I don't know you any more, Joe. You're sad. You're so, so sad. And you carry it around with you or it hangs over you like a cloud, infecting everyone around you.'

'I'm not sad.'

'You are. You worry about your disease. You worry about me. You worry about the girls. That's why you're sad. You *think* you're the same man, Joe, but it's not true. You don't trust people any more. You don't warm to them or go out of your way to meet them. You don't have any friends.'

'Yes I do. What about Ruiz?'

'The man who once arrested you for murder.'

'Jock, then.'

'Jock wants to sleep with me.'

'Every man I know wants to sleep with you.'

She turns and gives me a look of pity.

'For such a clever man, how do you manage to be so stupid and self-absorbed? I've seen what you do, Joe. I've seen how you study yourself every day, looking for signs, imagining them. You want to blame someone for your Parkinson's, but there's nobody to blame. It just happened.'

I have to defend myself.

'I *am* the same man. You're the one who looks at me differently. I don't make you laugh because when you look at me, you see this disease. And you're the one who's distant and distracted. You're always thinking about work or London. Even when you are at home, your mind is somewhere else.'

Julianne snaps back, 'Try psychoanalysing yourself, Joe. When did you last truly laugh? Laugh until your stomach hurt and you got tears in your eyes.'

'What sort of question is that?'

'You're terrified of embarrassing yourself. You panic about falling over in public or drawing attention to yourself but you don't mind embarrassing me. What you did tonight – in front of my friends – I've never been so ashamed . . . I . . . I . . .' She can't think of the words. She starts again.

'I know you're clever, Joe. I know you can read these people; you can rip apart their psyches and target their weaknesses, but these are good people – even Dirk – and they don't deserve to be ridiculed and humiliated.'

She squeezes her hands between her knees. I have to win something back. Even the worst reconciliation with Julianne will be better than the best pact I could make with myself.

'I thought I was losing you,' I say, plaintively.

'Oh, you have a bigger problem than that, Joe,' she says. 'I may already be lost.'

53

The minute hand has clicked past midnight and the second hand is racing away into a new day. The house is dark. The street is silent. For the past hour I have watched the moon rising above the slate rooftops and the latticed branches, creating shadows in the garden and beneath the eaves.

The sky has a sickly yellow glow from the lights of Bath and the smell of compost adds to the sense of decay and foulness. The mixture is too wet. Good compost is a combination of wet and dry: kitchen scraps, leaves, coffee grounds, eggshells and shredded paper. Too wet and it smells. Too dry and it doesn't break down.

I know these things because my pop had an allotment for thirty years on waste ground behind the railway yards at Abbey Wood. He had a shed and I remember standing among the tools and flowerpots and seed packets, my shoes cloyed with soil.

Pop looked like a scarecrow in the garden, dressed in rags and an old hat. He grew potatoes mainly and brought them home in a Hessian sack stiff with dried mud. I was made to wash them in the sink with a scrubbing brush. I remember him telling me a story of someone who dug up an old World War II hand grenade among their potatoes and didn't discover it until they were scrubbing the spuds. It blew them into the garden. I was always careful after that.

I look at my watch again. It's time.

Keeping low, I follow a grey stone fence along the right side of the garden .

347

until I reach the corner of the house. I push through the shrubs. Peer through the window. There are no alarms. No dogs. A forgotten towel flaps on the clothesline, waving to nobody.

Crouching at the back door, I unroll the fabric pouch, laying out my tools: the diamond picks, rakes, combs, snakes, shallow picks and a hand-made tension wrench of black sprung steel fashioned from a small allen key that I flattened at one end with a grinder.

I link my fingers and push them away until tiny bubbles of gas trapped in the fluid between the joints expand and burst making a cracking sound.

The lock is a double plug Yale cylinder. The plug will open clockwise, away from the doorframe. I slide a snake pick into the keyway, feeling it bounce over the pins and increase the torque on the tension wrench. Minutes pass. It's not an easy lock. I try and fail. One of the middle pins won't lift up far enough as the pick passes over it.

I reduce the torque on the wrench and start over, concentrating on the back pins. First I try a light torque and moderate pressure, trying to feel for the click when a pin reaches the sheer line and the plug rotates ever so slightly.

The last of the pins is down. The plug rotates completely. The latch turns. The door opens. I step inside quickly and close it behind me, taking a pencil torch from my shirt pocket. The narrow beam of light sweeps over a laundry and the kitchen beyond it. I edge forward, easing my weight on the floorboards, listening for creaks.

The kitchen benches are clear apart from a glass jar of teabags and a bowl of sugar. The electric kettle is still warm. The torch beam picks out labels on metal tins: flour, rice and pasta. There is a drawer for cutlery, another for linen tea towels and a third for odds and ends like hairgrips, pencils, rubber bands and batteries.

It's a nice house. Neat. A central hallway joins the front and rear. There's a lounge on my left.

The blue upholstered sofa has large cushions. It faces a coffee table and a TV on a stand. Small brass animals line the mantelpiece next to a wedding photograph and a craft project, homemade candles, a porcelain horse, a mirror surrounded by seashells. I catch sight of my reflection. I look like a long-legged black insect, a night creature hunting its prey.

They're sleeping upstairs. I am drawn towards them, testing the weight of each step. There are four doors. One must be a bathroom. The others are bedrooms.

There is a sound like an insect trapped against glass. It is a portable music player. Snowflake must have fallen asleep with it plugged into her ears. Her bedroom door is open. Her bed is beneath the window. The curtains only half-closed. A single square of moonlight paints the floor. I cross the room and kneel next to her, listening to her soft sweet breath. She looks like her mother, with the same oval-shaped face and dark hair.

I lean close to her face, breathing as she breathes. Her stuffed animals have been relegated to a box in the corner. Pooh has been usurped by Harry Potter and overpaid football stars.

I used to live in a house like this. My daughter slept down the hall from me. I wonder what she's doing now? I wonder if she bites her nails; does she sleep on her side; has she grown her hair long; does she wear it out; I wonder if she's bright, if she's courageous, if she thinks of me?

Backing away, I gently close her door and turn to other rooms, pressing my ear against the panelled wood, listening for the sounds of sleep or silence. Easing open another door, I find it empty. The queen-sized bed has a patch-work quilt, topped with throw pillows. I run my hands beneath them, looking for a nightdress. Nothing.

I turn to the wardrobe, a hand on the brass handle, my face in the mirrored door and listen to the house again. Nothing. Pushing through the clothes, I find her smell, the one I want, her deodorant and perfume. Fake smells. During my jungle training we were taught never to use soap, or shaving foam, or deodorant. Artificial smells can give a soldier away to the enemy. To survive in the jungle you must become one with the jungle, like the animals.

Women don't smell like women are supposed to. It comes from a bottle. Manufactured. Deodorised. This one has some nice clothes, but there is a curious formality about her: the mid-length skirts, dark tights and cardigans. She's as formal as a flight attendant but not so glossy. I'm going enjoy breaking her.

There are boxes of shoes at the base of the wardrobe. Flipping open the lids, I sort through them. Slingback sandals. Peep-toe mules. Court shoes. Flats. Wedges. She likes boots. There are four pairs, two of them with pointy toes and fuck-me heels. Soft leather. Italian. Expensive. I put my nose inside and inhale.

I sit at her dressing table and sort through her lipsticks. The dark vermilion is best; it complements her skin colour. And the malachite necklace in the velvet box will look very pretty on her naked skin.

Stretching out on the bed, I gaze at the ceiling. A square hatch in the corner leads to the attic. I could hide there. I could watch over her like an angel. An avenging one.

There are footsteps on the landing. Someone is awake. A woman. I wait, wondering if I will have to kill her. A toilet flushes across the landing. Pipes rumble and the cistern refills. Whoever it is, has gone back to bed, with her foul breath and bleary eyes. She won't find me.

Rising from the bed, I close the wardrobe door, making sure everything is back in its place. Returning to the landing, I retrace my steps downstairs, along the hallway, into the kitchen, out the back door.

Pausing at the end of the garden, I watch the wind testing the pines and feel the first drops of icy rain. I have marked my territory and drawn invisible battlelines. Hurry morning.

54

When we first married, Julianne and I promised ourselves that we would never go to sleep angry at each other. It happened last night. My apologies were ignored. My overtures were brushed aside. We slept back to back on the same white sheet but it could have been an icy wasteland.

We checked out of the hotel at ten; our romantic weekend cut short. On the train back to Bath Spa Julianne read magazines and I stared out the window, pondering what she said to me last night. Maybe I am miserable or looking to blame somebody for what's happened to me. I thought I was past the five stages of grieving. Perhaps they never go away.

Even now, sitting next to her in a minicab on the journey home from the station, I keep telling myself that it was just an argument. Married couples survive them all the time. Idiosyncrasies are forgiven, routines adopted, criticisms left unsaid.

The taxi pulls up outside the cottage. Emma comes tearing down the path, wrapping her arms round my neck. I hoist her onto my hip.

'I saw the ghost last night, Daddy.'

'Did you. Where was he?'

'In my room; he told me to go back to sleep.'

'What a sensible ghost.'

Julianne is paying the taxi driver with her company credit card. Emma is still talking to me. 'Charlie said it was a lady ghost but it wasn't. I saw him.'

'And you had a chat.'

'Not a long one.'

'What did you say?'

'I said, "Who are you?" and he said, "Go back to sleep".'

'Is that all?'

'Yes.'

'Did you ask his name?'

'No.'

'Where's Charlie?'

'She went for a bike ride.'

'When did she go?'

'I don't know. I can't read the time.'

Julianne has paid the fare. Emma squirms out of my arms and slides down my chest. Her sneakers touch the grass and she runs to her mother.

Imogen has come outside to help us with the overnight bags. She has two messages for me. The first is from Bruno Kaufman. He wants to talk to me about Maureen and whether they should go away for a few weeks when she gets out of hospital.

The second message is from Veronica Cray. Five words: 'Tyler is a trained locksmith.'

I call her at Trinity Road. The seesaw whine of a fax machine punctuates her answers.

'I thought locksmiths had to be licensed.'

'No.'

'Who trained him?'

'The military. He's been working nights for a local company, T.B. Henry, and driving a silver van. We have matched the plates to a vehicle that crossed Clifton Suspension Bridge twenty minutes before Christine Wheeler climbed the fence.'

'Does he work from an office?'

'No.'

'How do they contact him?'

'A mobile phone.'

'Can you trace it?'

'It's no longer transmitting. Oliver is keeping a close watch. If Tyler turns it on we'll know.'

There's another phone ringing in her office. She has to go. I ask if there's anything I can do but she's already hung up.

Julianne is upstairs unpacking. Emma is helping her by bouncing on the bed.

I call Charlie. She still has my mobile.

'Hi.'

'You're home early.'

'Yep. Where are you?'

'With Abbie.'

Abbie is also twelve and the daughter of a local farmer who lives about mile out of Wellow along Norton Lane.

'Hey, Dad, I got a joke,' says Charlie.

'Tell me when you get home.'

'I want to tell you now.'

'OK, hit me with it.'

'A mother gets on a bus with her baby and the bus driver says, "That's got to be the ugliest baby I've ever seen." The mother is really angry but she pays the fare and sits down. Then another passenger says, "You can't let him get away with that. You should go back and tell him off. Here, I'll hold the monkey for you".'

Charlie laughs like a drain. I laugh too.

'See you soon.'

'I'm on my way.'

55

*It begins with a number: ten digits, three of them sixes. (Unlucky for some.)
Next comes the ringing . . . then the answering.*

'Hello?'

'Is that Mrs O'Loughlin?'

'Yes.'

'Professor O'Loughlin's wife.'

'Yes, who is this?'

'I'm afraid your daughter Charlie has had a little accident. She fell off
her bike. I think she lost control on a bend. She's quite the daredevil on that
bike. I want you to rest assured she's completely all right. In good hands.
Mine.'

'Who are you?'

'I told you. I'm the person who's looking after Charlie.'

*There's a tremor in her voice, a dim stirring of approaching danger, some-
thing large and black and dreadful on the horizon, rushing towards her.*

'She's such a pretty thing, your Charlie. She says her real name is Charlotte.
She looks like a Charlotte but you let her dress like a tomboy.'

'Where is she? What have you done to her?'

'She's right here, lying next to me. Aren't you, Snowflake? Pretty as a peach,
a sweet, sweet peach . . .'

Inside she is screaming. Fear has filled every warm wet place in her chest.

'I want to talk to Charlie. Don't touch her. Please. Let me speak to her.'

'I can't. I'm sorry. She has a sock in her mouth, taped in place.'

That's when it starts, the first fracture in her mind, a tiny fissure that exposes the soft unprotected parts of her psyche. I can hear the hysteria vibrating through her body. She calls out Charlie's name. She begs. She cajoles. She cries.

And then I hear another voice. The Professor takes the phone from her.

'Who are you? What do you want?'

'Want? Need? I want you to put your wife back on the phone.'

There's a pause. I've never understood what people mean when they say a pause is pregnant. Not until now. This one is pregnant. This one is pregnant with a thousand possibilities.

Julianne is sobbing. The professor puts his hand over the mouthpiece. I can't hear what he's saying to her but I imagine he's issuing instructions telling her what to do.

'Put your wife back on the phone or I will have to punish Charlie.'

'Who are you?'

'You know who I am, Joe.'

There's another pause.

'Gideon?'

'Oh, good, we're using first names. Put your wife back on the phone.'

'No.'

'You don't think I have Charlie. You think I'm bluffing. You told the police I was a coward, Joe. I tell you what I'm going to do. I'm going to hang up and fuck your little girl and then I'll call you back. In the meantime, I suggest you try to find her. Go on. Run along. Try Norton Lane, that's where I found her.'

'No! No! Don't go!'

'Put Julianne back on the phone.'

'She's too upset.'

'Put her back on the phone or you'll never see Charlie again.'

'Listen to me, Gideon. I know why you're doing this.'

'Put your wife on the phone.'

'She's not capable of . . .'

'I DON'T GIVE A FUCK WHAT SHE'S CAPABLE OF.'

'OK, OK. Just give me a minute.'

He covers the phone again. He's telling his wife to call the police on the fixed line. I pick up another mobile and punch in the number. The phone rings. Julianne picks up.

'Hello, Mrs O'Loughlin.'

A sob catches in her throat.

'If you let your husband take this phone from you your daughter will die.'

Her next sob is louder.

'Stay with me, Mrs O'Loughlin.'

'What do you want?'

'I want you.'

She doesn't answer.

'May I call you Julianne?'

'Yes.'

'Let me tell you something, Julianne. If your husband takes this phone out of your hand, I will rape your daughter for a while. Then I'll slice pieces off her body and hammer nails in her hands. And afterwards, I promise you this, I will cut out her pretty blue eyes and mail them to you in a box.'

'No! No! I'll talk to you.'

'Only you can save Charlie.'

'How?'

'You remember when you were pregnant, how you kept those babies alive in your womb? Baby Emma and baby Charlie. Well, this phone is like an umbilical cord. You can keep Charlie alive only by staying on this line. Hang up and she dies. Let someone take the phone from you and she dies. Understand?'

'Yes.'

She takes a deep breath, steeling herself. She's strong this one. A challenge.

'Is your husband there, Julianne? Is he whispering in your ear like I'm whispering in Charlie's ear? What's he saying? Tell me what he's saying or I'll have to bruise her skin.'

'He says you don't have her. He says you're bluffing. He says Charlie is at her friend's house.'

'Has he tried to phone her?'

'Her number is engaged.'

'He should go and look for her.'

'He's gone.'

'That's good. He should look outside . . . in the village. He should go to Abbie's house. What about your nanny?'

'She's looking too.'

'Maybe they'll find her. I could be bluffing. What do you think?'

'I don't know.'

356

'Do you have caller display on this phone, Julianne?'

'Yes.'

'Look at the number. Do you recognise it?'

Her answer is not so much spoken as groaned. The strangled affirmation is trapped in her throat, barely able to get out.

'Whose number is it?'

'My husband's mobile.'

'What is Charlie doing with Joe's phone?'

'They swapped.'

'Now you believe me.'

'Yes. Please don't hurt her.'

'I'm going to make her into a woman, Julianne. All mothers want their daughters to grow up and become women.'

'She's just a child.'

'Now, yes, but not when I'm finished.'

'No. No. Please don't touch her. I'll do anything you want.'

'Anything?'

'Yes.'

'Are you sure?'

'Yes.'

'Because if you don't do it, Charlie will.'

'I'll do as you say!'

'Take off your clothes, Julianne, your skirt and that pretty top – the one with the metallic thread through it. Yes, I know what you're wearing. I know everything about you, Julianne. I've already taken off Charlie's jeans. I'm sorry but I had to cut them. I was very careful. I'm very good with scissors and a razor. I could carve my initials into her stomach. She'd have a souvenir to remember me by. And every man who ever looks at her naked will know that I was there first . . . in every hole.'

'No, don't.'

'Are you taking off your clothes?'

'Yes.'

'Show me.'

She hesitates.

'Stand at the bedroom window, open the curtains – I'll be able to see you.'

'Will you let her go?'

'That depends on you.'

'I'll do what you want.'

'Charlie is nodding. It's so cute. Yes, that's right, Mummy's on the phone. Do you want to say hello? I'm sorry. Mummy hasn't done what I asked, so you can't talk to her. Are you at the window, Julianne?'

'Yes.'

'Open the curtains so I can see you.'

'And you won't hurt Charlie?'

'Just open the curtains.'

'OK.'

'You need make-up. On your dressing table; the vermilion lipstick, I want you to put it on and I want you to wear the malachite necklace in the velvet box.'

'How do you——?'

'I know all about you . . . all about Charlie . . . all about your husband.'

'Please let Charlie go. I did what you asked.'

'Nakedness isn't enough, Julianne.'

'What?'

'It's not enough. Charlie can give me more.'

'But you said——'

'Surely you can't expect me to give up a prize like this one. Do you know what I want to do, Julianne? Now that I've cut off your daughter's clothes, I want to open up her flesh. I want to unzip her from her throat to her cunt so I can climb inside her. Then I'm going to hold her heart in my hands and feel it beating as I fuck her from the inside out.'

The long slow scream is like a mortar shell detonating in my ears.

Another pin has fallen.

The lock is almost open.

Her mind is giving way.

Memory feels like substance now. Memory is the only thing that's real. I am running down Mill Hill, across the bridge, up the next rise between the hedgerows.

I talked to Charlie twenty minutes ago. Her friend Abbie lives about a mile along Norton Lane. How long does it take her to ride a mile? Any moment she'll come around the corner, legs pumping, head down, tail up, imagining that she's in the Tour de France.

I keep trying her mobile. My mobile. I gave it to her. We swapped so I could talk to Darcy. It's engaged. Who is she talking to?

Norton Lane is a narrow strip of twisting bitumen, hugged by hedgerows, hawthorn bushes and fences. Vehicles have to reverse or pull into culverts to allow other cars or tractors to pass. In some sections the hedges are high and unruly, turning the lane into a green gorge, broken occasionally by farm gates leading to fields.

I see a flash of colour between the twisting branches. It's a woman walking her dog. Mrs Aymes. She cleans houses in the village.

'Have you seen Charlie?' I yell.

Angry at being startled, she shakes her head.

'Did she come along here? She was riding her bike.'

'Ain't seen no bike,' she says, in a thick accent.

I keep moving, crossing a small bridge above a stream, which drops away over rapids.

Gideon doesn't have her. Gideon only pretends to abduct children. Physical confrontation isn't his style. Manipulation. Exploitation. He's probably watching me now, laughing. Or he's watching Julianne. He's talking to her.

On the brow of the hill I look back at the village. I call Veronica Cray. Words tumble out between snatched breaths.

'Tyler says he has my daughter. He says he's going to rape and kill her. He's on the phone to my wife. You have to stop him.'

'Where are you?' asks the DI.

'Looking for Charlie. She should be home by now.'

'When did you last speak to her?'

I can't think straight. 'Thirty minutes ago.'

DI Cray tries to calm me down. She wants me to think rationally. Tyler has bluffed people before; it's what he does.

'He must be somewhere close,' I say. 'He's probably been watching the house. You should seal off the village. Close the roads.'

'I can't seal off a village unless I'm sure a child has been taken.'

'Trace his signal.'

'I'm sending cars. Go back to your wife.'

'I have to find Charlie.'

'Go back home, Joe.'

'What if he's *not* bluffing?'

'Don't leave Julianne alone.'

The farm buildings are silhouetted against the sky on the crest of the next ridge. A half-dozen barns and machinery sheds made of tin, brick and wood squat in the centre of muddy tracks. Old farm machinery lies abandoned in one corner of the yard with weeds growing beneath the rusting chassis. I have no idea what most of these machines do. The main house is nearest the road. Dogs bark excitedly from kennels.

Abbie opens the door.

'Is Charlie here?'

'No.'

'When did she leave?'

'Ages ago.'

'Which way did she go?'

She looks at me oddly. 'There's only one way.'

'Did you see her leave?'

'Uh-huh.'

'Was there anyone else on the road?'

She shakes her head. I'm frightening her. Already I'm turning, running back across the yard to the lane. I couldn't have missed her. Where else would she go? It's two miles to Norton St Philip. Surely Charlie wouldn't have ridden in the opposite direction to home.

I call her mobile again. Why is she still on the phone?

The return journey is mostly downhill. I stop at farm gates, hoisting myself on the metal rail to get a better view of the fields.

Crossing the bridge again, I peer into the ditches on either side of the road. In some sections the brambles and nettles are thigh high. There are tyre tracks at the side of the asphalt. A vehicle must have pulled over to let another one pass.

That's when I see a bicycle, half-hidden by weeds. I wanted to buy Charlie an aluminium frame, but she chose the matt black steel, with fireballs on the crossbar and shock absorbers on the front forks.

I wade into the nettles and thorns, dragging the bike free. The front wheel is twisted and buckled by an impact. I scream her name. Crows explode from the trees in a flurry of beating wings.

My arm is shaking. My leg. My chest. My head. I take a step and almost collapse. I take another and fall. I try to get up. I can't. Swallowing hard, I let the bike fall and climb back to the road. Then I sprint down the asphalt like a madman. The horrors of hindsight and regret have stolen my oxygen and I can't get Charlie's name out any more.

Climbing Mill Hill my left leg suddenly locks as it swings forward and I land on my face. I don't feel the pain. Dragging myself onto my feet, I start running again with a strange stumbling goosestep.

Two girls on horseback are clip-clopping towards me. One of them I recognise. She knows Charlie. I wave my arms. One of the horses grows skittish. I yell at them to look for Charlie, angry they don't instantly obey.

I can't stay. I have to get home. I have tried to phone Julianne. The number is engaged. Gideon is talking to her.

I reach the High Street and cross over, scanning the footpaths. Charlie might have fallen off her bike. Someone might have picked her up. Not Gideon; someone else – a *good* Samaritan.

I'm nearing the cottage. I look up and see Julianne naked in the bedroom window, her mouth smeared with lipstick. I take the stairs two at a time, flinging open the door, pulling her away from the window. I take the quilt and wrap it around her shoulders, taking the phone from her fingers. Gideon is still on the line.

'Hello, Joe, did you find Charlie? Still think I'm bluffing? I hate to say I told you so.'

'Where is she?'

'With me, of course, I wouldn't lie to you.'

'Prove it.'

'I'm sorry?'

'Prove that you have her.'

'Which part of her do you want me to post to you?'

'Put her on the phone.'

'Put Julianne back on the line.'

'No. I want to hear from Charlie.'

'I don't think you're in any position to make demands, Joe.'

'I'm not going to play games with you, Gideon. Prove to me

that you have Charlie and we'll talk. Otherwise I'm not interested.'

I press a button on the handset, ending the call.

Julianne screams and throws herself at me, trying to take the handset.

'Trust me. I know what I'm doing.'

'Don't hang up! Don't hang up!'

'Sit down. Please. Trust me.'

The phone is ringing. I answer: 'Put my daughter on the phone!'

Gideon explodes, 'DON'T YOU EVER FUCKING DO THAT AGAIN!'

I hang up.

Julianne is sobbing, 'He'll kill her. He'll kill her.'

The phone rings.

'DO THAT AGAIN AND I SWEAR I'LL—'

I hit the button, cutting him off.

He calls back.

'YOU WANT HER DEAD? YOU WANT ME TO KILL HER? I'LL DO IT RIGHT NOW!'

I hang up.

Julianne is fighting me for the phone, hammering her fists on my chest. I have to hold the handset out of her reach.

'Let me talk to him. Let me talk,' she cries.

'I know what I'm doing.'

'Don't hang up.'

'Just get dressed and go downstairs. The police are coming. I need you to let them in.'

I'm trying to sound confident but inside I'm so frightened I can barely function. All I know for certain is that Gideon has been pulling strings like a master puppeteer, in total control. Somehow I have to stop his momentum, to slow him down.

The first rule of hostage negotiation is to demand proof of life. Gideon doesn't want to negotiate. Not yet. I have to make him rethink his plans and change his methods.

The phone rings again.

Gideon is ranting: 'LISTEN YOU COCKSUCKER. I'M GOING TO CUT HER OPEN. I'M GOING TO WATCH HER INSIDES STEAM—'

362

I hang up as Julianne lunges for the handset and finishes on the floor. I reach down to pick her up. She slaps my hand away and turns on me, her face contorted with fury and fear.

'YOU DID THIS! YOU BROUGHT THIS ON US,' she screams, stabbing her finger at me. Her voice drops to a whisper. 'I *warned* you! I told you not to get involved. I didn't want you infecting this family with your sick, twisted patients or the sadists and psychopaths you know so much about.'

'We'll get her back,' I say, but Julianne isn't listening.

'Charlie, poor Charlie.' She groans, collapsing on the bed in great snorting sobs. Her head is hanging over her naked thighs. There's nothing I can say to comfort her. I cannot comfort myself.

The phone rings. I pick up.

'Hello, Daddy, it's me.'

My heart breaks.

'Hello, sweetheart, are you all right?'

'I hurt my leg. My bike is busted. I'm sorry.'

'It's not your fault.'

'I'm fright—'

She doesn't finish the statement. Her words are cut off and I hear masking tape being ripped from a spool.

Gideon's voice replaces hers.

'Say goodbye, Joe, you're not going to see her again. You think you can fuck with me. You have no idea what I'm capable of.'

'Charlie has nothing to do with this!'

'Call her collateral damage.'

'Why take her?'

'I want what you have.'

'Your wife and daughter are dead.'

'Is that so?'

'Take me instead.'

'I don't want you.'

I hear more tape being pulled off the spool.

'What are you doing?'

'I'm wrapping up my present.'

'Let's talk about your wife.'

'Why? Have you found her?'

'No.'

'Well, I have a new girlfriend to play with. Tell Julianne I'll call her later and give her all the details.'

Before I can ask another question the lines goes dead. I dial the number. Gideon has turned off the mobile.

Julianne doesn't look at me. I wrap the quilt around her shoulders. She's not crying. She's not screaming at me. The only tears are mine, falling on the inside. They've never come so easily.

56

A dozen detectives and twice that many uniforms have sealed off the village and the access roads. Vans and trucks are being searched and motorists questioned.

Veronica Cray is in the kitchen, along with Safari Roy. They look at me with a mixture of respect and pity. I wonder if that's how I appear when I confront someone else's misfortune.

Julianne has showered twice and dressed in jeans and a pullover. She has the body language of a rape victim with her arms crossed tightly over her chest as if desperately holding on to something she can't afford to lose. She won't look at me.

Oliver Rabb has two new mobiles to trace – mine and the one Gideon used when he first called Julianne. He should be able to track the signals up until an hour ago when Gideon broke off contact.

There is a ten-metre GSM tower in the middle of a field, two hundred yards north-west of the village. The next nearest tower is on Baggridge Hill a mile to the south; and the next closest on the outskirts of Peasedown St John, two miles to the west.

'We need Tyler to phone back,' says DI Cray.

'He will,' I answer, staring at Julianne's mobile, which is sitting on the kitchen table. He knew her number. He knew the house number. He knew what clothes she was wearing, what lipstick and jewellery she had on her dressing table.

Julianne hasn't told me exactly what Gideon said to her. If she were a patient in my consulting room, I'd be asking her to talk, to put things into context, to deal with her trauma. But she's not a patient. She's my wife and I don't want to know the details. I want to pretend it didn't happen.

Gideon Tyler has been inside my house. He has taken everything important – trust, peace of mind, tranquillity. He has watched my children sleeping. Emma said she saw a ghost. She woke and talked to him. He isolated Julianne. He told her what lipstick and jewellery to wear. He made her stand naked at the bedroom window.

I have always tried to put dark thoughts aside and imagine only good things happening to my family. Sometimes, looking into Charlie's sweet, pale, changing face, I have almost come to believe that I could protect her from pain or heartbreak. Now she's gone. Julianne is right. It's my fault. A father is supposed to protect his children, to keep them safe and lay down his life for them.

I keep telling myself that Gideon Tyler won't hurt Charlie. It is like a mantra in my head, but the message brings no comfort. I also try to tell myself that people like Gideon – sadists and psychopaths – are few and far between. Does that make Charlie one of the unlucky few? Don't tell me there's a price to be paid for living in a free society. Not *this* price. Not when it involves *my* daughter.

Recording devices are being attached to the landline of the cottage and a scanner programmed to pick up conversation on our mobile phones. Our SIM cards have been transferred to handsets with GPS tracking capabilities. I ask why. The DI says it's a contingency. They may want to try a mobile intercept.

The village is framed through the window, looking like a page from a storybook with great billowing clouds, streaked by the sun. Imogen and Emma have gone next door to Mrs Nutall's house. Neighbours have come outside to look at the police cars and vans parked in the street. They're having casual conversations, exchanging pleasantries and pretending not to gawk at the detectives going door-to-door. Their children have been shooed inside, locked away from the unknown danger stalking their streets.

I hear the shower running upstairs again. Julianne is under the water, trying to wash away what happened. How long has it been? Three hours. No matter what happens Charlie will remember this day. She will be haunted by Gideon Tyler's face, by his words, by his touch.

Monk ducks as he enters the kitchen, making it suddenly appear smaller. He glances at DI Cray and shakes his head. The road-blocks have been up for more than two hours. Police have knocked on every door, interviewed residents and retraced Charlie's steps. Nothing.

I know what they're thinking. Gideon has gone. He managed to get away before police sealed off the roads. Neither of the mobiles Gideon used has transmitted since 12.42. He must know we can trace the signals. That's why he changes phones so often and turns them off.

As if on cue, Oliver Rabb arrives, shuffling up the front path like a nervous bag lady. He's carrying a laptop computer in a shoulder case and is wearing a tweed cap to warm his smooth head. He wipes his feet three times on the doormat.

Setting up his laptop on the kitchen table, he downloads the latest information from the nearest base stations, triangulating the signals.

'It's harder in areas like this,' he explains, brushing invisible creases from his trousers. 'There are fewer towers.'

'I don't want excuses,' says Veronica Cray.

Oliver goes back to the screen. Outside in the garden detectives are congregating in the patches of sunshine, stamping their feet to stay warm.

Oliver sniffs.

'What is it?'

'Both calls arrived through the same tower – the nearest one.' He pauses, 'But they originated from a tower outside the area.'

'What does that mean?'

'He wasn't in the village when he called you. He was already out of the area.'

'But he knew what Julianne was wearing. He made her stand at the bedroom window.'

Oliver shrugs. 'He must have seen her earlier in the day.'

He checks the screen again and explains Charlie's movements. She was carrying my mobile, which was pinging a tower about a mile south of Wellow while she was at Abbie's house. The signal changed when she left the farmhouse just after midday. According to the strength analysis, she started moving towards home. That's when Gideon knocked her off her bike and took her in the opposite direction.

Oliver pulls up a satellite image and overlays a second map showing the locations of phone towers.

'They headed south as far as Wells Road and then west through Radstock and Midsomer Norton.'

'Where did the signal die?'

'On the outskirts of Bristol.'

DI Cray begins issuing orders, unsealing the village and re-assigning officers. Her voice has a metallic quality, as if bouncing off one of Oliver's satellites. The focus of the investigation is shifting away from the house.

She waves a hand at Oliver. 'We know Tyler has two mobiles. If he turns either one of them on, I want you to find him. Not where he was yesterday or an hour ago – I want to know *now*.'

Julianne is waiting on the landing, hanging back in a corner between the window and the bedroom door. Her dark hair is still tangled and damp from the shower.

She has changed again, wearing black trousers and a cashmere cardigan with just enough make-up to darken her eyelids and shape her cheekbones. It shocks me how beautiful she is. By comparison, I feel decrepit and ancient.

'Let me know what you're thinking.'

'Believe me, you don't want to know,' she replies. I can barely recognise her voice any more.

'I don't think he wants to hurt Charlie.'

'You don't know that,' she whispers.

'I know *him*.'

Julianne glances up, her gaze challenging me. 'I don't want to hear that, Joe, because if you *know* a man like this – if you understand why he's doing this – then I wonder how you can sleep at night. How you can . . . can . . .'

She can't finish the statement. I try to hold her, but she stiffens and twists away from me.

'You *don't* know him,' she says accusingly. 'You said he was bluffing.'

'Up until now he has been. I don't think he'll hurt her.'

'He's hurting her now, don't you see. Just by taking her.'

Her face turns back to the window and she says accusingly, 'You brought this on us.'

'I never expected this. How could I have known?'

'I warned you.'

I can feel my voice failing. 'I'm forty-five, Julianne. I can't live my life on the sidelines. I can't turn my back on people or refuse to help them.'

'You have Parkinson's.'

'I still have a life to live.'

'You *had* a life . . . with us.'

She's speaking in the past tense. This isn't about Dirk or the hotel receipt or my jealous outburst at her office party. This is about Charlie. And amid the fear and uncertainty in her face, there's something I don't expect to see. Contempt. Loathing.

'I don't love you any more,' she says blankly, coldly. 'Not in the right way – not how I used to.'

'There isn't a right way. There's just love.'

She shakes her head and turns away. It feels as though something vital has been cut out of my chest. My heart. She leaves me on the landing; an unseen string is pulling at my fingers, worked by a twitching puppeteer. Maybe he has Parkinson's too.

The doors are open. The house is cold. SOCO have been examining the cottage for the past hour, dusting the smooth surfaces for fingerprints and vacuuming for fibres. Some of the officers I recognise. Nodding acquaintances. They do not look at me now. They have a job to do.

Gideon is a trained locksmith. He can open almost any door: a house, a flat, a warehouse, an office . . . There are thousands of properties lying empty in Bristol. He could hide Charlie in any one of them.

Veronica Cray has been conferring with Monk and Safari Roy in the kitchen. She wants a meeting to discuss tactics.

'We have to decide what we're going to do when he calls back,' she says. 'We have to be ready. Oliver needs time to pinpoint the source and location, so it's important that we keep Tyler on the phone for as long as possible.'

She looks at Julianne. 'Are you up for this?'

'I'll do it,' I say, answering for her.

'He might only speak to your wife,' says the DI.

'We *make* him talk to me. Don't give him any another option.'

'And if he says no?'

'He wants an audience. Let him talk to me. Julianne isn't strong enough.'

She reacts angrily, 'Don't speak about me as though I'm not in the room.'

'I'm just trying to protect you.'

'I don't *need* protecting.'

I'm about to argue but she explodes, 'Don't say another word, Joe. Don't talk *for* me. Don't talk *to* me.'

I feel myself sway back, as if dodging punches. The hostility silences the room. Nobody will look at me.

'You should both calm down,' says the DI.

I try to stand but feel Monk's hand on my shoulder, forcing me to stay seated. Veronica Cray is addressing Julianne, outlining the possible scenarios. Up until now the DI has always treated me with respect and valued my advice. Now she thinks my judgement has been compromised. I am too closely involved. My opinions can't be relied upon. The whole scene has become dreamlike and slightly askew. The others are businesslike and thoughtful. I am dishevelled and out of control.

Veronica Cray wants to move the operation to Trinity Road to make it easier for the police to respond. The landline will be re-directed to the incident room.

Julianne begins asking questions, her voice barely audible. She wants to know more details of the strategy. Oliver needs at least five minutes to track any call and triangulate the signals from the nearest three phone towers. If the clocks in the base stations are synchronised perfectly, he may be able to pinpoint the caller to within a hundred metres.

It isn't foolproof. Signals can be affected by buildings, terrain and weather conditions. If Gideon moves indoors the signal strength will change and if the clocks are out by even a microsecond it could mean a difference of tens of metres. Microseconds and metres – that's what my daughter's life is coming down to.

'We've installed a GPS tracker and a hands-free phone cradle in your car. Tyler may issue instructions. He may want you to jump through hoops. We're not ready for a mobile intercept so you have to stall him.'

'For how long?' she whispers.

'A few more hours.'

Julianne shakes her head adamantly. It has to be sooner.

'I know you want your daughter back, Mrs O'Loughlin, but we have to secure *your* safety first. This man has killed two women. I need a few hours to get helicopters and intercept teams ready. Until then we have to stall him.'

'This is crazy,' I say. 'You know what he's done before.'

DI Cray nods towards Monk. I feel his fingers close around my arm. 'Come on, Professor, let's take a walk.'

I try and twist out of the big man's hand, but he takes a firmer hold. His other arm hooks over my shoulder. From a distance it probably looks like a friendly gesture, but I can't move. He walks me into the kitchen and out the back door, along the path to the clothesline. A lone towel flaps in the breeze like a vertical flag.

There is a stale, unsavoury smell in my lungs. It's coming from me. My medication has switched off suddenly. My head, shoulders and arms are writhing and jerking like a snake.

'Are you OK?' asks Monk.

'I need my pills.'

'Where are they?'

'Upstairs, beside my bed. The white plastic bottle. Levodopa.'

He disappears inside the cottage. Police officers and detectives are watching from the lane, looking at the freak show. Parkinson's sufferers talk a lot about preserving dignity. I have none of it now. Sometimes I imagine this is how I'm going to finish up. A writhing, twisting snake man or a life-sized statue, trapped in a permanent pose, unable to scratch my nose or shoo the pigeons away.

Monk comes back with the pill bottle and a glass of water. He has to hold my head still to get the tablets on my tongue. Water spills down my shirt.

'Does it hurt?' he asks.

'No.'

'Did I do something to make it worse?'

'It's not your fault.'

Levodopa is the gold standard treatment for Parkinson's. It's supposed to reduce the tremors and stop the sudden frozen moments when my body locks up, unable to move.

My movements are becoming steadier. I can hold the glass of water to take another drink.

'I want to go back inside.'

'Can't do that,' he says. 'Your wife doesn't want you around.'

'She doesn't know what she's saying.'

'She looked pretty sure to me.'

Words, my best weapons, have suddenly deserted me. I look past Monk and see Julianne wearing an overcoat, being led towards a police car. Veronica Cray is with her.

Monk lets me get as far as the gate.

'Where are you going?' I shout.

'To the station,' says the DI.

'I want to come.'

'You should stay here.'

'Let me talk to Julianne.'

'She doesn't want to talk to you just now.'

Julianne has ducked into the back seat of the car. She tucks her coat under her thighs before the door closes. I call her name, but she doesn't respond. The engine starts.

I watch them leave. They're wrong. Every fibre of my being says they're wrong. I know Gideon Tyler. I know his mind. He's going to destroy Julianne. It doesn't matter that she's the strongest, most compassionate, intelligent woman I've ever known. That's what he preys upon. The more she *feels*, the more he's going to damage her.

The rest of the cars are leaving. Monk is going to stay. I follow him back to the cottage and sit at the table as he makes me a cup of tea and collects phone numbers for Julianne's family and mine. Imogen and Emma should stay somewhere else tonight. My parents are closest. Julianne's parents are saner. Monk sorts it out.

Meanwhile, I sit at the kitchen table with my eyes closed, picturing Charlie's face, her lop-sided smile, her pale eyes, the tiny scar on her forehead where she fell from a tree at age four.

I take a deep breath and call Ruiz. A crowd roars in the background. He's watching a rugby match.

'What's up?'

'It's Charlie. He's taken Charlie.'

'Who? Tyler?'

'Yes.'

'Are you sure?'

'He called Julianne. I talked to Charlie.'

I explain about finding Charlie's bike and the phone calls. As I tell the story, I can hear Ruiz walking away from the crowd, finding somewhere quieter.

'What do you want to do?' he asks.

'I don't know,' I croak. 'We have to get her back.'

'I'm on my way.'

The calls ends and I stare at the phone, willing it to ring. I want to hear Charlie's voice. I try to think of the last words she said to me, the ones before Gideon took her. She told me a joke about a woman on a bus. I can't remember the punchline but she laughed and laughed.

Someone is ringing the front doorbell. Monk answers it. The vicar has come to offer his support. I've only met him once, soon after we moved to Wellow. He invited us to attend a Sunday service, which still hasn't happened. I wish I could remember his name.

'I thought you might want to pray,' he says softly.

'I'm not a believer.'

'That's all right.'

He takes a step forward and gets down on his knees, crossing himself. I look at Monk, who looks back at me, unsure of what to do.

The vicar has lowered his head, clasping his hands.

'Dear Lord, I ask you to look after young Charlotte O'Loughlin and bring her home safely to her family . . .'

Without thinking, I find myself on my knees next to him, lowering my head. Sometimes prayer is less about words than pure emotion.

57

When a man has nothing to call his own, he finds ways of acquiring other men's possessions.

This house is an example. The Arab businessman is still away, gone south for the winter like a migrating bird. A housekeeper opens the place up when he's due back, fluffing up the pillows and airing the rooms. There's also a gardener who comes in twice a week during the summer, but only once a month now because the grass has stopped growing and the leaves have been raked into moulding drifts.

The house is as I remember, tall and ungainly with a turret room over-looking the bridge. A weathervane faces permanently east. The curtains are drawn. Windows and doors are secured.

The garden is soggy and smells of decay. A rope swing is broken, frayed at one end, dangling halfway between a branch and the ground. I cross beneath it, skirting the garden furniture, and stand before a wooden shed. The door is padlocked. Crouching on my haunches, I press a pick into the keyhole and feel it bounce over the pins. The first lock I ever learned to pick was like this one. I practiced for hours sitting in front of the TV.

The barrel turns. I unhook the padlock from the latch and pull the door open, letting light leak across the dirt floor. Metal shelves hold plastic flower-pots, seed trays and old paint tins. Garden tools stand in the corner. A ride-on lawnmower is parked at the centre.

I step back and look at the dimensions of the shed. There's just enough room for me to stand. Then I start clearing the metal shelves and wrestling them to one side. I roll the lawn mower onto the grass and begin moving the paint cans and bags of fertiliser to the garage.

The back wall of the shed is now clear. I take a pickaxe and swing it at the floor. The compacted earth breaks into a jagged jigsaw of dried mud. I swing the pick again and again, pausing occasionally to shovel the soil away. After an hour I stop and rest, crouching and holding my forehead to the handle of the spade. I drink from the hosepipe outside. The hole in the floor is ten inches deep and almost as long as the wall. It's long enough to fit the sheet of plasterboard I found in the garage. I want to make it deeper.

Setting to work again, I carry buckets of earth to the end of the garden and hide the soil amid the compost heap. I am ready to build the box now. The sun is dropping through the branches of the trees. Perhaps I should check on the girl.

Inside the house, in a second floor bedroom, she is lying on an iron-framed bed with a bare mattress. Dressed in a striped top, a cardigan, jeans and sneakers, she is curled up in a ball, trying to make herself invisible.

She cannot see me – her eyes are taped. Her hands are secured behind her back with white plastic ties and her feet are chained together with just enough width to allow her to hobble. She cannot go far. A noose is looped around her neck, tied off on a radiator, with just enough slack to allow her to reach a small bathroom with a sink and toilet. She doesn't realise it yet. Like a blind kitten she clings to the softness of the bed, unwilling to explore.

She speaks.

'Hello? Is anyone there?'

She listens.

'Hello . . . anyone . . . can you hear me?'

Louder this time: 'HELP! PLEASE HELP! HELP!'

I press record. The tape turns. Scream, little one, scream as loud as you can.

A small lamp throws light across the room but not as far as my corner. She tests the bindings on her wrists, twisting her shoulders to the left and right, trying to slide her hands free. The plastic ties are cutting into her skin.

Her head hits the wall. She turns on her back, raising her legs and kicks both feet at once against the wood panelling. The whole house seems to shake. She kicks again and again, full of fear and frustration.

She arches backwards, bending her spine, forming a bridge between her

376

shoulders and her feet. Raising her legs in the air in a half shoulder stand, she pivots at the waist, dropping her knees to her chest and then further until they touch the bed on either side of her head. She has folded herself into a ball. Now she slides her bound wrists past the small of her back, over her hips and under her backside. Surely she's going to dislocate something.

Her hands squeeze past her feet and she can unfurl her legs again. How clever! Her hands are now in front of her instead of behind. She pulls off her tape blindfold and turns towards the lamp. She still cannot see me in my dark corner.

Hooking her fingers through the noose around her neck, she lifts it free and then stares at her chained feet and the plastic ties on her wrists. She's broken the skin. Blood weeps over the white strips.

I cup my hands and smash them together. The mock applause echoes like pistol shots in the quietness of the room. The girl screams and tries to run but the chains around her ankles send her sprawling to the floor.

I grab the back of her neck and pin her down under my weight, straddling her body, feeling the air being squeezed from her lungs. Grabbing her hair, I pull her head backward and whisper in her ear.

'You're a very clever girl, Snowflake. I'm going to have to do a better job this time.'

'No! No! No! Please. Let me go.'

The first loop of masking tape covers her nose, sealing off the airway. The next loop covers her eyes. I do it roughly, dragging her hair. She thrashes her head as more tape loops around her forehead and her chin, encasing her in plastic. Soon only her mouth is exposed. When she opens it to scream, I slide the hose pipe between her lips and teeth, into the back of her throat. She gags. I pull it out a little. More tape loops around her head, screeching as I drag it from the spool.

Her world has become dark. I can hear her breath whistling through the hose.

I speak to her softly. 'Listen to me, Snowflake. Don't fight. The harder you struggle, the more difficult it is to breathe.'

She is still wrestling at my arms. I hold a finger over the end of the hose, blocking off her air supply. Her body stiffens in panic.

'That's how easy it is, Snowflake. I can stop you breathing with one finger. Nod, if you understand.'

She nods. I take my finger away. She sucks air through the hose.

'Breathe normally,' I tell her. 'It's a panic attack, nothing more.'

I lift her back onto the bed: she curls into a ball.

'Do you remember the room?' I ask.

She nods.

'There's a toilet about eight feet to your right, beside a sink. You can reach it. I'll show you.'

Hauling her upright, I put her feet on the floor and count the steps as she hobbles forward to the sink. I put her hands on the edge of the basin. 'The cold tap is on the right.'

Then I show her the toilet, making her sit.

'I'm going to leave your hands in front of you but if you take off the mask, I will punish you. Do you understand?'

She doesn't respond.

'I will close off the hosepipe unless you acknowledge my question. Will you leave the mask alone?'

She nods.

I take her back to the bed and sit her upright. Her breathing is steadier. Her narrow chest rises and falls. Stepping backwards, I turn on her mobile phone and wait for the screen to light. Then I press the camera function and capture the image.

'Be quiet now. I have to go out for a while. I'll bring you back something to eat.'

She shakes her head, sobbing into the mask.

'Don't worry. I won't be long.'

I walk out of the house and down the steps. There is a garage within a copse of trees. My van is parked inside, next to a Range Rover that belongs to the Arab. He very helpfully left the keys on a hook in the pantry, alongside a dozen others, neatly labelled for the electricity box and the mailbox. Strangely, I couldn't find one for the shed. Not to worry.

'We shall take the Range Rover today,' I announce to myself.

'Very good, sir.'

A Ferrari Spider one day, a Range Rover the next – life is good.

The garage door rises automatically. Gravel murmurs beneath the tyres.

When I reach Bridge Road I turn right and right again into Clifton Down Road, weaving through Victoria Square and along Queen's Road. Shoppers are spilling onto the footpaths and Sunday afternoon traffic clogs the intersec-

tions. I turn into a multi-storey car park beside the Bristol Ice Rink and swing up the concrete ramps, looking for an open space.

The Range Rover locks with a reassuring clunk and a flash of lights. I walk down the stairs and out into the open, following Frogmore Street until I can mingle with the shoppers and tourists.

The curving façade of the Council House is ahead of me and beyond that the cathedral. Traffic lights change. Gears engage. An open-top bus trundles past spouting diesel fumes. I wait at the lights and turn on the mobile. The screen lights up with a singsong tune.

Menu. Options. Last number dialled.

She answers hopefully. 'Charlie?'

'Hello, Julianne, did you miss me?'

'I want to speak to Charlie.'

'I'm afraid she's busy.'

'I need to know she's OK.'

'Trust me.'

'No. Let me hear her.'

'Are you sure?'

'Yes.'

I press the play button. The tape turns. Charlie's screams are filling her ears, shredding her heart; opening the cracks a little wider in her mind.

I stop the tape. Julianne's breath is vibrating.

'Is your husband listening?'

'No.'

'What did he say about me?'

'He says you won't hurt Charlie. He says you don't hurt children.'

'And you believe him.'

'I don't know.'

'What else did he say about me?'

'He says you want to punish women . . . to punish me. But I've done nothing to hurt you. Charlie has done nothing. Please, let me talk to her.'

Her whining voice is starting to annoy me.

'Have you ever been unfaithful, Julianne?'

'No.'

'You're lying to me. You're just like all the others. You're a conniving, two-faced, backstabbing slut with a pesthole between your legs and another on your face.'

379

A woman pedestrian has overheard me. Her eyes go wide. I lean closer and say, 'Boo!' She trips over herself trying to get away.

Crossing the road, I walk through the gardens in the cathedral plaza. Mothers push prams. Older couples sit on benches. Pigeons flutter in the eaves.

'I'm going to ask you again, Julianne, have you ever been unfaithful.'

'No,' she sobs.

'What about with your boss? You make all those phone calls to him. You stay with him in London.'

'He's a friend.'

'I've heard you talking to him, Julianne. I heard what you said.'

'No . . . no. I don't want to talk about that.'

'That's because the police are listening to the call,' I say. 'You're terrified your husband might learn the truth. Shall I tell him?'

'He knows the truth.'

'Shall I tell him you grew tired of lying in his bed, looking at his spotty back, and had an affair?'

'Please don't. I just want to talk to Charlie.'

I peer through the misty rain at the buildings on the far side of Park Street. Silhouetted on the roof of the Wine Museum is a phone tower. It's probably the closest.

'I know this call is being recorded, Julianne. It must be a real party line. And your job is to keep me on the phone for as long as possible so they can track the signal.'

She hesitates. 'No.'

'You're not a very good liar. I've worked with some of the best liars, but they never lied to me for long.'

Crossing College Green in the shadow of the cathedral, I glance along Anchor Road. There must be fifteen phone towers within half a mile of here. How long will it take them to find me?

'Charlie is very flexible, isn't she? The way she can bend her body. She can put her knees behind her ears. She's making me very happy.'

'Please don't touch her.'

'It's far too late for that. You should be hoping I don't kill her.'

'Why are you doing this?'

'Ask your husband.'

'He's not here.'

380

'Why's that? Have you two had a fight? Did you kick him out? Do you blame him for this?'

'What do you want from us?'

'I want what he has.'

'I don't understand.'

'I want what's mine.'

'Your wife and daughter are dead.'

'Is that what he told you?'

'I'm very sorry for your loss, Mr Tyler, but we haven't done anything to hurt you. Please let Charlie go.'

'Have her periods started?'

'What difference does that make?'

'I want to know if she's ovulating. Maybe I'll put a baby in her. You can be a grandmother, a glamorous granny.'

'Take me instead.'

'Why would I want a grandmother? I'll be honest with you, Julianne, you're a fine looking woman, but I prefer your daughter. It's not that I'm into little girls. I'm not a pervert. You see, Julianne, when I fuck her, I'm going to be fucking you. When I hurt her, I'm going to be hurting you. I can touch you in ways that you can't even imagine, without laying a finger on you.'

I look up and down the street and cross over. People walk around me, occasionally jostling my shoulder and apologising. My eyes scan the street ahead.

'I'll do anything you want,' she sobs.

'Anything?'

'Yes.'

'I don't believe you. You're going to have to prove it.'

'How?'

'You have to show me.'

'OK, but only if you show me Charlie.'

'I can do that. I'll let you see her right now. I'm sending you something.'

I press a button and the photograph transmits. I wait, listening for her reaction. There it is! It's a sharp intake of breath, the strangled cry. She is lost for words, staring at her daughter's head, encased in masking tape, breathing through a tube.

'Give my regards to your husband, Julianne. Tell him he's running out of time.'

Police cars are heading south along St Augustine's Parade. I step onto a

381

bus heading north, watching the police pass in the opposite direction. I lean my head against the window and look down the Christmas Steps, falling away to my right.

Five minutes later, I step off the bus in Lower Maudlin Street before the roundabout. Stretching my arms above my head, I feel the vertebrae crack and pop along my spine.

The bus has turned the corner. Wedged between two seats, in a hamburger wrapper, the mobile phone is still transmitting. Out of sight and out of mind.

58

Sniffy nudges her bony head into my ankle, purring as she rubs her body along my calf and twirls to come back again. She's hungry. I open the refrigerator and find a half-open can of cat food covered in foil. I spoon some into her bowl and pour her some milk.

The kitchen table is covered with the debris of the day. Emma had cheese sandwiches and juice for lunch. She didn't eat the crusts. Charlie used to be the same. 'My hair is curly enough,' she told me at age five. 'I think I've had enough crusts.'

I will never forget seeing Charlie born. She arrived two weeks late, on a bitter January night. I guess she wanted to stay somewhere warm. The obstetrician induced her with Prostaglandin and told us the drug would take eight hours to work so he was going home to bed. Julianne went into accelerated labour and was fully dilated within three hours. There wasn't enough time for the obstetrician to get back to the hospital. A big black midwife delivered Charlie, ordering me around the delivery suite like a puppy that needed housetraining.

Julianne didn't want me looking 'at the business end', she said. She wanted me to stay up next to her face, wiping her brow and holding her hand. I didn't follow orders. Once I saw the dark-haired crown of the baby's head appear between her thighs, I wasn't going anywhere. I had a front row seat for the best show in town.

'It's a girl,' I said to Julianne.

'Are you sure?'

I looked again. 'Oh, yeah.'

Then I seem to remember there was competition to see which of us would cry first – the baby or me. Charlie won because I cheated and hid my face. I had never been so satisfied taking total credit for something I had so little to do with.

The midwife handed me the scissors to cut the umbilical cord. She swaddled Charlie and handed her to me. It was Charlie's birthday, yet I was the one getting all the presents. I carried her across to a mirror and stared at our reflections. She opened the bluest of eyes and looked at me. To this day, I have never been looked at like that.

Julianne had passed out, exhausted. Charlie did the same. I wanted to wake her up. I mean, what child sleeps through her birthday? I wanted her to look at me just like before, like I was the first person she had ever seen.

The humming refrigerator rattles into stillness and in the sudden quietness I feel a small ceaseless tremor vibrating inside me, expanding, filling my lungs. I am disconnected. Cold. My hands have stopped shaking. Suddenly, I seem to be paralysed by an odourless, colourless, invisible gas. Despair.

I don't hear the door open. I don't hear footsteps.

'Hello.'

I open my eyes. Darcy is standing in the kitchen, wearing a beanie, a denim jacket and patched jeans.

'How did you get here?'

'A friend brought me.'

I turn to the door and see Ruiz, rumpled, careworn, still wearing his rugby tie at half-mast.

'How are you doing, Joe?'

'Not so good.'

He shuffles closer. If he hugs me I'll start to cry. Darcy does it for him, putting her arms around my neck and squeezing me from behind.

'I heard it on the radio,' she says. 'Is it the same man – the one I met on the train?'

'Yes.'

She takes off her rainbow-coloured gloves. Her cheeks are flushed with the change in temperature.

'How did you two find each other?' I ask.

Darcy glances at Ruiz. 'I've sort of been staying with him.'

I look at the two of them in amazement.

'Since when?'

'Since I ran away.'

Then I remember the clothes in the dryer in Ruiz's laundry; a tartan skirt in the wicker basket. I should have recognised it. Darcy was wearing it when she first turned up at the cottage.

I look at Ruiz. 'You said your daughter was home.'

'She is,' he replies, shrugging away my anger as easily as he does his overcoat.

'Claire's a dancer,' adds Darcy. 'Did you know she trained with the Royal Ballet? She says there's a special hardship scholarship for people like me. She's going to help me apply.'

I'm not really listening to the substance of what she's saying. I'm still waiting for Ruiz to explain.

'The kid needed a few days. I didn't think there was any harm.'

'I was worried about her.'

'She's not your concern.'

There's an edge to the statement. I wonder how much he knows.

Darcy is still talking. 'Vincent found my father. I met him. It was pretty weird, but OK. I thought he'd be better looking, you know, taller or maybe famous, but he's just an ordinary old guy. Normal. He's a food importer. He brings in caviar. That's fish eggs. He let me try some. Talk about gross. He said it tasted like ocean spray, I thought it tasted like shit.'

'Language,' says Ruiz. Darcy looks at him sheepishly.

Ruiz has taken a seat opposite me, placing his hands flat on the table. 'I checked the guy out. Lives in Cambridge. Married. Two kids. He's all right.'

Then he changes the subject and asks about Julianne.

'She's gone with the police.'

'You should be with her.'

'She doesn't want me there and the police think I'm a liability.'

'A liability – that's an interesting analysis. Then again, I've often thought your ideas were dangerously subversive.'

'I'm hardly a radical.'

'More like a candidate for Rotary.'

He's teasing me. I can't find the energy to smile.

Darcy asks after Emma. She's gone. My parents have taken her to Wales, along with Imogen. My mother burst into tears when she saw Charlie's room and didn't stop sobbing until my father gave her an oversized box of tissues and told her to wait in the car. Then God's-personal-physician-in-waiting gave me his stiff upper lip speech, which sounded like something Michael Caine delivered in *Zulu*.

Everyone means well. I've had calls from three of my sisters, who each told me I was being stoic and they were saying prayers. Unfortunately, I'm not interested in hearing clichés or comforting words. I want to be kicking open doors and shaking trees until I get my Charlie back.

Ruiz tells Darcy to go upstairs and run a bath. She obeys immediately. Then he leans close.

'Remember what I told you about staying sane, Professor? Don't you go dying of the disease.' He's sucking a boiled sweet which rattles against his teeth. 'I know about tragedy. One of the things it teaches you is that you *have* to keep moving. And that's exactly what you're going to do. You're going to wash, get changed and we're going to find your daughter.'

'How?'

'We'll think about that when you come back downstairs. But I'm going to make you a promise. I'm going to find this bastard. I don't care how long it takes. And when that happens I'm going to paint the walls with his blood. Every last drop of it.'

Ruiz walks behind me as I climb the stairs. Darcy has found a fresh towel. She watches us from the door of Charlie's room.

'Thank you,' I tell Ruiz.

'Wait till I've done something to deserve it. When you're finished come downstairs. I've got something to show you.'

59

Ruiz unfolds a page and smooths it on the coffee table.

'This was faxed through this afternoon,' he says. 'It came from the Maritime Rescue and Coordination Centre in Piraeus.'

The facsimile is of a photograph – a woman with short dark hair and a round face, who looks to be in her mid to late thirties. Her details are typed in small print in the bottom corner.

Helen Tyler (nee Chambers)
DOB: June 6, 1971
British National
Passport No: E754769
Description: white Caucasian, 175 cms tall, slim build, brown hair, brown eyes.

'I called to make sure there hadn't been a mistake,' he says. 'This is the photograph they were working off when they were looking for Tyler's wife.'

I stare at the image as if expecting it to suddenly become more familiar. Although roughly the right age, the woman depicted looks nothing the one in the passport photograph Bryan Chambers gave me. She has shorter hair, a higher forehead and different shaped eyes. It can't be the same person.

'What about Chloe?'

Ruiz opens his notebook and pulls out a Polaroid snapshot. 'They used this one. It was taken by a guest at the hotel they were staying in.'

This time I recognise the girl. Her blonde hair is like a beacon. She is sitting on a swing. The building in the background has whitewashed walls and wild roses on a trellis.

I go back to the faxed photograph, which is still displayed on the coffee table.

Ruiz has poured himself a scotch. He sits opposite me.

'Who provided the Greeks with this photograph?' I ask.

'It came through the Foreign Office and the British Embassy.'

'And where did the Foreign Office get it?'

'Her family.'

The authorities were searching for Helen and Chloe; they needed to identify bodies in the morgue and survivors in the hospitals. The wrong photograph could have been sent by mistake but surely someone would have picked it up before now. The only other explanation reeks of cover-up.

Three people gave evidence that placed Helen and Chloe on board the ferry: the navy diver, the Canadian student and the hotel manager. Why would they lie? Money is the obvious answer. Bryan Chambers has enough to make it happen.

It had to be organised quickly. The ferry accident was an opportunity for Helen and Chloe to disappear. Luggage had to be tossed into the sea. Mother and daughter were reported missing. Bryan Chambers flew to Greece four days after the sinking, which means that Helen must have done most of the groundwork using her father's money to cement the deception.

Surely someone on the island must have seen them. Where would they hide?

I take Helen's photograph from my wallet – the one Bryan Chambers gave me at his lawyer's office. The picture was taken for a new passport – one in her maiden name – according to Chambers.

From the moment she fled from Germany in May, Helen avoided using credit cards or making phone calls home or sending emails or letters. She did everything she could to hide her whereabouts from her husband, yet surely one of the first things she should have done was to ditch her married name. Instead she waited until mid-July to apply for a new passport.

I stare at the faxed photograph sent from Greece.

'What if nobody on Patmos knew what Helen and Choe Tyler really looked like?' I ask.

'What do you mean?' asks Ruiz.

'What if mother and daughter were already travelling under different names?'

Ruiz shakes his head. 'I'm still not with you.'

'Helen and Chloe arrived on the island in early June. They booked into a hotel, kept a low profile, paid for everything in cash. They didn't use their real names. They called themselves something different because they knew Gideon was looking for them. Then, through a terrible twist of fate, a ferry sinks on a stormy afternoon. Helen sees a way of disappearing. She throws their luggage into the sea and reports the disappearance of Helen and Chloe Tyler. She bribes a backpacker and a navy diver to lie to the police.'

Ruiz picks up the thread. 'And this backpacker suddenly has the money to keep travelling when his parents expect him home.'

'And a disgraced Navy diver facing a misconduct tribunal might be in need of money.'

'What about the German woman,' he asks, 'what does she have to gain?'

I flick through the statements and pull hers to the top of the pile. Yelena Schafer, born 1971. I look at the date of birth and feel the flush of recognition.

'How long did Helen spend in Germany?'

'Six years.'

'Long enough to speak the language fluently.'

'You think . . . ?'

'Yelena is a variation of Helen.'

Ruiz leans over his knees, his hands hanging between them, looking like an ancient bewildered statue. His eyes close for a second, trying to see the details as I do.

'So you're saying the hotel manager – the German woman – is Helen Chambers?'

'The hotel manager was the most credible witness the police had. What reason did she have to lie about an English mother and daughter who were staying at the hotel? It was a perfect cover. Helen could speak German. She could pretend to be Yelena Schafer and announce the death of her former self.'

Ruiz opens his eyes. 'The caretaker sounded nervous when I talked to him. He said Yelena Schafer had gone on holiday. He didn't mention a daughter.'

'What's the number of the hotel?'

Ruiz finds the page on his notebook. I dial the hotel and wait. A sleepy voice answers.

'Hello, this is Athens International Airport. We have recovered a bag that failed to make a flight several days ago. The luggage tag indicates it was checked in by Miss Yelena Schafer, but there is some confusion. Was she travelling with anyone?'

'Yes, her daughter.'

'A six year old.'

'Seven.'

'Where were they flying to?'

The caretaker is more awake now. 'Why have you called so late at night?' he asks angrily.

'The bag was put on the wrong flight. We need a forwarding address.'

'Miss Schafer must have reported the bag missing,' he says. 'She should have given a forwarding address.'

'We don't seem to have one.'

He smells a rat. 'Who are you? Where are you from?'

'I'm looking for Yelena Schafer and her daughter. It's crucial that I find them.'

He shouts something unintelligible and hangs up. I hit redial. The phone is engaged. He's taken it off the hook or he's calling someone. Perhaps warning them.

I phone Trinity Road. Safari Roy is in charge of the incident room. DI Cray has gone for dinner. I give him Yelena Schafer's name and the most likely date she flew from Athens with her daughter.

Passenger lists won't be available until the morning, he tells me. How many flights are there from Athens every day? Hundreds. I have no idea where mother and daughter have gone.

I hang up and stare at the photographs, wishing they could talk to me. Would Helen risk coming home while Gideon Tyler is still looking for her?

Ruiz drapes his hand over the top of the steering wheel as if letting the Merc do the navigating. He looks relaxed and pensive, but I know his mind is working overtime. Sometimes I think he pretends that he's not a deep thinker or he's slow on the uptake as a way of fooling people into underestimating him.

Darcy is in the back seat, plugged into music. Perhaps I was wrong to worry so much about her.

'You hungry?' Ruiz asks.

'No.'

'When did you last eat?'

'Breakfast.'

'You should eat something.'

'I'm OK.'

'You keep saying that and maybe one day you *will* be OK, but that's not today. You shouldn't expect to be OK. You're not going to be OK until you get Charlie home . . . and Julianne home and you can play happy families again.'

'It might be too late for that.'

He gives me a sidelong glance and looks back at the road.

After a long silence, he says, 'We'll get her back.'

I haven't heard from Julianne since she left the cottage. Monk has been in touch with the incident room. Gideon called again, using my mobile. He was somewhere in central Bristol, near the cathedral. Oliver Rabb couldn't locate him before the handset was left on a bus. The phone was recovered from the Muller Road Bus Depot an hour ago.

There's no word on Charlie. According to Monk everything that *can* be done is being done, but that's not true. Forty detectives are working on the case. Why not four hundred or four thousand? A TV and radio appeal has been launched. Why not sound sirens from the rooftops and search every residence, warehouse, farmhouse, henhouse and outhouse? Why not get Tommy Lee Jones out there, organising the search?

Ruiz pulls into the driveway of Stonebridge Manor. The metal gates are bleached white by the high beam headlights. Nobody answers the buzzer. Ruiz holds it down for thirty seconds. Silence.

Getting out of the car, he peers through the bars. There are lights on in the house.

'Hey, Darcy, how much you weigh?' asks Ruiz.

'You're not supposed to ask a girl questions like that,' she replies.

'Think you can climb over that wall?'

She follows his gaze. 'Sure.'

'Be careful of the broken glass.'

Ruiz throws his coat over the wall to protect her hands.

'What are you doing?' I ask.

'Attracting attention.'

Darcy puts her right foot in his cupped hands and is hoisted upwards onto the wall. She holds on to a branch and scrambles to her feet, balancing between the broken half-bottles embedded in the concrete. Her arms are outstretched to keep her steady, but there's no chance of her falling. Her poise and balance comes from hours of practice.

'She'll get herself shot,' I tell Ruiz.

'Skipper couldn't aim that straight,' he replies.

A voice answers him from the darkness. 'I can shoot the eyes out of a squirrel at fifty paces.'

'And I had you down as a nature lover,' replies Ruiz. 'Guess you're a redneck through and through.'

Skipper emerges into the glow of the headlights, cradling a rifle across his chest. Darcy is still standing on the wall.

'Get down, miss.'

'Are you sure?'

He nods.

Darcy obeys, but not the way he expects. She jumps towards him and Skipper has to drop his rifle to catch her before she lands. Now she's on his side of the gate. It's a problem he hasn't bargained on.

'We need to speak to Mr and Mrs Chambers,' I say.

'They're not available.'

'You said that last time,' says Ruiz.

Skipper is holding Darcy by the arm. He doesn't know what to do.

'My daughter is missing. Gideon Tyler has taken her.'

The way his eyes flash to mine I know that I have his full attention. That's why he's here – to stop Gideon getting inside.

'Where's Tyler now?'

'We don't know.'

He looks at the car, as if worried that Gideon might be hiding inside. Reaching into his pocket, he pulls out a two-way radio, signalling the house. I don't hear the message, but the gates begin to open. Skipper circles the car. He checks the boot and looks both directions along the lane before waving us through.

Security lights trigger on either side of the drive as the Merc floats by. Skipper is sitting in the passenger seat, with his rifle resting on his lap, pointed towards Ruiz.

I look at my watch. Charlie has been missing for eight hours. What am I going to say to Bryan and Claudia Chambers? I'm going to beg. I'm going to clutch at straws. I'm going to ask for exactly what Gideon Tyler wants – his wife and daughter. He has made me believe what he believes. They're alive. I have no choice but to accept this.

Skipper escorts us up the steps, through the main door and across the foyer. Wall lamps reflect off the polished wooden floor and brighter lights spill from the sitting room.

Bryan Chambers rises from a sofa, squaring his shoulders.

'I thought our business was finished.'

Claudia is opposite him. She rises, adjusting the waistband of her skirt. Her pretty almond-shaped eyes don't make contact with mine. She married a powerful man, thick-skinned and heavy-footed, but her own strength is more self-contained.

'This is Darcy Wheeler,' I say. 'Christine's daughter.'

Claudia's face bears all her sadness. She takes Darcy's hand and pulls her gently into her arms. They're almost the same height.

'I'm so sorry,' she whispers. 'Your mother was a wonderful friend to my daughter.'

Bryan Chambers looks at Darcy with a kind of wonderment. He sits down and leans forward, resting his hands between his knees. His jaw is stubbled and flecks of white spit are gathered in the corners of his mouth.

'Gideon Tyler has kidnapped my daughter,' I announce.

The shudder of silence that follows reveals more about the Chambers than an hour in a consulting room could possibly tell me.

'I know that Helen and Chloe are alive.'

'You're crazy,' says Bryan Chambers. 'You're as mad as Tyler is.'

His wife stiffens slightly and her eyes meet her husband's for just a moment. It's a micro-expression. The barest trace of a signal passing between them.

That's the thing about lies. They're easy to tell but difficult to hide. Some people can perform them brilliantly but most of us struggle because our minds don't control our bodies completely. There are thousands of automatic human responses from a beating heart to a prickling skin that have nothing to do with free will, things that we can't control, that give us away.

Bryan Chambers has turned away. He pours himself a scotch from a crystal decanter. I wait for glass to touch glass. His hand is almost too steady.

'Where are they?' I ask.

'Get out of my house!'

'Gideon found out. That's why he's been harassing you, stalking you, tormenting you. What does he know?'

Rocking on his heels, he squeezes the tumbler in his fist. 'Are you calling me a liar? Gideon Tyler has made our lives a misery. The police have done nothing. Nothing.'

'What does Gideon know?'

Chambers looks ready to erupt. 'My daughter and grand-daughter are dead,' he hisses through clenched teeth.

Claudia stands alongside him, her eyes a cold shade of blue. She loves her husband. She loves her family. She'll do whatever it takes to protect them.

'I'm sorry about your daughter,' she whispers. 'But we've already given enough to Gideon Tyler.'

They're lying – they're both lying – but all I can do is shuffle and clear my throat with a sort of helpless croaking sound.

'We can stop him,' argues Ruiz. 'We can make sure he doesn't do it again.'

'You can't even find him,' scoffs Bryan Chambers. 'Nobody can. He melts through walls.'

I look around the room, trying to summon a reason, an argument, a threat, anything that might change the outcome. The images of Chloe are everywhere, on the mantelpiece, the side tables, framed and hung on the walls.

'Why did you give the Greek authorities the photograph of someone other than Helen?' I ask.

'I don't know what you're talking about,' says Bryan Chambers.

I take the faxed photograph from my pocket and unfold it on the table.

'It's a criminal offence to provide false information to a police investigation,' says Ruiz. 'And that includes an investigation in a foreign country.'

Bryan Chambers face turns three shades darker, blood up. Ruiz doesn't back down. I don't think he understands the concept of giving ground, not when it comes to missing children. There have been too many in his career; children he couldn't save.

'You sent them the wrong photograph because your daughter is still alive. You faked her death.'

Bryan Chambers sways backwards to throw the first punch. It's a giveaway. Ruiz dodges it and slaps him on the back of the head like cuffing a naughty schoolboy.

This just fires him up. With a bellow and a loping charge, the bigger man drives his head into Ruiz's stomach and wraps his arms around him, running him backwards into the wall. The collision seems to shake the entire house. Photographs topple over in their frames, falling like dominos.

'Stop it! Stop it!' screams Darcy. She is standing near the door, fists bunched, eyes shining.

Everything slows down. Even the ticking of the grandfather clock sounds like a slow dripping tap. Bryan Chambers is holding his head. He has a cut above his left eye. It's not deep but it's bleeding heavily. Ruiz is nursing his ribs.

I lean down and begin picking up the photographs. The glass has broken in one of the frames. It's a snapshot of a birthday party. Candles spark in Chloe's eyes as she leans over a cake with her cheeks puffed out like a trombone player. I wonder what she wished for.

The photograph is not unusual, yet something jars as being wrong. Ruiz has a memory like a metal trap that seems to lock up facts and hold them. I'm not talking about useless ephemera like pop songs or Grand National winners or right-backs who've played for Manchester United since the war. Important details. Dates. Addresses. Descriptions.

'When was Chloe born,' I ask him.

'July 27, 2000.'

Bryan Chambers is now violently sober. Claudia has gone to Darcy, trying to console her.

'Explain this to me,' I say, pointing to the photograph. 'How can your granddaughter be blowing out seven candles on a birthday cake if she died two weeks before her seventh birthday?'

The button beneath the floor has summoned Skipper. He's carrying a shotgun but this time it's not resting in the crook of his arm. He points the barrel at chest height, moving it in an arc.

'Get them out of my house,' bellows Bryan Chambers, still holding his forehead. Blood has leaked over his eyebrow and the side of his cheek.

'How many more people are going to get hurt unless we stop this now?' I plead.

It makes no difference. Skipper waves the rifle. Darcy steps in front of him. I don't know where she gets the courage.

'It's all right,' I tell her. 'We'll go.'

'But what about Charlie?'

'This isn't helping.'

Nothing is going to change. The wrongness of the situation, the imminent catastrophe, is lost on the Chambers who seem to be caught in a permanent twilight of fear and denial.

I'm being escorted out of this house for a second time. Ruiz goes first, followed by Darcy. As I cross the foyer, in the very periphery of my vision, I catch sight of something white, pressed against the railings of the stairs. It's a barefoot child in a white nightdress peering through the turned wooden railings. Ethereal and almost otherworldly, she's holding a rag doll and watching us leave.

I stop and stare. The others turn.

'You should be asleep,' says Claudia.

'I woke up. I heard a bang.'

'It was nothing. Go back to bed.'

She rubs her eyes. 'Will you tuck me in?'

I can feel the rhythm of my blood beneath my skin. Bryan Chambers steps in front of me. The stock of the rifle is tucked against Skipper's shoulder. There are footsteps on the stairs. A woman appears, looking agitated, scooping up the child.

'Helen?'

She doesn't react.

'I know who you are.'

She turns to me, lifting a hand to brush a fringe from across her eyes. Her head is drawn down between her shoulders and her thin arms are tightly folded around Chloe.

'He has my daughter.'

She doesn't answer. Instead she turns to climb the stairs.

'You've come this far. Help me.'

She's gone, back to her room, unseen, unheard, unconvinced.

60

Crossing a carpet of dead leaves on the paving stones, I let myself through the French doors into the dining room. *The furniture is covered in old sheets that turn armchairs and sofas into shapeless lumps.*

A cast iron coal grate, forever black, sits in the small fireplace beneath an old mantelpiece that is dotted with pinholes left by dozens of Christmas stockings, none of them owned by the Arab.

I climb the stairs. The girl is lying quietly. She hasn't tried to take tape from her head. How obedient she's become. How compliant.

The wind outside is blowing branches against the walls, scratching at the paintwork. Occasionally, she lifts her head, wondering if the sound is something more. She lifts her head again. Perhaps she can hear me breathing.

Sitting up, she lowers her chained feet cautiously to the floor. Then she leans forward until her hands touch the radiator. Feeling her way, she hops sideways until she reaches the toilet. She stops and listens, then pulls down her jeans. I hear the telltale tinkle.

Pulling up her jeans, she manages to find the sink. There are two taps, hot and cold. Left and right. She turns on the cold tap and puts her fingers beneath the stream. Lowering her head, she tries to position the hose in her mouth into the stream of water. It's like watching an awkward bird take a drink. She has to hold her breath and suck at the water. It goes down the wrong way, triggering a coughing fit that leaves her sobbing on the floor.

I touch her hand. She screams and tries to scramble away, banging her head against the plumbing.

'It's only me.'

She cannot answer.

'You've been a very good girl. Now I want you to hold still.'

She flinches as I touch her. Leading her to the bed, I make her sit. Using a pair of dressmaker's scissors, I hook the lower blade beneath the tape at the nape of her neck and begin snipping upward, a little at a time.

Her sweat and body heat have glued her hair to the tape. I have to cut it away. I slice through her locks, pulling at the balls of tape and hair. It must hurt. She doesn't show it until I wrench it away from her face, trying to do it quickly to spare her pain. She screams into the hose and spits it out.

I put the scissors down. The 'mask' is off, lying on the floor like the skin of a gutted animal. Tears and snot and melted glue cover her face. There are worse things.

I hold a bottle of water to her lips. She drinks greedily. Droplets fall onto her cardigan. She wipes her chin with her shoulder.

'I've brought you food. The hamburger is cold, but it should taste OK.'

She takes a mouthful. No more.

'Can I get you anything else?'

'I want to go home.'

'I know.'

I pull up a chair and sit across from her. It's the first time she has seen me. She doesn't know whether to look.

'Do you remember me?'

'Yes. You were on the bus. Your leg is better.'

'It was never broken. Are you cold?'

'A little.'

'I'll get you a blanket.'

I take a quilt from one of the chairs and drape it around her shoulder. She shrinks from my touch.

'Want some more water?'

'No.'

'Maybe you'd prefer a soft drink. Some Coke?'

She shakes her head.

'Why are you doing this?'

'You're too young to understand. Eat your burger.'

She sniffles and takes another small bite. The silence seems too big for the room.

'I have a daughter. She's younger than you.'

'What's her name?'

'Chloe.'

'Where is she now?'

'I don't know. I haven't seen her in a while.'

The girl takes another bite of the burger. 'I had a friend called Chloe when we lived in London. I haven't seen her since we moved.'

'Why did you leave London?'

'My dad is sick.'

'What's wrong with him?'

'He's got Parkinson's. It makes him shake and he has to take pills.'

'I've heard of it. Do you get on OK with your dad?'

'Sure.'

'What sort of stuff do you do with him?'

'We kick a ball around and go hiking . . . just stuff.'

'He read to you?'

'I'm a bit old for that.'

'But he used to.'

'Yeah, I guess. He reads to Emma.'

'Your sister.'

'Uh-huh.'

I look at my watch. 'I have to go out again in a little while. I'm going to tie you up but I won't tape your head like before.'

'Please don't go.'

'I won't be long.'

'I don't want you to leave.' Tears shine in her eyes. Isn't it strange: she's more frightened of being alone than she is of me.

'I'll leave the radio on. You can listen to music.'

She sniffles and curls up on the bed, still holding the half-eaten burger.

'Are you going to kill me?' she asks.

'Why do you think that?'

'You told my mum that you were going to cut me open . . . that you were going to do things to me.'

'Don't believe everything you hear a grown up say.'

'What does that mean?'

'What it says.'

'Am I going to die?'

'That depends upon your mother.'

'What does she have to do?'

'Take your place.'

She shudders. 'Is that true?'

'It's true. Be quiet now or I'll put the tape back on your mouth.'

She pulls the quilt over her and turns her back to me, shrinking into the shadows. I move away, putting on my shoes and my coat.

'Please, don't leave me,' she whispers.

'Shhh. Go to sleep.'

61

The Merc floats through dark streets, which are empty except for the occasional figure scurrying for a late bus or going home from the pub. These strangers don't know me. They don't know Charlie. And their lives will never touch mine. The only people who can help me are unwilling to listen or to risk exposing themselves to Gideon Tyler. Helen and Chloe are alive. One mystery is solved.

Even before I reach the cottage, I notice different cars parked in the street. I know what my neighbours drive. These belong to others.

The Merc pulls up. A dozen car doors open in unison. Reporters, cameramen and photographers close around the Merc, leaning over the bonnet and shooting through the windscreen. Reporters are yelling questions.

Ruiz looks at me. 'What do you want to do?'

'Get inside.'

I force open the door and try to push through the bodies. Someone grabs my jacket to slow me down. A girl bars my way. A tape recorder is thrust towards me.

'Do you think your daughter is still alive, Professor?'

What sort of question is that?

I don't answer.

'Has he been in contact? Has he threatened her?'

'Please let me go.'

I feel like a cornered beast being circled by a pride of lions waiting to finish me off. Someone else yells, 'Stop and give us a quote, Professor. We're only trying to help.'

Ruiz takes hold of me. His other arm is around Darcy. Head down, he forces his way through like a rugby prop in a rolling maul. The questions continue.

'Has there been a ransom demand?'

'What do you think he wants?'

Monk opens the front door and closes it again. TV spotlights are still bathing the cottage in brightness, shining through cracks in the curtains and blinds.

'They arrived an hour ago,' says Monk. 'I should have warned you.'

Publicity is a good thing, I tell myself. Maybe someone will spot Charlie or Tyler and tip off the police.

'Any news?' I ask Monk.

He shakes his head. I look past him and see a stranger standing in my kitchen. Dressed in a dark suit and a crisp white shirt, he doesn't look like a policeman or a reporter. His hair is the colour of polished cedar and silver cufflinks catch the light as he brushes his fingers through his fringe.

The stranger seems to stand at attention as I draw near, hands behind his back. It is a posture perfected on parade grounds. He introduces himself as Lieutenant William Greene and waits until my hand is offered for a handshake before he proffers his own.

'What can I do for you, lieutenant?'

'It's more a matter of what I can do for you, sir,' he says in a clipped public school accent. 'My understanding is that you have been in contact with a Major Gideon Tyler. He is a person of interest.'

'Of interest to whom?'

'To the Ministry of Defence, sir.'

'Join the queue,' laughs Ruiz.

The lieutenant ignores him. 'The army is cooperating with the police. We wish to locate Major Tyler and facilitate your daughter's safe return.'

Ruiz mocks his language. 'Facilitate? You bastards have done nothing so far except put obstacles in our way.'

Lieutenant Greene isn't fazed. 'There are certain issues that have prevented full disclosure.'

'Tyler worked for military intelligence?'

'Yes, sir.'

'What was he doing?'

'I'm afraid that information is classified.'

'He was an interrogator.'

'An intelligence gatherer.'

'Why did he leave the military?'

'He didn't. He went AWOL after his wife left him. He faces a court martial.'

The lieutenant is no longer standing to attention. His feet are a dozen inches apart, polished shoes turned slightly outwards, and hands at his sides.

'Why is Tyler's service record classified?' I ask.

'The nature of his work was sensitive.'

'That's a bullshit answer,' says Ruiz. 'What did the guy do?'

'He interrogated detainees,' I say, second-guessing the lieutenant. 'He tortured them.'

'The British government doesn't condone the use of torture. We abide by the rules set out by the Geneva Convention . . .'

'You trained the bastard,' interrupts Ruiz.

The lieutenant doesn't respond.

'We believe Major Tyler has suffered some form of breakdown. He is still a serving British officer and my job is to liaise with the Avon and Somerset Police Service to facilitate his prompt arrest.'

'In return for what?'

'When Major Tyler is detained he will be handed over to the military.'

'He murdered two women,' says Ruiz incredulously.

'He will be examined by army psychologists to see if he is fit to stand trial.'

'This is bollocks,' says Ruiz.

Right now, I'm past caring. The MOD can have Gideon Tyler as long as I get Charlie back.

The lieutenant addresses me directly. 'The military can bring certain resources and technology to a civilian investigation like this one. If I have your co-operation, I am authorised to provide this help.'

'How am I meant to co-operate?'

'Major Tyler had certain special duties. Did he talk to you about them?'

'No.'

'Did he mention any names?'

'No.'

'Did he mention any locations?'

'No. He was a very quiet soldier.'

Lieutenant Greene pauses a moment, choosing his words carefully.

'If he has revealed sensitive details to you, unauthorised disclosure of such information to a third person could result in you being charged under the Official Secrets Act. Penalties for such an offence include imprisonment.'

'Are you threatening him?' demands Ruiz.

The lieutenant has been well trained. He maintains his composure. 'As you can already appreciate, the media is taking an interest in Major Tyler. There are likely to be questions from reporters. There will be inquests into the deaths of Christine Wheeler and Sylvia Furness. You may be asked to give evidence. I advise you to be very careful about what statements you make.'

Suddenly I'm angry. I'm tired of the whole pack of them: the military for their double-speak and secrets, Bryan and Claudia Chambers for their blind loyalty, Helen Chambers for her weakness, the reporters, the police and my own sense of helplessness.

For the second time tonight Ruiz wants to hit someone. I can see him squaring up to the younger man, who regards the threat with a weary inevitability. I try to defuse the situation.

'Tell me this, lieutenant. How important is my daughter to you?'

He doesn't understand the question.

'You want Gideon Tyler. What if my daughter is in your way?'

'Her safety is our primary concern.'

I want to believe that. I want to believe that Britain's finest military minds and personnel will do everything in their power to save Charlie. Unfortunately, Gideon Tyler was one of their best. Look what happened to him.

I feel myself stumble slightly and catch a trembling hold of the table.

'Thank you for your help, lieutenant, you can assure your superiors of my co-operation. I will give them as much help as they have given me.'

Greene looks at me, unsure of how to interpret the statement.

'Gideon Tyler's wife and daughter are alive. They're staying at her parents' house.'

I study his reaction. Nothing. I get a tingling sensation in my fingertips. I haven't revealed a secret. I've uncovered one. He knew already about Helen and Chloe.

In the waiting stillness, the truth comes splattering like rain into my consciousness. The army is guarding the Stonebridge estate. Ruiz picked it on our first visit. He said Skipper was ex-military. Not 'ex'; he's current – a serving soldier. The cameras, motion detectors and the security lights are part of ongoing protection. The British army has been looking for Gideon Tyler for a lot longer than the police have.

Julianne is sedated and is sleeping according to Veronica Cray. The doctor thought it best that she wasn't interrupted.

'Where is she staying?' I ask.

'At a hotel.'

'Where?'

'Temple Circus. Don't try to call her, Professor. She really does need to rest.'

'Is anyone with her?'

'She's under guard.'

The DI breathes gently into the receiver. I can picture her square head, short hair and brown eyes. She feels sorry for me, but that's not going to alter her decision. My marriage is not her concern.

'If you see Julianne . . .' I try to think of a message for her to

406

pass on, but nothing comes to me. There aren't any words. 'Just check on her – make sure she's OK.'

The call ends. Darcy has gone to bed. Ruiz is studying me, his stare sliding loosely over everything.

'You should get some sleep.'

'I'm OK.'

'Lie down. Close your eyes. I'll wake you in an hour.'

'I won't sleep.'

'Try. There's nothing more we can do tonight.'

The stairs are steep. The bed is soft. I stare at the ceiling in a sort of conscious daze, exhausted yet frightened of closing my eyes. What if I do sleep? What if I wake in the morning and none of this has happened? Charlie will be sitting at the kitchen table in her school uniform, half-awake, grumpy. She'll launch into a long story about a dream and I'll only be half-listening. The content of Charlie's stories is never the important thing. What's important is that she's a bright, singular and amazing girl. What a girl.

I close my eyes and lie still. I have no expectation of sleep but hope the world might leave me alone for just a few moments and let me rest.

A phone is ringing somewhere. I look at the digital clock on the bedside table. It's 3.12 a.m. My whole body is trembling as if struck like a tuning fork.

The cottage phone has been diverted to Trinity Road and it's not the ringtone for my mobile. Maybe Darcy's mobile is ringing in the guest room. No, it's coming from somewhere closer. I slip out of bed and step across cold floorboards.

The ringing has stopped. It starts again. The sound is coming from Charlie's room . . . her chest of drawers. I pull open the top drawer and rifle through socks and school tights rolled into balls. I feel something vibrating inside a pair of striped football socks: a mobile phone. I pull it free and flip it open.

'Hey, Joe, did I wake you? How can you sleep at a time like this? Man, you're cold.'

I groan Charlie's name. Her mattress sinks beneath me. Gideon must have planted the mobile when he broke into the cottage. The police looked for fingerprints and fibres, not mobile phones.

'Listen, Joe, I've been thinking you must know a hell of a lot about whores – being married to one. '

'My wife's not a whore.'

'I've talked to her. I've watched her. She's hot to trot. She would have fucked me. She told me so. She was begging me to bang her. "Take me, take me," she said.'

'That's the only way you can get a woman – by kidnapping her daughter.'

'Oh, I don't know. Her boss is banging her. He signs her pay cheques, so I guess that makes her a whore.'

'It's not true.'

'Where was she Friday night?'

'In Rome.'

'Funny. I could have sworn I saw her in London. She stayed at a house in Hampstead Heath. Arrived at eight, left next morning at eight. Owned by a rich guy called Eugene Franklin. Nice place. Cheap locks.'

My chest tightens. Is this another one of Gideon's lies? He does it so effortlessly, mixing in just enough truth to create doubts and sow confusion. Suddenly I feel like a stranger in my own marriage. I want to defend Julianne. I want to produce evidence that he's wrong. But my arguments sound puny and my excuses taste bad even before they leave my lips.

Charlie's pyjamas are spilling out from beneath her pillow, a pink vest and flannelette trousers. I rub the brushed cotton between my thumb and forefinger, almost trying to conjure her up, every detail.

'Where's Charlie?'

'Right here.'

'Can I speak to her?'

'She's tied up right now. Trussed up like a Christmas turkey. Ready for the stuffing.'

'Why did you take her?'

'Work it out.'

'I know about you, Gideon. You're AWOL from the army. You worked in military intelligence. They want you back.'

'It's nice to be wanted.'

'Why are they so keen to get you?'

'Can't tell you that, Joe, or I might have to kill you. I put the word secret into secret service. I'm one of those soldiers that isn't supposed to exist.'

'You're an interrogator.'

'I know how to ask the right questions.'

He's getting bored with the conversation. He expects more of me. I'm supposed to provide him with a challenge.

'Why did your wife leave you?'

I can hear the slow, relentless sound of his breathing.

'You frightened her away,' I continue. 'You tried to lock her up like a princess in a tower. Why were you so convinced she was having an affair?'

'What is this – a fucking therapy session.'

'She left you. You couldn't keep her happy. How did that make you feel? Till death do us part, isn't that what you both promised.'

'That bitch walked out. She stole my daughter.'

'The way I hear it, she didn't walk – she ran. She punched that accelerator and got the hell out of there – left you running down the driveway, trying to put on your pants.'

'Who told you that? Did she tell you that? Do you know where she is?' He's yelling at me now. 'You really want to know what happened? I gave her a child. I built her a house. I gave her everything she wanted. And do you know how she showed her gratitude? She left me and she stole my Chloe. May she piss red-hot pokers, may she rot in hell . . .'

'You hit her.'

'No.'

'You threatened her.'

'She's a liar.'

'You terrified her.'

'SHE'S A WHORE!'

'Take a deep breath, Gideon. Calm down.'

'Don't tell me what to do. You miss your daughter, Joe, well I haven't seen mine in five months. I once had a heart, a soul, but a woman tore it out. She shattered me into a thousand pieces and left nothing but a glowing filament, but it's still burning, Joe. I'm nursing that light. I keep it burning against the whores.'

'Maybe we should talk about that light.'

'And how much do you charge for a session, Joe?'

'For you it's free. Where do you want to meet?'

'How does someone become a Professor of psychology?'

'It's just a title.'

'But you use it. Is that because it makes you sound clever?'

'No.'

'Do you think you're cleverer than I am, Joe?'

'No.'

'Yes you do. You think you know all about me. You think I'm a coward – that's what you told the police. You drew up a profile on me.'

'That was before I knew who you were.'

'Was it wrong?'

'I know you better now.'

His laugh is spiteful. 'That's the bullshit thing about psychologists. Guys like you never come down off the fence and give an opinion. Everything is couched in parenthesis and inverted commas. Either that or you turn everything into a question. It's like your own opinion isn't good enough. You want to hear what everyone else has to say. I can picture you banging your wife, hammering away between her legs, and saying, "Obviously, it's good for you, dear, but how is it for me?"'

'You seem to know a lot about psychology.'

'I'm an expert.'

'Did you study it?'

'In the field.'

'What does that mean?'

'It means, Joe, that fuckers like you who call yourself professionals don't know how to ask the right questions.'

'What sort of question should I be asking?'

'Torture is a complicated subject, Joe, a hell of a subject. Back in the fifties, the CIA ran a research project and spent over a billion dollars to crack the code of human consciousness. They had the most brilliant minds in the country working on it – people at Harvard, Princeton and Yale. They tried LSD, mescaline, electroshock, sodium pentothal. None of it worked.

'The breakthrough came at McGill. They discovered that a person deprived of his or her senses will begin to hallucinate within forty-eight hours and ultimately break down. Stress positions accelerate the process, but there's something even more effective.'

Gideon pauses, wanting me to ask, but I won't give him the satisfaction.

'Imagine if you were blind, Joe, what would you prize most?'

'My hearing.'

'Exactly. Your weakest point.'

'It's sick.'

'It's creative.' He laughs. 'That's what I do. I find the weakest point. I know yours, Joe. I know what keeps you awake at night.'

'I'm not going to play games with you.'

'Yes you will.'

'No.'

'Choose.'

'I don't understand.'

'I want you to choose between your whoring wife and your daughter. Which one would you save? Imagine they're in a burning building, trapped inside. You dash in, through the flames, kick open the door. They're both lying unconscious. You can't carry two of them. Which one do you save?'

'I'm not playing.'

'It's the perfect question, Joe. That's why I know more about psychology than you'll ever know. I can break open a mind. I can take it apart. I can play with the bits. You know I once convinced a guy that he was rigged up to a power socket when all he had was a couple of wires in his ears. He was a would-be suicide bomber but his vest bomb didn't blow up. Thought he was going be a martyr and go straight to heaven. Thought he'd get blowjobs from the vestal virgins for the rest of eternity. By the time I was finished with him, I convinced him there was no Heaven. That's when he started praying. Crazy, isn't it. Convince a guy there's no Heaven and the first thing he does is start praying to Allah. He should have been praying to me. He didn't even hate me in the end. All he wanted to do was to die and to take something into death that wasn't my voice or my face.

'You see, Joe, there is a moment when all hope disappears, all pride is gone, all expectation, all faith, all desire. I own that moment. It's mine. And that's when I hear the sound.'

'What sound?'

'The sound of a mind breaking. It's not a loud crack like when bones shatter or a spine fractures or a skull collapses. And it's not something soft and wet like a broken heart. It's a sound that makes you wonder how much hurt can be visited upon one person; a sound that shatters the strongest of wills and makes the past leak into the present; a sound so high only the hounds of hell can hear it. Can you hear it?'

'No.'

'Someone is curled up in a tiny ball crying softly into an endless night. Isn't that fucking poetic? I'm a poet and I don't know it. Are you still there, Joe? Are you with me? That's what I'm going to do to Julianne. And when her mind breaks, so will yours. I'll get two for the price of one. Maybe I'll give her a call now.'

'No! Please. Talk to me.'

'I'm sick of talking to you.'

He's going to hang up. I have to say something to stop him.

'I've found Helen and Chloe,' I blurt.

Silence. He waits. I can wait, too.

He speaks first. 'You've talked to them?'

'I know they're alive.'

Another pause.

'You get to see your daughter, when I get to see mine.'

'It's not that easy.'

'It never is.'

He's gone. I can hear the hollow echo of my own breath in the emptiness of the bedroom and see my reflection in a mirror. My body is shaking. I don't know if it's the Parkinson's or the cold or something more elemental and deep-seated. Rocking back and forth on her bed, clutching Charlie's pyjamas in my fists, I howl without making a sound.

62

The service lift rises from the lower basement through the floors. A light floats through the numbers on the panel.

It is 5.10 a.m. and the corridor is deserted. I tug at the sleeves of my jacket. When was the last time I wore a suit? Months ago. It must have been when I visited the army chaplain because my wife had been to see him. He told me that I could have all the love in the world but without trust, honesty and communication a marriage wouldn't work. I asked him if he'd ever been married. He said no.

'So God didn't marry, Jesus didn't marry and you've never been married.'

'That's not the issue,' he said.

'Well, it fucking well should be,' I replied.

He wanted to argue. The thing with chaplains and priests and religious fuckers is that every lesson you get is about marriage and the importance of family. You could be discussing artificial grass, global warming or who killed Princess Diana and they would still bring it round to some crazy lesson about family being the bedrock of domestic bliss, racial tolerance and world peace.

Turning into another passageway, I notice the emergency door and check the stairwell. Empty. At the far end of the passage there is a small lobby where the main lift doors open. Two armchairs are arranged one each side of a small polished table with a lamp. A detective is sitting in one of the armchairs, reading a magazine.

My fingers slide easily into the loops of a brass knuckleduster in my trouser pocket. The metal has grown warm against my thigh.

He looks up as I approach and unfolds his legs. His right hand is out of sight.

'Long night.'

He nods.

'Is she ready?'

'I was told not to wake her.'

'Boss wants her at the station.'

He doesn't recognise me. 'Who are you?'

'Detective Sergeant Harris. Four of us drove up last night from Truro.'

'Where's your badge?'

His right hand is still hidden. I drive my fist into his throat and he subsides again, sucking bubbles of blood through a crushed windpipe. I slip the knuckleduster back into my pocket and take his gun, tucking it into the waistband of my trousers.

'Breathe long and slow,' I tell him. 'You'll live longer.' He can't speak. I take the radio from his pocket. He has an entry card for her room. A weak groan and brittle breath signal unconsciousness. His head drops. Opening the magazine, I rest it over his face, crossing his legs again. He could be sleeping.

Then I knock on the door. She takes a moment to answer. The door opens a crack. She is silhouetted against a haze of white light from the bathroom behind her.

'Mrs O'Loughlin, I've come to take you to the station.'

She blinks at me. 'Has something happened? Have they found her?'

'Are you dressed? We have to leave.'

'I'll get my bag.'

I hold my foot against the door to stop it closing as she disappears, her bare feet making little slapping sounds on the tiled bathroom floor. I want to follow her inside to make sure she isn't calling someone. I glance up and down the passage. What's taking her so long?

She reappears. Little things about her appearance show that she's struggling. Her movements are slow and exaggerated. Her hair hasn't been brushed. The sleeves of her cardigan are stretched and bunched in her fists.

'Is it cold outside?'

'Yes, ma'am.'

She looks at me. 'Did we meet yesterday?'

'I don't think so.'

I hold the lift door open for her. She glances at the sleeping detective and steps inside. The doors close.

Holding her handbag to her stomach, she doesn't look at her reflection in the mirrored walls.

'Has he called again?' she asks.

'Yes, he has.'

'Who did he call?'

'Your husband.'

'Is Charlie all right?'

'I have no information.'

We emerge in the hotel foyer. I hold my right hand an inch from the small of her back and point my left hand towards the glass revolving door. The foyer is empty except for a receptionist and a cleaner who is polishing the marble floor with a machine.

The Range Rover is parked on the corner. She's moving too slowly. I have to keep stopping and waiting for her. I open the car door.

'Are you sure we haven't met before? Your voice sounds very familiar.'

'We may have talked on the phone.'

63

Trinity Road police station sleeps with one eye open. The lower floors are deserted but the lights remain on in the incident room where a dozen detectives have worked through the night.

Veronica Cray's office door is closed. She's sleeping.

It's still dark outside. I woke Ruiz and told him to bring me here. First I took a cold shower and put on my clothes and took my medication. It still took me twenty minutes to get dressed.

The death photos of Christine Wheeler and Sylvia Furness are watching from the whiteboards. There are aerial photographs of the murder scenes, post mortem reports and a tangle of black lines drawing links between mutual friends and business contacts.

I don't need to look at the faces. I turn my head away and notice a new whiteboard, a new photograph – this one of Charlie. It's a school portrait with her hair pulled back and an enigmatic smile on her face. She hadn't wanted the photograph taken.

'We get one every year,' Julianne had said.

'Which means we don't need another one,' countered Charlie.

'But I like to compare them.'

'To see how much I've grown.'

'Yes.'

'And you need a *photograph* for that?'

'Where did you learn to be so sarcastic?' At this point, Julianne had looked at me.

Monk arrives with the morning papers. There's a picture of me on the front page, holding my hand up to the cameras as though reaching to rip it from the photographers' hands. There's also a picture of Charlie, a different one, taken from the family album. Julianne must have chosen it.

Someone has ordered croissants and pastries. The fresh coffee smell is enough to wake the DI, who emerges from her office in rumpled clothes. Her hair is cut so short it doesn't need a comb. She reminds me of a carthorse, heavy footed, slow to anger but immensely powerful.

Monk briefs her on what happened at the cottage. It doesn't improve her mood. She wants the house searched properly this time, every cupboard and crawl space in case there are more surprises.

The DI has summoned Oliver Rabb, wanting him to trace the call. He arrives in the incident room in the same baggy trousers and bow tie as yesterday, complemented by a muffler to keep his neck warm. He stops suddenly, frowning and patting his pockets as though he's lost something on his way upstairs.

'I had an office yesterday. I seem to have misplaced it.'

'End of the corridor,' answers Veronica Cray. 'You have a new partner. Don't let him boss you around.'

Lieutenant William Greene is already at work behind panes of glass in a booth-like office alongside the radio room.

'I'm not very good at working with people,' says Oliver glumly.

'Sure you are. Ask nicely and the lieutenant will let you play with his military satellites.'

Oliver bucks up and straightens his glasses before heading off down the corridor.

I want to talk to Veronica Cray before Julianne arrives. She closes her office door and sips a coffee, grimacing as though nursing a toothache. Outside I can see gulls wheeling above the distant docks and a chink of light opening on the horizon. Helen and Chloe Chambers are alive, I tell her. They're home.

The information washes over the DI seemingly without effect.

She puts two tubes of sugar in her coffee, hesitates and adds a third. Then she picks up the cup and looks at me over the steaming lip, regarding me with a level stare.

'What do you want me to do? I can't arrest them.'

'They've conspired to fake two deaths.'

'Right now I'm more interested in finding *your* daughter, Professor. One case at a time.'

'It's the same case. That's why Tyler is doing this. We can use Helen and Chloe to negotiate with him.'

'We're not swapping your daughter for his.'

'I know that, but we can use her to draw him out into the open.'

She strikes a match and lights a cigarette. 'Worry about your own daughter, Professor, she's been missing since lunchtime yesterday.' A coil of smoke curls from her fist. 'I can't force Helen Chambers to co-operate but I'll send someone to the house to talk to her.'

She walks to the door of her office. Opens it. Her voice booms across the incident room: 'Full briefing at 7.00 a.m. I want answers, people.'

Julianne will be here soon. What am I going to say to her? There are no words she wants to hear unless they come from Charlie's mouth, whispered in her ear, with her arms embracing her.

I find an empty office and sit in the dark. The sun is beginning to show, putting drops of colour into the water of the world. Until a few days ago, I had never heard of Gideon Tyler, but now I feel as though he has been watching me for years, standing in the darkness, staring down at my sleeping family, blood dripping from his fingers to the floor.

Although not physically powerful, not a bodybuilder or a strong man, Gideon's strength lies in his intellect and his planning and his willingness to do what others cannot comprehend.

He is an observer, a cataloguer of human characteristics; a collector of clues that can tell him about a person. The way they walk and stand and talk. What car they drive. What clothes they wear. Do they make eye contact when they talk? Are they open, trusting, flirtatious or more enclosed and introspective? I do the same – observe people – but in Tyler's case it's a prelude to harm.

Any sign of weakness is preyed upon. He can recognise a flagging heart, distinguish inner strength from a charade and find the fault lines in a psyche. We're not so different, he and I, but we aspire to different ends. He tears minds apart. I try to repair them.

Oliver and Lieutenant William Greene are at work in their goldfish bowl-like office, leaning over laptops and comparing data. They make an odd couple. The lieutenant reminds of one of those wind-up toy soldiers with a stiff legged gait and a fixed look on his face. The only thing missing is a large key rotating between his shoulder blades.

A large map takes up the entire wall, dotted with coloured pins and crisscrossed with lines that join them, forming series of overlapping triangles. The last call from Gideon Tyler originated from Temple Circus in the centre of Bristol. Police are studying CCTV footage from four cameras to see if it can link the call to a vehicle.

The mobile phone hidden in Charlie's bedroom went missing from a boating supply shop in Princes Wharf on Friday. The handset Gideon used to make the call has been traced to a phone shop in Chiswick, London. The name and address of the buyer were those of a student living in a shared house in Bristol. A gas bill and credit card receipt (both stolen) were used as proof of identity.

I study the map, trying to acquire the nomenclature to read the red, green and black pins. It's like learning a new alphabet.

'It's not complete,' says the lieutenant, 'but we've managed to trace most of the calls.'

He explains that the coloured pins represent phone calls made by Gideon Tyler and the nearest transmitting tower to each signal. The duration of each call has been logged, along with the time and signal strengths. Gideon hasn't used the same handset more than half a dozen times and he never calls from the same location. In almost every case the handset was turned on only moments before he made the call and turned off immediately afterwards.

Oliver talks me through the chronology, starting with Christine Wheeler's disappearance. The signals can place Gideon Tyler in Leigh Woods and near the Clifton Suspension Bridge when she jumped. He was also within a hundred metres of Sylvia Furness when her body was handcuffed to the tree and in Victoria Park in Bath when Maureen Bracken aimed a pistol at my chest.

I study the map again, feeling the landscape rise up from the paper, becoming solid. Amid the predominantly red, green and blue pins, a lone white pin stands out.

'What does that one mean?' I ask.

'It's an anomaly,' explains Oliver.

'What sort of anomaly?'

'It wasn't a phone call. The handset pinged for a tower and then went dead.'

'Why?'

'Perhaps he turned the phone on and then changed his mind.'

'Or it could be a mistake,' suggests the lieutenant.

Oliver looks at him irritably. 'In my experience mistakes happen for a reason.'

My fingertips brush the pinheads as reading a document in Braille. They come to rest on the white pin.

'How long was the phone turned on for?'

'No more than fourteen seconds,' says Oliver. 'The digital signal is transmitted every seven seconds. It was picked up twice by the tower we've marked. The white pin is the location of the nearest tower.'

Errors and anomalies are the bane of behavioural scientists and cognitive psychologists. We look for patterns in the data to support our theories, which is why anomalies are so damaging and why, if we're very lucky, a theory will hold together just long enough for a better one to come along.

Gideon has been so careful about not leaving footprints, digital or otherwise. He has made precious few mistakes that we know of. Patrick's sister ordered a pizza with Christine Wheeler's mobile – that's the only mistake I can remember. Perhaps this was another one.

'Can you trace it?' I ask.

Oliver has pushed his glasses up his nose again and tilted his head back to bring my whole face into focus.

'I suppose the signal may have been picked up by other towers.'

The lieutenant looks at him incredulously. 'The phone was only turned on for fourteen seconds. That's like trying to find a fart in a windstorm.'

Oliver raises his eyebrows. 'What a colourful analogy! Am I to assume that the army isn't up to the job?'

Lieutenant Greene knows that he's being challenged, which he finds vaguely insulting because he clearly thinks Oliver is a chinless, pale, limp-wristed boffin who couldn't find his arse with both hands.

I take some of the tension out of the moment. 'Explain to me what's going to happen when Tyler calls again.'

Oliver explains the technology and the benefit of satellite tracking. The lieutenant seems uncomfortable discussing the subject, as though military secrets are being revealed.

'How quickly can you trace Tyler's call?'

'That depends,' says Oliver. 'Signal strengths vary from place to place in a mobile network. There are dead spots created by buildings or terrain. These can be mapped and we can make allowances, but this isn't foolproof. Ideally we need signals from at least three different towers. Radio waves travel at a known rate, so we can work out how far they've travelled.'

'What if you get a signal from only one tower?'

'This gives us DOA – direction of arrival – and a rough idea of the distance. Each kilometre delays the signal by three microseconds.'

Oliver takes a pen from behind his ear and begins drawing towers and intersecting lines on a piece of paper.

'The problem with a DOA reading is the signal could be bouncing off a building or an obstacle. We can't always trust them. Signals from three base stations give us enough information to triangulate a location as long as the clocks at each of the base stations are synchronised exactly.'

'We're talking microseconds,' adds Oliver. 'By calculating the difference in the arrival times it's possible to locate a handset using

421

hyperbolas and linear algebra. However, the caller must be stationary. If Tyler is in a car or on a bus or a train it won't work. Even if he walks into a building there will be a change in signal strength.'

'How long does he have to stay in one place?'

Oliver and the lieutenant look at each other. 'Five, maybe ten minutes,' says Oliver.

'What if he uses a landline – something fixed?'

The lieutenant shakes his head. 'He won't risk it.'

'What if we make him?'

He raises his eyebrows. 'How you plan to do that?'

'How easy is it to shut down mobile phone towers?'

'The phone servers would never agree. They'd lose too much money,' says Lieutenant Greene.

'It won't be for long. Ten minutes maybe.'

'That's going to stop thousands of phone calls. Customers are going to be very pissed off.'

Oliver seems more open to the idea. He looks at the map on the wall. Most of Gideon's calls have come from central Bristol where most of the phone towers are concentrated. More servers would have to co-operate. He thinks out loud. 'A limited geographical area, fifteen towers maybe.' His interest is sparked. 'I don't know if it's ever been done.'

'But it's possible.'

'Feasible.'

He turns and sits at a laptop, his fingers dancing on the keyboard, as his glasses slip further and further down his nose. Oliver, I sense, is happier in the company of computers. He can reason with them. He can understand how they process information. A computer doesn't care whether or not he brushes his teeth or cuts his toenails in the bath or wears socks to bed. Some would say this is true love.

64

There are shouts and people running. Veronica Cray is yelling orders above the commotion and police officers are heading for the stairs and the lift. I can't hear what she's saying. A detective almost knocks me over and mumbles an apology as he picks up my walking stick.

'What's happened?'

He doesn't answer.

A shiver of alarm swarms across my shoulder blades. Something is wrong. I hear Julianne's name mentioned. I yell above the voices.

'Tell me what's happened.'

Faces turn. They're looking at me, staring. Nobody answers. The soft wetness of my own breathing is louder than the ringing phones and shuffling feet.

'Where's Julianne? What's happened?'

'One of our officers has been seriously injured,' says Veronica Cray, hesitating for a moment before continuing. 'He was guarding your wife's hotel room.'

'Guarding her.'

'Yes.'

'Where is she?'

'We're searching the hotel and surrounding streets.'

'She's missing?'

'Yes.' She pauses. 'There are cameras in the foyer and outside on the street. We're retrieving the footage . . .'

I'm watching her mouth move but not hearing the words. Julianne's hotel was near Temple Circus. According to Oliver Rabb, that's the same area that Gideon phoned me from at 3.15 a.m. He must have been watching her.

Everything has changed again, shivering and shifting, detaching from my conception like a fragment of sanity jarred loose in the night. I close my eyes for a moment and try to picture myself free, but instead witness my own helplessness. I curse myself. I curse Mr Parkinson. I curse Gideon Tyler. I will not let him take my family from me. I will not let him destroy me.

The morning briefing is standing room only. Detectives are perched on the edge of desks, leaning on pillars and looking over shoulders. The sense of urgency has been augmented by disbelief and shock. One of their own is in hospital with a collapsed windpipe and possible brain damage from oxygen deprivation.

Veronica Cray stands on a chair to be seen. She outlines the operation – a mobile intercept involving two-dozen unmarked vehicles and helicopters from the police air wing.

'Based on previous calls, Gideon will use a mobile and keep moving. Phase one is protection. Phase two is to trace the call. Phase three is contact with the target. Phase four is the arrest.'

She goes on to explain the communications. A radio silence will operate between the cars. A codeword and number will identify each unit. The phrase, 'Pedestrian knocked down' is the signal to move, accompanied by a street and cross street.

A hand goes up. 'Is he armed, boss?'

Cray glances at the sheet in her hand. 'The detective guarding Mrs O'Loughlin was carrying a regulation sidearm. The pistol is now missing.'

The resolve in the room seems to stiffen. Monk wants to know why it's an intercept and arrest. Why not follow Tyler?

'We can't take the risk of losing him.'

'What about the hostages?'

424

'We'll find them once we have Tyler.'

The DI makes it sound like the logical course of action, but I suspect her hand is being forced. The military want Tyler in custody and know exactly how to apply pressure. Nobody questions her decision. Copies of Tyler's photograph are passed from hand to hand. Detectives pause to look at the image. I know what they're wondering. They want to know if it's obvious, if it's visible, if someone like Tyler wears his depravity like a badge or a tattoo. They want to imagine they can recognise wickedness and immorality in another person, can see it in their eyes or read it on their faces. It's not true. The world is full of broken people and most of their cracks are on the inside.

From across the incident room comes the sound of a toppling chair and the clatter of a wastepaper bin being kicked through the air. Ruiz comes raging between desks, stabbing his finger at Veronica Cray.

'How many officers were guarding her?'

DI Cray gives him an icy stare. 'I would advise you to calm down and remember who you're talking to.'

'How many?'

She matches his anger. 'I will not have this discussion here.'

Around me, the detectives are transfixed, bracing for the clash of egos. It's like watching two wildebeest charge at each other with lowered heads.

'You had *one* officer guarding her. What sort of three ring bloody circus are you running?'

Cray launches into a spluttering, head-shaking tirade. 'This is *my* incident room and *my* investigation. I will NOT have my authority questioned.' She barks to Monk. 'Get him out of here.'

The big man moves towards Ruiz. I step between them.

'Everyone should calm down.'

Cray and Ruiz glower at each other in sullen defiance and in some unspoken way agree to back down. The tension is suddenly released and the detectives dutifully turn away, returning to their desks and making their way downstairs to waiting cars.

I follow the DI back to her office. She clicks her tongue in annoyance.

'I know he's a friend of yours, Professor, but that man is a prize-winning pain in the arse.'

'He's a passionate pain in the arse.'

She stares fixedly out the window, her face fleshy and pale. Tears suddenly sparkle in the rims of her eyes. 'I should have done better,' she whispers. 'Your wife should have been safe. She was my responsibility. I'm sorry.'

Embarrassment. Shame. Anger. Disappointment. Each is like a mask but she's not seeking to hide. Nothing I can say will make her feel any better or alter the violent, rapacious longing that has infused this case from the beginning.

Ruiz knocks lightly on the office door.

'I want to apologise for my outburst,' he says. 'It was out of order.'

'Apology accepted.'

He turns to leave.

'Stay,' I tell him. 'I want you to hear this. I think I can make Gideon Tyler stop moving.'

'How?' asks the DI.

'We offer him his daughter.'

'But we don't have her. The family won't co-operate, you said so yourself.'

'We bluff him just like he bluffed Christine Wheeler and Sylvia Furness and Maureen Bracken. We convince him that we have Chloe and Helen.'

Veronica Cray looks at me incredulously. 'You want to *lie* to him.'

'I want to bluff him. Tyler knows his wife and daughter are alive. And he knows we have the resources to get them here. If he wants to talk to them or see them, he has to give up Charlie and Julianne first.'

'He won't believe you. He'll want proof,' says the DI.

'I just have to keep him on the line and make him stay in one place. I've read Chloe's journal. I know where she's been. I can bluff him.'

'What if he wants to talk to her?'

'I'll tell him that she's on her way or that she doesn't want to talk. I'll make excuses.'

426

DI Cray sucks air through nostrils that pinch and then flare as she exhales. Her jaw muscles are working under her flesh.

'What makes you think he'll buy this?'

'It's what he *wants* to believe.'

Ruiz suddenly pipes up. 'I think it's a good idea. So far Tyler has had us running around like our butts are on fire. Maybe the Professor's right and we can light a fire under him. It's worth a try.'

The DI pulls a packet of cigarettes from her drawer and glances dismissively at the NO SMOKING sign.

'On one condition,' she says pointing an unlit cigarette at Ruiz. 'You go back out to see Helen Chambers. Tell her what we're doing. It's about time someone in that bloody family stood up to be counted.'

Ruiz steps back and lets me leave the office first.

'You're crazy,' he mutters, once we're out of earshot. 'You can't really think you can bluff this guy.'

'Why did you agree with me?'

He shrugs and gives me a rueful sigh. 'Ever heard the joke about the nursery school teacher who stands up in front of the class and says, "If anyone feels stupid, I want you to stand up." Well this little boy, Jimmy, gets to his feet and the teacher says, "Do you really feel stupid, Jimmy?"'

'And Jimmy says, "No, miss, I just didn't want you standing up there all alone."'

65

Lying on a thin mattress on the far side of the room I watch the girl sleeping. She whimpers in her dreams, rocking her head from side to side. My Chloe used to do that when she had a nightmare.

I get up and cross the floor. The dream has taken hold. Her body heaves beneath the quilt as she fights to get away. My hand reaches out and I touch her arm. She stops whimpering. I go back to my mattress.

Later, she wakes properly and sits up, peering into the darkness. She's looking for me.

'Are you there?'

I don't answer.

'Talk to me, please.'

'What do you want?'

'I want to go home.'

'Go back to sleep.'

'I can't.'

'What was your nightmare about?'

'I didn't have a nightmare.'

'Yes, you did. You were moaning.'

'I don't remember.'

She turns her face to the closed curtains. Light is leaking around the edges. I can make out more of her features. I have ruined her hair but it will grow back again.

'Am I a long way from home?' she asks.

'What do you mean?'

'I mean in miles. Is it a long way?'

'No.'

'Could I make it if I walked all day?'

'Perhaps.'

'You could let me go and I could walk home. I wouldn't tell anyone where you live. I wouldn't know how to find it again.'

I move across the room and turn on a bedside lamp. Shadows run away. I hear a sound from outside. I hold a finger to my lips.

'I didn't hear anything,' she says.

In the distance I hear a dog bark.

'Maybe it was the dog.'

'Yes.'

'I have to go to the toilet. Please don't watch me.'

'I'll turn my back.'

'You could go outside.'

'Is that what you want?'

'Yes.'

I leave the bedroom and stand on the landing. I can hear her shuffling across the floor and the tinkle of her urine in the bowl.

She's finished. I knock on the door.

'Can I come back in?'

'No.'

'Why not?'

'I had an accident.'

I push open the door. She is standing in the bathroom, trying to dab a dark stain from the crotch of her jeans.

'You should take them off. I'll dry them.'

'That's OK.'

'I'll get you something else to wear.'

'I don't want to take them off.'

'You can't stay in wet jeans.'

I leave her and look in the main bedroom, which has built-in wardrobes and chests of drawers. The trousers and sweaters are too big for her. I find a white bathrobe on a hanger. It belongs to a hotel. Even a rich Arab isn't beyond stealing a hotel robe. Maybe that's why he's so rich.

I bring it back. I have to unchain her feet so she can pull off her jeans. She makes me leave the room.

'The window is locked. You can't escape,' I tell her.

'I won't.'

I listen at the door until she tells me I can come back in. The bathrobe is too big for her, falling past her knees to her ankles. I take her jeans and wash them in the sink. There is no hot water. The boiler has been turned off. Twisting the jeans into a coil, I wring out the water and hang them over the back of a chair.

I can feel her watching me.

'Did you really kill Darcy's mother?'

It's a nervous question.

'She jumped.'

'Did you tell her to jump?'

'Could someone make you *jump?'*

'I don't know. I don't think so.'

'Well, I guess you're safe.'

Rummaging in my backpack, I take out a small can of pears and open it with a tin opener.

'Here. You should eat something.'

She takes the can and eats the slippery pieces of fruit, sucking the juice from her fingers.

'Be careful. The edges are sharp.'

Lifting the can to her lips she drinks the juice, wiping her mouth on her sleeve. Then she leans back, wrapping the robe around her. The sky is growing brighter outside. She can see more of the room.

'Are you going to kill me?'

'Is that what you think?'

'I don't know.' Her bottom lip is bitten.

It's my turn to ask a question. 'Would you kill me *if you had the chance?'*

She frowns. There are twin creases above the bridge of her nose. 'I don't think I could.'

'What if I was threatening your family – your mother or your father or your sister – would you kill me then?'

'I don't know how.'

'What if you had a gun?'

'Maybe. I guess.'

430

'So we're not so different, you and me. We'll both kill if the circumstances are right. You'll kill me and I'll kill you.'

A tear squeezes silently from the corner of her eye.

'I have to go out again in a little while.'

'Don't leave.'

'I won't be long.'

'I don't like being alone.'

'I have to chain your feet again.'

'Don't cover my face.'

'Just your mouth.'

I rip a length of masking tape from the spool.

'I heard you before,' she says, before I can cover her mouth. 'You were doing this to someone else.'

'What do you mean?'

'I heard you pulling tape from a spool thing like this one. You were downstairs.'

'You heard that.'

'Yes. Is there someone else here?'

'You ask too many questions.'

I push the loop of the padlock until the chains on her ankles are secure.

'I'm going to trust you again not to take this tape off your mouth. If you disappoint me, I will put the hose back down your throat and cover your head. Do you understand?'

She nods.

I put a large square of tape across her mouth. Her eyes are brimming now. She slides sideways down the wall until she's lying curled up on the mattress. I cannot see her face any more.

66

The handset rattles on the desk. I glance through the glass partition at Oliver Rabb and William Greene. Oliver nods.

'Hello.'

'Good morning, Joe, did you sleep well?'

Gideon is calling from a car. I can hear the road drumming beneath the tyres and the sound of the engine.

'Where's Julianne?'

'Don't tell me you've lost her. How careless – losing a wife and a daughter in less than twenty-four hours. It must be some sort of record.'

'It's not so unusual,' I tell him. 'You lost yours.'

He falls silent. I don't think he appreciates the comparison.

'Let me talk to Julianne.'

'No. She's sleeping. What a great fuck she is, Joe. I think she really appreciated getting banged by a real man instead of a retard like you. She went off like a string of firecrackers, especially when I shoved my thumb up her arse. I'm going to do her again later. Maybe I'll do them both together, mother and daughter.'

'Charlie has been a very good girl. Obedient. Subservient. You'd be proud of her. Every time I look at her I go all warm and fuzzy inside. Do you know she whimpers the way a lover does when she sleeps? Have you found my wife and daughter?'

'Yes.'

'Where are they?'

'On their way.'

'Wrong answer.'

'I talked to Chloe this morning. She's a bright girl. She had a question for you.'

He hesitates. Oliver and William Greene are crouched over their laptops. Dozens of police units are in place across Bristol and two helicopters are in the air. I look at my watch. We've been talking for three minutes.

'What question?' asks Gideon.

'She wants to know about her cat, Tinkle. I think she said it was short for Tinkerbell. She asked if Tinkle was OK. She hopes you left her with the Hahns to look after. She said the Hahns had a farm next door.'

Gideon's breathing has altered slightly. I have his full attention. Through an earpiece, I listen to Oliver Rabb's progress.

['We got a powerful level of seven dBm. The signal strength is eighteen decibels higher than the next nearest tower. The handset is less than a hundred and fifty metres away from the base station . . .']

'Are you still there, Gideon? What will I tell Chloe?'

He hesitates. 'Tell her I gave Tinkle to the Hahns.'

'She'll be pleased.'

'Where is she?'

'Like I said, she's on her way.'

'This is some sort of trick.'

'She told me about a postcard that she wrote to you from Turkey.'

'I didn't get a postcard.'

'Her mother wouldn't let her send it. Remember how you taught her to snorkel? She went snorkelling off a boat and saw underwater ruins. She thought it might be Atlantis, the lost city, but she wanted to ask you.'

'Let me talk to her?'

'You'll talk to her when I talk to Charlie.'

'Don't fuck with me, Joe. Put Chloe on the line. I want to speak to her now.'

'I told you, she's not here.'

433

Oliver's voice is in my ear again:

[*'We have BMS signals from three towers. I can estimate DOA but he keeps moving, leaving the range of one tower and getting picked up by another. You have to make him stop.'*]

'They were living in Greece. But they came home a few days ago. They're being protected.'

'I knew they were alive.'

'Your voice keeps breaking up, Gideon. You might want to stop somewhere.'

'I'd prefer to keep moving.'

I've exhausted everything I can remember from Chloe's journal. I don't know how long I can keep up the charade. On the far side of the incident room, Ruiz appears, half-running and out of breath. Behind him, Helen Chambers clutches her daughter's hand and struggles to keep up. Chloe looks goggle-eyed at the speed with which she's been woken, dressed and brought from the warmth of her bed to this place.

Gideon is still on the line.

'Your daughter is here.'

'Prove it.'

'Not until I talk to Charlie and Julianne.'

'You think I'm an idiot. You think I don't know what you're trying to do.'

'She has blonde hair. Brown eyes. She's wearing skinny-leg jeans and a green cardigan. She's with her mother. They're talking to Detective Inspector Cray.'

'Let me talk to Chloe.'

'No.'

'Prove she's there.'

'Let me speak to Charlie or Julianne.'

He grinds his teeth. 'I want you to understand something, Joe. Not everyone you love is going to live. I was going to let you choose which one, but you're pissing me off.'

'Let me speak to my wife and daughter.'

His cold composed unyielding tone has changed. He's enraged. Ranting. He screams down the line.

'LISTEN, YOU COCKSUCKER, PUT MY DAUGHTER

ON THE PHONE OR I'LL BURY YOUR PRECIOUS WIFE SO DEEP YOU'LL NEVER FIND HER BODY.'

I can imagine his mouth twisting and flecks of spit flying. Brakes squeal and a car horn sounds in the background. He's losing concentration.

Oliver Rabb is also talking to me.

['He's just been handed on to a new tower. Signal strength five dBm and falling. Radius three hundred yards. You have to make him stop moving.']

I nod through the glass partition.

'Calm down, Gideon.'

'Don't tell me what to do. Put Chloe on the line!'

'What do I get in return?'

'You get to choose if your wife or your daughter survive.'

'I want both of them back.'

I hear a tight-lipped laugh. 'I'm sending you a souvenir. You can have it framed.'

'What sort of souvenir?'

The mobile vibrates against my ear. I hold the handset at arm's length, as though it might explode. An image appears in the small backlit square. Julianne, naked and bound, her body as pale as candle wax, lies in a box with her mouth and eyes taped shut and clods of earth crumbling over her stomach and thighs.

A thin rancid stink of fear fills my nostrils and something small and dark scuttles inside my chest, burrowing into the chambers of my heart. I can hear it now: the sound Gideon talked about. A tiny creature crying softly into an endless night. The sound of a mind breaking.

'Stay with me, Joe,' he says, in a soft insinuating tone. 'She was still alive when I last saw her. I'll still let you choose.'

'What have you done?'

'I gave her what she wanted.'

'What does that mean?'

'She wanted to take her daughter's place.'

The grotesque image is beyond words. My imagination paints pictures instead. And in my mind's eye I see Julianne's breathing

435

body, sipping the darkness, unable to move, her hair spread out beneath her head.

'Please, please, don't do this,' I beg, my voice breaking.

'Put my daughter on the phone.'

'Wait.'

Ruiz is standing in front of me. Chloe and Helen are with him. He pulls two chairs to the desk and motions for them to sit. Helen is dressed in jeans and a striped top. Clutching Chloe's hand, she sits with her head drawn down between her shoulders, her face a crumpled mask. Worn down. Defeated.

I cover the phone. 'Thank you.'

She nods.

Chloe's blonde fringe has fallen across her eyes. She doesn't push it back. It is a physical barrier she can hide behind.

'He wants to talk to Chloe.'

'What's she going to say?' asks Helen.

'She just has to say hello.'

'Is that it?'

'Yes.'

Chloe rocks her legs beneath the chair, chewing at a fingernail. A baggy green cardigan hangs down to her thighs and narrow jeans make her legs look like sticks in denim.

I motion to her. She circles the desk on tiptoes, as if frightened of bruising her heels. I cover the mouthpiece and silently mouth the words I want her to say.

Then I raise my hand to Oliver, giving him a countdown by closing my fingers one at a time. Five . . . four . . . three . . .

Chloe takes the handset and whispers, 'Hello, Daddy, it's me.'

. . . two . . . one . . .

I drop my arm. Through the window Oliver presses a button or flips a switch and a dozen mobile phone towers are silenced.

I can picture Gideon staring at his handset, wondering what happened to the signal. His daughter was right there but her words were snatched away. Fifteen police units are within a hundred and fifty yards of his last known location, near the Prince Street Bridge. Veronica Cray has gone to join them.

Chloe doesn't understand what's happened.

'You did really well,' I say, taking the mobile from her.

'Where's he gone?'

'He's going to call back. We want him to use another telephone.'

I glance through the window at Oliver and Lieutenant Greene. Both seem to be holding a collective breath. It has been two minutes. We can't keep the phone towers blacked out for any longer than ten. How long will it take Gideon to find a landline?

Come on.

Make the call.

67

One of the few lessons I remember from physics class at school is that nothing travels faster than the speed of light. And if a person could move at light speed for long distances, time would slow down for them and even stand still.

I have my own theories on time. Fear expands it. Panic collapses it to nothing. Right now my heartbeat is racing and my mind is alert, yet everything else in the incident room has the stillness of a hot Sunday afternoon and a fat dog sleeping in the shade. Even the second hand on the clock seem to hesitate between ticks, unsure whether to go forward or stop completely.

In front of me, the desk is clear except for two landlines attached to the station switchboard. Oliver Rabb and Lieutenant Greene are sitting in the comms room next door. Helen and Chloe are waiting in Veronica Cray's office.

Picking at a patch of flaking paint on the chair, I stare at the phones, willing them to ring. Perhaps if I stare hard enough I can picture him calling. Through the earpiece, I hear Oliver count down another minute. Eight have gone. My chest rises and falls. Relax. He'll call. He just has to find a landline.

It takes me a moment to realise the phone is ringing. I glance at Oliver Rabb. He wants me to let it ring four times.

I pick up.

'Hello.'

'Where the fuck is Chloe?'

'Why did you hang up on her?'

Gideon explodes: 'I didn't hang up. The line went dead. If this is some fucking stunt . . .'

'Chloe said you hung up on her.'

'There's no signal, arsehole. Look at your mobile.'

'Hey, yeah.'

'Put Chloe on the phone.'

'I'll send someone to get her.'

'Where is she?'

'Next door.'

'Get her.'

'I'll put the call through to her.'

'I know what you're doing. Get her on the line now!'

I glance at Oliver and William Greene. They're still trying to trace the call. It's taking too long. My left side is trembling. If I keep my leg on the ground, I can stop it shaking.

Ruiz ushers Chloe into the room. I cover the phone.

'You OK?'

She nods.

'I'm going to be listening. If you get frightened, I want you to cover the phone and tell me.'

She nods and picks up the second phone.

'Hello, Daddy, it's me.'

'Hi, how are you?'

'Good.'

'I'm sorry we got cut off, baby. I can't talk long.'

'I lost a tooth.'

'Did you?'

'The tooth fairy gave me two bits of money. I left the tooth fairy a note. Mummy helped me write it.'

Chloe is a natural at this. Without even trying, she's holding his attention completely, keeping him on the line.

'Is your mum there?'

'Yeah.'

'Is she listening?'

439

'No.'

Beyond the glass, Oliver turns and raises both thumbs. They've traced the call. Chloe has run out of things to say. Gideon is asking her questions. Sometimes she nods rather than answers.

'Are you in trouble?' she asks him.

'Don't worry about me.'

'Did you do something wrong?'

In the background I hear the wail of approaching sirens. Gideon has heard them too. I take the handset from Chloe.

'It's over,' I say. 'Where are Charlie and Julianne?'

Gideon screams down the phone. 'You cocksucker! You scumbag! I'm going to rip you a new arsehole! You're dead! No, your wife's dead! You're never going to see her alive.'

There are more sirens, along with screeching brakes and car doors opening. Glass breaks and a gunshot echoes through the handset. Please, God, don't shoot him.

There are cheers from the incident room. Fists punch the air. 'We've got the bastard,' someone declares.

Chloe looks at me, bewildered, terrified. I'm still pressing the phone to my ear, listening to the sound of at least twenty weapons being cocked. Someone is yelling at Gideon to lie on the ground, to put his hands on his head. More voices. Heavy boots.

'Hello? Is anyone there? Hello?'

Nobody is listening.

'Can someone hear me? Pick up!' I scream down the line. 'Tell me what's happened.'

Suddenly, there's a voice on the end of the line. It's Veronica Cray.

'We got him.'

'What about Charlie and Julianne?'

'They're not with him.'

68

Gideon Tyler looks different. Fitter. Leaner. He is no longer a stuttering confabulator and constructor of deceits. There are no invisible mousetraps on the floor. It's almost as though he can physically transform himself by taking on a new persona, his real one.

Some things are the same. His thin blond hair hangs limply over his ears and his pale grey eyes blink at the world from behind a pair of small rectangular glasses with metal frames. His hands are cuffed and placed palm-down on the surface of the table. The only signs of stress are the circles of perspiration beneath the arms of his shirt.

Strip-searched and examined by a doctor, his belt and shoelaces have been confiscated along with his watch and personal effects. Since then he's been alone in the interview suite, staring at his hands as if willing the metal cuffs to break and the door to open and the guards to dissolve.

I am watching him through an observation window – a one-way mirror into the interview room. Although he can't see me, I sense that he knows I'm here. Occasionally, he looks up and stares into the mirror – not examining his own features as much as looking beyond it, imagining my face.

Veronica Cray is meeting upstairs with a brace of military lawyers and the Chief Constable. The army is demanding the right to interrogate Gideon, claiming it has national security concerns. DI Cray isn't likely to cede ground. I don't care who asks the questions. Someone should be in there now, demanding answers, finding my wife and daughter.

A door opens behind me. Ruiz steps from the darkness of the corridor into the darkness of the observation room. There are no lights. Any luminosity could leak through the mirror and reveal the hidden room.

'So that's him.'

'That's him. Can't we do something?'

'Like what?'

'Make him talk. I mean, if this were the movies you'd go in there and beat the crap out of him.'

'Perhaps in the old days,' says Ruiz, sounding genuinely nostalgic.

'They still arguing?'

Ruiz nods.

'The military are sending a chopper. They want to take him to an army base. They're scared he might tell us something. Like the truth.'

Surely, there's no way Veronica Cray will surrender jurisdiction. She'll take it to the Home Secretary or the Lord Chamberlain. She has two murders, a shooting and two kidnappings on her patch, on her watch. The arguments and legal manoeuvrings are taking up too much time. Meanwhile, Gideon sits twelve feet away, humming to himself and staring into the mirror.

He doesn't look like a man who's going to spend the rest of his life in prison. He looks like a man without a care in the world.

DI Cray enters the interview suite. Monk is sitting second chair. A third person, a military lawyer, takes up a position behind them, standing ready to intervene at any moment. Microphones have been removed from the room. There are no pads or pencils. The interview isn't being recorded. I doubt if there's a record any longer of Gideon's arrest or his fingerprinting. Somebody is determined to remove all trace of him.

Veronica Cray pours water from a plastic bottle into a plastic cup. Leaning her head back, she takes a long deep draught. Tyler seems to look at her throat with interest.

'As you can probably tell, this isn't a formal interview,' she says. 'Nothing you say is being taken down. It can't be used against you. You only have to answer one question. Tell us the whereabouts of Julianne and Charlotte O'Loughlin.'

Gideon presses his back against the chair and pushes his arms forward, fingers splayed on the table. Then slowly he raises his head, his eyes disappearing in the wash of fluorescence reflecting from his glasses.

'I will not talk to you,' he whispers.

'You *have* to talk to me.'

His head moves from side to side.

Gideon stares at the mirror, through it.

'Where are Charlie and Julianne O'Loughlin?'

He sits to attention. 'My name is Major Gideon Tyler. Born October six, 1969. I am a soldier in Her Majesty's First Military Intelligence Brigade.'

He is following the Conduct Under Capture rules – name, age and rank.

'Don't give me this bullshit,' says Veronica Cray.

Gideon fixes her with a milky grey stare, searching her eyes. 'It must be hard being a dyke in the police force, liking the black triangle, being a member of the tongue and groove club. Must get a lot of snide remarks. What do they call you behind your back?'

'Answer the question.'

'You answer mine. Do you get much? I often wonder about dykes and if you get much sex. You're as ugly as a hat full of arseholes so I shouldn't think so.'

Veronica Cray's voice remains smooth but the back of her neck is blazing. 'I'll hear your fantasies another time,' she says.

'Oh, I never leave anything to fantasy, detective. You must know that by now.'

There is something horribly truthful about the statement.

'You're going to prison for the rest of your life, Major Tyler. Things happen in prison to people like you. They get changed.'

Gideon smiles. 'I'm not going to prison, Detective Inspector. Ask him.' He motions to the military lawyer who doesn't hold his gaze. 'I doubt if I'll even get out of this place. Ever heard the word rendition? Black prisons? Ghost flights?'

The lawyer steps forward. He wants the interview terminated.

Veronica Cray ignores him and keeps talking. 'You're a soldier, Tyler, a man who lives by rules. I'm not talking about military regulations or regimental codes of honour. I'm talking about your own rules, what *you* believe, and hurting children doesn't come into it.'

'Don't tell me what I believe,' Gideon says, his heels scraping on the floor. 'Don't talk about Honour, or Queen and Country. There *are* no rules.'

'Just tell me what you've done with Mrs O'Loughlin and her daughter.'

'Let me see the Professor.' He turns to the mirror. 'Is he watching? Are you there, Joe?'

'No. You'll talk to me,' says the DI.

Gideon raises his arms above his head, stretching his back until his vertebrae pop and crack. Then he slams his fists into the table. The combination of his strength and the metal cuffs creates a sound like a gunshot and everybody in the room flinches except for the DI. Gideon crosses his wrists, holding them in front of himself as though warding her off. Then he flicks his hands apart and a long splash of blood flies across the table and lands on her shirt.

Using the edge of the handcuffs, Gideon has opened a gash across his left palm. DI Cray says nothing but her face is suddenly pale. She pushes back her chair and stands, looking at the crimson slash of blood on her white shirt. Then she excuses herself from interview while she changes.

With three quick stiff steps she reaches the door. Gideon calls after her. 'Tell the Professor to come and see me. I'll tell him how his wife died.'

69

I meet Veronica Cray in the passageway outside the interview suite. She looks at me helplessly and lowers her gaze, sagging under the weight of what she knows and doesn't know. The bloodstain is drying on her shirt.

'They're sending a military chopper. I can't stop them. They have a warrant signed by the Home Secretary.'

'What about Charlie and Julianne?'

Her shoulder blades flinch beneath her shirt. 'There's nothing more I can do.'

It's what I feared. The MOD cares more about silencing Gideon Tyler than it does about a missing mother and daughter.

'Let me talk to him,' I say. 'He wants to see me.'

Time shimmers for a moment. The hubbub of the world disappears.

The DI takes a cigarette from a packet in the pocket of her trousers. She rests it between her lips. I notice a tiny tremor in her hand. Anger. Disappointment. Frustration. It could be all of them.

'I'll get rid of the military lawyer,' she says. 'You might only have twenty minutes. Take Ruiz with you. He'll know what to do.'

The insinuation in her voice has not been there before. She turns and moves slowly along the passage towards the stairs.

I enter the interview suite. The door swings shut behind me.

We're alone for a moment. The very air in the room seems to have congregated in distant corners. Gideon can no longer jump to his feet or pace the floor. His handcuffs have been secured on the surface of the table, fixed with bolts and recessed screws. A doctor has bandaged the cut to his palm.

I move closer and take a seat opposite him, placing my hands on the table. My left thumb and forefinger are beating a silent tattoo. I take the hand away and press it between my thighs. Ruiz has slipped into the room behind me, shutting the door softly.

Gideon gazes at me steadily with a formless smile. I can see the ruins of my life reflected in his glasses.

'Hello, Joe, heard from your wife lately?'

'Where is she?'

'Dead.'

'I don't believe you.'

'You killed her the moment I was arrested.'

I can smell the very odour of his insides, the rancid, festering, misogyny and hatred.

'Tell me where they are.'

'You can only have one of them. I asked you to choose.'

'No.'

'I wasn't given a choice when I lost my wife and daughter.'

'You didn't lose them. They ran away.'

'The slut betrayed me.'

'You're making excuses. You're obsessed with your own sense of entitlement. You believe because you've fought for your country, done terrible things for them, that you are owed something better.'

'No. Not better. I want what everyone else wants. But what if my dream conflicts with yours? What if my happiness comes at your expense?'

'We make do.'

'Not good enough,' he says, blinking slowly.

'The war is over, Gideon. Let them come home.'

'Wars don't end,' he laughs. 'Wars thrive because enough men still love them. You meet people who think they can stop wars, one person at a time, but that's bullshit. They complain that inno-cent women and children get killed or wounded, people who don't

446

choose to fight, but I'm betting a lot of them wave their sons and husbands off to war. Knit them socks. Send them food.

'You see, Joe, not every enemy combatant carries a gun. Old men in rich countries make wars happen. And so do the people who sit on the sofas watching Sky News and voting for them. So spare me your bullshit homilies. There are no innocent victims. We're all guilty of something.'

I'm not going to argue the morals of war with Gideon. I don't want to hear his justifications and excuses, sins of commission and omission.

'Please tell me where they are.'

'And what are you going to give me?'

'Forgiveness.'

'I don't want forgiveness for what I've done.'

'I'm forgiving you for who you *are*.'

The statement seems to shake him for a moment.

'They're coming to get me, aren't they?'

'A chopper is on its way.'

'Who did they send?'

'Lieutenant Greene.'

Gideon looks at the mirror. 'Greenie! Is he listening? His wife Verity has the sweetest arse. She spends every Tuesday afternoon in a budget hotel in Ladbroke Grove fucking a lieutenant colonel from acquisitions. One of the lads from ops put a bug in the room. What a tape! It's been passed round the whole regiment.' He smirks and closes his eyes, as if reliving the good times.

'Could you adjust my glasses for me, Joe?' he asks.

They've slipped down his nose. I lean forward and place my thumb and forefinger on the curved frame, pushing it up to the bridge of his nose. The fluorescent lights catch in the lenses and turn his eyes white. He tilts his head and his eyes are grey again. There doesn't seem to be any magnification from the lenses.

He whispers. 'They're going to kill me, Joe. And if I die, you'll never find Julianne and Charlie. The ticking clock – we all have one, but I guess mine is running a little faster than most and so is your wife's.'

A bubble of saliva forms and bursts on my lips as I open them but no words come out.

'I used to hate time,' he says. 'I counted Sundays. I imagined my daughter growing up without me. That was mechanical time, the stuff of clocks and calendars. I deal in something deeper than that now. I collect time from people. I take it away from them.'

Gideon makes it sound as though years can be traded between individuals. My loss can be his gain.

'You love your daughter, Gideon. I love mine. I can't possibly understand what you've been through, but you won't let Charlie die. I know that.'

'Is that who you want?'

'Yes.'

'So you're making a choice.'

'No. I want them both. Where are they?'

'No choice is a choice, remember?' He smiles. 'Did you ask your wife about her affair? I bet she denied it and you believed her. Look at her text messages. I've seen them. She sent one to her boss saying that you suspected something and she couldn't see him any more. Do you still want to save her?'

A blood-dark shadow shakes my heart and I want to lean across the space between us, one arm drawn back like a bow, and smash my fist into his face.

'I don't believe you.'

'Look at her text messages.'

'I don't care.'

His voice erupts in a hoarse laugh. 'Yes, you do.'

He glances at Ruiz and back to me. 'I'm going to tell you what I did to your wife. I gave *her* a choice too. I put her in a box and told her that your daughter was in a box next to her. She could breathe through a hose and stay alive but only by taking her daughter's air.'

His hands are bolted to the table, yet I can feel his fingers reaching into my head, wedging between the two halves of the cerebellum, levering them apart.

'What do you think she'll do, Joe? Will she steal Charlie's air to stay alive a little longer?'

448

Ruiz launches himself across the room and hurls his fist into Gideon's face with a force that would knock him down if his wrists weren't bolted in place. I hear breaking bones.

Gripping Gideon beneath his lower ribs, he drives his knee into his kidneys, sending bolts of pain shooting through his body. Perspiration. Empty lungs. Fear. Faeces. Ruiz is screaming at him now, pounding his face with his fists, demanding to know the address. For a violent, bloody minute he takes out all his frustrations. He's no longer a serving member of the police force. Rules don't apply. This is what Veronica Cray meant.

Waves of pain break and crash on Gideon's body. His face is already beginning to bruise and swell from the beating, yet he's not complaining or crying out.

'Gideon,' I whisper. His eyes meet mine. 'I'll let him do it. I promise you. If you don't tell me where they are, I'm going to let him kill you.'

A bloody froth forms on his lips and his tongue rolls across his teeth, painting them red. An unearthly smile forms on his face as the muscles contract and relax.

'Do it.'

'What?'

'Torture me.'

I look at Ruiz, who is rubbing his fists. His knuckles are torn.

Gideon goads me. 'Torture me. Ask me the right questions. Show me how good you are.'

He sees me hesitate and bows his head in the posture of the confessional. 'What's wrong? Don't tell me you're a sentimentalist. Surely you're justified in torturing me.'

'Yes.'

'I have the information you need. I know exactly where your wife and daughter are. It's not like you're uncertain or half-sure. Even if you were fifty per cent certain, you'd be justified. I tortured people for far less. I tortured them because they were in the wrong place at the wrong time.'

He stares at his hands like a man considering his future and discounting it.

'Torture me. Make me tell you.'

I feel as though someone somewhere has opened a sluice gate and my hostility and anger are draining away. I hate this man more than words can describe. I want to hurt him. I want him dead. But it's not going to make any difference. He won't tell me where they are.

Gideon doesn't want forgiveness or justice or understanding. He has bathed in the blood of a terrible conflict, done the bidding of governments and secret departments and shadowy organisations operating beyond the law. He has broken minds, obtained secrets, destroyed lives and saved countless more. It changed him. How could it not? Yet throughout it all, he clung to the one pure, innocent, untainted thing in his life, his daughter, until she was taken away from him.

I can hate Gideon, but I cannot hate him more than he hates himself.

70

'There's another anomaly,' says Oliver Rabb, adjusting his crooked bowtie and dabbing at his forehead with a matching handkerchief.

When I don't answer he keeps talking. 'Tyler turned on his mobile and turned it off again at 7.35 a.m. It was on for just over twenty-one seconds.'

The information rises and falls over me.

Oliver is looking at me expectantly. 'You wanted me to check for anomalies. You seemed to think they were important. I think I know what he was doing. He was taking a photograph.'

Finally there is awareness. It's not a grand vision or a blinding insight. Things have become clearer, clearer than yesterday.

Gideon took photographs of Julianne and Charlie. He used a mobile phone camera, which had to be turned on for the pictures to be taken. The anomalies can been explained. They support a theory.

Oliver follows me upstairs, through the incident room. I don't notice if detectives are back at their desks. I don't notice if my left hand is pill rolling or my left arm is swinging normally. These things are unimportant.

I go straight to the map on the wall. A second white pin is stuck alongside the first. Oliver is trying to explain his reasoning.

'Yesterday's anomaly happened at 3.07 p.m. The mobile was

turned on for fourteen seconds but he didn't make a call. Later, he transmitted a photograph from the same phone to your wife's mobile.'

He pulls the image up on screen showing Charlie with her head encased in tape and a hosepipe in her mouth. I can almost hear the rasp of her breath through the narrow opening.

'The second anomaly was this morning. Tyler sent another photograph from the same mobile – the picture of your wife.'

Gideon knew police could trace a mobile every time he turned it on. He didn't make mistakes. In each case he turned on the mobile phone for a reason. Two signals. Two photographs.

'Can you trace the signals?' I ask.

'I was struggling when there was only one, but now it might be feasible.'

I sit alongside him, unable to comprehend most of what he's doing. Waves of numbers cross the screen as he quizzes the software, overrides error messages and circumvents problems. Oliver seems to be writing the software as he goes along.

'Both signals were picked up by a ten metre GSM tower in The Mall, less than half a mile from the Clifton Suspension Bridge,' he says. 'The DOA points to a location west of the tower.'

'How far?'

'I'm going multiply the TOA – Time of Arrival – with the signal propagation speed.'

He types and talks, using some sort of equation to do the calculation. The answer doesn't please him.

'Anywhere between two hundred and twelve hundred metres.'

Oliver takes a black marker pen and draws a large teardrop shape on the map. The narrow end is at the tower and the widest part covers dozens of streets, a section of the Avon River and half of Leigh Woods.

'A second GSM tower picked up the signature and sent a message back but the first tower had already established contact.' Again he points to the map. 'The second tower is here. It's the same one that carried the last mobile call to Mrs Wheeler before she jumped.'

Oliver goes back to his laptop. 'The DOA is different. North to north-east. There's an overlapping connectivity.'

The science is beginning to lose me. Rising from his chair again, Oliver goes back to the map and draws a second teardrop shape, this one overlapping the first. The common area covers perhaps a thousand square yards and a dozen streets. How long would it take to doorknock every house?

'We need a satellite map,' I say.

Oliver is ahead of me. The image on his laptop blurs and then slowly comes into focus. We appear to be falling from space. Topographical details take shape – hills, rivers, streets, the suspension bridge.

I walk to the door and yell, 'Where's the DI?'

A dozen heads turn. Safari Roy answers. 'She's with the Chief Constable.'

'Get her! She has to organise a search.'

A siren wails into the afternoon, rising from the crowded streets into a coin-coloured sky. This is how it began less than four weeks ago. If I could turn back the clock would I step into that police car at the university and go to the Clifton Suspension Bridge?

No. I'd walk away. I'd make excuses. I'd be the husband Julianne wants me to be – the one who runs the other way and shouts for help.

Ruiz is alongside me, holding on to the roof handle as the car swings through another corner. Monk is in the front passenger seat, yelling commands.

'Take the next left. Cut in front of this bastard. Cross over. Go round this bus. Get that arsehole's number plate.'

The driver punches through a red light, ignoring the screeching brakes and car horns. At least four police cars are in our convoy. A dozen more are coming from other parts of the city. I can hear them chattering over the two-way.

The traffic is banked up along Marlborough Street and Queens Road. We pull on to the opposite side of the road onto the footpath. Pedestrians scatter like pigeons.

The cars rendezvous in Caledonia Place alongside a narrow strip of parkland that separates it from West Mall. We're in a wealthy area, full of large terraces, bed & breakfast hotels and boarding houses. Some of them are four storeys high, painted in pastel shades, with outside plumbing and window boxes. Thin wisps of smoke curl from chimneys, drifting west over the river.

A police bus arrives carrying another twenty officers. DI Cray issues instructions, unshakeable amid the mêlée. Officers are going door to door, talking to neighbours, showing photographs, making a note of any empty flats and houses. Someone must have seen something.

I look again at the satellite map unfurled across a car bonnet. Statistics don't make science. And all human behaviour cannot be quantified by numbers or reduced to equations, no matter what someone like Oliver Rabb might think. Places are significant. Journeys are significant. Every excursion or expedition we take is a story, an inner narrative that we sometimes don't even realise we're following. What was Gideon's journey? He boasted that he could melt through walls, but he was more like human wallpaper, able to blend in and become simply background while he watched houses and broke into them.

He was there when Christine Wheeler jumped. He whispered in her ear. He must have been somewhere close. I look at the terraces, studying the skyline. The Clifton Suspension Bridge is less than two hundred yards to the west of here. I can smell the sea stink and gorse. Some of these addresses are likely to have a view of the bridge from the upper floors.

A man rides past on a bicycle with elastic around his trouser legs to stop the fabric getting caught in the chain. A woman walks her black spaniel on the grass. I want to stop them, grasp them by the upper arms and roar into their faces, demanding to know if they have seen my wife and daughter. Instead, I stand and study the street, looking for something out of the ordinary: people in the wrong place, or the wrong clothes, something that doesn't belong or tries too hard to belong or draws the eye for another reason.

Gideon would have a chosen a house, not a flat; somewhere away from the prying eyes of neighbours, isolated or shielded, with a driveway or a garage so he could take his vehicle off the road and move Charlie and Julianne inside without being seen. A house that is up for sale, perhaps, or one that is only used for holidays or weekends.

I step across the muddy patch of grass and begin walking along the street. The trunks of trees are wreathed in wire and the branches shiver in the wind.

'Where the hell are you going?' yells the DI.

'I'm looking for a house.'

Ruiz catches up to me and Monk is not far behind, having been sent to keep us out of trouble. I keep looking at the skyline and trying not to stumble. My cane click-clacks on the pavement as I head down the slight hill past a row of terraces and turn into Sion Lane. I still can't see the bridge.

The next street across is Westfield Place. A front door is open. A middle-aged woman is sweeping the steps.

'Can you see the bridge from here?' I ask.

'No, love.'

'What about the top floor?'

'The estate agent called it "glimpses",' she laughs. 'You lost?'

I show her the photographs of Charlie and Julianne. 'Have you seen either of them?'

She shakes her head.

'What about this man?'

'I'd remember him,' she says, when the opposite is probably true.

We keep moving along Westfield Place. The wind is whipping up leaves and sweet wrappers that chase each other along the gutter. Abruptly I cross the street to a brick wall with stone capping.

'Give me a leg-up,' says Ruiz, before stepping into Monk's cupped hands and being hoisted upwards until his forearms are braced along the white painted capping.

'It's a garden,' he says. 'There's a house further along.'

'Can you see the bridge?'

'Not from here, but you might be able to see it from the top of the house. There's a turret room.'

He jumps down and we follow the wall, looking for a gate. Monk is now ahead. I can't match his stride and have to run every few yards to catch up.

Stone pillars mark the entrance to a driveway. The gates are open. Tyres have crushed leaves into the puddles. A car has been here recently.

The house is large and from another age. Overgrown with ivy on one side, it has small dark windows poking through the leaves. The roof is steep with an octagonal turret on the western corner.

The place looks empty. Closed up. Curtains are drawn and leaves have collected on the main steps and entrance portico. I follow Monk up the steps. He rings the doorbell. Nobody answers. I call Charlie's name and then Julianne's, pressing my face against a slender pane of frosted glass, trying to catch the tiny vibrations of a reply. Imagining it.

Ruiz has gone to check out a garage at the side of the house, beneath the trees. He disappears through a side door and then appears again immediately.

'It's Tyler's van,' he yells. 'It's empty.'

My head fills with tumbling and leaping emotions. Hope.

Monk is on the phone to DI Cray. 'Tell her to get an ambulance,' I say.

He relays the message and snaps the phone shut. Then he raises his elbow and drives it hard against the glass pane, which shatters and falls inward. Reaching gingerly inside, he unlocks the door and swings it open.

The hall is wide and paved with black and white tiles. It has a mirror and an umbrella stand, as well as a side table with a Chinese takeaway menu and list of emergency numbers.

The lights are working, but the switches seem to be camouflaged against the floral wallpaper. The place has been closed up for the winter, with sheets and rugs covering the furniture and the fire grates swept clean. I imagine figures lurking unseen, hiding in corners trying not to make a sound.

Behind us a trio of police cars streams through the gates and up the gravel driveway. Doors open. DI Cray leads them up the front steps.

Gideon said Julianne and Charlie were buried in a box, breathing the same air. I don't want to believe him. So much of what he said to people was designed to wound and to break them.

I stand swaying in the dining room, watching a spill of light from the patio doors. There are muddy footprints on the parquetry squares.

Ruiz has climbed the stairs. He calls to me. I mount the stairs two at a time, gripping the banister and dragging myself upwards. My cane falls from my hand and clatters down the steps to the black and white tiles.

'In here,' he yells.

I pause at the door. Ruiz is kneeling beside a narrow cast iron bed. A child is curled on a mattress, her eyes and mouth taped shut. I do not remember uttering a sound, but Charlie's head rises and turns to my voice and she lets out a muffled sob. Her head rocks from side to side. I have to hold her still while Ruiz finds a pair of dressmaking scissors lying on a thin mattress in another corner of the bedroom.

His hands are shaking. So are mine. The blades of the scissors open and close gently and I peel back the tape. I am staring at her with a kind of wonderment, mouth open, still not able to believe it's her. I meet Charlie's blue eyes. I am seeing her through a shining fluid that will not be blinked away.

She is dirty. Her hair has been hacked to her skull. Her skin is torn. Her wrists are bleeding. She is the most beautiful creature to ever draw breath.

I crush her to my chest. I rock her in my arms. I want to hold her until she stops crying, until she forgets everything. I want to hold her until she remembers only the warmth of my embrace and my words in her ears and my tears on her forehead.

Charlie is wearing a bathrobe. Her jeans are on a chair.

'Did he . . . ?' The words get caught in my throat. 'Did he touch you?'

She blinks at me, not understanding.

'Did he make you do things? You can tell me. It's OK.'

She shakes her head and wipes her nose with her sleeve.

'Where's your mum?' I ask.

She frowns at me.

'Have you seen her?'

'No. Where is she?'

457

I look at Monk and Ruiz. They're already moving. The house is being searched. I can hear doors being opened, cupboards explored, heavy boots sound from the attic and the turret room. Silence. It lasts half a dozen heartbeats. The boots start moving again.

Charlie puts her head back on my chest. Monk comes back with a set of 24" bolt cutters. I hold her ankles still as he eases the jaws around the shackles, pushing the arms together until the metal breaks and the chain snakes to the floor.

An ambulance has arrived. The paramedics are outside the bedroom door. One of them is young and blonde, carrying a first aid box.

'I want to get dressed,' says Charlie, suddenly self-conscious.

'Sure. Just let these officers take a look at you. Just to be sure.'

I tear myself away from her and go downstairs. Ruiz is in the kitchen with Veronica Cray. The house has been searched. Now detectives are scouring the garden and the garage, poking at dead leaves with heavy boots, squatting to peer at the compost heap.

The trees along the northern border are skeletal and the shed has a derelict forsaken look. A wrought iron table and matching chairs are rusting under an elm tree, where colonies of toadstools have sprung up after the rains.

I walk out the back door, past the laundry and across the sodden lawn. I have the uncanny sense of the birds falling silent and the ground sucking at my shoes. My cane sinks into the earth as I walk between flowerbeds and past lemon trees in enormous stone pots. An incinerator built from breezeblocks is against the back fence, alongside a pile of old railway-sleepers meant for garden edging.

Veronica Cray is alongside me.

'We can have ground-penetrating radar here within the hour. There are cadaver dogs in Wiltshire.'

I stop at the shed. The lock has been smashed open in the search and the door sags on rusting hinges. Inside smells of diesel, fertiliser and earth. A large sit-on lawnmower squats in the centre of the floor. There are metal shelves along two walls and garden tools propped in the corner. The blade of the shovel is clean and dry.

Come on, Gideon, talk to me. Tell me what you've done with her. You were talking half-truths. You said you'd bury her so deep I'd never find her. You said she and Charlie were sharing the same air. Everything you did was practiced. Planned. Your lies contained elements of the truth, which made them easier to maintain.

Leaning on my cane, I reach down and pick up the padlock and broken latch, brushing away mud. Tiny silver scratches are visible against the tarnished metal.

Then I look back into the shed. The wheels of the mower have been turned, wiping away the dust. My eyes study the shelves, the seed trays, aphid sprays and weedkiller. A garden hose is looped on a metal hook. I follow the coils, growing dizzy. One end of the hose droops downward against the upright frame of the shelf.

'Help me move the mower,' I say.

The DI grabs the seat and I push from the front, steering it out the door. The floor is compacted dirt. I try to move the shelf. It's too heavy. Monk pushes me aside and wraps his arms either end, rocking it from one side to the other, walking it towards the door. Seed trays and bottles topple to the floor.

Dropping to my knees, I crawl forward. The compacted earth becomes softer near the wall where the shelf used to stand. A large piece of plywood has been screwed into place. The hosepipe hangs down the plywood and seems to disappear inside it.

I glance back at Veronica Cray and Monk.

'There's something behind the wall. Get some lights in here.'

They won't let me dig. They won't let me watch. Teams of two officers are taking turns, using shovels and buckets to scrape away the floor. A police car has been driven across the lawn and its headlights are allowing them to see.

Shielding my eyes to the brightness, I can see Charlie through the kitchen window. The blonde paramedic has given her something warm to drink and wrapped a blanket around her shoulders.

'Someone you love is going to die,' Gideon told me. He asked me to choose. I couldn't do it. I wouldn't do it. 'No choice is still a choice,' he said. 'I'm going to let Julianne decide.' The other thing Gideon said was that I would remember him. Whether he died today or spent a lifetime in prison, he wouldn't be forgotten.

Julianne told me that she didn't love me any more. She said that I was a different person to the one she married. She was right. Mr Parkinson has seen to that. I *am* different – more pensive, philosophical and melancholic. This disease has not broken me against a rock, but it is like a parasite with tentacles coiling inside me, taking over my movements. I try not to let it show. I fail.

I don't want to know if she's had an affair with Eugene Franklin or Dirk Cresswell. I don't care. No, that's not true. I *do* care. It's just that I care more about getting her back safely. I am to blame, but this is not about seeking redemption or easing a swollen conscience. Julianne will never forgive me. I know that. I will give her whatever she wants. I will make her any promise. I will walk away. I will let her go. Just let her be alive.

Monk calls for help. Two more officers join him. The digging has exposed the lowest edge of the plywood. They're going to rip down the wall.

Dust and dirt reflect in the beams of the headlights, penetrating the cavity. Julianne's body is inside, curled in a foetal ball, with her knees touching her chin and hands cradling her head. I catch a whiff of the urinous smell and see the blueness of her skin.

Other men's hands reach into the cavity and lift her body out. Monk takes her from the others and carries her into the light, stepping over a mound of earth and placing her on a stretcher. Her head is encased in plastic tape. The headlights have turned her body to silver.

A blonde paramedic pulls a hose from Julianne's mouth, replacing it with her lips, forcing air into her lungs. They're cutting the tape from her head.

'Pupils dilated. Her abdomen is cold. She's hypothermic,' says the paramedic, yelling to her partner. 'I got a pulse.'

They roll Julianne gently onto her back. Blankets cover her nakedness. The blonde paramedic is kneeling on the stretcher putting heat packs on Julianne's neck.

'What's wrong?' I ask.

'Her core body temperature is too low. Her heartbeat is erratic.'

'Make her warm.'

'I wish it were that easy. We have to get her to hospital.'

She's not shivering. She's not moving at all. An oxygen mask is pulled over her face.

'Coming through.'

Julianne's eyes flutter open, blind as a kitten in the brightness. She tries to say something but it comes out as a weak groan. Her mouth moves again.

'Charlie's safe. She's fine,' I tell her.

The paramedic issues instructions. 'Tell her not to talk.'

'Just lie still.'

Julianne isn't listening. Her head moves from side to side. She wants to say something. I press my cheek close to the oxygen mask. 'He said she was in a box. I tried not to breathe. I tried to save the air.'

'He lied.'

Her hand snakes out from beneath the blankets and grabs my wrist. It's like ice.

'I remembered what you said. You said he wouldn't kill Charlie. Otherwise I would have stopped breathing.'

I know.

We're almost at the doors to the ambulance. Charlie comes sprinting out of the house, across the grass. Two detectives try to stop her. She feints left and goes right, ducking under their arms.

Ruiz hooks her around the waist and carries her the final few yards. She throws herself at Julianne, calling her Mummy. I haven't heard her use the word in four years.

'Be careful. Don't squeeze her too hard,' warns the young blonde paramedic.

'Do you have children?' I ask her.

'No.'

'You'll learn it doesn't hurt when they squeeze you hard.'

Epilogue

It's a typical spring day with the mist being burned away early and the sky so high and blue it seems impossible that space is a dark domain. The stream looks clear, shallow at the edges where the gravel is clean and eddies swirl around the grasses.

On the far side of the valley the road is visible through the budding trees, curling around a church and dipping out of sight over the ridge.

'Any bites?'

'Nope,' says Charlie.

I keep an eye on Emma who is playing with Gunsmoke, a gold-coloured Labrador I rescued from the pound. He is a very earnest dog who regards me as the cleverest human being he has ever met. Unfortunately, apart from loyalty, he is almost totally useless. As a guard dog he barks whenever I get home and completely ignores strangers until they've been in the house for upwards of an hour at which point he howls as though he has just discovered Myra Hindley coming through the window. The girls love him, which is why I got him.

We're fishing in a stream about a quarter of a mile from the road, through a farm gate and across a field. A picnic rug is spread out on a grassy bank, just near the gravel beach.

Charlie has adopted the Vincent Ruiz mode of fishing, eschewing bait, lures or hooks. This is not for philosophical reasons (or beer drinking), it is because she cannot bring herself to putting a 'living breathing' earthworm on a hook.

'What if he has a whole earthworm family who will miss him if he gets eaten?' she argued.

At this point I tried to explain that earthworms were asexual and didn't have families but that just confused the issue.

'It's just a worm. It doesn't have any feelings.'

'How do you know? Look, it's squirming, trying to get away.'

'It's squirming because it's a worm.'

'No. He's saying, "Please, please don't stick that big hook in me."'

'I didn't know you could speak worm.'

'I can read his body language.'

'Body language.'

'Yes.'

I gave up after that. Now I'm fishing with bread, watching Emma, who has managed to sit in a puddle and get pondweed in her hair. The worm debate is lost on her. Gunsmoke is off chasing rabbits.

The changing seasons are more obvious since we moved out of London, the cycle of death and rebirth. There are blossoms on the trees and daffodils in every garden.

It has been six months since that afternoon on the bridge. Autumn and winter have gone. Darcy is dancing at the Royal Ballet School in London. She's still living with Ruiz and constantly threatening to leave if he doesn't stop treating her like a child.

I haven't heard any news of Gideon Tyler. There has been no military court martial or official statement. Nobody seems to know where Gideon is being held and if he'll ever stand trial. I did hear from Veronica Cray that the military chopper had to land after leaving Bristol. Apparently, Gideon managed to pick the lock on his handcuffs using the frames of his glasses. He forced the pilot to put down in a field, but according to the Ministry of Defence he was recaptured quickly.

I also heard from Helen Chambers and Chloe. They sent me a postcard from Greece. Helen has opened the hotel for the season and Chloe is going to a local school on Patmos. They didn't say very much in the card. Thank you seemed to be the gist of it.

'Can I ask you something?' says Charlie, tilting her head to one side.

'Sure.'

'Do you think you and Mum will ever get back together?'

The question snags like a hook in my chest. Maybe this is how an earthworm feels?

'I don't know. Have you asked your mum?'

'Yes.'

'What does she say?'

'She changes the subject.'

I nod and raise my face, feeling the warmth of the sunshine on my cheeks. These warm cool clear days bring me comfort. They tell me that summer is coming. Summer is good.

Julianne hasn't filed for divorce. Maybe she will. I made a deal. A pact. I said that if she were alive, I would do anything she asked. She asked me to move out. I have. I am living in Wellow, opposite the pub.

She was still in the hospital when she told me what she wanted. Rain streaked the windows of her room. 'I don't want you coming back to the cottage,' she said. 'I don't want you ever coming back.'

She kicked me out once before but that was different. Back then she said she loved me, but couldn't live with me. This time she hasn't offered me any similar crumb of comfort. She blames me for what happened. She's right. It was my fault. I live with that knowledge every day, watching Charlie closely, looking for any sign of post-traumatic stress. I watch Julianne too and wonder how she's coping. Is she having nightmares? Does she wake in a cold sweat, and check the locks on the windows and doors?

Charlie winds in her fishing line. 'I got a joke for you, Dad.'

'What's that?'

'What did one saggy breast say to the other saggy breast?'

'What?'

'If we don't get some support soon we'll be nuts.' She laughs. I laugh too. 'Do you think I should tell it to Mum?'

'Maybe not.'

I still regard myself as being married. Separation is a state of mind and my mind hasn't come to terms with it. Hector the publican wants me to join the Divorced Men's Club of which he's the unofficial president or chairman. There are only six of them and they meet every month and go to the movies or sit in the pub.

'I'm not divorced,' I told him, but he treated that like a minor technicality. Then he gave me the speech about getting over the shoals and heading back into the mainstream. I told him I'm not a classic joiner of things. I've never been a member of anything, not a gym or a political party or a religion. I wonder what they do at a divorced men's club?

I don't want to be alone. I don't want the long empty moments. It reminds me too much of crappy dorm rooms at university, after I left home and couldn't find a girlfriend.

It's not that I can't live on my own. I'm OK with that. But I keep imagining that Julianne is thinking the same thing and will come to realise that she was happier together than apart. Mum, Dad, two children, the cat, the hamsters, and I could bring the dog. We could shop, pay bills, choose schools, watch movies and romance each other like normal married couples, with flowers on Valentine's Day and anniversaries.

Speaking of anniversaries, today is a special one: Emma's birthday. I have to get her back to the cottage by three for a party. We pull in the fishing lines and pack up the picnic basket. Gunsmoke is filthy and smelly and neither of the girls want to sit next to him in the car.

The windows are kept open. There are lots of shrieks and girlish laughter until we get to the cottage, where they tumble out the doors and pretend that I've gassed them. Julianne is watching from the doorway. She's put coloured balloons over the trellis and the letterbox.

'Look at you,' she says to Emma. 'How did you get so wet?'

'We went fishing,' says Charlie. 'We didn't catch anything.'

'Except pneumonia,' says Julianne, shooing them upstairs for a bath.

There is an abstract sort of intimacy in our conversations now. She is the same woman I married. Brown-haired. Beautiful. Barely forty. And I still love her in every way but the physical one where we exchange bodily fluids and wake up next to each other in the morning. Whenever I see her in the village I am still struck by wonder: what did she ever see in me and how could I have let her go?

'You shouldn't have let Emma get wet,' she says.

'I'm sorry. She was having fun.'

Gunsmoke is tearing through her garden, chasing a squirrel and trampling her spring flowers. I try to call him back. He stops, lifts his head, looks at me as though I am extremely wise and then takes off again.

'Everything ready for Emma's party?' I ask.

'They should be here soon.'

'How many are coming?'

'Six little girls from day care.'

Julianne's hands are stuffed into the front pocket of an apron. Both of us know we could pass our time like this, chatting about storms or whether to clean the gutters or fertilise the garden. Neither of us has the vocabulary or the temperament to share what remains of our intimacy. Maybe this is a form of mourning.

'Well, I'd better get Emma cleaned up,' she says, wiping her hands.

'OK. Tell the girls I'll come and see them during the week.'

'Charlie has exams.'

'Maybe on the weekend.'

I smile a winning smile at her. I am not shaking. I turn and walk to the car, swinging my arms and holding my head up.

'Hey, Joe,' she calls. 'You seem to be happier.'

I turn back to her. 'You think so?'

'You're laughing more.'

'I'm doing OK.'